"Looks like you need help," said a rumbling baritone from behind her.

Could the morning get any worse?

"Oh no, I'm fine," Ava said.

"Fine, huh? Aren't those your car keys inside the car?"

"I believe so."

Brice studied her for a moment. "Hey, it's no big deal. This kind of thing happens, right?" Tender feelings came to life and he couldn't seem to stop them. Maybe Ava's keys getting locked inside the car was providential. Just like the fact that he was here to help at just the right moment.

"Let me help. It'll just take a minute, and then you can be on your way," he added.

Why was her every sense attuned to this man? Ava felt his presence like the bright radiant sun on her back, almost as if she was interested in him. But of course, she couldn't be. And she especially couldn't be falling in love with Brice Donovan.

Books by Jillian Hart

Love Inspired

Heaven Sent #143
**His Hometown Girl* #180
A Love Worth Waiting For #203
Heaven Knows #212
**The Sweetest Gift* #243
**Heart and Soul* #251
**Almost Heaven* #260
**Holiday Homecoming* #272
**Sweet Blessings* #295
For the Twins' Sake #308
**Heaven's Touch* #315
**Blessed Vows* #327
**A Handful of Heaven* #335
**A Soldier for Christmas* #367
**Precious Blessings* #383
**Every Kind of Heaven* #387

*The McKaslin Clan

JILLIAN HART

makes her home in Washington State, where she has lived most of her life. When Jillian is not hard at work on her next story, she loves to read, go to lunch with her friends and spend quiet evenings with her family.

Jillian Hart

Every Kind of Heaven

Published by Steeple Hill Books™

STEEPLE HILL BOOKS

ISBN-13: 978-0-373-81301-8
ISBN-10: 0-373-81301-5

EVERY KIND OF HEAVEN

This edition published by arrangement with Steeple Hill Books.

www.SteepleHill.com

Printed in U.S.A.

I consider that our present sufferings
are not worth comparing with the glory
that will be revealed in us.

—*Romans* 8:18

Chapter One

Baker Ava McKaslin stopped humming as she stepped back from the worktable to inspect the wedding cake. Her footsteps echoed in the industrial kitchen, nearly empty except for a few basics—the sink, countertops and the few pieces of equipment she'd managed to buy off the previous tenant. They'd considered it too cumbersome and expensive to move the industrial oven and fridge, which was just her luck.

She might not have the bakery of her dreams *yet,* God willing, but it was a start. Besides, her cake was spectacular, if she did say so herself.

But what was with all the silence? She cut a look to the long stretch of metal counter behind her. The CD had come to an end. She'd probably forgotten to hit Repeat again. Okay, she forgot most things most of the time. Since her hands were all frosting coated, she hit the Play button with her elbow. The first beats of percussion got her right back into the creative mode. Although some people found it hard to think with bass blasting from her portable boom box, she thought it helped her brain cells to fire…or synapse…or do whatever brain cells did.

As the Christian music pulsed with an upbeat rhythm, she went back to work on the top tier. The delicate scrollwork took patience, not to mention stamina. Her wrist and arms were killing her, since she'd been at this for six hours straight. Ah, the price of being a baker. She ignored the burn in her exhausted muscles. Pain, that didn't matter. What mattered was *not* failing.

Before she'd bought this place, she'd been unofficially in business by using her oldest sister Katherine's snazzy kitchen off and on for a few months. This was her very first wedding cake in her own bakery. How great was that? And it was actually going well—a total shocker. So far there were no disasters. No kitchen fires. No last-minute cancellation of the wedding. It was almost as if this business venture of hers was meant to be.

Maybe she hadn't made a disastrous mistake by jumping into this entrepreneurial thing with both feet. And, best of all, the remodeling contractor would start work soon transforming this drab commercial space into a cheerful bakery shop in less than a couple of weeks. That was another reason why she was in such a great mood.

"Hello?" a man's voice—a stranger's voice—yelled over the booming music.

She screamed. The spatula slipped from her grip. What was a man doing in her kitchen? A man she'd never seen before. Her brain scrambled and her body refused to move. She could only gape at him in wide-eyed horror.

Oh, no. What if he was the backdoor burglar? The thief that had been breaking into the back doors of restaurants and assaulting and stealing? What if this dude was him?

It would be smart to call 9-1-1, but she had no idea where her cell was. There was no business phone installed yet. Even if she did have her cell or a working landline, it wouldn't matter since she was paralyzed in place.

"Uh...uh..." That was the best speech she could manage? Get it together, Ava. You're about to be robbed. "I've seen your face, so I can identify you in a lineup."

The burglar stared at her. Wow, he was really handsome. And he looked startled. His strong, chiseled jaw was clenched tight in, perhaps, fury and his striking dark eyes glittered with viciousness...or maybe that was humor. The left corner of his mouth quirked up as if he were holding back a grin.

Great, she had to get an easily amused thief.

"I've got two bucks in my purse. That's it, buddy. There's not another cent on the premises. You've picked the wrong place to rob. So t-t-turn around r-right now and go away. Go on. Shoo."

There, that ought to scare him off *or* confuse him. She really didn't care which. Adrenaline—or maybe it was terror—started to spill like ice into her veins.

"Go ahead, call the cops." He called her bluff, crossing his arms over his wide chest. He had the audacity to lean one big shoulder against the doorframe, as if he had all the time in the world. He looked more like a movie star than a criminal. "Explain to the police how you left the front door unlocked."

"No, I—" Wait, she *did* forget to lock stuff. And if he'd come in the *front* door, then he wasn't the backdoor thief. Maybe. Unless he'd changed his M.O. and was that very likely? She didn't think so. "I did leave the door unlocked, didn't I?"

"Anyone could walk right in. Even the backdoor burglar. That's who you thought I was, right?"

Okay, her mind was starting to unscramble. He didn't look like any criminal she'd seen on TV. To make matters worse, he looked *better* than any man she'd seen on TV. He was handsome to a fault. His thick black hair fell with disregard for convention over his collar. He wore a short-sleeve polo shirt—black—with the little expensive insignia. His clothes—including his baggy khaki shorts and exclusive manly leather sandals—were top of the line. Expensive.

It was likely that the backdoor thief didn't dress like that or have such a perfect smile. She hit Pause on the boom box. "Okay, I feel dumb now. What were you doing surprising me like that? You just can't go walking into any place you want."

"I'm looking for you, Ava McKaslin." His grin broadened enough to show off a double set of dimples.

Oops. This must be about business, and mistaking a potential customer for a burglar was so not professional. "You've come with a cake order, haven't you, and after meeting me, you've changed your mind."

"No, but it's tempting." The sets of dimples dug deeper as his grin widened. "I've been sent to check on the cake."

"Chloe's cake?" Oh, no. That can't be good. Suddenly her great mood tumbled. "Has she called off her wedding?"

"Nope."

"Changed her mind and eloped?"

"Not to my knowledge."

"Has she gone with another baker and forgot to tell me? Has she postponed the wedding?"

"Let me guess. You're more of a glass-is-half-empty kind of girl, aren't you?"

"Hey, disasters happen. I'm a realist."

Ava knelt to retrieve the spatula. She

tossed it into the sink and washed her hands, turning her back to the guy. He wasn't a burglar. She'd leapt to a wrong conclusion, but his being a thief might be better because he'd come with bad news. She knew, although he had yet to admit it, that he'd come to cancel the first cake she'd made in her bakery.

Total doom.

She grabbed a paper towel to dry her hands. "Tell Chloe I appreciate that she went with me, even if it didn't work out. Is she all right?"

"I hope so, since she's getting married tomorrow."

"The wedding's still on?"

"Sure it is."

She was as cute as he remembered. Brice Donovan took a step closer, trying to act like he wasn't stunned. He'd never met any woman who looked so funny and gorgeous all in the same moment. It was the eyes. Those big violet-blue eyes filled with one hundred percent vibrant emotion. They radiated such heart and spirit that he was sucked right in, like being caught in the vortex of a black hole.

It ought to be terrifying, but he didn't mind

it so much. He was glad to see her again. She didn't seem to remember seeing him at Chloe's wedding shower, considering she'd mistaken him for a burglar. But he sure remembered her. How could he not? She was unforgettable.

And absolutely adorable. Not that he could see much of her; she was standing behind the most unusual cake he'd ever seen. One large heart-shaped layer was stacked off-center on another, and another over that. Satin-textured, smooth ivory frosting adorned with amazing gold lace and ribbons of some kind of frosting, and colorful sugar flowers everywhere.

Unlike her cake, the designer wasn't as perfectly arranged. She had globs of icing all over her. A streak on her cheek, a dried crown of it in her light blond hair, which was neatly tied back, and a blob just above the tip of her cute little nose.

When he'd agreed to check on the cake's progress for his sister, he'd thought the address was familiar. He knew why the instant he'd pulled into the lot. His construction company had won the bid for renovation—starting next week. The moment he'd spotted the shop's proprietor hard at work, he'd known why Chloe had sent him. She was meddlesome, but then a guy had to tolerate that from his baby sister. Not that he wasn't grateful.

Over the past year, he'd noticed Ava McKaslin around town a couple of times. They didn't belong to the same social circle or church, and didn't live in the same parts of town, so he'd never had an opportunity to talk to her before. There was something about her that always made him smile. Just like he was doing now.

"I've been sent to make sure the cake is on schedule." He stalked forward, wanting to get closer to that smile of hers. "It looks on schedule to me."

"I'll need thirty minutes tops, and then it's done. Chloe doesn't have to worry about a thing. I'll deliver it bright and early at the country club, just as I promised, no sweat."

"She'll be thrilled." He splayed both hands on the table and leaned toward her, drawn by those eyes, by everything.

Up close, there was nothing artificial about her. She was radiant. She had a fresh-faced complexion and dazzling beauty, sure, but she was unique. She was like the light refracting off a flawless diamond. Hers was a brilliance that was impossible to touch or to capture.

He'd really like to get to know her. "You said you've got thirty minutes until you're done?"

"I promise. You and Chloe have nothing to worry about. Your wedding cake will be perfect." Ava crossed her heart like a girl scout, as cute as a button.

Captivated, Brice felt blinded in a way he'd never been before. He definitely would like to see what this violet-eyed, flawless Ava was really like. He took in the little gold cross at her throat and the sweet way she looked. What was such a good, amazing woman doing single?

She scooped a short spatula into a stainless steel bowl, fluffy with snow-white frosting. "Did you want to come back when I'm done?"

"I'd rather stay, if you don't mind."

"Stay? You don't want to do that. You'd be bored."

"I doubt that. I could watch you work. I've never seen anything like this. It's beautiful, the work you do." He took a breath. Gathered his courage. "If you don't mind, when you're done, we could talk, just you and me."

Ava stared over the top frills of the cake. She blinked hard, as if she were trying to bring him into focus. Or make sense of what he was saying. "Talk?"

"Sure. We've met before, don't you remember? Maybe we can go down the street for a cup of coffee. Get to know each other better."

"*What?*" The spatula dropped from her supple artist's fingers and clattered on the metal tabletop. "You want to get to know me *better?*"

Uh-oh. She didn't look happy about that. He'd never had that reaction from a woman before. Okay, maybe he'd jumped the gun. "Do you have a boyfriend? I should have asked first. I noticed you weren't wearing a wedding ring and I assumed—"

She cut him off, circling around the table like a five-star army general. "You *assumed?* What's wrong with you?"

He couldn't believe how mad she looked. "Hey, what did I do? I just wanted to talk."

"Talk? Oh, is that what men like you call it? You need to get some morals."

Well, at least she was a lady with serious principles. He liked that. He respected Ava's inner fiber. It was a little passionate, but he liked that, too. He held up both hands, a show of surrender. "Hey, I didn't know you were attached. Why wouldn't you be? Look at you. Of course you have a boyfriend. He probably worships at your feet."

"No I don't have a boyfriend, but what about you and Chloe? You're getting married! You should leave. Go."

Normally, he might take offense at her dismissal, but he didn't seem to mind.

No boyfriend, huh? Okay, call him interested. No, call him dazzled, that's what he was. She fascinated him, all pure inner fire and feeling. But this wasn't going well. Usually he got a better response than this.

"What am I going to have to tell your bride?" Her sweetheart-shaped face turned pink with fury. "The poor woman thinks she's getting married to Mr. Right. Little does she know you're Mr. Yuck, wanting to get to know me the evening before your wedding. I don't think you want to chat, either!"

So, that was it. Whew. For a minute there,

he was afraid she really didn't like him. "You misunderstood."

"Misunderstood? Oh, I don't think so."

Men, Ava fumed. What was wrong with the species? *This* was why she wasn't married. Too many of the gender were just like this guy, and nothing made her madder. Spitting mad. "I'm a good Christian girl. Get a clue, buddy. Are you misunderstanding me now?"

"Uh, no. I noticed the gold cross. You look like a very nice Christian girl to me."

He was being agreeable now, but it didn't matter. "Poor Chloe. Now what do I do? Do I tell her? Or do I make you do it? A man like you doesn't deserve a nice wife like her. What kind of man would do that to the woman he was about to marry?"

He chuckled. Actually chuckled, the sound rich as cream. His dimples deepened. Tiny, attractive laugh lines crinkled around his kind, warm brown eyes.

That was the problem. He didn't look like a cheater. He looked like a nice guy. What did a girl do in a world where icky men could look as good as the nice ones?

She'd had this problem before. This is why she had a newly instated policy of staying away from every last one of them, unless they needed to buy a cake from her, of course. She intended to stick to her current no-man policy one hundred percent. "This is the last time I'm telling you to leave."

"Okay, stand down soldier." He held up both hands as if he were surrendering. "I'll go. But please accept my apology. I'm sorry. I don't know what I was thinking."

"Obviously you weren't thinking at all. Or you thought that I looked easy, and let me tell you, you couldn't be more wrong."

"Ava McKaslin, you look like class to me. I can't help noticing that you aren't happy with my interest."

"You got that right. Hey! You're not heading toward the door."

"We're not done discussing the cake." He had the audacity to grin again.

That grin became more charming each time he used it, Ava thought, making him look like the absolute perfect guy.

She'd been fooled by dimples and charm too many times before. "The cake will be ready and delivered at the country club's service entrance by nine tomorrow morning, as agreed. There. Discussion done."

"Chloe will be relieved. You aren't going to mention this little misunderstanding to her, right?"

Didn't that take the prize? "I don't know. I may have to consult my sisters and my minister on this one. She should know the kind of man she's marrying."

"I'm not the groom."

"Oh, *sure* you're not." Ava rolled her eyes. Some men would resort to anything. Men like him had made her give up dating. Perhaps forever. Good thing she'd vowed to turn all her energy to making a success of her business, because it would be impossible to make marriage work considering the men running around these days.

She reloaded her spatula with frosting. "You're not gone yet."

He sighed, resigned as he backed through the kitchen doorway. "I guess I'll see you at the wedding, huh?"

"Not if I can help it." Really, what gave this guy the idea that she was interested? "I'd better follow you to the door to make sure you really leave. Then I'm going to lock it, so no more riffraff can get in."

"At least I'm not the backdoor burglar, or

you would have really been in trouble. That spatula loaded with frosting wouldn't be much of a weapon against a revolver." He paused in the front door, framed by the brilliant June sunshine. His grin went cosmic. "By the way, you have frosting on your nose. It's cute. Real cute."

"You're not so attractive, Mr. Yuck."

"Ava, listen. I'm *not* the groom. When you deliver the cake, stick around for the wedding. You'll see I'm the best man. So, how about it?"

She grabbed his arm and gave him a shove. It was impossible not to notice he felt like solid steel. Once he'd rocked backwards a step, she was able to slam the door. Not that he was harmful, she thought as she threw the deadbolt, but she'd had enough of not-so-stellar men.

So why did she gravitate to the front windows that gave her a perfect view of the parking lot?

Because she wanted to make sure he left, the horrible man, trying to pick up a woman on the night before his wedding. Despicable.

It was hard to believe a human being was capable of behaving so badly, but she'd been propositioned like that before. Three wedding cakes ago. Darrin Fullerton had thought that when she delivered the two-tier caramel coconut cake that she was ready to serve up something else, too. It still shocked her. Too many men needed to spend more time reading their Bibles. Filling their minds with uplifting and spiritual subjects. Learning to recite the Psalms. List the seven deadly sins. That kind of thing.

The groom climbed into a bright red luxury sports car—not surprising—and zipped away. As he passed by the shop's glassed front, his driver's side window whipped down and he lifted his designer aviator sunglasses to give her a wink.

Horrible. Anger turned her vision to pure crimson. Seconds passed until she could see normally again. The parking lot was empty, the red sports car long gone.

Her cell phone chimed. The cheerful jingle came from very near. She looked down and found it in her apron pocket. The display said it was her twin sister, Aubrey. "Howdy."

"I'm just pulling up into the lot. I can see your frowny face from here."

"I have more than a frowny face on. It's my down-on-men face."

"Wow. What happened?"

"Oh, another groom trying to get one last party in before he commits." Ava spotted her bright yellow SUV cautiously creeping across the empty lot. Her sister had borrowed it and was coming closer. "What is it with men and commitment? I don't get why it's so terrifying. It's not any more frightening than a lot of things. Like premature baldness."

"Crow's feet."

"New car payments. Now *that's* scary. Which is why I'm glad I've given up on dating. Who cares if I ever get married?"

"*You* do."

"Too true." Ava sighed. "I've got a few more minutes to finish up, and then I'm good to go."

Aubrey brought the vehicle to a slow stop at the curb outside the window. She leaned forward, squinting through the windshield. "You brought a change of clothes, right? Or are you going to the movies like that?"

"I knew I forgot something." Ava snapped the phone shut. Who needed a man when she had enough disaster in her life?

Too bad the kind of man she needed—perfect in every way, no selfishness, no flaws or questionable morals—didn't exist.

So what was a nice girl to do? Settle for Mr. So-So or Marginally Moral? As if!

Ava unlocked the door for Aubrey and went back to work. There was the wedding cake in all its loveliness, fresh and beautiful like the new promise a wedding should be. But would she ever know what that new promising love felt like? No.

Disappointed, she grabbed a clean spatula from the drawer by the sink and went back to work, making sugar roses. Trying not to dwell on the sadness that was buried so deep inside she could *almost* pretend it didn't exist. She didn't want to live her life without knowing true love.

But with the men she kept running into, she had no other choice.

Chapter Two

The next morning, Brice pulled into the country club's parking lot and killed the engine. It was 8:53 a.m. Hadn't Ava promised the cake would be delivered by nine?

He climbed out into the hot sunshine, made hotter by the monkey suit he had to wear. He hooked a finger beneath his tie and tugged until he had a little more breathing room. After remoting the door locks, he hadn't gone five steps before his cell rang. He thumbed it from his pocket. Seeing his sister's number on the call screen made his step lighter. "Having cold feet yet?"

"No way. I can't wait to get married. I don't have a single doubt. Where are you?"

"Where do you think?"

"Ha! You're up to something. You're not answering me." She sounded happy, her voice light and easy.

Brice was glad for his little sister. He wouldn't mind having that kind of happiness in his life. He checked his Rolex. Another minute had ticked by. He shouldered through the club's main door. "Where I am is none of your business. Is Mom giving you problems?"

"When isn't she giving me problems? She means well. At least, that's what I keep telling myself so I don't flip out. She's made two of my bridesmaids cry. She's decided the wedding planner isn't capable and is trying to take over."

"Do you need me to come run interference?"

"Do you know what I need you to do?" Chloe sounded as if she was very glad he'd asked. "I'd love it if you could swing by the club and check on the cake."

I know what you're up to little sister, he thought. But he didn't mind. He hadn't been able to stop thinking of Ava since he'd left her shop yesterday.

It ate at him that she thought he was the groom. She was right—from her mistaken perspective he did look like a Mr. Yuck. Now, that was a misperception he had to change, even if he had to show her two forms of ID to do it.

Because he didn't want to encourage his sister, he tried to sound indifferent. Not at all interested. "Tell me what you know about this baker you went with."

"Ha! You like her. I know you do."

"I don't know her." *Yet.* But he intended to change that.

As he began looking around the room, he spotted her through the closed French doors into the ballroom and he froze in place. Ava. Seeing her was like the first light of dawn rising, and that was something he'd never felt before. *Ever.*

"I met Ava when we were volunteering at the community church's shelter kitchen." Chloe sounded very far away, although the cell connection was crystal clear. "She's sweet and kind and hysterical. We had a great time, until they asked her to leave."

What had she said? Brice's mind was spinning. He couldn't seem to focus. All he could think of was Ava. Her thick, shiny hair was tied up into a haphazard ponytail, bouncing in time with her movements. She was busily going over the cake, checking each colorful flower and sparkling golden accent.

She hadn't noticed him yet and seemed lost in her own world. She had a set of ear buds in, probably listening to a pocket-sized digital music player. She wore jeans and a yellow T-shirt that said on the back "Every Kind of Heaven" in white script.

Was the saying true? It had to be. She *did* look like everything sweet and good in the world.

"Brice? Are you listening to me?"

He felt dazed, as if he'd been run over by a bus. He couldn't orient himself in place and time. Any minute Ava would look up, and when she saw him, she'd leap to the same conclusion as before—that he was Mr. Yuck. If he didn't act quickly, would she start lobbing frosting at him?

He'd never quite had that affect on a woman before.

"Look, Chloe. I gotta go. Call if you need anything, okay?"

"Sure. You'll make sure Ava doesn't need

any help, right? She's just starting her business and she hasn't hired anyone yet. She'll need some assistance with all the favors we ordered. Remember, if you change your mind and decide to bring a date to my wedding, feel free."

"Sure. Right," he said vaguely.

Ava. He was having the toughest time concentrating on anything else. His thoughts kept drifting to the woman on the other side of the door.

When he opened it, he heard a lightly muttered, "Oops!"

Ava's voice made his senses spin.

Think, Brice. He clicked off his phone and stepped into the ballroom.

Morning light spilled through the long row of closed French doors and onto her. She looked tinier than he remembered. Maybe it was that she had such a big personality that she gave the impression of stature. She was surprisingly petite with slender lines and almost skinny arms and legs. There was no one else helping. How she'd delivered that big cake by herself was a mystery. It had to be heavy.

He knew the moment she sensed his presence. The line of her slender shoulders stiffened. Every muscle went completely rigid. She pulled the ear buds out of her ears, turning toward him in one swift movement.

"You." If looks could kill, he'd at least be bleeding. "What are you doing here? You're just like Darrin Fullerton. He showed up when I was delivering the cake to beg me not to say anything to his bride. He'd been drunk, he'd said, and didn't know what he was doing when he propositioned me. As if that's any excuse!"

Quick, Brice, look innocent. He held up both hands in surrender. "Wait. I'm nothing like that Fullerton guy. I'm a completely innocent best man. Really."

"Innocent? I don't think so."

Ava gave him her best squinty-eyed look. He was bigger than she remembered, a good six feet tall. When she'd shoved him out the door of her bakery, it had been like trying to move a bulldozer.

She went up on tiptoe so she could glare at him directly, not exactly eye to eye, but it was the best she could manage, being so short. "Are you ashamed of yourself? At all?"

He didn't look unashamed. "Chloe's going to love that cake. You did an amazing job."

"Now if only I can control the urge to lob the top tier at you."

"Do you think you can restrain that urge for a few seconds? I've got something to show you." He reached into his back pocket.

Men were much more trouble than they were worth, she concluded. But why did he have to have such an amazing grin? That's probably what Chloe saw in him; it obviously blinded her to all his multitude of faults. Poor Chloe. "You should be getting ready for your wedding, but what are you doing? Trying to get me not to tell—"

He flashed a card at her. "This ought to clear up the confusion."

"I'm not the one who's confused. You owe me an apology and your bride an enormous apology and—"

He waved the card in front of her. "Look closer."

She squinted to bring the card into focus. Not a card. It was a driver's license. Some of her fury sagged as she realized the picture, which was, of course, perfect, matched the man standing before her. The name to the left of the photo was Brice Donovan.

What? Her mind screeched to a sudden

halt. She sank back onto her heels, staring, feeling her jaw drop. Brice Donovan. Chloe Donovan's *brother.* Not the groom.

"I'm the best man," he said, wagging the card. "Do you finally believe me?"

His eyes darkened with amusement, but they weren't unkind. No, not at all. A strong warmth radiated from him as he leaned close, and then closer.

That thought spun around in her brain for a moment, like a car's engine stuck in neutral. Then it hit her. She'd insulted, yelled at and accused a perfectly innocent man.

It was hard to know just what to say. Talk about being embarrassed. Had she really said all those things to him? She felt faint. Wasn't he on the city's most eligible bachelor's list? It was just in last weekend's paper. She couldn't believe she hadn't recognized him.

Why did these things always happen to her? She clipped her case closed. He was probably waiting for an apology. An apology for the accusations. The fact that she'd been beyond rude to him, one of the wealthiest men from one of the most prominent families in Montana.

Lovely. Her face heated from the humiliation starting to seep into her soul. "Oops. My bad."

"You think?" He crooked one brow, amusement softening the impressive impact of all iron-solid six feet of him.

The effect was scrambling her brain cells, and that wasn't helping her to think.

"Chloe's going to really love what you've done with this cake." He jammed his hands into his pockets, looking like a cover model come to life. "It's going to make her so happy. Thank you."

Now what did she say? She'd been awful to him and he was complimenting the cake she'd worked so hard on. It made her feel even worse. "I'm trying to figure out how to apologize, but *sorry* seems like too small a word."

"Don't even worry about it."

"Thanks," she said shyly.

Brice Donovan's smile made her even more muddled. Before he'd walked into the ballroom she'd been so happy, thinking how pleased Chloe was going to be. But now? Her heart twisted with agony. Her face was so hot and red from embarrassment, she could feel her skin glow. What she could see of her nose was as bright as a strawberry.

This was no way for a professional baker to behave. Feeling two inches tall, she looked up to Brice's kind eyes. He wasn't laughing at her. No. That was one saving grace, right?

"I am sorry. Really. Tell Chloe best wishes. This cake is my gift to her."

"But she hired you to bake it."

"So she thinks. I've got to go, I have another project to work on, but this, the groom's cake and the favors, it's all from me to her. She was a good friend to me when I really needed one." Her chest felt so tight, she felt ready to burst. Embarrassment had turned into a horrible, sharp pain right behind her sternum.

Doom. She'd just made a mess of this. Would there ever be one time—just *once*—when she didn't make a mess of something? There was no way to fix this, and the cake was finished. There was nothing else to do but grab her case and her baseball cap.

Somehow she managed to speak without strangling on her embarrassment. "Goodbye, Mr. Donovan. And I am s-sorry again."

"Wait, don't go yet, I—"

"I have to." She was already walking away. She had work waiting and she couldn't face him a second longer. She'd humiliated herself enough for one day and it was only 9:15 a.m. She hadn't even had breakfast yet. Way to go, Ava.

She wasn't aware of crossing the room, only that she was suddenly at the kitchen. But she was aware of him. Of his presence behind her in the spill of light through the expansive windows. She didn't have to look at him as she pushed through the kitchen door to know that he was watching her. She could feel the tangible weight of his touch between her shoulder blades. What was he thinking?

Lord, I don't want to know. She kept going. She hit the back service doors and didn't slow until she felt the soothing morning sun on her face.

She skidded to a stop in the gravel and breathed in the fresh morning air. The scents of warm earth and freshly mowed grass calmed her a little. She breathed hard, getting out all the negative feelings. There were a lot of them. And trying not to hear her mother's voice saying, *You wreck everything you touch. Can't you stop making a mess for two seconds?*

She'd been seven, and she could still hear the shrill impatience. She still felt like that little girl who just didn't know how things went wrong no matter how hard she tried.

You're just a big dope, Ava, she told herself. What kind of grown adult had the problems she had? Wasn't she going to turn over a new leaf? Start out right this time? Stop making so many dumb mistakes?

Well, no more. She wasn't going to think about the way she'd embarrassed herself back there. She'd been hoping that by doing a good job with Chloe's cake, she'd get some word-of-mouth interest and her business would naturally pick up.

But after this, what were the chances that anyone was going to remember what the cake looked like?

None. All Brice Donovan was going to do was to talk about the dingbat cake lady who mistook him—the city of Bozeman's golden boy—for a philandering groom.

Her SUV blurred into one bright yellow blob. She blinked hard until her eyes cleared and reached into her pocket for her keys.

The only thing she could do was go on from here. Simply write off this morning as a lesson learned. What else could she do? She reached into her other pocket, but it was empty. No, it couldn't be. Her heart jack hammered. Where were her keys?

She did another search of her pockets. Jeans front pockets. No key. Back pockets. No key. Those were the only pockets she had. Panic began to stutter in her chest. *Where were her keys?*

There. Sitting right in plain view on the rear passenger seat. *Inside* the locked vehicle. Right next to her cell phone and her sunglasses.

Super-duper. What did she do now?

"Looks like you need help," said a rumbling baritone from behind her. A baritone she recognized. Brice Donovan.

Could the morning get any worse? How was she going to save her dignity now—or what was left of it? "H-help? Oh, no, I'm fine."

"Fine, huh? Aren't those your car keys inside the car?"

"I believe so."

"I don't know too many people who can actually lock their keys in the car with a remote. Don't you need the remote to lock the door?"

"Yes." She plopped her baseball cap on her head and pulled the bill low, trying to hide what she could of her face. Her nose was bright red again.

Brice studied her for a moment before realization dawned. Oh, he knew why she was acting this way, shuffling away from him, head down, avoiding his gaze. She was embarrassed. Well, she didn't need to be. "Hey, it's no big deal. This kind of thing happens, right?"

The tension eased from her tight jaw and rigid shoulders. She shrugged helplessly. "I've only had this car for a few months and I haven't figured out all the settings yet. It's too technologically advanced for me."

"I doubt that." Tender feelings came to life and he couldn't seem to stop them. Maybe her keys getting locked inside the car was providential. Just like the fact that he was here to help at just the right moment. "I have a knack for this kind of thing."

"Thanks, but please don't bother."

She still wouldn't look at him. Instead, she stared hard at the toes of her sunshine-yellow sneakers. Yellow, just like her SUV. There was nothing mundane about Ava McKaslin.

He liked that. Very much.

She surprised him by sidestepping away, heading back to the service doors.

"Hey, where are you going?"

"To find a phone."

"To call…?"

"My sister to come with the extra set of keys."

Wow. She really didn't want his help. Getting a woman to like him used to be easier than this, although he *had* been out of the dating circuit for a long time. After all, he'd dated Whitney two years before he'd proposed to her, which had turned out to be a much longer engagement period than either of them had expected. That put him nearly four, no, almost five years out of practice.

But still, he just didn't remember it being so difficult. "Your sister doesn't need to go to the trouble of driving out here. I'll break in for you."

She paused midstride.

He could sense her indecision, so he tried again. "Let me help. It'll take a minute and then you can be on your way."

"But I was so rude to you."

"So? If you're worried about retaliation, forget it. I'm a turn-the-other-cheek kind of guy. And I won't leave a scratch on your new car. Promise."

"And just why does a man like you know how to break into a car without leaving any evidence?"

"Chloe used to lock herself out of her car, too. I need a coat hanger. I'll be right back." He shouldered past her, pausing at the base of the concrete steps.

Why was her every sense attuned to this man? She felt Brice's presence like the bright radiant sun on her back, almost as if she was interested in him, but, of course, she couldn't be. She was done with thinking about any guy, and done with dreams of falling in love.

She was done with dreams like Brice Donovan.

Chapter Three

"Mission accomplished. No trouble at all."

His voice moved through Ava like a warm breeze. She turned toward him as her car's alarm went off. While the vehicle honked and the headlights flashed, he calmly opened the back door, grabbed the key ring with the remote and pressed the button. The horn silenced, the headlights died.

For him, it had been simple. But for her? She'd had to stand here and watch him, knowing he was helping her out of sympathy. Because he'd felt pity for his little sister's friend.

She would rather fall through a big black hole in the ground than to have to look Brice Donovan in the eye one more time. Sure, he was being gallant and incredibly nice, but it wasn't as if she could erase the things she'd said to him. She heard all the adjectives she'd called him roll around in her head. *Mr. Yuck. Riffraff.* She'd told him to *get some morals.* How could she have not recognized him? How could she have made such a mistake?

"All done. And without any damage, thanks to the caterer." He finished bending a wire hanger back into place, but his gaze seared her from six feet away. "Lucky for us she had this in her van."

"Yep, lucky for us." But she didn't feel fortunate. Her nose was still strawberry red, but now it felt hot, too, as if it were glowing under its own energy source.

He opened her driver's side door, looking every inch the handsome millionaire in the designer tux he wore, which fit him like a vision. Of course. He appeared every inch the proverbial prince. And suddenly she knew how Cinderella felt in her ragged dress, wishing she could put on a fancy dress and change her circumstances.

"Here are your keys." They rested on his wide, capable palm.

She couldn't help but notice how strong

his hand was. Calluses roughened his skin, as if he worked hard for a living. But that couldn't be. Wasn't he a trust fund kind of guy?

"Thanks, again."

It took all her willpower to meet his gaze. His eyes were so kind and tender. Clearly, he wasn't holding the mistaken identity thing against her. What a relief.

"Goodbye, Brice." She scooped the keys from his hand as quickly as she could, but her fingertips brushed his hand.

It was like touching a piece of heaven. A corner of serenity. The shame within her faded until there was only a hush in her soul. She didn't know why this happened, but it couldn't be a good sign. She hopped into her car, grabbed her belt as Brice closed her door. Their gazes met, held through the tempered glass, and her world stilled. Her heart forgot to beat.

Probably from the aftereffects of a lethal dose of embarrassment and nothing else—surely not interest, she told herself as she started the engine. But she knew, down deep, that wasn't the truth. The truth wasn't something she could examine too closely.

She drove away, into the sun, purposefully

keeping her gaze on the road ahead. She resisted the urge to peek at her rearview mirror and see if he was standing there, watching her go.

Chloe had cried in happiness at her first glimpse of the wedding cake. The cake had been cut, pictures taken, and everyone in the ballroom had been served, and still he could hear the conversation buzzing about the unbelievable cake. It had looked like a porcelain creation of art and beauty, impossible that it was edible. But every piece, from the intricate lace ruffles to the golden beads to the delicate curls of rose petals, had tasted as sweet as heaven.

Each of the two hundred carefully stacked serving boxes, printed to match the lacework of the cake, held an individual cake for the guests to take home. A heart-shaped version with sugary miniature rosebuds and golden ribbons. He thought of the woman who had done so much work as a gift to his sister. Chloe didn't know it yet since he hadn't found the moment to tell her. She looked as happy as a princess in her frosty white gown at her husband's side.

Brice thanked God for his sister's happiness. He wouldn't mind having some of that kind of joy of his own. He took a gulp of sparkling cider, draining the glass. This was the spot where Ava had stood earlier this morning, with the pale morning sunshine sprinkling over her like a blessing.

Then she'd driven away. What had she been thinking? Did she like him at all? She hadn't acted like it, and yet he'd thought he'd glimpsed something in her eyes. Something that made him think she might be feeling this, too.

Then again, she'd driven off pretty fast. That couldn't be the best sign.

"*There* you are, big brother. You've been hiding." Chloe swept close in her cloud of a dress.

"You know me. All this fancy stuff makes me itch."

She slipped her arm through his. "You look dashing. Five of my former sorority sisters asked me if you were seeing someone."

"And you said…?"

"That you seem to be interested in someone. But if I'm wrong, I have a long list of available women I can set you up with, Mr. Most Eligible Bachelor."

"You know I had nothing to do with that. It's not me." That only made him feel more out of place. Like he was a rich playboy looking for a fast lifestyle or a great catch for a debutante—both equally wrong.

All he wanted was to trade in this getup for his favorite T-shirt, jeans and his broken-in work boots. That's who he really was, and all this glam and glitter made his palms sweat. He swept his hand toward the cake. "You don't need to set me up with a date. I can do it myself."

"Would you rather Mom did it? She's working on it, you know. I was just trying to help out."

"I know." If anyone knew how rough of a time he'd had after the breakup with Whitney, it was Chloe. She meant well. "I can handle it from here."

"I never doubted it." She rose up on tiptoe to brush a sisterly kiss to his cheek. "I want you to be happy. I saw how you looked at Ava at my shower."

"Exactly how was that?"

"Like you were glimpsing heaven. Don't

worry, I haven't said anything to her, but you should ask her out. I bet she says yes."

"I've tried that, but I don't think she likes me." Like he needed his baby sister's dating advice. He could handle his own love life just fine. "She said no."

"And since when does Brice Donovan take no for an answer?" She flounced away, grinning over her shoulder at him. "Try again, silly. Look out, here comes Mom."

The problem was, his mother had been dropping some pretty strong hints lately. Now that she had Chloe successfully matched, she must be refocusing her energy on him. She seemed determined as she barreled through the crowd. Flawless, dressed in diamonds and flowing silk, she looked deceptively like a genteel upper-class lady instead of the five-star general she really was.

"Brice. You have been hiding again." She tugged at his tie, unknotted and hanging loose. "This isn't a barnyard. And what are you doing all the way over here? What are people going to think?"

He accepted the china dessert plate a server handed him. "Maybe people will think that I'm having a second piece of cake."

"Yes. The cake. Horrible, that's what it is. I don't know what Chloe was thinking going with that McKaslin girl."

"That she wanted her friend to make her wedding cake."

"Ridiculous. That cake is unsophisticated and completely unacceptable. And the taste of it, why, it's much too sweet. What is wrong with that girl? I told Chloe. I said, you're going to regret going with her."

"Mom, stop. You're doing it again."

"But did she listen to me? No, she had to have her own way. We ought to have gone with a professional, not some iffy girl who thinks because our family is richer than hers, she has the right to charge us an arm and a leg."

He laid a hand on his mom's arm to stop her. Sometimes she got such a wind going—sort of like gravity's effect on a snowball rolling downhill—that she simply couldn't realize what she was saying. "Chloe's happy, and that's all that matters. Besides, how much did Ava charge?"

"Ava, is it?" Mom's face pinched, something only she could do and still look dignified. "I wouldn't be so familiar with her if I were you. Her family has money, goodness, but that mother of hers."

"People have been known to say the same thing about Chloe." He said it gently, because he knew his mother didn't mean to be harsh. She simply wasn't aware of it. "I think Ava did an amazing job. So does everyone else in the room. Maybe you should learn to like sweet. You're awfully fond of the bitter."

"That had better not be a veiled reference to me, young man." His mom smiled and tried to hide it, but her eyes were twinkling. "I work hard for this reputation. If people aren't afraid of you, they take advantage. Now, come with me and say hello to a few of my dear friends."

"To the *daughters* of your friends, you mean."

"Crystal Frost is back from her disastrous divorce to that big real estate broker in Seattle. She's perfect for you."

"Perfect? I don't think so." He took a bite of cake, and sweetness flooded his mouth. The frosting was as rich as cream cheese, and the cake was delicious and buttery. *Perfect.*

"Hello, Brice. Excuse me." One of his mother's friends had sauntered over and gestured toward the cake. "Lynn, this is all so lovely. I came to plead for the name of the designer. My Carly must have a cake like this for her wedding."

Brice knew it would probably drain his mother of her life energy to say something kind about anyone. She was his mom, so he tried to save her from herself. And he wanted to help the cute baker, even if she didn't want to have coffee with him. "Ava McKaslin is the designer and I highly recommend her. Chloe loved working with her."

"Oh, let me think which McKaslin girl. Oh, of course. The friend of your sister's. One of the twins?"

"Yep. She has a shop off Cherry Lane. My company starts renovation on it this week."

"I know which shop you mean. Why, thank you, Brice. You do know that my Crystal is back from Seattle. She's here somewhere." Maxime scanned the room. "Where did she go?"

Uh-oh. Time to escape while he could. "I have to go. Mrs. Frost, it was good seeing you again. Bye, Mom."

He left quickly and didn't look back. It wasn't until he hit the foyer that he realized he still had hold of his dessert plate. Ava's cake. As if he couldn't quite let her go.

The only reason Ava heard her cell ring was because of the break between songs. The electronic chime echoed in the silence of her shop's kitchen. She set down her pastry cone, hit the Pause button on her CD player and went in search of her phone.

Not in her apron pocket. Not on the kitchen counter. She followed the electronic ringing to her gym bag. She unzipped the outside compartment and *ta da,* there it was.

As she grabbed her phone, she realized it was after four. Mrs. Carnahan was supposed to drop by for the birthday cake in ten minutes! Good thing it was almost done. Well, it *would* be done if she'd stop fussing. But after this morning's disaster, she wanted this cake to be perfect.

She flipped open the phone. "I'm late, I know. I was supposed to call an hour ago. My bad."

Instead of her sister's sensible response, a

man's resonant chuckle vibrated in her ear. "Keeping your boyfriend waiting?"

It took her a moment to place that voice. Brice Donovan. If he was calling, that could only mean one thing. "Chloe wasn't happy with the cake?"

Disappointment drained her and she sank onto the floor next to her gym bag. Not only had she failed at something she'd tried her hardest at, something that she was good at, but she'd let down a friend. "I'm so sorry."

"Now, wait one minute. That's not why I'm calling."

"It's not?"

"No." His voice warmed like melting chocolate, kind and friendly. "I'm calling to thank you. You made her very happy. She didn't want to cut into the cake because it was too pretty."

"Really? Chloe was happy? Whew!" That was a relief. Now, if she could just forget flinging insults, she'd be doing well. Don't even think about what happened, she told herself. Look forward, not back. Don't dwell on what went wrong.

Problem was, that was easier said and not so easy to do. She took a quivering breath. "Good. Then my work is done."

"And your work is?"

"To make this world a sweeter place one cake at a time. I know it's not solving world strife, but it's the only talent I seem to have, so I'm going with it."

"Surely that's not your only gift."

"Uh, you don't want to hear the long list of disasters I've left in my wake. Speaking of which, I have a cake to get ready and box for a client."

"You can't do that and talk to me?"

"If I want to drop the cake. I need two hands."

Don't think of him in that tux, she thought. Or how amazing he looked. Or how kind he'd been when he'd helped her recover her keys. What had he been thinking when she'd driven away? That unreadable expression in his eyes came back to her now and unsettled her. Why?

Just forget it, Ava. Just forget him. "I appreciate the call. Thank you."

"Well, now, I'm not done with you yet."

"Why am I not surprised?" She couldn't keep the curiosity out of her voice. Or the smile. Both the humiliation she'd felt and the failure seemed far away. Maybe it was because she knew this was a pity call. He felt sorry for the dopey cake lady. Face it, he was Mr. Wow, and she was lucky to keep the date and time straight.

That meant this was a business call. How great was that? She hadn't totally embarrassed herself beyond redemption after all. Cool. "Hopefully you're interested in placing an order?"

"You've got a renovation coming up. How are you going to fill your orders?"

He probably knew about the upcoming renovation because Chloe had been the one to recommend a construction company. "I'm planning on using my sister's kitchen. She's spending most of her evenings with her fiancé and his daughter, so I've commandeered her condo."

"Then maybe you and I can talk later. Say, Monday morning, bright and early?"

"Oops. Can't. I have construction dudes coming by bright and early."

"That's a coincidence because I—"

"I'm totally sorry, but my customer is here. Can I call you back and we can make an appointment? I can show you my catalogue and have some samples ready."

"Why don't I come by on Monday sometime?" Brice leaned back in his car seat and could see the bakery's front door over the curve of the side mirror. There was a grandmotherly woman at the front door, waving at Ava through the glass.

"Thanks, Mr. Donovan. I really appreciate this. Bye!" There was a click in his ear.

He slid his sunglasses down his nose to get a better view as the front door swung open and there was Ava, dressed in her jeans and that yellow T-shirt, her hair tied back and her genuine smile bright as she waved her hands, talking away to her customer.

Okay, this isn't how he figured things would go. Again. Ava wasn't going to make this easy for him.

She caught his gaze again, moving back into sight with a cake made like a giant dump truck. The red chassis and the bright blue bed made it look like the real toy. Even from a distance, he could see the details. The driver behind the steering wheel, the big black tires, and real-looking dirt.

When she opened the other box, he watched the grandmother's face brighten a notch. There were what had to be small cake rocks about the size of his thumb in chubby yellow buckets. One for each little guest, he figured.

The grandmother looked delighted. But it was the sight of Ava that drew him, multi-faceted and flawless, shining like one perfect jewel. She probably didn't realize how she shone from the inside out when she was happy. How caring she was as she refolded the side panels and tucked the lids of the boxes into place. How she waved away what was probably a compliment with ease. She was like no one he'd ever seen before.

Something happened inside him when he looked at Ava. Something that made his spirit come more alive.

He was going to try again. She was a sparkle he could not resist.

He put the car into gear and started driving. Her cheerful words replayed in his mind. *Hopefully you're interested in placing an order?* She'd sounded so full of joy. How was he going to tell her he hadn't meant he wanted to order a cake, but to talk to her about that cup of coffee he'd mentioned earlier?

And what about the renovation? She'd

sounded as if the construction guys who were coming had nothing to do with him and his company. She did know he was a part owner, right?

Then again, Ava might not have noticed. His business partner, Rafe, had handled the contracts and the scheduling, and was supervising this project.

Brice hit the speed dial on his cell and waited for it to connect. He'd see if Rafe wouldn't mind switching jobs. Being around Ava every working day for the next two weeks sounded like a good idea. No, a brilliant idea, considering how much he wanted to get to know her.

How would she take it? He was definitely anxious to see the look on her face when he walked into her shop bright and early Monday morning. What would happen then? Only God knew.

One thing was for sure, it was going to be a whole lot of fun to find out.

"Good news!" Ava announced as she sailed through the front door of their apartment. "Mrs. Carnahan loved the cake. She said her little grandson was going to be so happy. And your idea about adding bonus party favors at no charge—it was brilliant. She loved the little rocks I made."

Her twin, Aubrey poked her head out of the kitchen. "What did I tell you?"

"I know, you're *always* right. I don't deny it." Ava rolled her eyes, shut the door with her foot and dropped her purse, gym bag and keys on the floor. "Instead of takeout burgers, I splurged and got Thai. Cashew chicken, stir-fried rice and that noodle dish you love."

"Well done." Aubrey's smile turned full-fledged as she reached for the big takeout sack. "Hurry up, get changed. I'll get us all set up."

"I'm late, I know. But it was an excellent day despite it all. Who knew?" Ava took off for her bedroom, a total disaster. One day when she got enough time, it would be the epitome of orderliness. But since she wasn't sure when that would be, she had to go with the flow.

Knowing Aubrey was waiting, she tossed her clothes on the floor, kicked her sandals toward the closet and dug around in the laundry basket of clean clothes for her favorite sweatpants and T-shirt. After she found her fuzziest socks, she flew down the little hall.

Aubrey was in the living room setting two heaping plates of food onto two TV trays facing the widescreen TV they couldn't afford but got anyway. Not smart, and her poor credit card was bent from the weight of debt, but it was nice to watch Clark Gable in forty-two-inch glory.

"If you would have remembered to call before I hit the video store, you would have had some say in tonight's movie," Aubrey said as she settled down on the couch.

"Hey, the cell waves work both ways. You could have called me."

"I'm always calling you." Aubrey reached for her napkin and shook it open over her lap. "So, I take it the Donovan cake delivery went well this morning. You haven't mentioned the groom. What happened with that?"

"Oh, that's a disaster. Total doom. You know me." While she'd told her sister about insulting Brice Donovan, she hadn't given her the day's full update.

"Men." Aubrey shook her head, disapproving. "And to think Chloe's groom, Mark

Upton, is supposed to be like last year's most eligible bachelor. Philanthropic. An upstanding Christian. I guess it just shows, you never know about some men. They show one face when they really have another."

"Well, now, that's not exactly the case." Ava slipped behind the TV tray and plopped onto the couch. "Whew, I'm starved. Your turn to say the blessing."

"What happened? Are you telling me that he showed up this morning at the country club and apologized? Or no, there was a mix up. He didn't proposition you, did he? You jumped to conclusions like you always do and accused him of it. Right? When it wasn't true?"

"You're partly right. I was asked out to coffee, sure, but it wasn't by Mr. Upland. I thought it was, but you know me, like I can remember everyone I've ever met."

"We went to school with Mark *Upton.* Don't you remember?"

"I was busy in high school. How was I supposed to know everyone? Besides, I don't recognize a lot of people. I'm not good with faces."

"Or names."

"Or names." How could she argue with

that? She wanted to keep things light and funny, that's the way she felt comfortable with everything. Anything serious or painful, well, that made her feel way too much. And once you started really feeling, then you had to face all the other emotions you were trying to avoid.

Avoidance was a very good policy. At least, she was doing fine avoiding the things that hurt the most. Take today. She didn't have to think about the fact that Brice Donovan might think she was a disaster, too, but he wanted to order a cake. She'd concentrate on the cake part, and try hard not to think about anything else.

Not that she was having the greatest luck with that.

"So what really happened?" Aubrey asked, taking possession of the remote before Ava could grab it and divert her with the movie. "It's okay. You can tell me. It isn't as bad as you think. Really."

Easy for Aubrey, who thought things through before she opened her mouth. Aubrey who never made a mistake of any kind, who never embarrassed herself, who never locked her keys in the car.

Remembering how Brice Donovan's voice had sounded, kind and not belittling, made the yuck of her morning fade a few shades.

"I'll tell you after the movie." Ava shrugged. Some things she didn't even want to talk about, even with her twin. That wasn't the way it was supposed to be, and she knew it made Aubrey sad to be shut out like that, but she didn't want to share every detail.

She wanted to do things right for a change—not just try really hard and then fail, but to really stay focused and careful and committed. One day, maybe she could be the girl who didn't make a mess, who didn't insult Bozeman's most eligible bachelor or who frustrated people so much they simply left her for good.

As Aubrey bowed her head, beginning the blessing, Ava bowed her head, too. But she added a silent prayer to Aubrey's. *Show me the way, Lord. Please, I don't want to mess up anymore. Show me how to be different. Better.*

There was no answer, just the click of the remote as Aubrey hit a button. The TV flared to life, showing a classic movie with a silver-screen hero. Maybe if she met a man like that, she might make an exception to her no-man policy.

She grabbed her fork and dug into the cashew chicken, but did she pay attention to the movie? No. Who was she thinking about?

Brice Donovan and how he'd looked like a real gentleman in his tux. How he'd looked like one of her forgotten dreams when he'd been standing in the full brightness of the morning sun, looking as vibrant and as substantial as a legend come true. But it was just a trick of the light. Legends didn't exist in real life, and real love didn't happen to her.

Chapter Four

It was a beautiful Monday morning, and Ava was on her way to meet the construction dudes. Okay, in truth, she was going to ply them with her special batch of homemade doughnuts and signature coffee. She might not be the brightest bulb in the pack, but she wasn't the dimmest. It was only common sense that people worked better when they were well fueled.

This renovation was a step toward her dream. Tangible and real, and all the hammering and sawing and dust to come would transform the dingy little place into a baker's delight. This was fabulous, something to celebrate, right?

Right. At least, she *should* be feeling so

buoyant with happiness that she ought to be floating. But sadly her happiness felt subdued and superficial like icing on the cake, and nothing deeper. Why?

She'd been down a little ever since Brice Donovan's call. Did that make any sense?

No. So what was all this being sad stuff about?

Concentrate on the positive, Ava.

She screeched into the closest parking space since her favorite spot—right beneath the shade of a broad-leafed maple—was already taken by a big forest-green pickup truck. It was the ostentatious kind that looked as if it cost more than a house. There was a lot of chrome glinting in the low-rising sun and big lights on top of a custom cab. It probably belonged to one of the construction guys.

Yep, there was one standing on the sidewalk with his back to her. He seemed to be looking over the front of the shop with a contractor's discerning eye.

She cut the engine and grabbed her cell from the console and her bag from the front passenger seat. It was still early, only ten minutes to seven. She'd have time to get the coffee canisters set up and the doughnuts laid out before the rest of the workers arrived. She elbowed the door open, stepped down from the seat and the second her shoe touched the ground she felt it. Something was wrong, but she couldn't put her finger on what.

The construction worker hadn't moved. He was still staring at the front windows—and she could see his reflection as clearly as she could see her own. He looked remarkably like Brice Donovan. That handsome face, sculpted cheekbones and chin, straight nose and strong jaw were all the same. Except for one thing—how could that be Brice? It made no sense. She gave the door a shove to close it.

She had Brice Donovan on the brain. *That's* why her emotions were all off kilter. *That's* why she wasn't fully enjoying the beautiful morning or this first momentous day of construction.

Brice Donovan. It wasn't as if she even liked him a tiny bit. Really. So what was going on? Maybe it was stress, she decided as she circled around to the back of the vehicle and realized she hadn't hit the door release.

No problem. She looked down at her cell phone. Where were her keys?

The automatic locks clicked shut all on their own.

Great. Wonderful. Terrific. She'd done it again! Why wasn't she paying better attention?

Well, if she hadn't have been thinking of Brice Donovan then she wouldn't have been distracted. See? *This* is why she had to stick to her no-man policy—all the way. No exceptions. Even thinking of him just a little caused problems.

She leaned her forehead against the rear window and took a deep breath. All she needed was to call Aubrey. Plus, there was a silver lining in all this. At least this time she hadn't locked her cell phone in, too. Hey, it could be worse.

She flipped open her phone when a startling familiar baritone rumbled right behind her. "Let me guess. You're in need of rescuing again."

Brice Donovan? She turned around and there he was, looking totally macho in workmen's clothes. The lettering on the light gray T-shirt he wore said it all: D&M Construction, the name of the company she'd hired for the renovation. How on earth did he have a shirt with that company name? Did he work for them?

Then it hit her. Maybe the *D* stood for Donovan. *Wow.*

He jammed his hands into his pockets, emphasizing the muscled set of his shoulders. "You don't look happy to see me."

"Surprised." So surprised she had to lean against the fender for support. "What are you doing here?"

"Rafe Montgomery was going to do the job, but I sweet-talked him into trading."

"Lucky me." Ava's mind swirled. Montgomery must be the *M* in the company. Rafe had been a nice man who'd been her contact. "But why are you here in workman's clothes. Aren't you like an investment broker or something?"

"That would be my dad. Rafe Montgomery and I got to talking one night while we were studying for our graduate school exams. What we were really dreading wasn't taking the test, it was being cooped up in an office all day. Just like our dads. Don't get me wrong, I don't mind putting in a good hard day's work, but I felt put in a box. It wasn't for either of us. So we pooled our resources and went into business."

That was the most unlikely story she'd ever heard. MBA dudes who built stuff? "I'd like to think you had woodworking training. A certificate of carpentry competence."

"I'm good at what I do, believe me."

Oh, she did believe him. And how was it possible that he looked even better dressed for work than he had the other day in a tux? Today he looked genuine, capable and very manly.

"Let me get a coat hanger." He strode to the green pickup and opened the crew-cab door. A big golden retriever tumbled out and ping-ponged in place in front of Brice, tongue lolling. "Whoa there, boy."

Okay, she melted. She couldn't help it—she was a softy when it came to dogs. "What's his name?"

Goofy brown eyes fastened on her. That big doggy mouth swung wide, showing dozens of sharp teeth. The huge canine launched toward her, tongue out and grinning, moving so fast he was a golden-brown blur.

"Rex, no! Come back here." Brice reached for his collar to catch him.

Too late.

Ava didn't have time to brace herself, because the dog was already leaping on her, plopping one front paw on either side of her neck, almost hugging her. His tongue swiped across her chin. Happy chocolate eyes studied hers with sheer joy.

"Brice, I'm in love with your dog." She couldn't help it. The big cuddly retriever hugged her harder before dropping down on all four paws. As if he knew how much he'd charmed her, he posed handsomely, staring up adoringly with those sweet eyes.

"Excuse him. He's very friendly. Too friendly." Brice grabbed his collar. "This may come as a shock to you but he failed every obedience class he's been in. From puppy school all the way up to the academy."

"Academy?"

"I hired professionals, but in the end, he won." Brice turned his attention to the retriever, his face softening, his big hand stroking over the crown of the canine's downy head. He received a few swipes of that lolling tongue and laughed. "Life's hard enough, isn't it? Without being told what to do every second of the day."

Ava couldn't believe it. The big, macho, most eligible bachelor was tough looking with all his masculine strength and charm, but she knew his secret. He was a big marshmallow underneath.

Not that she was interested. Really.

"This'll only take a second, now that I have the routine down." He took a wire hanger—she hadn't even noticed when he'd fetched it from his truck—and unbent it enough to slide it between the frame of the door and the roof.

True to his word, a few seconds later he'd hit the lock and was pulling her key from the ignition and silencing the alarm. He hit the back door release for her.

Okay, he was really a decent guy. On the surface anyway, and that's the only level on which she intended to know him. He was the *D* in D&M Construction, so that meant for better or worse, she was stuck with him. Not that she thought for a moment he actually did the hard work. No, he was probably more of a figurehead. He probably just oversaw projects. He was Roger Donovan's son, right?

She lifted the back and slid out the bakery box, and Rex bounded up to sniff at it.

"Hey, buddy, these are not for you." Ava might be charmed by the big cuddly dog, but she wasn't that big of a pushover. "Sit."

The retriever grinned up at her with every bit of charisma he possessed.

"Look at him drool. That can only mean one thing. There must be doughnuts in that box." There was Brice, as large as life, wrapping one big, powerful hand around the canine's blue nylon collar. "Need any help carrying those?"

"I suppose you like doughnuts, too."

"Guilty." His warm eyes and dazzling grin, those dimples and personality and his hard appearance made him look good down to the soul.

She had been fooled by this type of guy before, but not this time. "These are not for you. They are for your crew. For the men who actually work for a living instead of walking around owning companies."

"Hey, I work hard."

"I don't see a hammer." She reached for a second box, but he beat her to it. It was heavy with big thermos-type coffee canisters. "I see you eyeing the thermoses and no, you may not have any of that, either. Not unless you're a construction dude, and I don't see a tool belt strapped to your waist."

"That's not fair. My tools are in my truck."

She rolled her eyes. "Oh, *sure* they are."

Brice shut the door and hit the remote. Rex bounced at his hip, the dog's gaze glued to the pink bakery box. "You know I'm the on-site manager of this project, right?"

"I'll have to see it to believe it." She snapped ahead of him with that quick-paced walk of hers, her yellow sneakers squeaking with each step. "I still don't get why you're here. Why I'm plagued with you and that dog of yours."

She eyed him like a judge awaiting a guilty verdict, but she didn't fool him. Not one bit. He saw in her eyes and in the hint of her smile what she was trying to hide. He wasn't the only one wondering.

Maybe he wasn't the only one wishing.

"Where do you want these?" he asked of the stuff he carrying.

She gestured to the worn wooden counter in front of them, where she'd set the bakery box and was lifting the lid.

He did as she asked and nearly went weak in the knees at the aroma wafting out from the open box. Sweet cake doughnuts, the comforting bite of chocolate, the richness of custard and the mouth-watering sweet huckleberries that glistened like fat blue jellybeans.

"Where did you get these?" The question wasn't past his lips before he knew the answer. "You made these. You."

"Okay, that's so surprising? I'm a baker. Hel-*lo*." She rolled her eyes at him, but it was cute, the way she shook her head as if she simply didn't know about him. Yep, he knew what she was trying to do. Because whatever was happening between them felt a little scary, like standing on the edge of a crumbling precipice and knowing while the fall was certain, the how and what of the landing was not.

She pulled a bag of paper plates from her big shoulder bag, ripped it open and pulled out a plate. She slid the berries-and-cream-topped doughnut onto the plate and handed it to him. "I saw you eyeing it."

Had she noticed how he'd been looking at her? He thought she was two hundred times sweeter than that doughnut. "How about some cups?"

"Here." She pulled a bag of them from her mammoth bag. "Which doughnut should I give your dog?"

Rex gave a small bark of delight and sat on his haunches like the best dog in the world. His doggy gaze was glued on the bottom corner of the bakery box.

"He'd take every last one. Don't trust him if you leave that box uncovered."

"Oh, he's a good guy. It's you I don't trust," she said with a hint of a grin. "You said you traded with Mr. Montgomery. I want to know why."

Just his luck. He filled two cups with sweetened, aromatic coffee and handed her one. "How about grace, first?"

"I've already had my breakfast." She took the coffee.

Their fingertips brushed and it was a little like being hit by a lightning strike from a blue sky. His heartbeat lurched to a stop. What was it about Ava that seemed to make his world stand still?

She gave him another judgmental look like a prim schoolmarm as she put a glazed doughnut on a second plate. Rex's tail thumped like a jackhammer against the scarred tile floor. She knelt to set the plate on the floor.

"What a nice polite gentleman," she praised, and gave him a pat.

Rex sat a moment to further fool Ava into thinking he was a perfect dog before he wolfed down the doughnut in two bites.

"You're welcome," she said as she patted him again and removed the plate. "Oh, some of the men are driving up now. Good."

Brice tried not to let it bother him that she disregarded him completely as she disappeared through the kitchen door. This was *not* how most single ladies reacted to him. He considered the steaming cup of coffee he held and the plate with the delectable doughnut.

Lord, I'm gonna need help with this one. If it's Your will, please show me the way.

The doors swung closed as if in answer, swinging open again to show a glimpse of Ava, washed in sunlight from the large window. Inexplicably, the sun shone brighter.

Could the morning be going any more perfectly? The homemade doughnuts were a hit. With promises of more sweet surprises for tomorrow morning, Ava made sure the fridge was stocked with plenty of liquids—it was important to keep the workers hydrated—and gathered up her stuff.

Time to get out of their way. Dust was already flying. Walls were already missing. As curious as she was to see absolutely everything, she knew she'd only be in the way. Besides, she had to work at her family's bookstore because she had her share of the rent and utilities to pay at month's end. Not to mention her car payment. Oh, and credit card payments. And her school loans. She grabbed her bag and was in the middle of hunting down her keys when she suddenly realized she wasn't alone.

"Ava, I'm glad I caught you." There was Brice, shouldering through the door. "Before you go, I want to go over your final plans."

"I already did that with Mr. Montgomery. When we talked the other day on the phone, you know, after Chloe's wedding, you said you wanted to stop by on Monday morning. I assumed that meant you were interested in ordering a cake. But this is why, isn't it?"

"I can order a cake if you want."

"It isn't what I want that's the question." Really, that grin of his was infectious. Dashing and charming and utterly disarming. What was a girl to do? How was she supposed to *not* smile back? She was helpless here. *Lord, give me strength, please.* "I haven't forgotten that you tried to ask me out. I mean, I know you changed your mind once I started insulting you."

"The post traumatic stress is better, by the way. Although standing in this kitchen might give me a flashback or two." His grin deepened right along with his dimples. "You're questioning why I'm here, right? Remember I said that you made my sister happy with her wedding cake?"

"I do." Leery, that's what she had to be. On guard. The kindness of his smile was like a tractor beam pulling her in. If she wasn't careful, she was going to start liking this man.

Liking men at all—even platonically—wasn't a part of her no-man policy. Because that's how it had happened with Ken, the chef she dated about five months back, and that had ended in disaster. If she didn't learn lessons from her ten billion mistakes, how was she ever going to feel better about herself?

Brice came closer, his dog trailing after him. “You made Chloe happy, and now I want to return the favor.”

Okay, she could buy that reason. It was actually a nice reason. Which only made him a nicer man in her eyes.

He set a coffee cup down on the metal table between them and gave it a shove in her direction, obviously meant for her. She hadn’t noticed what he’d been carrying.

How could she have not noticed that he was hauling with him a rolled up blueprint, too?

Keep your mind on business, Ava, she ordered herself. Really, it was that smile of Brice’s. It ought to come with a surgeon general’s warning. Beware: Might Have The Gravitational Pull Of A Black Hole And Suck You Right In.

“I know you’ve gone over the plans with my partner.” Brice plopped the blueprints on the metal work table and spread out them out with quick efficiency. He anchored each corner with a battered tape measure and hammer he plucked from his tool belt. “But what I want to know is the dream of what you want. The heart of it. Beyond the computer-generated drawings of this place."

Okay, that wasn't what she expected and it disarmed her even more. Emotions tangled in her throat and made her voice thick and strange sounding. "I showed Mr. Montgomery a few pictures of what I had in mind."

"I'd like to see them."

Their gazes met, and a connection zinged between them. A sad ache rolled through her and she didn't know why. She refused to let herself ask. Instead, she fumbled through the top drawer in the battered cabinets. She'd left the magazine pictures here to show the woodworker, just in case.

But turning her back to him gave her no sense of privacy or relief from the aching she felt. Somehow she managed to face him again, but her hands were shaking. She didn't want to think too hard on the reason for that, either. "Here. I'm not looking for exactly this. But something warm and whimsical and unique. In my price range."

She spread the three full-color pictures on the metal table, turning them so they were right side up for his inspection. Long ago, she'd torn them from magazines she'd come across, tucking them away for the when and if of this dream. The white frame of the pages had dulled to yellow over time, and the ragged edges where she'd torn them from the magazine looked tattered. But the bright glass displays and the intricate woodwork remained as bright and as promising as ever.

"It's probably beyond my budget, I know, that's what Mr. Montgomery said. But he thought he could scale it down and still get some of the feeling of the craftsmanship."

Brice said nothing as he studied the photos, sipping his coffee, taking his time. "Why baking? Why not open a bistro? Or stay working at your family's bookstore?"

Surprise shot across her face. "You know about the bookstore? Wait, Chloe knows. She probably told you."

That wasn't exactly true. Everyone knew about the bookstore. Ava's grandmother's family, a wealthy and respected family and one of the area's original settlers, had owned the store forever. "I need to know what this means to you before I start on the woodwork. Isn't that what you do before you design a cake for someone?"

"Exactly." She took a sip of the sweetened coffee and studied him through narrowed eyes, as if she were truly seeing him for the first time.

He could see her heart, shining in her eyes, whole and dazzling. He leaned closer. Couldn't stop himself.

She turned one of the pictures around to study. "You wouldn't understand what I want, being Bozeman's most eligible bachelor and all."

"You know, I have relatives who work on the local paper. That's where the list came from. I had nothing to do with it. I'm just a working man, so I bet I can understand. Try me."

A cute little furrow dug in between her eyes, over the bridge of her nose. Adorable, she shrugged one slim shoulder, and for a moment she looked lost. *Sad.* "My mom really wasn't happy being a wife and mother. I know that. But when I was little it felt like I was the one who made her unhappy. I was always spilling stuff and knocking into furniture and forgetting things. Not that I've changed that much." She shrugged again. "This isn't what you want to hear."

"This is exactly right. Exactly what I want to know."

He laid his hand over hers, feeling the warm silk of her skin and the cool smoothness of the magazine page. One picture was of bistro tables washed in sunlight, framed by golden, scrolled wood and crisp white clouds of curtains. It looked like something out of a children's story book, where evil was easily defeated, where every child was loved and where love always won.

That's what he knew she saw on the page, he knew because he could see her heart so clearly.

She drew in a ragged breath, her voice thin with emotion, her eyes turning an arresting shade of indigo. "One thing that always went right was when I was with Mom in the kitchen. She wasn't much of a baker, but I had spent a lot of time with Gran in the kitchen, she taught me to bake, and I liked the quiet time. Measuring sugar and sifting flour. Getting everything just right."

She paused as if noticing for the first time that his hand still covered hers. She didn't try to move away. Did she know how vulnerable she looked? How good and true? He didn't think so. He feared his heart, hurting so much for her, would never be the same.

"This reminds you of baking with your Mom," he said.

"Sort of. I remember the kitchen smelled wonderful when the cookies or the cakes were cooling. And afterwards there was the frosting to whip up and the decorating to do. It's the one thing I could always do right. It made everyone happy, for how ever little time that happiness lasted, it was there."

"And then your mother left?"

Ava gently tugged her hand out from beneath his. She lowered her gaze, veiled her heart. That was a scandal of huge proportion. Everybody had known at the time, and in a small city that was really just one big small town, everybody still remembered although twenty years had passed. "I want this to be like a place where customers feel like they've stepped into a storybook. Not childish, just—" She couldn't think of the word.

"You want a place where it feels as if wishes can come true."

How did he know that? Ava took a shaky breath and tucked away the honesty she shouldn't have hauled out like dirty laundry in a basket. She was *so* not a wishing kind of girl. Not anymore.

She grabbed her bag again, not remembering when exactly it had slipped from her shoulder to the floor. "I'd better get going. I'm late for my shift at the bookstore."

"Do I make you uncomfortable?"

"Yes." The word popped out before she could stop it.

He winced. "Well, that's not my intention. We got off on the wrong foot. Is that's what's bothering you?"

"No. Yes."

"Which is it?"

"I don't know." All she knew was that he felt *way* too close, although she'd crossed half of the kitchen on the way to the door and it still didn't make any difference. She took a shaky breath. "I should have recognized you. I mean, I'm usually so busy in my own little world, I don't notice everything I should."

"Well, I didn't introduce myself, so when you think about it, it could be all my fault."

"You're being too nice."

"That's better than being Mr. Yuck, right?"

"Maybe."

That made his dimples flash. "What do you do with your time, besides baking incredible cakes?"

"Hang out with my sisters, mostly. Doing my part to contribute to consumer debt. That kind of thing." And that was all she was going to share with him because anything else would be way too personal. "Okay, what did I do with my keys?"

"I might have 'em." He reached into his back pocket and then there they were in the palm of his hand.

Oops. It looked like she would have to move closer to him to get them. Her chest tightened and her emotions felt like one big aching mess. Was it because of the story she'd told him, about baking with her mother? Or was he the reason?

She knew the answer simply by looking at him. His appearance—the worn T-shirt, battered Levi's and beat-up black workboots—all shouted tough guy, but in a really good, hard-working way. Add that to his kindness and class—and he was totally wishable.

Not that she was wishing.

As he strode toward her with the slow

measured gait of a hunter, she didn't feel stalked. No, she felt *drawn.* As if he'd gathered up her tangled heartstrings and gave them a gentle shake. There were no more knots, just one simple, honest feeling running up those strings and straight into her heart.

She didn't want to be drawn to any man. Especially not him.

She grabbed the keys, careful to scoop them from his hand without any physical contact. But something had changed between them and she couldn't deny it.

"Thanks," she said in a practically normal-sounding voice. "You have my cell number if there's a problem, right?"

"Right."

She could feel him watching her as she yanked open the door. Rex bounded toward her and she almost forgot about Brice. She knelt down to give his head a good rubbing. "It was very nice meeting you, boy. I'll bring some muffins tomorrow. Is that all right by you?"

Rex lapped her cheek and panted in perfect agreement.

She had one foot over the threshold when Brice's voice called her back. "See you tomorrow, Ava. And thanks for sharing a cup of coffee with me."

Coffee. That made her screech to a total halt. Her mind sat there, idling. Isn't that what he'd wanted to do in the beginning? He'd wanted to get to know her over a cup of coffee.

And he had.

She wanted to leap to the quick conclusion that she'd been tricked. But it wasn't that simple. She'd been the one to bring the coffee in the first place. It was her coffee, her kitchen, her renovation project. It was her heart she had to hold onto as she took the other step through the door and closed Brice Donovan from her sight.

Chapter Five

Ava burst through the employee's entrance door in the back of the Corner Christian Bookstore. The big problem? Her oldest sister was heating a cup of tea in the break room's microwave and she had *that* look. The one where she frowned, shook her head slowly from side to side as if this was exactly what she expected.

"Oops, I'm late." Ava slid the bakery box onto the small battered Formica table. "My bad. But I brought chocolate."

"That doesn't begin to make up for it." The corner of Katherine's mouth twitched, as if she were holding back a smile. "What am I going to do with you?"

"Nothing. I'm your little sister and you love me."

"Not at much as Aubrey," she teased. "Aubrey showed up twenty-three minutes early for her shift."

"True." Aubrey appeared from the other doorway that led to the floor. "I smell doughnuts. The doughnuts that were missing from our kitchen this morning. I came back from the stables and had nothing to eat. You didn't have to take every last one with you."

"Hey, the real question is why would you walk by a kitchen full of boxed doughnuts and not take any in the first place?" With a wink, Ava shoved open the small employee's closet and dumped her bag on the floor.

"What could have possessed me, I wonder?" Aubrey flipped open the box and stole a chocolate huckleberry custard. "The construction dudes were—"

"Cool. Loved the doughnuts. Started beating down walls with their sledgehammer thingies right away." Ava grabbed a cup from the upper cabinet and filled it from the sink tap.

Don't think of Brice, she ordered herself. Too late. There he was in her mind's eye. Standing in her kitchen, looking like a good man, radiating character. Normally, she'd be *so* interested, but if she let herself like him, that would be just another huge mistake in a long, endless string of disasters.

Don't start wishing now, she told herself, letting her big sister Katherine take the mug from her hands and slip it into the microwave to heat.

"You look down," Katherine commented as she added honey to her steaming teacup, her engagement ring sparkling. "That can't be good. This is your first day of renovation. You should be excited. What's going on?"

"Uh-oh." Aubrey had a twin moment.

Great. Somehow she had telebeamed her thoughts to her twin; they seemed to share brain cells. Ava felt the humiliation creeping through her all over again. "Don't say it. Let's just not go into it."

Ava could sense Katherine's question hovering in the air unspoken between them, wanting to know what was wrong and how she could help. Dear Katherine meant well, wanting to take care of everyone and fixing what she could, but what do you do when you know there's no solution to a problem?

You refocus yourself, that's what, and concentrate on preventing disasters. There was Brice Donovan again, flashing across her brain pan. Definitely disaster material.

Hayden, Katherine's soon-to-be stepdaughter, poked her head around the door. "Hey, like, Spence is totally freaking out. There's no one out there to ring up and stuff."

"So? Our brother is always freaking out."

"I'll go," Aubrey said. "I'm supposed to be watching the front anyway. I'll take this with me, though." With a grin she slipped past the teenager with her chocolate-covered doughnut in hand.

"Like that's going to make Spence happy." The kid shrugged her gangly shoulders. "Maple bars, too? Cool, Ava."

"I knew they were your favorite, not that I like you or anything." Ava hid her smile, knowing she wasn't so successful.

Hayden grinned, snatched a doughnut. "Thanks!" she called over her shoulder as she disappeared back into the stacks.

Talk about weird. "Are you ready to be a stepmom?" Ava already knew the answer, but it was called a diversionary tactic. She *so* did not want to talk about her shop, her dreams, and how it had all gotten tangled up with Mr. Wishable. “You’ll be marrying Jack in two more months.”

“I know. Time is melting way and it feels as if I’m never going to have everything ready for the wedding.” Katherine waited for the microwave to ding. She opened the door, dropped a tea bag into the steaming water and left it on the counter to steep. “But I’m more than ready to be a stepmom. Hayden is a part of Jack. How could I not love her? Speaking of which, how are the designs for my cake coming along?”

Okay, another topic to avoid. “I’m working on it. Honest.”

“I have all the faith in the world in you, sweetie.”

Wasn’t that the problem? “I’ve got some great sketches, but I’ve got a few more ideas I want to work out before we sit back down.”

“Do you know what we should do?” Katherine pushed the plastic bear-shaped bottle of honey along the counter. “We’ll all go out to a nice dinner, my treat. To celebrate.”

“Celebrate what?”

Katherine shook her head, as if she couldn’t believe it. “The first day of construction on your shop? This has been your dream forever, right?"

"I can't tonight. I have a consultation. Maybe later, though? Besides, you're just in a good mood because you've found Mr. Dream Come True. Not everyone is as lucky." She didn't mean to sound wistful, really. She was deeply happy for her sister. Katherine deserved a good man and a happy marriage. And, seeing that it had happened for her sister after all this time, it *almost* gave a girl a little hope it could happen to her.

Not that she'd go around praying for it, because she'd tried that route before. She had a gift for prayer. She might make a mess of everything she touched, she might show up late for work and forget where she put her keys, but what she prayed for almost always happened. Hence her last relationship disasters with Mike, Brett and Ken. Before that, Isaiah, Christian and Lloyd. It was that old adage, be careful what you wish for. Which was why she wasn't, not even silently, wishing. Really.

"I know something isn't right." Katherine frowned as if she were trying to figure out what. "I know you've got to be under a lot of pressure getting your business off the ground, but you know you're not alone, right? You say the word and we're right with you. In fact, you might not have a chance to say the word before we barge in."

Was she blessed with her awesome family or what? Ava's eyes burned. She was grateful to the Lord for her wonderful sisters. "You know me. I know how to holler."

"Excellent." Katherine brushed some of Ava's windblown hair out of her eyes. "Whatever's got you down, remember you are just the way God made you. And that makes you perfectly lovable, sweetie. Trust me."

She didn't know about being perfectly lovable but she did know that her sister—her family—was on her perfectly lovable list. Blessings she gave thanks for every day of her life. Katherine's words meant everything.

The morning had been perfect. The construction workers were hard-working family men who were very happy with the box of doughnuts. And—surprise!—Brice looked like a good boss and a hard worker himself. She was confident that the renovation would be terrific when it was done.

She was the problem since she wavered on what she said she wanted. No, she wasn't exactly wavering. But she'd *almost* given in to wishing and that was just as bad. She had to be more careful. More determined.

A deep, frustrated huff sounded at the inner door. It was Spence, glowering. "There you two are. Ava, you're late. For, what, the fifteenth shift in a row?"

"Probably. Sorry." Ava couldn't argue. She upended the plastic bear over her cup and gave it a hard squeeze. "But I'm here now, so that's good, right? I mean, it could be worse. I could be even later."

That was the logic that always confounded Spence. His Heathcliff personality couldn't seem to understand and he stormed away.

She wasn't fooled. His bark was much worse than his bite.

"He's under a lot of pressure," Katherine excused him as she grabbed a cinnamon twist from the box on her way to the front. "Thanks for the goodies, cutie."

Alone in the break room, Ava took a sip of her tea, but the chamomile blend didn't soothe her. She dumped in more honey, and that didn't do the trick either. A big piece of sadness sat square in the middle of her chest, stronger after having been with Brice.

His words came back to her now. *You want a place where it feels as if wishes could come true.* He'd said what was in her heart.

How had he known?

At a loss, she headed out front. She had bills to pay and dreams to dream—and a no-man policy to stick to.

Ava had lingered in his thoughts all through the work day, all of Brice's waking hours and into the next morning. He hadn't looked forward to strapping on his tool belt this much in a long time. Though he liked his work, it was the prospect of seeing Ava that made the difference.

His commitment to this renovation project was about more than work. He wanted to do a good job with it—hands down, customer satisfaction was job one. But beyond that, he wanted to do his best to give Ava her dream. Listening to her talk about baking with her mom—the mom who had run off to Hollywood with the youngest daughter decades ago and had never been heard from since—

was like a sign from above pointing the way to win her heart.

He wondered if Ava had any idea how purely her inner beauty shone when she talked about being happy like that? In wanting again, for others and for herself, a joy-filled place where wishes could come true?

She was a different kind of woman than he was used to. Whitney had been exactly what his mom had wanted for him. She was from a respectable family, from money older than the state of Montana. The right schools and the proper social obligations and charity work. But in the end, she'd been wrong for him. Wrong for the man he really was, not Roger Donovan's son, but a Montanan born and raised, who liked his life a little more comfortable and far less showy.

The shop had a decimated look to it, even gilded by the golden peach of the newly rising sun. The interior walls were bare down to the studs, which glowed like honey in the morning light. The white dip and rise of electrical wire ran like a clothesline the length of the room. Dust coated the windows, but he could see the promise. See her dream.

Rex romped to the front door, springing in place with excitement. His tongue rolled out of his mouth as he panted, and since Brice was taking too long, pawed at the door handle.

"Hold on there, bud. I'm eager to see Ava, too."

The retriever gave a low bark when he heard Ava's name.

Yeah, at least the dog liking her won't be an issue the way it was with Whitney. Yet another sign, Brice figured as he picked through his mammoth ring of work keys, found the one for the shop and unlocked the door. Whitney hadn't been fond of big, bouncing, sometimes slobbery dogs. Brice was.

The second the door was open an inch, Rex hit it at a dead run and launched through the open kitchen doors. There on the work table was a bright pink bakery box. That explained the retriever's eagerness. They may have missed Ava, but she'd left a consolation prize.

She'd come before his shift started, left her baking and skedaddled. Apparently, there was a good reason. Like maybe the comment he'd made about finally getting to talk with her over coffee. Maybe—just maybe—he shouldn't have pointed that out.

Right when he'd thought he was making progress with her, getting to know her, letting her know the kind of man he was, he'd hit a brick wall.

Apparently Ava wasn't as taken with him as he was with her.

Wow. That felt like a hard blow to his sternum. Here was the question: Did he pursue this or not? Sure, they'd gotten off on the wrong foot when she'd mistaken him for Chloe's groom, but even after that, she'd been determined to put some distance between them.

Face it, this was one-sided. He'd stood right here in this kitchen and got to know her, seen right through to her dreams. He was captivated by her. He was falling in serious like with her.

But now? She was missing in action.

Rex's bark echoed in the vacant kitchen.

"Okay, okay." Brice popped open the huge bakery box. "Only one, and I mean it this time. All this baked stuff can't be good for you—"

He fell silent at the treats inside the box. She'd promised muffins, but these weren't like anything he'd ever seen. They were huge muffins shaped like cute, round monsters. They had ropy icing for hair, big goofy eyes, a potato nose and a wide grin. Two dozen monster faces stared up at him, colorful and whimsical.

Ava made the ordinary unusual and fun. He liked that about her. Very much.

He'd been praying, to find a good woman to love and marry. Have a few kids. Live a happy life. That had been part of his plan for a long time, but it just hadn't worked out for one reason or another. In fact, it hadn't worked out for such a length of time that began to feel as if his prayer was destined to remain unanswered.

The front door swung open and heavy boots pounded against the floor, echoing in the demolished room. It was Tim, the electrician. "Hey, where are those muffins she promised?"

"In here."

"I gotta tell ya," Tim said as he dropped his tool bags on the floor, "this might be the best job we've done yet. The doughnuts yesterday were something. You think she's gonna keep bakin' for us?" Tim's jaw dropped in disbelief when he saw the muffins. "Look at that. Think anyone would mind if I took one home for my little girl? She'd get a kick out of that."

Brice realized that Ava had made five times the number of muffins they needed for their small work crew. "Go for it."

"Cool." Tim grabbed a mammoth monster muffin and took a bite. "Mmm," he said around a full mouth, as if surprised by how good it tasted.

Not that Brice was surprised by that. He flipped open his phone and dialed. While he waited for the call to connect, he took a muffin for Rex on the way out the back door. The sunshine felt hot and dry as he sat on the back step and unwrapped the muffin. The dog gobbled his muffin in three bites.

Ava picked up on the sixth ring. "Hi there. Is there a problem at the shop?"

Caller ID, he guessed. "A problem? You could say that."

"What's wrong? I was there and everything looked fine. Okay, it was like a total wreck, but it's supposed to look like that, right?"

"Right. That wasn't the kind of problem I meant." He leaned back, resting his spine against the building. He wondered where she was. A lot of clanging sounded in the background. "You left a box of monsters behind. Why didn't you stay and say hello?"

"I didn't want to be in the way."

"I hope you didn't feel uncomfortable with me yesterday. You know I like you."

"I'm trying to ignore that."

"Is there any particular reason for that?"

"Well, you're doing the renovation on my shop, for starters."

"Good reason. Look, I don't want you to feel uncomfortable. Not around me. Not around my men. Not when it comes to the work we're doing for you."

"Sure, I know that."

It didn't seem as if she did. She sounded as vulnerable as she'd looked yesterday when she'd been talking about her baking. Okay, so maybe what he felt wasn't a two-way street. "How about you and I agree to be friends. Would that make you more comfortable?"

"Friends? Uh, sure. Wait." He could imagine her biting her bottom lip while she thought, the cute little furrow digging in between her eyes. "You mean like platonic friends."

"I mean that whatever this is going on between us, let's put in on hold until your renovation is done. That way you don't have to come to your own shop before 6:45 a.m. just to avoid me."

"I wasn't necessarily avoiding *you.*" Ava knew her voice sounded thin and honest. She was no good at subterfuge of any kind. Another reason she'd never understood men who had hidden agendas. "You see, it's not you. It's me. All me."

"You want to explain that?" he asked in that kind way he had, but he obviously didn't understand.

There it was, doom, hovering right in front of her, and its name was Brice Donovan.

"It's just that—" she blurted out, nearly losing hold of her grocery cart in the dairy aisle. "I have the worst luck dating. If there's a loser anywhere near me, he'll be the one I think is nice. I'm like a disaster magnet. That's why I have a policy."

"What policy? I don't understand."

She felt her heart weakening. She liked

this man—and wasn't that the exact problem? She had to be totally tough. Cool. Focused. Strong. That's what she had to be. Strong enough to stick to her guns. "It's an iron-clad, non-negotiable no-man, no-dating policy."

"That's a pretty strict policy. There's a good reason for it, huh?"

Her throat tightened. When she spoke, she knew she sounded as if she were struggling. "Yeah. Nothing horrible, just disappointing. I don't want to spend my life believing in a man's goodness and being blind to any terrible faults that I just can't see until it's too late. You see, it's like being color-blind. I'm just..." She didn't know what to say.

Apparently Brice didn't either. No sound came from his end of the connection. Nothing at all.

"I'm sorry." That came out strangled sounding.

So she was never going to be a tough business woman. She wasn't a tough anything. Sadness hit her like the cold from the refrigerated dairy case. Was she disappointed?

Surprisingly, yes.

"Okay, then. I'll call you if we have any

questions over here." He broke the silence, sounding business as usual, but beneath, she thought she heard disappointment, too.

Maybe it was best not to think about that, she thought as she closed her phone, dumped it into her bag and put the milk jug into her cart. She couldn't say why she would be feeling deflated, because she did the right thing by putting him off. She just had to stay focused on her goals and her path in life, she thought as she grabbed a carton of whipping cream.

Her phone rang again and she went fishing for it in her messy tote. Luckily it was still ringing when she found it. She didn't recognize the number on the screen. "Hello?"

"Uh, yes," came a refined woman's voice. "My name is Maxime Frost and I was at Chloe Donovan's wedding. Brice highly recommended you, and I just *had* to call. We simply must have one of your cakes for my Carly's wedding."

"I'm sure I can design something both you and Carly will love."

She wrote down an appointment time on the inside of her checkbook and ended the call. How about that? Brice had recommended her in spite of the mistaken identity incident.

Just when she thought she was sure she'd made the right decision to stick to her no-date policy, look what happened. He made her start wishing all over again—and reconsidering.

Chapter Six

Everyone was at the restaurant by the time she got there, seated in a big table at the back, between a cozy intersection of booths. Of course, she was late because she was time-challenged. From the head of the table, Spence spotted her first and his dour frown darkened a notch. He highly prized timeliness. Katherine sat between him and her fiancé, Jack Munroe. Seated next to her dad, the teenaged Hayden gave a finger wave.

Ava lifted her hand to finger wave back but the sight of the appetizers in platters placed in three parts of the table stopped her in her tracks. "I can't believe you ordered without me."

"You're twenty minutes late." Spence

huffed. "The assistant manager wasn't going to hold the reservation just for you."

Personally, this was why she thought Spence wasn't married, but now was probably not the time to mention it. "Oops. Sorry." She didn't bother to explain the extra appointment she squeezed in, and that she'd left a message on Aubrey's phone that she'd be late, and there had been a major traffic snarl from some wild moose who was wandering Glenrose Street. It was easier to endure Spence's scowl.

She dropped into the empty seat next to her twin. "Do you check your messages?"

"I was out at the studio and lost track of time. I barely got here myself." Aubrey grabbed the platter in front of her and began sliding a stack of deep-fried zucchini slices onto Ava's plate. "Don't worry about Spence. It's that assistant manager who works here. The one that had that date with Katherine long ago and it didn't go well? He's always snippy with us. The construction—"

"Is going well." Ava paused to bow her head and gave a quick grace, since she'd missed Spence's blessing.

Aubrey spooned a heap of creamy dip next to the zucchini slices on Ava's plate. "And how's Brice?"

"Fine, I guess. I didn't see him today."

"And that wouldn't be because you're avoiding him?"

"I'm not avoiding him." It wasn't true but she wanted it to be. "Fine, I just avoided him for the day. Maybe I'll try again tomorrow."

"He's supposed to be this great guy. Wasn't he this year's most eligible bachelor or something?"

"Let's not talk about him." She glanced around the table to see if everyone was straining to listen. They were. "Later, okay?"

Katherine spoke up. "Didn't you do a wedding cake for Brice's sister?"

"Yeah. Just." Like she wanted to talk about it? *This* was the downside of being in a big family. Nothing was secret for long. "He's the contractor doing the renovation."

Spence leaned in. "You mean it's his *company* doing the renovation. He's not doing the actual work. He's an owner."

"No, he's like the on-site manager guy. Trust me, he had a hammer and everything." She hedged because everyone in her family but Aubrey was *way* too eager to marry her off. "Chloe recommended the company."

It didn't look like anyone at the table was fooled by that.

Katherine passed her hunky fiancé a platter of mozzarella sticks. "I thought Brice Donovan was engaged."

"No," Aubrey dragged a zucchini slice through a puddle of dip. "I read in the paper over a year ago that she called it off. The wedding was cancelled something like two days before it was supposed to happen. That had to be very hard for both of them."

Ava couldn't seem to swallow. The part of her that was afraid of getting close to him wanted to use this new piece of news as a reason to keep away from him. He'd already had one failed relationship. He was probably at fault, and she didn't need some flawed guy, right? On the surface, it sounded like the best reasoning.

But she knew it wasn't. Brice was a good guy—that much was clear. The real question was, how far down did that kindness go? Was it superficial, or the real thing?

The cracked pieces of her heart ached with a wish she couldn't let herself voice. Brice had a lot of redeeming qualities, so what? She had to resist. What she had to do was clear every thought of him from her mind. His every image from her memory. No more thoughts of Brice Donovan allowed.

"Good evening, McKaslin family," said a familiar voice behind her. Brice's voice.

Of course.

Why did it have to be him? She felt as if she'd been hit with the debris from a fast approaching tornado. She couldn't outrun it, escape it and there was no hope of avoiding it as Brice Donovan stepped into sight.

To her surprise her brother stood, nodding a greeting. "Good to see you again, Brice. Would you care to join us, or are you here with your family?"

"With family. It's my mother's birthday, but thanks for the invite. I just spotted Ava and I thought I'd come over. Let her know a few things about the job today, if she's got time before her meal arrives."

Ava could feel the power of his presence, stronger than the earth's gravity holding her feet to the floor. "Do I have time?" she asked her twin.

"I ordered for you," Aubrey explained.

"Take your phone and you two go talk. I'll call you when the meal arrives."

Okay, it sounded like a good plan, but there was a downside here—did she want to be alone with Brice? No. Was she mentally prepared to be alone with him? Not a chance.

She grabbed her plate and her phone and followed him to the more casual patio area, where there were plenty of tables available. Brice nodded toward one of the waiters, who gestured to a set of unoccupied tables along the railing.

"I was hoping to catch you tomorrow morning." Brice was entirely too close as he leaned to pull out a chair for her. "But seeing you charge through the restaurant a few minutes ago seemed like a sign. I hope you don't mind the intrusion."

"Nope." What she minded was being alone with him. How was she going to hold onto her policy now? She caught a hint of his spicy aftershave. "After all, we've agreed to be friends."

"Exactly." He smiled his killer smile, the one with the dimples.

Did he know what that did to a woman? It made every innocent, friendly thought vanish and the ones about sweet romance and marriage proposals surge forth like a hurricane hitting shore. That part of her, which always panicked when she got too close to anyone new, started to tremble.

There was no need to panic. This was only business, right? Except as he helped her scootch her chair up to the table, it definitely didn't feel friendly.

He took the chair across the table from her, and a girl might think that would be safer, with the span of the table between them, but somehow he seemed closer. Much too close.

Don't wish, she reminded herself and bit into a zucchini slice. "If it's bad news about the renovation, you can't just spring it on me. It's best to work up to it. Want some?"

"Sure." He grabbed a coated, deep-fried slice and crunched into it. "I have some suggestions for changes for the finished woodwork. What Rafe drew up for you is nice, but it's plain."

"It's what I can afford."

"You can afford this, too." He took another slice. His manner was casual, his overall tone was friendly, but there was something intense beneath the surface, something that hadn't been there before. "I think you'll be happier with it. It won't add any time if I get started now. I mostly do the jobs with custom woodwork."

"I'm still trying to picture that. I know, I've seen you with a tool belt, but it doesn't still compute." She said this without thinking and watched his face harden. Not in a mean way, but guarded, like she'd struck a sore spot. "Don't get me wrong. There's a lot of integrity working to perfect a craft and doing your best. It's how I justify my baking. But I look at you and think, white-collar professional."

"It's a big issue in my family right now. My mom and dad have always just assumed I'd step into place at the family business and take over the firm when Dad's ready to retire. And he's starting to think about it, so they're starting to get serious."

"Aren't they supportive of what you're doing now?"

"They're tolerating it."

"I can't imagine that." Ava dragged a zucchini slice through the dip and bit into it. "My family is everything to me. I would be nothing without them."

"You seem tight with your sisters."

"Yeah. I'd never be able to open my own bakery without my family's help. I got my business loan from my grandmother—talk about fear of failure. I don't want to let her down. And Spence helped me with my business plan and buying the property. My sisters are helping me with the finishing stuff. Katherine took me to all the flea markets and swap meets and secondhand stores in the state, I think, and we got a bunch of bistro tables and chairs that Aubrey is refinishing for me in her studio. My stepsister Danielle has promised to make the window blinds and valences. That kind of thing. And that's not including the pep talks when I need them."

"So, they've got a lot of confidence in you. It must be nice to have the people you love most wanting what will make you happy."

"It is." Ava's eyes shone with emotion and she dunked her zucchini into the dip. "It's also a lot of people to disappoint. Something I could never stand to do."

He could see that about her. Brice's throat tightened. "I can't stand how much this has upset my parents either. It's been a huge strain on our relationship."

"They want the best for you, though?"

He could see from the hopeful trust in her eyes that she didn't understand. "They do. I know they love me, but the truth is, I'm not what they hoped for in a son. I wrestled with it for a long time. I tried things their way, but I'm not cut out for spending a day in an office, investing other people's money. I like the work I do, but they see it as too blue collar."

"And that would be wrong because…?"

He swallowed his embarrassment over his parents. They were too set in their ways and opinions to change. He tried to dismiss the pain behind it, and the weight of his father's disappointments. His father who was a good, loving dad. Love and family were always complicated. "Dad thinks I'm not going to be happy unless I have a white-collar career, but I think it's the appearance thing. They care too much what other people think."

"It's hard to know other people think you're a dope or a loser. It has happened to me too many times to count. I've become sort of numb to it."

He choked down a hoot of laughter. She said it with a twinkle in her eyes. She always surprised him. "Exactly. I've become a little numb on this subject, where my parents are concerned. My mom is still holding out hope I'll come to my senses and go to law school or medical school. Or into the seminary."

"I can't picture you doing any of that. I'm sure you'd be good at any profession you chose, but you can only be yourself. Who God meant you to be." She lowered her gaze and stared hard at the table's surface between them. "At least, that's what my older sister keeps telling me."

"She's right."

He considered the woman across from him, with her blond hair windblown and going every which way. She was lovelier every time he saw her. Today her cheeks were slightly flushed from what he guessed to be a busy day. She had that breathless look about her. Her words had been rolling around in his head all day. *It's an iron-clad, non-negotiable no-man, no-dating policy.*

He couldn't give up hope completely. Business first. And when the renovation was done, then he'd see where he stood with her.

At that exact moment her cell rang. She checked it and turned it off. "It's Aubrey. Food's served. I'm sorry, but I'm starving."

He stood to help her with her chair. "You'll stop by tomorrow when I'm there so I can show you what I have in mind?"

"I can do that."

"No more drive-by bakings?"

"Now, I can't promise that." She swished away.

She was so small and fragile, so whimsical and feminine, that a vibrant, steel-like emotion came to life in his heart, overtaking him. He watched her go with a mix of care and affection. He really liked her.

She stopped at the end of the row of tables. "Oh, I forgot to ask about the muffins. Did the men like them?"

"The monsters were the hit of the day."

She flashed him her brightest smile, the one that showed her dazzling spirit. The one that caught his heart like a hook on a line and dug deep. The hook did not leave as she walked away with her gait snapping and her golden hair swaying across her back. Even when she was out of his sight it remained, inexplicably.

Without Brice Donovan anywhere around, it was like a thousand times easier to remember her policy. Later that day, Ava jammed her Bible study materials into her tote and heaved it off the floor. The classroom in the church's auxiliary building was pleasant and serene, but then she always felt peaceful after spending an hour in fellowship, studying her Bible. She was focused and calm and everything seemed clear.

Aubrey fell in beside her and they trailed the small crowd filing out the door. "I'm in the mood for chocolate. Want to stop by the ice creamery and pig out on sundaes?"

"Like I would ever think that was a bad idea." Really. Did Aubrey even have to ask? She staggered under the weight of her mammoth bag. She was really going to have to find the time to go through it and clean it out—not that she was skilled at stuff like that. "I need sustenance if I'm going to be able to face my day tomorrow. It's jam-packed."

"You remembered we were going to babysit for Danielle, right?" Aubrey waited a beat before rolling her eyes. Their stepsister was happily married with two great kids. "It's okay. Don't even bother. I'll babysit and you'll do it next Friday. I've got that church retreat thing. So, tomorrow's packed?"

"It's just that I got this referral from Chloe's wedding. It was Brice, really—"

"Ex-boyfriend alert," Aubrey cut in, although by the interested lift of her eyebrows she'd caught the Brice reference. "It's Mike, directly ahead, in the hall."

They were still safely stuck in doorway of the classroom, in a small queue, but she was definitely visible. Ava could feel his smug gaze sweeping over her. She didn't have to look to know he had some poor clueless woman hanging on his arm. Two years ago, she'd been there, believing the stories he told about what a moral Christian guy he was on the surface.

Unfortunately, his supposed values were pure fabrication, and every time she spotted him she felt beyond foolish. Yep, even years later, her nose was turning glowing strawberry red again. Why couldn't she have noticed right away that he wasn't what he seemed? It was her fault-blindness. She just couldn't see the big glaring signs of trouble that other people could.

"That poor woman," Aubrey said with sympathy and kindness. Good, gentle Aubrey never made a fool of herself and never made any mistakes at all, much less mistakes of gargantuan proportion. "I'm going to add both of them to my prayers. She's bound to be heartbroken one day."

Just like I was. Ava could still feel the crack in her heart from him. "I'll pray for her, too."

She purposely didn't look ahead down the hall, so she wouldn't have to see him. Or to remember she'd really fallen hard for Mike. Discovering who he really was had been tough.

"And there's Ken." Aubrey grabbed Ava's wrist and steered her toward the far wall. "No, don't look up."

Great. Ken was probably with someone, too. He'd been the chef who, on the third date, said he'd waited long enough and tried to take liberties. She'd accidentally broken two fingers on his right hand when she'd bolted from the passenger seat of his car and slammed his hand in the door.

Really, did she look like the kind of girl who said one thing and did another?

No—it was some men. See? It went right back to them. They needed to think faithful, pious thoughts. Study their Bibles even more. She was really starting to get disillusioned about men. *All men.*

What about Brice? a little voice asked—a voice that seemed to come straight from her heart.

What about him? So, he'd been a gentleman so far, but wasn't that the problem? How deep did the gentleman thing go? She'd been fooled too many times by how a man *seemed.* So, he was Mr. Eligible Bachelor. Did that mean he was really good at fooling others? Or was he truly a good man, soul-deep?

Well, if she was interested in him, maybe that was a sign right there. Ken and Mike were excellent examples of her flaw-blindness. What if she was doing the same exact thing with Brice? If the man was interested in her, as time had proved over and over again, there had to be something wrong with him.

It was as simple as that. And if the tiny hope in her heart wished for more, that he truly was what he seemed, did she risk finding out? Face it, she didn't have Aubrey's quiet beauty or her sister Katherine's classic poise. She'd driven her own mother away.

Don't think about that. She squeezed the pain from her heart. Erased the thought from her mind. Purposefully turned her thoughts from her failures and to her business. Her shop. She had more sketching to do tonight when they got home. And breakfast treats to bake for the construction dudes.

Maybe she'd do a batch of scones. She'd lose herself in the kitchen. Baking always made everything right. Baking made her problems and failures turn from shouts into silence.

There would be no dreaming. She'd lost too many dreams to waste them on what could never truly be. Brice had given her the perfect solution. He'd said he was happy to be friends. He didn't want anything to complicate their business relationship, and she was going to hold him to it, whether her heart liked it or not.

Pleased with that plan, she led Aubrey out of the church hall and through the parking lot, beeped the SUV unlocked and headed straight to the ice creamery.

Chapter Seven

Brice climbed out of his truck and into the morning. The hiss of the sprinkler system in the city park diagonally across the street provided enough background noise to drown out the faint hum of distant traffic. It was early enough yet that only an infrequent car motored down the nearby street. Birds took flight from the tree overhead when Rex hopped onto the sun-warmed blacktop. The parking lot was empty, except for them. He'd beat Ava here. Again.

Ava. Spotting her in the restaurant last night had given him a chance to clear the air. The only problem was, nothing felt clearer. Their agreement to keep it to business, sure, that was crystal clear. But his feelings for her became more complicated every time he was around her.

Lord, You know I'm in over my head. Please, I need some help. If it's not too much trouble, show me the way.

As if in answer, he felt a shift in the calm peace of the morning. It was as if the nearly non-existent breeze had completely vanished, as if the world stopped spinning on its axis. As if for one nanosecond, the rotation of the earth ceased. Brice felt an odd prickling at the back of his neck. When he turned around, there she was.

Or, more accurately, there she was in her yellow SUV driving straight toward him. The morning light cut at an angle through her windshield, illumining her clearly. Those sunglasses were perched on her nose again, and the bill of the baseball cap—pink, today—framed her heart-shaped face. She whipped into the parking space closest to the front door. Right beside his truck.

Her nearness was like taking an unexpected punch to the chest. Brice rocked back on his heels from the impact. He watched her through the windshield as she chattered on her cell while cutting the engine, pulling the e-brake and gathering up her things.

Knowing there would be more bakery boxes and careens of coffee and spiced tea, he moved to help. Rex bounded ahead, whining in anticipation of being with Ava.

"I know just how you feel, buddy." He scrubbed his dog's head with his knuckles.

Her driver's side door was open, but she'd turned away, still busy gathering her things and absorbed in her phone conversation. Her dulcet, cheerful tone was as soft as the morning breeze. "Yes, Madeline, I'd be happy to bring by my catalogue. If your client wants something unique, then I'm the right baker. I specialize in one-of-a-kind designs."

She backed out of the vehicle, dragging her enormous purse with her. The bulk of it clattered over the console and snagged on the emergency brake, which stopped her progress. No one was cuter. Captivated, he could not look away as she freed her bag from the snag. Once it was free, she hooked the big bag over her shoulder, absently, and went to slam the door. With the keys inside.

Suddenly it wasn't a mystery how she

kept locking herself out. He caught the edge of the door.

"Goodbye, Madeline and—" She stopped, apparently startled to find him latched onto her door. For the tiniest part of a millisecond she gazed up at him unguarded, forgetting to finish her conversation. "Uh…thanks again, Madeline, for this opportunity. I won't let you down. Bye!"

She snapped her phone shut. "Thank you, too. You keep showing up right when I need rescuing."

"It's a knack of mine." He waited for her to step out of the way before he settled behind the steering wheel and snagged the keys from the ignition. He started fiddling with the remote.

"And now what are you doing?"

"Reprogramming this for you. So it won't auto lock. There."

He was starting to look more and more like a fictitious knight in shining armor… well, more like a knight with a tool belt. It was nice to be rescued by such a good guy.

"Who was on the phone?" he asked over a few electronic beeps that came from inside the SUV.

"That was Madeline from Madeline's

Catering. She provided the food for your sister's wedding reception. She asked me to make the desserts for a baby shower she's catering. The funniest thing, though. She said you had highly recommended me."

"I might have." He angled out from behind the wheel and closed the door.

"Thank you. I met with Maxime Frost yesterday, and her daughter Carly chose one of my designs. Also because of your recommendation."

"I'm just glad it worked out. If you want to head in, I'll bring in the boxes. Take a look at the plans. They're on the work table."

"Oh. Well, okay." Ava tried so hard not to like Brice more, but found it impossible. Fighting her feelings, she accepted Rex's good morning jump up, hugged him and promised him his own scone. Thrilled, his doggy tongue hanging, he bounded ahead of her on the way to the front door as if to say, hurry, faster!

"It's too bad I really don't like your dog," she said, not quite comfortable saying the truth, of how very much she adored Rex.

"Yeah, I don't like him either," Brice said with a wink.

She ducked her head to dig for her office

keys in the mess of her bag. Truth was, she didn't want to keep looking at Brice. And see more and more good things to like about him. But her attempts were futile. There was Brice's reflection in the glass as she went to unlock the door.

My, he was such a fine man. Her heart gave a little tumble—just the tiniest fall.

It's just business. That's all. That's what it had to be.

So, why didn't that rationale feel convincing? Best not to think about that too much. She pushed open the door. Rex sprung in, expertly dodging the sawhorses and piles of fresh wallboard, and she lingered, turning to watch Brice. It was hard not to notice the powerful agile way he hefted the boxes, shut the back of the SUV and locked up.

He was a great guy—wait, rephrase that. He was a really awesome man. Why did that make her panic?

"It's starting to take shape." His voice and his boots echoed in the big empty shop. "You can see we've got the rewiring done. The inspector's supposed to be here in an hour. Once we get that okayed, the wallboard goes up. Do you like the cathedral ceilings? We were able to punch up a few feet higher than we'd first thought."

See? Just business. Ava managed to push aside the lump of feelings all wadded up in her chest. Did her best not to notice how she felt happy when he was near.

"I love the ceilings. It's better than I hoped for." She walked around, giving Brice time to head into the kitchen with the mornings treats, and to put space between them. "The guys have done a great job."

She could see her dreams of the new shop taking shape in the shell of the old. She'd have warm honeyed woods, cheerful yellow walls and the scent of happiness in the air. It was finally happening. For real. She thought of Madeline's call—was it a sign her business would boom? Maybe.

She had a business to build, not more mistakes to make. She caught sight of Brice unboxing the scones. A tiny question whispered inside her heart: What if he wasn't a mistake?

"Ava, you've topped yourself." He had one of the sunshine face scones in hand.

"I made a double batch, so the construction dudes can take some home to their families."

"Once you get this shop open, I hope you know that you're going to be in demand."

"From your lips to God's ears," she said, trying to stay focused on the business. The business. Not on Brice's kind words.

He took a bite. "Sheer heaven. You'll be open soon. Do you have hired help all lined up?"

"Are you kidding? I've got enough extended family to hire without even putting an ad in the paper. I'm just hoping this doesn't wind up being another failure."

"It won't be." Brice could see the burden of it weighing her down. "You have an excellent quality of product, and the decorating is top notch. It's all I heard at Chloe's reception. I think you should believe in yourself a little more. It will turn out fine."

"You're just saying that to be nice, mister."

"That's the idea. I want to be nice to you. This is business, remember? We have this business relationship, but after that, I'm hoping you'll want more."

"Oh, that's scarier than starting my own business." She swiped a lock of golden hair out of her eyes, looking adorable. "It's that fault-blind thing. You look perfect to me, but it's just because I can't see the flaws. It's like walking blind into a tornado."

"Good. No man wants you to see his flaws."

"Some people are better at hiding them than others." She followed him into the kitchen where sunlight highlighted the drawings he'd set out beside the bakery box. "Take me, my flaws are totally noticeable."

"I haven't noticed any flaws."

"Sure you haven't. What about those accusations?"

"Those were perfectly understandable considering you were confusing me with a Darren Fullerton."

Really, he was just trying to get her to like him, and it wasn't going to work. Absolutely not. The same way she *wasn't* going to notice how wonderfully tall he was. Solid. Substantial. How he looked like a man who could shoulder any burden. Solve any problem.

Okay, she was starting to notice, but only just a little. Really.

Rex, the perfect gentleman, was sitting

there with his big innocent eyes showing just how good and deserving he was of a scone. Ava turned her attention to the dog because there was no reason why she shouldn't fall in love with Rex. She grabbed one of the cheerful iced treats. "Here you go, handsome."

Rex delicately took the scone from her fingertips, gave her a totally adoring look and sucked the sweet down in one gulp.

"He seems to like your baking," Brice said with a grin. "Can you stay for a while? I can pour you a cup of coffee if you want to look over the—"

"*Oh.*" She was already looking at the drawings, and it was her turn to be utterly adoring. She couldn't believe her eyes. Could she talk? No. The penciled images had stolen every word from her brain. Her mind was a total blank except for a single thought.

Perfect.

He'd taken the photos she'd showed him yesterday and transformed them into her vision. Into exactly what she'd imagined. There it was. Curlicue scrollwork and rosebud-patterned moldings and carvings framing the wood and glass bakery case. "There's no way I can afford this."

"Custom woodwork is built into the estimate you signed. This would be for the same price. We've agreed to it."

"How can that be? I love this, don't get me wrong, but this can't be what was on the estimate. I know it's not."

"Rafe doesn't do woodwork, so pricing it is a mystery to him. Trust me. I can do this for the same price as he quoted you."

"Are you sure?"

"Positive. There's no hidden costs and no hidden agendas. With me, what you see is what you get."

"Business-wise, right?"

"Always."

She loved the sincerity in his words. The honesty he projected was totally irresistible. Now she *had* to like him. But just a pinch. A smidgeon. But not a drop more.

"I love this." She traced the drawn image of the bakery case with her fingertips. "This is my dream."

"That was the idea." He leaned closer to study the drawing, too, and to set a coffee cup in front of her. The steely curve of his upper arm brushed against her shoulder and stayed.

The trouble was, she noticed. She liked being close to him. She felt safe and secure and peaceful, as if everything was right in the world.

"If I have your approval, then I'll get started in the wood shop today. On one condition."

"Name it."

"Send two dozen of these scones to my office along with the bill." He moved away to take another treat from the box and broke it in half. Tossed one piece to the dog, who caught it like a pro ballplayer, and kept the other for himself. "Do you deliver?"

"For you, I could make an exception."

"Excellent. It's a pleasure doing business with you, Miss McKaslin."

"Anytime, Mr. Donovan." It was a good thing she had her priorities straight in life. Because otherwise, she could completely fall for him. Talk about doom!

She pushed away from the table, away from his presence and away from the wish of what could be. She grabbed her cup of coffee. "Later, Donovan."

"Later, McKaslin."

She gave Rex a pat and sauntered out of

her shop like a businesswoman totally in charge of her life and her heart.

It was a complete facade.

Rex's high yelping rose above the grind of the radial saw. Brice slipped down his protective glasses and glanced over his shoulder toward the open workshop door.

Maura, his secretary, had walked the twenty or so yards from the front office and stood staring at him, her arms crossed over her chest, looking like a middle-aged spinster despite the fact that they'd gone through public school together. "The scones you ordered are here. Talk about amazing. We're all taking a coffee break. You want to come join us?"

"Ava was here?" He hadn't expected her to be by so fast. He'd figured she would have to make another batch, but she must have made enough originally. He hadn't planned on that, he'd been busy working on her molding and now he'd missed her.

Maura shrugged. "I didn't know you wanted to see her. I'll make sure she doesn't run off next time."

She gave him that smile that women have, the knowing one that means you aren't fooling them one bit, and he was floored. Just how many people had guessed about his feelings for Ava?

"I've heard her cakes are heavenly." Maura paused in the doorway, giving that smile again. "When you order next time, remember—we all love chocolate. Don't forget, now."

"It's a business relationship." It was the truth. For now. "What makes you think it isn't?"

Maura arched one brow and stared pointedly at the pile of wood. "You always take the summer months off, but it's now June and look, you're still here. You aren't fooling me. And for your 4-1-1, she's really nice. She goes to my church and we're in the same Bible study. I could put in a good word for you."

"I can handle it, thanks."

"It's just that I know what happened with Whitney. It wasn't your fault." Maura kindly didn't say more on that topic. "I hope you know what you're doing. You haven't dated in a long time."

"Thanks, Maura, but I have a plan."

"Well, if you need a woman's opinion, you

can always run it by me." She hesitated again. "Thanks for the scones. They are wonderful." And finally she was gone, shutting the door tight behind her.

A plan? That wasn't what he'd thought to call it before now. He lifted the length of wood from the bench, a smooth piece of oak that would gleam like honey when he was through with it. He had a plan, of sorts. He intended to work hard. To deliver on his promise to Ava. To show her that he could help her with this dream. Maybe—God willing—with all her dreams.

The problem was, he didn't know if he could get her to go to dinner with him. It wasn't looking promising at this moment in time.

Based on his experience with her so far, he feared that Ava McKaslin might be the Mt. Everest equivalent of dating—a nearly impossible feat to accomplish and not for the faint of heart. A smart man would choose a much smaller mountain that required less effort.

He, apparently, wasn't a smart man, but he was a dedicated one and he recognized her value. He set his goggles in place, grabbed another length of oak from the lumber pile.

He had long hours of detailing to do and he intended to bring this in on time. He'd work on this dream first.

Then he'd try to tackle the rest of them.

Chapter Eight

In the serenity of her oldest sister's snazzy kitchen, Ava piped careful scrollwork across the final dozen cookies in the shape of a baby's shoe. Madeline, the caterer, had subcontracted with her for six dozen specialty cookies for a baby shower and they were going perfectly. It was a good feeling, a relieved feeling. The first she'd had in two days. That's how long she'd gone without seeing Brice.

You'd think that would be enough time to get her feelings under control, right? But no, she thought as she piped the final curlicue on the last cookie and stretched her aching back. She had feelings for him, and she liked him. But that didn't mean she had to actually do anything about it, right?

She'd been avoiding seeing him. Oh, she'd continued to deliver baked goods for the construction dudes, but she arrived way early, well before Brice was supposed to show, and just left the box in the kitchen. *Drive-by baking,* as he'd called it.

She hit the Off button on her digital music player and plucked the buds from her ears just in time. Katherine was tapping down the hall, coming her way. Since she was in big, deep favor-debt to her sister, Ava snatched a ceramic mug from the cabinet and poured a brisk cup of tea she'd had ready, steeping. The instant Katherine stepped foot in the kitchen, she had the cup on the breakfast bar and was heating a monster muffin in the microwave.

"Wow, it smells amazing in here." Dressed in a modest summer dress and sensible flat sandals, Katherine slid onto a breakfast bar stool. The classy act that she was, she didn't even comment on the shambles of her ordinarily super-tidy kitchen. "These cookies are too beautiful to eat. Your customer will be delighted, I'm sure."

Talk about a great sister. Ava rescued the muffin from the microwave and set it next to the tea. "Ta da! I promise I'll have this place spic-and-span by the time you get home today."

"I'm not worried about it in the slightest."

Katherine had so much faith in her, sometimes it was hard to get past the fear of letting her down. Ava went back to her cookies, boxing the ones that were ready, leaving the others to dry a few more minutes. The icing was still a tad tacky. Out of the corner of her eye she watched her sister bow her head and whisper a blessing over the meal. Her mammoth engagement diamond glinted in the overhead lights.

Katherine hadn't had the easiest time with things, but she'd made a success of her life. She'd become such a graceful woman. It was no wonder at all why she'd found a good man to fall love with her and promise her the real thing—true love—for a lifetime to come.

Katherine was the kind of lady true love happened to. Ava laid a sheet of waxed paper across the first layer of cookies in the box, not at all sure that true love would ever happen to her personally. She loved the dream, but all she had to do was to think of the long string of romantic disasters lying behind her like a desolate wasteland, and she knew, soul deep, it wasn't possible for her.

Or was it? Brice liked her. He had from the very start. Like he was either desperate, or maybe—*maybe*—this could be the start of something extraordinary. Something rare. Because she had to admit, what she felt for him was simply unusual. She had gotten to know him more, and he was a great guy—not just on the outside. He had a big heart, was an honorable character. He could see her dreams.

But was that enough to risk amending her no-dating policy? *That* was the million-dollar question.

"I love these." Katherine studied the muffin she'd bitten into. "Are you going to put these in your bakery? You'll have people beating down the door for them."

"From your lips to God's ears. Wouldn't that be something, if I actually succeeded at this? I've got a bunch of leftover muffins. Do you want to take some to the store? Maybe the early morning customers would like a muffin break."

"That'd be perfect. We have a reader's group this morning."

"Oh, and I've got the last of the cake sketches done. Do you want to see them now?"

"Are you kidding? Show me what you've got, sweetie."

Ava hauled out her mammoth sketch pad and removed the soft, pastel-colored drawings from the front. "I know you're going with a roses theme. Pinks and ivory. So I went with that."

She slid the drawings one by one onto the breakfast bar, carefully watching her sister's face for signs of dismay and abhorrence, but there was only a happy gasp of delight.

"Ava, these are so wonderful! I'm never going to be able to choose between them."

Whew. What a relief. The last thing she ever wanted to do was to disappoint her sister. Her family was all she had, and she loved them so much. "If you can't choose, maybe I should do a few more sketches. The right design should just jump out at you. It's something your heart decides."

"No, sweetie, you misunderstand. I feel that way about each one these. I love this rose garden theme. Can you really do this with frosting?"

"It's easy."

"I'm going to show these to Jack and see what he has to say. But…oh, the golden climbing roses on this ivory cake, with the leaves, that's stunning too."

"I can amend any of this, too. That's not carved in stone, you know. A little erasing and redrawing and *ta da*, the wedding cake of your dreams."

Katherine gathered up the sketches with care. "Are you okay? You seem a little down this morning."

"Down? No, not me. I'm always in a good mood." As long as she didn't think about Brice, that is. She moved away—quick—before Katherine figured it out, and started assembling a second bakery box. "I've got a lot on my mind. The renovation is stressful."

"I've heard nothing but renovation horror stories. What problems are you having?"

Katherine was watching her carefully over the rim of her teacup, so Ava did her best to steer the topic away from her confused, tangled up heart. "None. Not a single problem. The construction workers are organized. They've got their schedule, they do their work on time, they've already got the inspectors lined up, so there's hardly any downtime. I haven't been by yet, but they are supposed to have all the wallboard up and taped. Can you believe it? My shop is going to have brand new pretty walls and wiring that's up to code."

"I'm thrilled for you."

"I should be able to open on time. Danielle is going to help me set up my books. I've been throwing all my receipts into a shoebox in my closet. That's not going to work for a long-term bookkeeping solution, or so she tells me."

"No, sorry." Katherine smiled in that gentle, caring way of hers. "Now, tell me the truth. Something's bothering you. Is it the stress of getting a start-up business off the ground? You know you have us to help."

Ava nodded, slipping the last of the cookies into the box and snapping shut the lid. She deftly avoided mentioning her romantic confusion. "Tell Spence I might be a little late for my shift this afternoon. I have an ad to put into the church bulletin. The deadline's today. Oh, and I'm meeting Danielle for a bookkeeping session."

"Sure." She kept sipping her tea, assessing over the rim.

Ava knew what was coming. "Well, I've got a busy morning. See you—"

"Wait a minute. Don't run off just yet. You haven't told me what's wrong." Katherine was a sharp tack. "That leaves only one possibility left. You like Brice Donovan, don't you?"

"*Like?* That's a pretty strong word. Especially for a woman who has a brilliant no-dating policy." The smartest thing she'd ever done, hands down. Because without it, she'd be letting Brice charm her. Letting him close. Letting him into her heart. "I know you just want me to be happy, but I'm nothing but a country love song gone wrong."

"There's not one thing wrong with you. Maybe with some of the men you've spent time with, but you made the right decision in the end. Besides, you can't really get to know a man—any man, good or not so good—unless you spend time with him and get to know what he's really like."

That was the problem with Katherine. She always saw the good side. She believed that good things happened to good people, but she just didn't see the truth. Good men happened to *other* women, not her.

"Says the happily engaged woman. Get back to me on those sketches, right?" She grabbed the cookie box and her keys. If she left fast enough, Katherine couldn't say—

"Not every man is going to leave you, Ava. Not every man is going to let you down."

Too late. Ava stopped dead in her tracks, with her hand on the garage door. "I'm not going to give any man a chance to. I'll see you later, alligator."

Katherine said nothing, nothing at all, not that Ava gave her much of a chance to. She'd practically leaped into the garage and closed the inner door after her. Trying to shove out the words echoing in her head. *Not every man is going to leave you, Ava. Not every man is going to let you down*

And Brice's words, *With me, what you see is what you get.*

Business wise, right? she'd asked.

Always.

Would believing in him be the right thing? Heart pounding, she caught her breath in the echoing garage, feeling the pieces of her past rain down on her like soot and ash, willing away the sadness. It came anyway. Sharp and bone-deep and in her mother's voice.

Why, after all these years, did she still feel like that seven-year-old girl, standing in their old backyard beneath the snap of the clothes drying on the line, watching the blur of their 1960s Ford disappear down the alley? Why did she still feel the panic of being to blame? Why did it feel as if every failure just added to that pain?

She'd prayed for as long as she could remember with every fiber of her being for a good man to come into her life. But unlike all her other prayers, that one had remained unanswered. Over the years, her wishes had faded in luster and possibility until she couldn't see them anymore.

And she was better off that way, really. Her no-man policy had been working perfectly fine. She'd already taken the leap to start a business. Already bought a shop and had placed advertisements, and already word-of-mouth recommendations were starting to come in. Okay, people weren't exactly knocking down her door, but it was a start, right?

She'd finally learned to stop spending her life with her head in the clouds and now what?

Brice.

She'd finally stopped looking for the one man whose heart was stalwart enough to love her through all time and accepted that he didn't exist. At least, not for her. And then what?

Brice. He came into her life like the impossible dream she'd given up on. But was he so impossible?

"Ava? Hel-*lo?* Earth to Ava." Aubrey slowed the SUV to a crawl. "You've been a space cadet all day."

"I know. Sorry." Ava blinked, focusing. She'd been trying to think of everything but Brice all day, and what was she doing? Looking out the window to see if his pickup was in her shop's parking lot. Pathetic, she thought, undoing her seat belt. It looked as if the coast was clear. "Just park here at the curb."

"Are you kidding? I'm coming, too. I've been dying to see this all week." Aubrey cut the engine and pulled the e-brake. She never forgot to remove the keys. "Just think, this time next week it will be done. Can you believe it?"

"No. Yes. I don't have to be too terrified

of this venture failing until I open the doors, officially, for business." It wasn't the business she was terrified of, at the moment, but of not seeing Brice. Of turning down his more-than-friends offer to date, after the shop was done.

"You won't fail," Aubrey said with confidence. "You don't give yourself enough credit."

What did she say to that? Ava stumbled out into the stifling heat. The temperature was in the high nineties, and heat radiated off the pavement. She had to stop and dig through her purse to find her keys, no small feat. It gave her plenty of time to think over Aubrey's words.

She gave herself plenty of credit. But what did you do when you succeeded at attracting doom? Most of the time, she didn't let it bother her, but now….

Now, it was Brice. She could really fall for him, harder than any man she'd ever known. And that meant her heart could really be broken, right?

"Let me." Aubrey grabbed Ava's bag, plunged her hand in and pulled out the wallet so thick with debit and credit card receipts that it wouldn't snap shut. "There they are—at the bottom."

"I keep meaning to clean this bag out."

"I know." Aubrey dumped the wallet, papers and all, back into the bag and unlocked the door. She looked around the inside of the shop. "Wow, this looks *great.*"

"Wow. It does." Ava followed her sister inside. The cooled air washed over her as she stared in awe at the tall cathedral ceilings and real walls. All the mess had been cleaned up. The cement slab was perfectly swept. The taped and mudded wallboard wasn't pretty, but it took no imagination at all to add paint and trim and flooring to see the airy, sunny result.

Footsteps boomed in the kitchen behind them. Heavy, booted steps. Ava heard her sister yelp, felt Aubrey's instant fear, but she *knew* the sound and rhythm of that gait. The instant she'd stepped foot into the building, she should have recognized his presence.

"Your dream is taking shape." Brice Donovan filled the threshold between the kitchen and the main room looking like her dream come true in a simple black T-shirt, black jeans and boots. He looked stalwart and easygoing, like a guy a girl could always depend on.

Her heart wished for him a tiny bit more. It was a sweet twist of pain that moved through her. She stepped toward him and her spirit brightened. "Your construction guys have done a wonderful job. It's just right."

"The finish work starts Monday. We'll be done before you know it."

She gulped, unable to speak. There was only the magnetic draw of his gaze. Of his dimpled grin. Of his presence that drew her like an unsuspecting galaxy toward a black hole. That couldn't be a good thing, could it?

"This must be your sister." Brice broke his gaze, releasing her, to hold out his hand to her sister. "It's good to meet you."

"Ava hasn't said a word about me, has she?" Aubrey's hand looked engulfed by Brice's larger one.

Oh, no. Ava held her breath, sensing what would come next. Knowing that, like it or not, Aubrey would *know.* It was that twin thing. Their brain cells would fire and she would guess the horrible secret Ava was keeping from everyone, including herself.

Yep, there it was. In the change in

Aubrey's jaw line, her stance, her voice. Aubrey withdrew her hand, but there was an "ah ha" glint in her eyes. "I know why she hasn't said anything about you. In fact, she's refused to do a whole lot of talking about this very important renovation."

"It's all the stress," Ava added. The stress of the construction, the financing, getting a new business started, of being afraid she was falling in deep like with a man who was entirely wrong for her.

"I understand completely." The way Brice said it, it was like he had unauthorized access to that twin brain cell, and that was impossible. "Ava and I currently have a business-only policy."

"Ah, so that explains it," Aubrey said as she backed toward the door. "I'm probably just in the way here. Brice, you probably have a lot of construction things to go over with Ava."

"As a matter of fact, I do have a few things to show her."

"Oh, *sure* you do." Ava couldn't believe it. That didn't sound very business-like. She narrowed her eyes at him. "Why are you here, anyway?"

"I spent all day in the woodshop, and I wanted to stop by and see the progress for myself. Make sure nothing had been overlooked before the painters show up at seven Monday morning. I want this done right for you."

When he smiled, she couldn't stop the rise of her spirit, the tug of longing in her heart. She'd come by because she'd wanted to see the progress of her dream, and Aubrey had wanted to see it, too. Now Aubrey was at the door, tugging it open. What kind of world was this when your twin abandoned you? Panic rattled through her. She'd feel better if Aubrey would stay—

"Aubrey, why don't you stay with us?" Brice asked. "Unless you two have other plans?"

"Not at all," Aubrey said so fast. "None that can't be changed. We were just going to barbecue supper."

"*What?* Wait one minute." Ava had a bad feeling about this. It was four-thirty on a Saturday afternoon. Not exactly business hours. "Brice and I have a strict policy to adhere to."

"True. But we agreed to excuse dating and

romance from our business policy, right? That doesn't mean we can't be friends."

"Friends." Friendship did not begin to describe this swirl of confusing emotions she had for him. Emotions she did not want to analyze, thank you very much. What she wanted to do was to stay in denial about them. Denial was an excellent coping method.

"Sure, my business partner has been my best friend since kindergarten. Friendship and business don't have to be mutually exclusive. In fact, it can often be beneficial. If you two don't mind, come out to my place. I fix a mean steak. I was going to barbecue dinner tonight anyway, I'll just throw a few more steaks and shrimp on the barbie—"

"Shrimp?" Aubrey perked up.

Now there was no way to get out of this. Ava knew she *should* be sensible, like her sister Katherine. Stoic and self-disciplined like big brother Spence. Be calm and think things through like her twin. Her problems always came from leaping before she looked, and right now looking at his dark tousle of hair, the curve of his grin and the steady hope in his eyes made her want to leap into agreement.

"Lots of shrimp," Brice promised. "I've got a shop behind my garage, so I work at home a lot when I'm doing custom stuff like this. Hey, while you two are there, I'll show you a few new ideas I have. Something for the display case."

"Now I don't believe there's an allowance for even more custom stuff in the contract I signed."

"True. This is just because. This is what I want to do for you as a friend. We start as friends. See where it goes from there."

Didn't that sound harmless? It was like a test- drive of a new car. You got to see if you liked it first before you bought it. It was the same situation here. If she didn't like him for a friend, she wouldn't date him and marry him, right?

Ava felt her heart fall even more. There it was, that terrible urge to leap. To just tell him yes. Friends first, and then let's see where this goes. What could go wrong with that?

Chapter Nine

"Did you know he lived up here?" Aubrey asked from behind the wheel as she negotiated the curving road that led into the foothills where the posh people lived.

"Nope. I had no clue."

Ava couldn't seem *not* to look at Brice. There he was right in front of them in his snazzy red sports car.

Aubrey followed Brice into an exclusive gated community. "If you're falling for this guy, you have to stop this destructive thing you do."

"I tried my best at all my other relationships. It's my fault-blindness. Maybe it's a good thing you're here. I need your help. You can watch for his faults that I can't see."

"You *definitely* need help." Aubrey rolled her eyes and turned her full attention back to the road. "Look at this place. This is really wow. How rich is this guy?"

"He's a Donovan. How rich are they?"

"Well, his grandfather knew Grandpop. They played golf together."

Grandpop had been pretty rich. "It still hurts to think about him, doesn't it?"

"Yeah." Aubrey paused a moment, the sadness settling between them. He'd been gone two years now and it was a terrible hole in the family. It was why Gran had moved permanently to their winter home in Scottsdale. She'd found it so painful to be alone in the house he built for her when they were a young married couple, that she simply stayed down south where there were fewer memories to haunt her.

The quiet stayed between them as they followed Brice through a gate and along a grand driveway to a private house tucked into the hill, surrounded by lush trees and lawn. Views of the Bridger Mountains backed up behind him, and views of the Rockies rimmed the entire western exposure.

Brice parked in the third bay of a three-car

garage, and Ava was too busy looking around to realize Aubrey had parked the SUV and was already climbing out of the vehicle. Okay, pay attention. She joined her sister outside the wood and stone house that looked like something out of a magazine.

"That's nicer than Gran's house," Aubrey said.

True. Which only pointed out the plain truth. Brice was so wrong for her. He was going to look for the wife to fit into this house. Face it. It was such a good thing they had this friends-only policy.

He closed the car door and pocketed his keys. "C'mon in this way. I never use the front door."

"Not even when you entertain?" Aubrey asked.

"I never entertain. Having my folks over is about as elaborate as I get." There was that grin again, the inviting warmth, the good-guy charm that was so totally arresting.

He held open the door for them at the back of the garage. Ava saw a wide but short hallway with a laundry room to her right elbow and what had to be a huge pantry to her left. Ahead of her was an enormous kitchen with a family room off to the side, not that she noticed that. She was too busy salivating over the kitchen.

Gleaming, light maple cabinets and a gray granite countertop stretched for miles. She spotted a gas range, Sub-Zero refrigerator and a double oven. There were plenty of windows, a bay in a huge eating nook and then a row of them looking out to the green backyard. “This is better than Katherine’s kitchen.”

Brice went straight to the fridge. “Is that where you’ve been doing your baking?”

“Yeah. It’s working out okay, but sometimes I know I’m in her way.” Ava ran her hand over the expensive granite. “This is a nice work space you’ve got here.”

“It’s wasted on me. I don’t cook much. What do you want to drink? I’ve got soda, iced tea and lemonade. Oh, and milk.” He opened the door wide so she could see what was on the shelves.

Something pink caught her eye. “Wait one minute. You have strawberry milk?”

“Chocolate, too.”

“I never would have pegged you for a guy who would drink pink milk.”

“Hey, I like strawberries. Nothing wrong with that.”

“No, it’s just—” Did she tell him it was one of her very favorite things? “I’ll take a glass of pink milk. Aubrey will, too.”

“Do you always speak for her?”

“I’m just trying to be efficient. Where are your glasses?”

“Sit down. Both of you. You’re guests, let me do the fetching.” His words were deceptively light but when his gaze raked over her, tenderness charged the air between them.

Hmm. That didn’t feel like friendship. It felt like “more than friendship” in the nicest way she’d ever experienced. She took a shaky breath. Whatever she did, she had to remember not to start reading things into his actions. *Friends only,* he’d said. But she knew he wanted more.

“Wow,” Aubrey said somewhere behind her, and Ava turned.

“Look at that pool. It’s bigger than Gran’s.”

Ava went weak in the knees. “There’s my favorite guy.”

Rex was lounging in the cooling spray of the pool fountain. He looked up with a start, gave a goofy grin and heaved himself up on all fours. Dripping wet he took off for a run and disappeared from sight around a huge sixteen-foot awning that shaded a patio set, chaise lounges and a built-in brick grill.

"Rex!" Brice called out a second before a big golden streak charged into the kitchen.

The sound of heavy dog breathing drew Ava's attention to the archway where the retriever streaked toward her. She caught a faint glimpse of a sleek dining room and a comfortable living room in the background before the oaf lunged toward her, both front feet wrapping around her shoulders. His tongue roughened her face and she started to laugh. The dripping heap of retriever stopped licking to give her a goofy grin and then started over again.

"Stop! Stop!" Ava was laughing, but it was kind of hard not to like such a good-hearted dog.

Out of the corner of her eye she saw Brice round the long span of counter, coming to her rescue, but it was too late. Rex dropped to the floor in front of her and gave a huge shake. Water droplets rained everywhere.

If she wasn't soaked enough down the

front from his hug, she was now. The retriever dropped to his haunches looking from Brice's disapproving face to hers. Rex's eyebrows shot up, the goofy grin dropped from his cute face and the happiness faded from his chocolate-sweet eyes. His whine said, "Oh, no. I messed up again."

Ava's heart fell and she followed him to the floor where she wrapped her arms around Rex's wet neck. "I don't mind," she told him. "I know you didn't *mean* for disaster to happen."

"Speak for yourself," Aubrey commented on a laugh. "I was standing downwind and now I'm wet, too."

"But he was just excited." Ava kept one arm around the canine's neck. "I'm in love with this guy."

Rex gave a whine low in his throat and dropped his huge head on her shoulder.

"The feeling appears to be mutual." Brice. There he was, all six feet of solid male kneeling down, meeting her gaze with his. "Rex knows better than this. He just can't help himself sometimes."

"I think he's perfect."

"Another mutual sentiment."

Perfect, Brice thought, that's what Ava was. Dripping wet, her honey gold bangs tousled from wet dog kisses, sprayed with droplets, she'd never been more beautiful.

"I've always wanted a dog just like this, but Dad's allergic to dogs." She glowed with happiness as she hugged Rex, who looked like he was in heaven. "And then we've been in apartments and too busy for a pet. But one day, I want a handsome guy just like you."

Rex's eyes melted with adoration and gave Ava another swipe across the face.

"You are the best dog." She laughed, all spirit, all brightness and big loving heart.

Brice was enchanted. Tenderness blazed so strongly, it transformed him completely. His heart fell—a measureless, infinite tumble from which there was no return.

They were beneath the shady awning, seated at the poolside table with an impressive view of the sparkling azure water. Ava looked around, ignoring the full plate of food in front of her. The forest-like backyard and the rise of the Bridger Mountains spearing up to the sky were spectacular. She had to give Brice's home full marks.

But his cooking, wow. That deserved full marks plus. The juicy, flavorful steak was grilled to perfection. Talk about a total shocker. Who would have guessed that when Brice said he cooked a mean steak, he meant it?

He sat across the snazzy teak table, the breezes lazily ruffling his dark hair. He cut a strip off the fourth steak he'd barbecued—for Rex—and tossed it to him. Rex caught it neatly, gulped, swallowed and sat back down on his haunches.

The gentle waterfall of the fountain and the leaves rustling through the trees only added to the pleasantness of the evening.

Earlier, after readying the steaks in their marinade, Brice had brought their glasses of strawberry milk to the poolside and relaxed in the shade. Since their clothes were wet anyway, she and Aubrey did cannonballs into the pool, trying to see who could leave the biggest splash marks. Ava had won, but it had been an intensely close—and fun—competition.

Now, drying in the hundred-degree shade, she was just still damp enough from the pool to be comfortable temperature wise. But emotionally? Not so much. Brice dominated her field of vision. He was impossible to ignore.

"I read in the paper a while back that you were engaged," Aubrey said abruptly as she poked the tines of her fork into a cube of red herbed potatoes heaped on her plate. "Didn't the wedding get cancelled?"

What? Ava could not believe her ears. The fork tumbled out of her hand and fell into the three-bean salad. Hello? Aubrey did *not* just say that, did she? How could she stick her nose where it didn't belong?

Brice winced as if he'd taken a painful blow. "That's true. I was engaged to Whitney Phelps."

"Of the Butte Phelps," Aubrey nodded, as if coaxing Brice along.

Ava sank into the comfy cushions of her chair and felt as if a hundred-pound weight had settled onto her chest. Sympathy filled her.

Brice put down his steak knife and took a long pull of strawberry milk. "It was one of those things. I'd just turned twenty-five. I had this plan. I had my business started and it was going well, and I was ready to get married. I figured we'd date for two years, get engaged for a year, be married for a couple more and then have kids."

"It sounds like a good plan to me," Aubrey said in the gentle quiet way of hers that made anybody want to tell her anything. "What happened?"

Ava knew. She could see it play across his face. Feel the resonance of it in his heart. He'd really loved this woman. The right way—heart deep and honestly. She wasn't surprised when he spoke.

"The moment I saw Whitney, I thought she was classy. Poised. Polished. Just what I was looking for." His tone wasn't bitter. There was no anger in his words. Nor was there any pining. Just the pain of regret. "I must have been what she was looking for, too."

"I imagine so," Aubrey answered.

Poor Whitney, Ava thought. She must have felt something like this. Overwhelmed by his million-dollar grin and honesty. Helplessly sucked in by the pull of those deep dark eyes. Enamored by his decency and strength and manliness. Lost in too many wishes to find her way out.

Brice stared down at his plate for a

moment, as if gathering his thoughts. A muscle tightened in his square granite jaw. "We came from the same backgrounds. We seemed compatible. I cared for her, and she fit into my plan. Or, maybe I made her. I prayed for our relationship to work out. For it to progress. Sometimes I wonder if I imposed way too much too early when we were dating, instead of just trusting God to work things out for the best."

Oh, I so know what you mean. Ava felt the heavy pain radiate out from the center of her chest, into her throat, into her voice. "You have to be very careful what you pray for."

"Exactly." His gaze met hers, and she felt the connection, an emotional zing that opened her heart right up.

"I prayed," he said, "and while my prayers were answered in a way, I'll never know how much I messed up God's plan for me. Maybe He had someone better for me, a better match, and a better chance for happiness for both me and Whitney separately. I don't know."

I understand completely, Ava thought.

"I only know He answered my prayers, but I asked in the wrong way. Whitney and I would never have made each other happy in the end. It was hard, admitting that, because I cared for her deeply. I was a disappointment to her. She slowly became disappointed in me. These days when I pray, I ask for the Lord to show me the way He wants me to go."

You're not falling in total serious like with him, she commanded herself. She knew better than that. So, he was perfect in many ways. She could feel the weight of his pain and the honesty of his experience. Her heart tumbled a little more.

"It was a mess." He shrugged one big shoulder, looking vulnerable even for such a big, brawny guy. "My mom hasn't forgiven me completely for calling off the wedding. She was very attached to Whitney."

"Your mom still hasn't forgiven you?"

Brice studied Ava's dismay. "She'd come to love Whitney like a daughter and it was a severe loss for her. She loves me, but I'm different from my parents in a lot of ways. They just don't get me."

"You're talking about your construction company?"

"Yep. Like the dog. He's not a purebred."

He cut another piece of steak for Rex. "Not that it's good or bad, I just was looking for a best buddy, and went to the pound looking for a puppy. Rex and me, we connected."

When his gaze met hers, Brice couldn't tell if she knew that's how he felt about her. There'd been something special about her right from the beginning, something unique and amazing and rare that made him look and keep looking.

And it kept him riveted now. She made him take this risky step toward another relationship. It was hard opening himself up. But he took the risk. "Ava, it's your turn to tell the real story behind your no-man policy."

"What? Oh, you so don't want to hear about that." Ava averted her eyes, dismissing his question. Then, as she cut a small bite off her steak, she appeared to reconsider. "Maybe it is a good idea. Then you can see what I mean and you'll understand how important being just friends is to me."

"Tell me."

"Where to start?" She looked to Aubrey for help.

Aubrey took a sip of strawberry milk. "The high-school boyfriend. It's classic Ava."

"True." Ava set down her fork, looking even more adorable with the way her hair was drying in a flyaway tangle. "Okay, here's the scoop. Lloyd was in my earth sciences class. Now, I'm totally not a science whiz but I had to take some kind of science credit, and it was like the easiest science class in our high school. So there I was, trying to figure out some weird earth crust layer experiment, I don't know, I never did figure it out. Lloyd was cute, he saw me struggling and came over to help me. I need a lot of help."

"I'm beginning to see that." Big time. She clearly could take care of herself, but it didn't hurt to have, say, someone like him to look out for her. Help her find her keys, watch over her, make her happy. He was interested in that job. "Poor Lloyd. I bet he fell for you."

"Poor Lloyd," Aubrey agreed with a nod.

Just what he'd thought. Brice could picture it. The teenage boy probably had such an incredible crush on Ava to begin with, he'd been all vulnerable heart. "What did poor Lloyd do that made you dump him?"

"Oh, it wasn't me," Ava insisted. "I liked him. I mean, he was cute."

"Cute," Aubrey agreed, a mirror of Ava. "But clueless."

"He was like a big dopey puppy, sorry, Rex." Ava flashed him a smile and the big adoring dog tilted his head to one side, quirked his brows and gave a sappy grin. Totally besotted.

Yeah, Brice knew just how he felt.

"A girl wants a boyfriend with a clue. Aubrey, what was the first really nutso thing Lloyd did?"

"The utility pole."

"That's right, our first date. We were on our way for hamburgers at the drive-in, and he drove smack into a big light pole going twenty-five miles an hour. Not looking where he was going." Ava lifted both hands in a helpless gesture. "He wouldn't stop looking at me while he was driving. I kept telling him to keep his eyes on the road. I mean, even I know better than that. But his gaze just kept coming back to me and I said to him, 'Lloyd, turn. There's a utility pole.' But he just said, 'yeah, uh-huh' and didn't listen and didn't look. I was too smitten to notice that he didn't have a lick of common sense."

"He was nice, though. Unlike a few of your boyfriends." Aubrey began cutting her steak.

It was interesting, sitting with a view of both sisters. They were identical but the more he got to know Ava, the more different the two of them looked. Similar, but different. Aubrey was more composed and sensible, clearly the more responsible of the two, always there to watch over Ava. The way she studied him, as if he'd met with her approval, made him think she wouldn't mind handing over the caretaking of Ava to him. Good to know. It was nice feeling to have her sister's positive opinion.

"I didn't date for a while," Ava continued. "Until I was out of high school."

"That's because I had my accident," Aubrey added, setting down her steak knife. "I jump horses, and one day in the middle of a competition, my mare went down. On top of me. She broke her leg and I cracked my hip and back. It took us both a long time to recover. Ava was there helping me faithfully without complaint."

"It was my privilege to be there with you," Ava said.

There was no mistaking the affection between the sisters as their gazes met.

"Then there was Brett," Aubrey began.

Ava pealed with laughter. "Oh, Brett. He was the worst. He was like a stalker. But did I figure that out right away? No. We'd dated two years and he'd proposed. That's when he went really strange."

"Plus, he was mean to you."

"Yeah, but I was going to cooking school and working full-time at the bookstore. That was before Dad and Dorrie retired to Arizona, so I had to help out at home, I never had a spare minute to just sit down and think. Or I *might* have noticed it. It started out subtle at first."

"He was sarcastic right up front." Aubrey corrected. "Then it snowballed from there, especially after the proposal."

"Exactly." Ava rolled her eyes, adorable and sweet and as wholesome as the sunshine glittering on the spray of the fountain, a bright sparkle that he would never tired of watching.

Show me the way, Lord. He felt the conviction deep in his soul. *Do I have a chance here?*

"Well, he would get sharp or distracted or

gruff, but he'd be tired. He was going to school full-time, too. But it kept getting worse and there's no excuse for that. So I gave him his ring back, and then he started turning up wherever I went. Apparently, he thought I had another boyfriend on the side. Like I'd want another one. So it sounds like I've had boyfriend after disastrous boyfriend, but it hasn't been that many."

"Just that disastrous, but serious. Lloyd had proposed too," Aubrey commented. "This is why I don't date. Ava's experiences have scared me."

He watched the way the sisters laughed together, seeming amused and not traumatized by their experiences. "So you both have a no-man no-dating policy?"

"Well, mine is more habit," Aubrey said.

"Mine is a philosophy. I date guys that *seem* great."

"You have a talent for it—" Aubrey started.

"—But then when I really get to know them, it's not the truth," Ava finished. "They're marginally moral at best. Or so-so, or have secret habits like gambling. What's a girl to do? The Mr. Yucks look nice on the outside. It isn't until you get to know them that you see them for who they are, and see the things they are trying to keep hidden. It's that fault-blindness, not a good trait to have in the dating world."

Ava shrugged, and there it was, the hint of sadness at the corners of her eyes, dimming the wattage of her smile. There was a lot of pain there. More than she was going to talk about.

"I'm not like that," he said. "I don't run off, I don't leave, and I don't have destructive habits. Just so you know. I'm respectful toward women, I'm not mean and I try as hard as I can to be one of the good guys."

Ava sighed. Yeah, she was noticing that about him, and his words made her soul ache with longing. He could capture her heart, if she let him.

And wasn't that the problem? Brice Donovan could be her downfall. The one thing she could never do was amend her policy, because if she dated him and fell in love with him, he could hurt her most of all. He was like a dream man and too good to be true.

A few hours later, the sun was sinking into the amethyst peaks of the Rockies as Ava guided the SUV out of Brice's winding subdivision. Talk about gorgeous homes. She tried to focus her thoughts on the road, on how Rex had hopped into the driver's seat of the SUV when they went to leave, wanting to go with her.

She tried *not* to think of the man who'd grabbed his stubborn dog by the collar, kindly helping him down. He was a dream man. So where did that leave her? In more trouble than she'd been when she'd agreed to dinner. Now what? How was she going to resist him now?

"He's a great cook." Aubrey yawned. "I haven't had that good a dinner since Gran was up from Arizona."

One more thing to add to the growing list of the great things about Brice Donovan. Ava negotiated a corner, slowed to a stop and checked for traffic on the main road. "I know where you're going with this."

"He likes you, you like him. Why won't you go out with him? I wouldn't be surprised if he's asked you out and you turned him down."

"I never said I liked him."

"You don't have to. Do you know what your problem is?"

Ava stared extra hard at the road. "I don't need you to tell me."

"Yes, you do. That's why God assigned me to you. I'm telling you this for your own good."

"Please don't." Ava pulled to a stop at another stop sign, staring in frustration at the city laid out like glitter in the twilight valley. "I know you mean well, but I've got things under control."

"You never have *anything* under control. You like Brice so much, you're afraid of it."

"Not that I'll admit."

"Ha! See? You're in the denial stage. Remember? Katherine was there after she met Jack, and she wouldn't admit it either, but she was."

"Denial is a very effective coping method. Except for the fact that I'm totally *not* in denial. I have a policy, remember? I'm dedicating my life to making the world a sweeter place. I'm on a mission. I will not be distracted by anything."

Even she could hear how those words were hollow—they were no longer the whole truth. No matter how hard she willed them to be, they fell short of what she now knew to be honest.

How had that happened? It was like sand shifting beneath the rock of her foundation and now she had to readjust everything.

Aubrey was only being caring, kind and gentle in that way of hers; and she was always right. Ava knew it, but she wasn't ready to admit this to herself. Because as long as she was in denial, then she wouldn't have to make a decision. She wouldn't have to acknowledge that caring about Brice was no longer her choice. Her heart was just doing it.

"Ava, do you know how great this guy is? He's wonderful. He really cares about you. He invited me to come along tonight, and none of the other guys you've dated ever welcomed me and included me the way Brice has. The way he looks at you and the way he talks to you, it says one thing. He likes you. He didn't care that you drained half his pool of water with all your cannonballs."

"Hey, you helped with that."

"Yes, but I don't make as big of a splash. I lack your finesse and skill."

"True."

They smiled together.

"And what about the beautiful woodwork he's doing for you? Ava, he's working over the weekend. I don't think he has to work overtime to keep his personal budget in the black."

"Probably not." Did she tell Aubrey that Brice had wanted to give her this dream? And that was really starting to affect her?

"Ava, he had worked up two different scrollwork patterns for you to choose from. That's a big deal."

"Not if I don't think about it."

They had reached the outskirts of town, and the traffic was light. She concentrated on driving, which was a lot easier than concentrating on how Brice had brought her two two-foot lengths of wood, carefully detailed, from his home workshop. One had rosebuds and leaves, and the other had cabbage roses. He'd made no big deal about it, but she knew it was more. That was scaring her, too.

Aubrey hit her second wind when they turned into their apartment complex. "Okay, I have one more thing to say, and then I'm done. You've finally found a good guy. A man of substance who sees how special you are. He's not like the others."

"You mean, after I get to know him I won't see that he's not right for me, before my heart is broken?"

"At least you see the pattern."

"It isn't just me. We've all had such a hard time getting attached, I mean, Katherine's in her thirties and she's finally getting married. Spence? Well, look at him, he drives every nice woman away before she can say 'hi.' Do you think it's because Mom left us like that? We already know love ends."

"*Some* love ends. Mom wasn't happy. Don't you remember?"

Remember? Painfully. *You make a mess of everything. You ruin everything. I can't take it anymore.* Her mother's last words to her. Haunting her after all these years.

Ava maneuvered into their reserved covered spot and cut the engine. She even remembered to take the keys out of the ignition.

Aubrey didn't move to unbuckle her seat belt. "Not all love ends. Look at Dad. He stayed. He never left. He loved us enough to stick it out, even when things were devastating for him. After Mom left, he was so lost and overwhelmed with responsibility. Remember?"

It had been a tough time for all of them. Dad trying to hold it together, lost doing housework and cooking. His sadness was suffocating and Ava had felt the responsibility for their mom's leaving. Although what Aubrey said *was* true. Dad had stayed. He'd never let them down.

It hurt too much to dwell on that, too. She climbed outside into the stifling heat, the chlorine scent of the water from Brice's pool clung to her skin and clothes, reminding her. Of him. Of what her heart wanted. That Aubrey was right.

That still didn't mean it was the smartest thing to disregard common sense and believe in one man—to put all her heart and soul, and all the love she had, on the line. For some reason she felt that seven-year-old girl inside her, feeling small and alone and wishing she could be different, so that *everything* could be different.

The sun was setting through bright magenta and orange clouds, casting a mauve light that glowed on the ordinary asphalt shingle rooftops and changed them to shining satin. Rose-pink glinted along the white siding of the two-storey buildings and reflected in windows.

The light cast over her too, and she felt hope lift though her like grace.

Chapter Ten

The bookstore's after-hours' quiet made her little sigh sound like a hundred-mile-per-hour gust of wind, which wasn't her intention. Now everyone was going to stop their inventory work and come hunt her down and ask, "What's wrong, Ava?"

She could hear the question already—mostly because it's what they always asked. She was the kind of girl who had one kind of problem after another, and her family was slightly enmeshed in her affairs.

She crept forward a few inches on her rug-burned knees, ignoring the rough rasp from the industrial carpet. Did she remember her knee pads? No. She'd forgotten for the past four nights in a row straight. She'd been on the run, from sun up and well into the dark of night, working, trying to figure out the malicious concept of bookkeeping—to no avail—and baking. Running errands. Picking up as many hours here at the bookstore as she could, which was why she was helping with inventory. She hated inventory, but the sad truth was, she needed the money. Big time.

She may have borrowed a chunk from Gran, but she'd only borrowed what was absolutely necessary for start-up, not for her wages or anything else. *A shoestring start-up,* that's what Gran called it and while she'd offered more of a loan, Ava had refused. She'd appreciate the funds, but she wasn't out to take advantage of her grandmother, whom she loved very much. So, she was on a shoestring. She would just work harder to make ends meet, that's all.

The problem was, she wasn't as efficient as she could have been, and why? Who was to blame?

Brice Donovan. Thoughts of him were distracting her in a big way. Not that she'd seen him since they'd had dinner at his house. She'd run out of any hopes of actually seeing him. For four straight workdays she'd been by the bakery early every morning to drop off goodies. And every evening, except for today, she'd checked the work after the construction dudes had left. She'd been excited by the renovation's progress, but there'd been no sight of Brice. Sure, he'd left messages on her cell. And she'd left messages on his. But did they actually speak? No.

She'd even received a chocolate cake order from Brice's secretary for delivery to the office on Friday afternoon. Why hadn't he called with that? Or at least left a message? He'd given her the full court press with his charm and his cooking and now when she was considering softening her policy, was he available to hear it? No-oo.

Ava halted in mid-row and stared helplessly at the titles on the shelf and the clipboard on the floor beside her. Oops. Now she'd lost her place on the shelf, again. She stared down at the print out, and it started to blur. Probably because she'd been up since 4:45 a.m. that morning. It was now nearly nine—at night. She was totally beat.

"Ava?" Katherine rounded the corner of

the history section, concern on her face. "What's wrong? You look exhausted. Why don't you take a break?"

Spence's voice sounded muffled coming from the other side of the row. "It's not time for her break. And she came in late. *Again.*"

Katherine planted her hands on her slender hips and shook her head. She looked calm and classic, as always, even casually dressed for their late night work session in a simple butter-yellow knit top and black boot-cut jeans.

How did Katherine do it? She carried as much of the responsibility of the bookstore as Spence did, but with such serene, easy grace. No sharp words of frustration, ever. She looked gorgeous and totally put together and never missed her Bible study groups, had started a weekly woman's reading group program and found time to date, fall in love with Jack, get engaged and teach the teenager to drive.

"I don't need a break," Ava confessed, feeling so totally like a frumpy failure right then. She knew her hair was falling out of the comb holder thingy for the billionth time. Aubrey had talked her into wearing it this morning. She stood up to stretch and noticed that her linen blouse had wrinkled so much, it looked as if she'd been sleeping in it. "I need junk food."

"Pizza?" asked the teenager—more commonly known as Hayden, Jack's kid. "Or how about French fries?"

"Nachos," Aubrey hollered from four stacks over. "With the works."

"No food near the books!" Spence sounded particularly annoyed. "And no breaks. I want this done before midnight."

Before midnight. Ava didn't want to think about how little sleep that meant she was going to get. But the good news was that she'd be able to make her next month's car payment.

"You look like a mess." Aubrey appeared and went straight to the comb clip thingy. "You didn't put this in right."

"I don't know how to put it in right." Ava rolled her eyes. "I'm so glad this is the last night we have to do this. Tomorrow night, I'm going to crash in front of the TV. The only time I plan on moving will be to answer the door for the pizza delivery guy. You too, Aubrey?"

"No. I have plans, I know you forgot. I'm going to that singles church function in the valley." Aubrey ran her fingers through Ava's hair and gathered it up in a neat coil. "And you were going to babysit for Danielle, so she can go on a date with her husband? Remember?" Even the thought of those fried tater tots made her feel perky.

"I'm too exhausted and hungry to remember anything. I think mexifries will help."

"There there's only one solution. We need junk food if we're going to last until midnight." Aubrey repositioned the Venus-flytrap-looking comb. "Spence, we're going to take another break."

"No breaks." He sounded angry, and there was a thud, like a few books tumbling from a shelf. He made an even angrier sound.

Aubrey took a step back to consider the comb's positioning. "He's extra crabby tonight."

"You distract him, and I'll slip out the back. Maybe he won't notice I'm gone."

"I'll notice," Spence barked, closer than they thought.

"Go." Katherine took Ava's clipboard.

"I'll finish for you. Hayden, what do you want to order?"

"Uh..." The teenager poked her head around the corner. "I dunno."

"Hey, you come with me," Ava decided. "I'll need help carrying all that food. Katherine, I'm going to need money."

"I *knew* you were going to say that. Help yourself to a couple of twenties from my purse. Our late-night snack will be my treat."

Super-duper. It might not be the answer to her frustration about Brice, but there was nothing like a fast-food fix, right? If you order enough fried food, you could forget a lot of problems. Distraction, that was the key to coping.

After finding cash in Katherine's purse, she grabbed her own. The first thing she checked was her cell, already knowing what she'd see. One missed call. A voice mail message.

She hit the button and waited to connect as she went in search of her keys.

"Are these them?" Hayden asked standing in front of the open refrigerator. There they were, on the shelf next to the soda cans.

"Hey, you're pretty useful for a teenager,"

Ava winked at the girl while she listened to her one message.

Brice's deep baritone was a welcome sound. "Tag, you're it. Try me back when you're off work at the bookstore. I'll be up late."

Okay, at least there was hope. She dialed his number, pushed open the back door and held it for the teenager. Hayden bopped through with coltish energy and waited while Ava made sure the door locked after them. She didn't want the backdoor burglar to try to rob the place. Poor Spence had enough pressure without that.

She got Brice's voice mail. Big surprise. "It's your turn to call me," she said and turned her ringer to the loudest setting. For added measure, so the phone didn't get muffled by all the junk in her bag, she slipped it into an outside pocket. There. She was all set. "Kid, do you still have my keys?"

"Yep. I was kinda hopin' that you'd let me drive. You know, cuz I gotta practice so I can ace my driver's test."

"Deal." She opened the passenger's side door and hopped onto the seat. She was pretty exhausted and look, she had a chauffeur. Cool. "When Katherine marries your dad, I won't mind too much that you're my new niece. I mean, I could probably endure it."

"Like I guess I could, too." Hayden looked happy as she took control behind the wheel. "So, what taco place is it? And how do I get there?"

"You have much to learn. Lucky for you, you have me to teach you. We always go to Mr. Paco's Tacos. They have the best nachos and mexifries. If you turn left out of the driveway, we can go past my shop on the way there. I want to see how the final coat of paint looks."

"You'll hire me when you open up, right?"

"Are you kidding? I thought you were going to work for free. I *could* pay you, I guess." Ava winked.

Hayden's smile was pure happiness. "You gotta teach me how to make monster muffins."

"In good time. Just drive, kid." Ava pulled out her phone just to check it.

No call. She knew that because she would have heard it ringing, but she had to check. Thinking of Brice at least made her feel a little closer to him when he felt so far away. Not that she wanted to admit it, but she missed him.

Big time.

In the quiet of Ava's shop, Brice swiped the sweat from his forehead and uncapped a bottle of water. He downed half of it in one swig. He was hot, tired and hungry. But he didn't want to break until he'd installed the last of the ceiling moldings. He'd have to bust his hump tomorrow, put in a long day, to get this finished before the cleaning crew pulled up tomorrow—Friday—afternoon.

The week had gone by in a blur, too fast, and without Ava. He'd heard about the morning baked goods that she'd provided faithfully every morning. He'd heard about the free certificates she'd handed out to all the workers this morning along with the colorfully decorated little coffee cakes. He'd been busy in his shop, finishing the last of the intricate scrollwork.

He missed her. He knew she was working late shifts at the bookstore—she'd left a message on his voice mail telling him about it. They had been playing phone tag all week.

The lack of contact frustrated him, but he had to get this right for her. It was her dream, which was important to him. Important for her.

The soft yellow walls had warmed like sunshine during the day and now, with the honey glow of the varnished woodwork, the place was better than any picture. He couldn't wait for her to see it, but he wanted everything done first. He wanted it perfect for her.

Which meant only one thing. Time to get back to work. He recapped the bottle, set it on the sawhorse next to his cell and noticed a green light was flashing. A missed call.

No. He'd missed her again. He'd either been hammering or running the saw—he hadn't heard it ring. He snatched it up, ready to hit the speed dial, but before he could, he glanced up and there she was. She stood on the passenger side of her SUV, closing the door, looking through the windows directly at him. There was surprise on her face and disbelief in her eyes as she remained frozen in place.

He crossed to the door in three strides and threw the bolt. The night air was balmy as he moved toward her.

"Oh, I can't believe this. Brice, this is wonderful. What are you doing here, working so late?"

His heart rolled over. She looked so dreamy, so precious. It was hard to believe that she was real and that he hadn't imagined her here.

"I didn't expect you to show up here like this." He studied her dear face. She looked tired, but happy. That's why he'd worked long endless hours in his shop. He wanted her to be happy. With the woodwork. With the shop. With him. "It was supposed to be a surprise for you. I wanted it finished before you came by in the early morning."

"But—" Her fingers caught tightly around his. "It's nine-thirty at night and you're still working. Were you going to work all night?"

"However long it takes."

"But that's so much work."

"It's my pleasure, Ava."

"But—" Her lovely eyes shone, as if she understood, finally. "This is my dream. It's like you could look right into my heart and know."

"Amazing, don't you think?"

Ava was starting to believe it. She could

feel it in the marrow of her bones. Aubrey was right, okay, she was *always* right. *What about the beautiful woodwork he's doing for you? I don't think he has to work overtime to keep his personal budget in the black.*

This had to be so much work. This was such a big deal. This was more than business. More than friendship. This was everything that totally scared her.

"Want to go inside and see?" His hand was so strong as he guided her toward the door. He felt as invincible as titanium, like a man a woman could believe in.

She'd been fooled before, but those times faded like shadows to light. Looking at him—being with him—filled her with true hope. He awakened a part of her that had been never been wholly alive before—an optimistic part of her spirit. That positive force seemed to fill her senses, overwhelming all common sense, so that she couldn't think of anything else but Brice, standing so tall and good.

It would be easy to lose perspective. She had to move slow, be smart, think things through and not rush into anything too fast. "Let's go inside so I can see everything a little better."

"Sure." His hand moved to the middle of her back, guiding her.

She turned at the door and gestured to the teenager still behind the wheel. "Like I'm going to leave you out here? C'mon."

"Who are you talking to?" he asked.

"My personal chauffeur. Brice, meet Hayden Munroe, my future niece, she's driving tonight."

"Good to meet you," Brice said politely, but Hayden only stared at him in shock. "Munroe. Your dad wouldn't be Jack Munroe, would he?"

"Yep. He's a state trooper. Did he like pull you over and give you a speeding ticket?"

"No. I'm a faithful follower of all traffic laws. But I met him at a charity golf match last month. To benefit the children's hospital wing. He beat the socks off me."

"That's my Dad." Hayden gave a shy smile and stepped through the open door.

Ava followed her, taking in the full effect of Brice's work. Their footsteps echoed in the tall ceilings painted the faintest shade of yellow, so that they looked white as they angled upwards. There were gaping holes where the tract lighting was supposed to fit, but the ceiling moldings were already mounted around half of the room, separating the airiness of the ceiling from the warm buttery walls.

How many hours had all of this taken him? Ava could only stare in disbelief. The careful rosebud design was everywhere—not overdone, not ornate, but subtle and whimsical. Like something out of a country painting come to life.

His hand came to rest on her shoulder, a light touch, and a claiming one. She could feel the weight of it and his heart's question.

"What do you think?" His baritone rumbled dangerously close to her ear.

Dangerous because any amount of proximity was too close for her comfort. Panic beat with frantic, sharp edges against her ribs, but she held her ground. She stayed near to him instead of bolting away. "It's unbelievable. You must have worked so hard."

"True. And?"

"You know I love it." He'd done all this work, taken an infinite amount of care, done all of this. For her. How was she going to resist him now? She looked at the lovely work, the careful beveling, the meticulous detail, the perfection that glowed like varnished sunshine. "Thank you."

"You're welcome." His fingers curled into her shoulder, not bruising, not harsh, but tender. "You know what this means, don't you?"

A more-than-friends policy. "That's everything I'm afraid of."

"I know, but you don't need to be."

She could totally fall in love with Brice. Head over heels, the whole shebang. She was already halfway there.

"Hey, this is so cool," Hayden said from the corner where she was tracing some of the lovely scrollwork with her fingertips. "There's a heart inside some of these roses. Do you have to like carve this or something?"

"Or something," he answered the teenager, but he didn't take his eyes from Ava, who went to the kid's side for a closer look.

Ava was endearing. Her golden hair was pulled back at the crown of her head to bounce in a curling fall down the graceful column of her neck. Her gauzy top could have been something a fairy tale princess might wear, and her modest denim shorts and rubber flip flops made her seem even more wholesome and sweet. She traced the intricate scrollwork with her forefinger. Tears filled her eyes and did not fall. She stood still, studying the work, framed by the pale yellow walls and the dark rectangles of uncovered windows.

His heart filled with devotion for her. Afraid to scare her more with the seriousness of his affection, he waited, letting her have the time she needed to see what he'd done for her.

"This is amazing, Brice." Her smile was a little wobbly. "I love it."

She didn't say more. She didn't need to. The moment their gazes met, he could feel a rare, inexplicable connection forge between them. An emotional bond that was already so strong, what would it become if given more time?

He thought he knew the answer to that, too.

"I'm glad you like it," he said.

The niece-to-be wandered around, appraising. "I thought this was like supposed to be done tomorrow."

"We will be," he answered her but could not

look away from Ava. From her violet-blue eyes silvered with tears and her heart showing.

He brushed at her tears with the pads of his thumbs, feeling like he was ready for this.

He dropped a kiss on the tip of her nose. "Rex will be sad he missed you. He has a strict ten o'clock bedtime or he's grumpy the next day."

"I'll make an extra treat for him tomorrow. Will you be here?"

"To do the final walk-through with you. How does four o'clock sound? Will it work with your schedule?"

"I have no idea. Let me check." She pulled open the top of her enormous shoulder bag and began pawing through it. "No, no, no. Oh, here it is." She filed through a small appointment book and found the correct date. "It looks like I can make it at four. Will it take very long?"

"Not at all," he said. "I've got plans at five."

"Perfect." She ought to be done in plenty of time to babysit for Danielle. "This means that our business will be concluded. Done. Over."

"That's right." He flashed her that drop-dead gorgeous killer grin of his, full wattage, and showed both sets of dimples. "I guess it's time to work on amending our friends-only policy. I'll see you at four?"

"Four." Ava blinked, but that didn't help. Her mind had gone completely fuzzy. It was as if all her gray matter had turned into one big cotton ball. "If I could say thank you for the next decade without stopping, it wouldn't feel like enough."

"It's enough." He took a step back and held open the door. "Why are you two out and about this late?"

"The kid and I are on a fast-food run. It's our last night of inventory and we desperately need nachos to keep going."

"Let me guess. Mr. Paco's Tacos. One of my favorite places."

"Really? And here I thought after visiting your posh house and snazzy pool, that you ate only gourmet. Little did I know we share a love of Mr. Paco's nachos."

"The burritos, too."

"Don't even go there. My stomach is going to start growling and that would be so embarrassing." *Embarrassing.* That word hit her like a punch. She was gaping up at him like she was totally love-struck. How embarrassing was that? As if she'd let herself fall in love with him so fast. Not!

She was in total control of her emotions.

A distant ring penetrated her thoughts and broke the moment between them. Ava stepped back, fished through her bag again and came up with her cell. She saw the bookstore's number on her screen and she groaned. "It's Spence. I'm not going to answer this."

"Spence. He's a little wound up," Hayden said. She'd stationed herself by the door. "I don't like it when he's so mad. We better go."

"Yeah, or we'll be punished with that disappointed look of his." She dumped her phone back into her bag. Eventually it would stop ringing, but she had bigger concerns right now—and he was standing directly in front of her. Brice. "Should we come back with nachos for you? Or a burrito?"

"No, I'm good. Thanks."

"Okay." She took a step closer to the door, but she didn't want to say goodbye. She told herself it was the beautiful woodwork she couldn't tear herself away from. That wasn't the truth, but it was easier than admitting the truth.

She didn't want to leave Brice, because she knew she'd miss him. And in caring for him so much, she was terrified. "Good night," she said, as if she were in complete control of her heart, went up on tiptoe to brush a chaste kiss to his cheek and walked out of the shop. But when she'd settled in the passenger's side of her SUV, she realized she'd left something behind.

Her heart.

Chapter Eleven

Another drive-by baking. Brice had arrived just in time to see the back of a yellow vehicle far down the street, too far away for her to notice him. Rex seemed disappointed, too. He'd dashed to the kitchen only to find the box and a note on a star-shaped, bright-yellow Post-it note.

> Sorry, I promised the teenager monster muffins for her church thing today, so I'm running short on time. I've left gifts for the dudes and their families. And a special treat for my true love, Rex.

He wasn't surprised by her curlicue script or the fact that the note was written in glittery pink ink. There were a dozen medium-sized gift boxes set behind the regular baking box. One had his name on it, so he snooped beneath the lid. A small individually decorated cake and a gift certificate.

Rex whined with impatience, his tail thumping.

"You have one here, too." Curious, Brice peeked into the box with Rex's name written in glittery gold ink. It was full of large, bone-shaped snacks.

Ava *would* have a recipe for fancy dog treats. He tossed one to Rex, who caught it in mid-air and gobbled it in two bites. It had to be delicious because his eyes brightened and he sat perfectly, the very best behavior ever witnessed. This dog obviously wanted another one.

Okay, he was a sucker. Brice tossed him one more before he went straight to work. He had a few touch-ups to do and the display case glass to pick up.

He was totally beat. He'd put in a hard week's work, but it was worth it. At exactly four-thirty this afternoon, their final walk-through would be complete and their business over. Then their relationship could get personal.

And he'd planned in a big way. He had reservations. A jet. A limo. Everything all lined up. By the time the jet touched back down at the local private airport tonight around ten-thirty, he hoped that Ava would have a better idea just what she meant to him. What he wanted to mean to her.

This might be the hardest thing he'd ever done. To lay his heart on the line. But what choice did he have? He loved her. No holds barred. No going back. All the way until forever—if that's what she wanted.

The hard thing about falling in love was that it took two to get to there. Ava had to make a decision now. He knew she was afraid, she'd been hurt. It was hard for her to risk again. He knew how she felt. He was scared, too.

With God's help, maybe they could take that risk together.

The late afternoon sun was in Ava's eyes as she screeched to a stop in front of the bakery. Wow, no one was around, just one green pickup parked in the shade. The brand new windows were so clean they shone, and gave a perfect view into the cozy little shop space.

It was perfect, and her heart gave a little twist. She'd never dared dream as much as this. Even from the outside, the pale yellow walls warmed with the direct sunshine and seemed to invite a person right in. The empty display case sparkled, too, and the honey-colored wood was a comforting, homey touch.

Best of all, there was Brice, standing with his boots planted, wearing a knit black shirt and trousers, looking like a hundred on a scale of ten. There was no mistaking the intensity of his look or the reason why she felt joy light up in her heart.

It was his joy. His light.

Time to work on amending our friends-only policy, so think about the terms for our next agreement. His words had been troubling her since they'd talked last night.

So had Hayden's. Once they'd driven away, she'd said so innocently. "Wow, is that your boyfriend? Isn't he like rich and really cool?"

Yeah, so why was he interested in me? That was another insecurity that had plagued her every second, all day long. But seeing him coming toward her with his powerful athletic stride, knowing the gladness on his face was from seeing her made those insecurities whisper a little more quietly.

She grabbed her bag, tossed her phone inside and hopped out of the car. The door slammed shut before she realized her hand was empty—no keys. But the locks didn't automatically set, so she could open the door right back up and grab the keys from the ignition—thanks to Brice.

"You are so handy to have around, I can't believe it," she smiled at him.

"Good to know." The look he gave showed her he was glad to see her.

Somehow she had to *stop* liking him more every time she saw him. Otherwise, she was going to be a total goner. She'd fall all the way in love before the evening was over.

"I dropped the check for the last half of the payment at the office on my way here. Along with a dozen monster muffins."

"I bet the office staff was happy. That was nice of you. You must be awfully pleased with the work. Everybody waits until after the walk-through and the punch list is finished before they hand over that much money."

"It just felt strange to give you a check, so I left it with your bookkeeper."

"Because you're past the business-only phase, too?" he asked.

Okay, she could officially admit it. "Just a little bit. Maybe."

"Me, too. Just a little bit. *Maybe.*" But when he said it, the words sounded as if he didn't have a doubt in the world. He took her hand, twining his big strong fingers between hers, holding on to her as if she mattered, as if she had so much value to him.

For now, that pesky little voice whispered inside her. That'll change. Just give him time.

It took all her inner might to silence that voice. To accept the cherished feeling of having him at her side, of his hand to hers, palm to palm.

"Let's get this over with because I have plans for you." His fingers tightened on hers, strengthening their connection. "Are you ready?"

"As ready as I'll ever be."

He held the door for her, a gentleman all the way. She tried to keep her emotions in check, but the sunshine spilling over her made her feel more than hopeful. Made her intensely aware of her blessings.

What if this was a sign that her luck in life was changing? This charming shop with wood-wrapped windows, cathedral ceilings and whimsical warmth had once existed only in her dreams.

Now it was real.

Maybe it was time to see if more of her dreams in life could come true.

"Four twenty-nine." Brice checked his watch and glanced over the top of Ava's head. No sign of the limo yet, but the driver still had another minute. "I'm glad you're happy with our work."

"Happy doesn't begin to describe it. I still can't believe this was so painless. And the work your men did here. I'm grateful to all of you."

He could see that this transition from friends-only to more than friends was hard for her, too. She was nervously glancing toward the front door. Trying to escape before he hit the serious questions? he wondered. Or being afraid that he didn't have any?

This was tough for him, too. He'd never been this nervous. He'd never felt as if he had so much on the line. Everything was riding on this—his heart, his hopes and his future. It was tough letting go and trusting God's will for him. Brice took a shaky breath, gathering his courage. He'd have to see how this worked out. It wasn't easy not knowing.

"There's the limo now." He set the clipboard aside to cradle her chin in his hands. "Remember I said I had plans for you?"

"Y-yes. I vaguely recall something to that effect."

"And that we needed to renegotiate our friends-only policies?"

"Yes, but why the limo?" Panic coiled through her.

He could feel her fear. "It's okay. I have plans. Nice plans, involving dinner and watching the sun set. It should be painless, maybe even romantic. Are you interested?"

"Tonight? I c-can't."

His heart took a blow. He'd really thought she felt this, too. He took a step back and released his hold on her. "Well, I had to ask."

"Wait—no, I'm not saying 'no.'" She looked tortured. "When you said you had plans, I was thinking more of that next step. You know, like you'd ask me out sometime soon. I didn't know that you meant tonight. Now you're mad."

"I'm not mad."

"I told Danielle that I'd babysit for her. Aubrey has this church thing, and everyone else is busy. Spence could do it, but we don't want him to scare the children. So there's nobody else but me. You're looking madder."

"No. I just…made…plans."

See? Already she was messing this up. How did she do it? And so fast. They'd been officially more than friends for two minutes, maybe three? She twisted around to get a good look at the limo. It was shiny white and one of the long ones with sparkling windows and it looked expensive. "What kind of plans did you make?"

"Nothing that can't be rearranged for another time."

There it was, the terrible sense of foreboding, that everything so wonderfully right in her life was about to go totally wrong. Doom would strike and then it would all be over. She would never know what it would be like to be cherished by this man.

"I'll be back." Brice strode away, shoulders set, spine straight, purposefully.

Oh, no. Every last one of her hopes plummeted. What plans had she messed up? She closed her eyes, took a deep breath and tried to get centered enough to pray. But she couldn't. She was all messed up inside, as if someone had taken a big stick to her vat of negative feelings and was stirring it hard.

The door opened with a faint swoosh. Brice's powerful, wonderful presence filled the room.

"C'mon," he said in his kind voice, the one that made all the fears inside her melt like butter on a hot stove. His hand settled on her nape, and his touch, his kindness, seared through her like hope. He opened the door.

"Okay, call me confused." She stared at the driver in his suit and cap, holding open the passenger door for her. "What about Danielle?"

"Rick is going to take you to Danielle's house. I'm going to borrow your SUV and swing through and pick up take out so we all have something to eat. I'm coming with you tonight instead. My plans can change. Yours shouldn't."

"You mean...you're going to babysit with me?"

"Do you have a problem with that?"

She was vaguely aware her jaw was hanging open, but she couldn't seem to make it shut. She couldn't seem to move anything at all. All she could do was stare at this man—this perfect man—and feel even worse. How was she going to keep from falling one hundred percent in love with him *now?*

Brice held out his hand. "Your keys?"

She went in search and found them in her pocket. Did he know what this meant to her?

"I'll see you soon." He leaned close, so close she could smell the faint scent of fabric softener on his shirt.

Her spirit lifted from simply having him near.

He pressed a sweet kiss to her cheek. "I know family is important to you. That means, since we're dating, your family is important to me."

She sank onto the leather seat, dazed. This wasn't a dream, was it?

Brice knelt down on the sidewalk until they were eye to eye. "We are dating, right?"

"Right." Her entire soul smiled.

* * *

"All right," Danielle said, dragging Ava into the kitchen. "When did you start dating Brice Donovan?"

"Officially about twenty minutes ago." Ava leaned over the counter to get a good look out the kitchen window. There he was, as gorgeous as a wish come true. He'd climbed out of her SUV and was now carting with him a box of drinks and several big food bags bearing the Mr. Paco's Tacos emblem.

"Why didn't I know about this? You girls aren't supposed to leave me out of the loop!" Danielle looked rushed as she grabbed her purse and rummaged around for something. She pulled out her cell and hit the power button. "You have my number, call if there's a problem. I just can't believe this. Brice Donovan. He's *wonderful.* Jonas knows him from the community of united churches charities board. They served on it together for a few years. He just raved about him. Oh, look, he's here. And I've got to go. I'm completely late."

"Don't worry. Tell that great husband of yours that it's all my fault. I was late in the first place."

"He expects it." With a wink, Danielle rushed to the door. "Madison's not to have sugar. Tyler will try to talk you into too much television."

"I know the scoop. Go. Before your husband holds it against me. It's okay that he's here, right?"

"Uh, yeah." Danielle grabbed her keys and rushed into the living room. After a final kiss to her little ones she headed to the garage door.

It closed the same moment there was a knock on the front door. She swung it open and wasn't prepared for how good it was to find him there. He could be anywhere tonight, but he'd chosen to be with her. Which worked out just fine since she wanted to be with him.

She took the drink box. "Come on in. The kids are watching TV. I like your choice of take out."

"I figured we couldn't go wrong with tacos." He shouldered past her. "Do you want this on the table?"

"Yep. I'll round up the munchkins."

Brice set the bags of food on the table and glanced around. He wasn't surprised by the comfortable-looking furniture and pictures of cute kids on the wall. Several family vacation photos were framed in recognizable places like the Grand Tetons and Yellowstone. It felt like a real home. Cheerful checks and ruffles sparingly decorated the kitchen and what he could see of the living room. There was a TV in a cabinet tuned to a wholesome-looking cartoon. A couch faced it.

Ava knelt down to talk to the kids out of his view on the couch. She was pure tenderness, and his heart thudded to the floor. She was truly a kind woman. No doubt about it, she'd make a great mom. It was a side of her he hadn't seen but guessed was there.

A preschool-aged boy hopped up, stood on the cushions and threw his arms around Ava. The kid wore a plastic fireman's hat and the brim bonked her in the temple when he gave her a wet smacking kiss, which she pretended was gross just to have him laughing. Then she tickled his stomach, reminded him of the rule about the couch and standing and watched while he jumped down with a two-footed thud.

"Did ya bring lotza mexifries?" he asked

as he charged Brice's way. "Aunt Ava says I gotta have lotza mexifries or I'll get shorter insteada taller."

Yeah, he could see Ava telling that to the little guy. Funny. "Don't sweat it. I got the largest tub of them."

"Whew." As if that had been a big worry, the kid pulled back his chair, climbed up and settled into his booster seat.

Brice wasn't around kids very much, but this one was cute. He started unpacking the food. "You like tacos, kid?"

"Lots." The preschooler rested his elbows on the edge of the table and propped his chin on his hands. "Are you a fireman?"

"No. Are you?"

"Yep. I put out lotza fires today."

"Good work." Brice pulled the boxed kiddy meal from the giant bag.

He felt more than heard Ava's approach. It was as if his spirit turned toward her, recognizing her and only her. She had a curly-haired little girl on her hip, and the sight did something to him. She had the little girl laughing, her chubby cheeks pink with delight.

"Aunt Ava! Aunt Ava!" The boy shouted,

holding up three sticky-looking fingers. "I put out three fires today."

"Sorry, I can't hear you," she teased as she slid the little girl into a high chair. "I'm deaf from you yelling so loud."

"Oops. My bad."

Brice didn't need to wonder where the kid had learned that—his gaze landed on Ava again as she double-checked the little girl's lap belt on the high chair, and satisfied, straightened. "Brice, I hope you brought a lot of mexifries. We don't want anyone at this table to get any shorter than they already are."

"I brought the biggest tub."

"My hero. It's hard for a girl not to like a guy who knows what's important in life."

"Mexifries are one of the real secrets to true happiness."

"Exactly." She peered into one of the food bags. "Nachos. Burritos. Tacos. I'm speechless with gratitude."

"Not hunger?"

"That, too. Let me get milk for the kids. If you want to start doling out the food?"

"Sure." As he got to work, the little tot across the table stared at him like she wasn't too sure she approved of his presence.

"Aunt Ava! Aunt Ava!" The boy twisted around on his knees and hung over the back of his chair. "I getta say grace! I getta say grace!"

"Okay, okay. But what's your mom's rule?" Ava asked from behind the refrigerator door.

"Umm." The kid appeared to be thinking extremely hard.

This was not his experience of a family, Brice thought as he put the tubs of mexifries in the middle of the table. His mom would have a coronary at the noise level. No laughing at the table. No yelling. Sitting like a little gentleman—always. Use our best manners all the time.

All that had its place, but this was better. Comfortable. Fun. That was one of the things he cherished about Ava so much. She could make the simple things in life, like settling down to the dining room table, feel like a refreshing and cheerful kind of heaven on earth.

Ava slid a plate and a cup of milk in front of the boy. "No hats at the table, Tyler."

"Oh, yeah. I forgot." He handed her the bright red fireman's hat. "Can I say the blessing now?"

Ava dropped the hat on the back of the couch and returned to hand out another plate. "Brice, do you mind if Tyler does the honors?"

He could tell by the twinkling humor in her eyes that the boy's blessing was cute. Call him curious. He took the offered plate. "Sure."

"*Now,* Aunt Ava?"

"Hold on a minute." Ava rolled her eyes as she slid a cup on the toddler's tray.

"*Now?*" The kid sounded as if he were about to spontaneously combust.

"Now." Ava dropped into her chair.

Before Brice had time to bow his head, the little boy started in. *"Thanks for the eats, Lord. God bless us every one!"*

"Dickens' *A Christmas Carol* has made an impression on him," Ava explained after they'd muttered a quick "Amen." "He keeps watching this wholesome cartoon version of the movie over and over and it's driving Danielle insane."

Before Brice could answer, the boy hollered. "Aunt Ava! Hurry, I need mexifries. I'm shrinking."

"We can't have that. Brice, you look a little shorter, too."

He held out his plate. "Load me up."

What else could he say? This was exactly what he expected of an evening spent with Ava. Maybe not what he'd planned, but that didn't matter. All that mattered to him was being with her. For now and, he suspected, for his lifetime to come.

"I can't believe you're still talking to me," Ava said in the quiet of the warm night standing beside her SUV. It was dark out. Almost eleven o'clock. "Especially after Tyler squirted you with the hose."

"We were playing fireman, and it was an accident. I dried out pretty fast."

"You handled being drenched from head to toe in your snazzy clothes pretty well. Most men would have gotten really angry."

"I'm not like most men."

"I'm noticing that." It was hard not to.

Don't think about how perfect he is, she warned herself. That would just start making her nervous. Look at him, Mr. Fantastic, nice, wealthy and kind. He liked fast-food mexifries and went to church faithfully every Sunday. They'd talked about that after the kids had been in bed.

And after discussing faith, they went on to talk more about his family and hers. Chloe was still honeymooning in Fiji. His mom was ready to drive him nuts now that his sister was married off and she kept making elaborate plans for his upcoming birthday, and his dad was holding open a position at his investment firm, which Brice still didn't want.

She told of Katherine's upcoming wedding and all the planning that took, that she still hadn't picked a cake yet. She talked about their cousin Kelly who'd gotten married and was living in California on base with her marine husband. Then she mentioned the stress of owing her grandmother so much money.

Somehow they'd managed to avoid the more personal side of their conversation. Like, did he want kids? How many? She wanted children, but she had to find someone to get married to first. And wasn't that practically impossible? Certainly not a topic for a first date. If seeing her taking care of kids hadn't totally scared him off, talking about marriage and wanting kids would.

Then again, why risk it?

She dug through her purse for her keys. "It looks like you need a ride home."

"Nope, Rick should be arriving here in the next few minutes."

"Well, I don't want to leave you standing here alone."

"It's late. You've got to be tired from running after the kids. Go home." He smiled his billion mega-watt smile with the double dimples. "I'll be fine. I want you to drive safely."

"That's always my plan. I might not be the best driver, but I've never hit anything. Except for Grandpop's St. Bernard. I didn't see him in the rearview mirror."

Brice burst out laughing. "Does anything normal ever happen to you, or it is always a circus with you?"

"Always a circus. You've changed your mind about dating me. By the way, I didn't hurt Tiny at all."

"Tiny?"

"The St. Bernard. Not even a bruise. He didn't want us to leave and I couldn't see that he'd planted himself behind the car to stop us from going. He must have been in a blind spot because I checked the mirrors before I started backing up. There was this horrible thud. You should have seen the damage to Dad's bumper, though. It was the family car, and because they didn't want the insurance premium to go up, he didn't get it fixed. My family never let me live it down."

"And Tiny?"

"He learned to keep away from me when I was behind the wheel. I miss that guy. He passed away a month after Grandpop did." The pain of the loss still stole her breath. "Your grandparents are alive and well?"

"Thriving. They're vacationing at their home in Italy. They like to travel. They should be back for my birthday this week."

"I'm glad they are enjoying their lives. My grandparents always meant to do that, but they never got to travel much before they ran out of time to do it together."

"Our grandfathers were very close friends. I know he still advises your grandmother on her investments. Is she still living in Arizona?"

"She's stayed away since Grandpop passed. She said the house had too many memories of him, so she moved to their home in Scottsdale. They'd only had it for a few years, so I guess there weren't as many memories there. I think it helps her to be away, although we miss her. Dad's down there now, too, with Dorrie. They're all coming back at the end of summer for Katherine's wedding."

"My grandparents can't seem to breathe without the other. Were yours like that, too?"

"Gran said that losing her husband was like having her heart cut out. She's never been the same. They were very much in love. The real way."

"The way it's meant to be. My parents never managed to find that with each other." He shrugged. "They get along all right, they're compatible, but it's not what my grandparents have. They're tight."

"I know what you mean. Gran has always said Grandpop was her gift straight from heaven. She had all the best blessings in him." Okay, this was getting dangerously close to the topic she wanted to avoid, because she did not want to mess this up with Brice.

And yet, she couldn't seem to stop herself. "I've always thought they were the happily-ever-part of the fairy tale. You know, after Cinderella gets her shoe back *and* her prince, and Snow White is awakened by her prince, they end the stories. But I knew that kind of love was real because my grandparents lived for each other. They breathed together. It's what I always wanted."

Great going, Ava. She held her breath, *waiting,* just waiting, for him to start moving away.

But he didn't. "Me, too."

Headlights broke around the corner at that moment. It was Rick with his fancy limo and he pulled right up to the sidewalk, so Ava didn't know what else Brice had been about to say.

He brushed a kiss to her cheek. "Good night, beautiful."

Her soul sighed. "Wow, aren't you Mr. Perfect?"

"Oh, so it's working. Good to know I'm charming you."

"Only a tad. A smidgeon. A pinch."

Okay, that was an understatement. If she could measure how much Brice Donovan had impressed her, it would be the distance from the earth to the moon and back six hundred times.

Then he was gone, leaving her there in the light of the moon, unable to stop the full-blown wishes rising up from her soul.

Chapter Twelve

With hopeful cheer mid-afternoon light tumbled through the new larger front windows of her shop. But was she feeling hopeful? No. Astonished would be one word. Overwhelmed would be another.

She couldn't stop staring at the two dozen yellow, red-tipped roses Brice had sent. What was a girl to do when her hopes were already sky high, tugging like a helium balloon against the string? With every breath she took, she drew in the delicate fragrance of the lovely bouquet and tried to convince herself she wasn't scared.

The door behind her whispered open and there was Aubrey hefting a really big box.

Ava caught the door, holding it as her twin tumbled inside.

"Whew, it's a scorcher out there. The air conditioning feels nice." Aubrey slid the box to the ground. "Those flowers are gorgeous. From Brice?"

It wasn't exactly a question. And it wasn't exactly what Aubrey was asking. Ava could feel their shared brain cells firing. Her sister knew how she felt. She knew what those roses meant.

It was a shocker how calm her voice actually sounded. "Yes, they just arrived. Isn't it a totally nice gesture?"

"Nice, sure. But a bunch of daisies is nice. Roses say something much more. Like the *L* word."

"The *L* word is none of your business, nosy." No sense in getting into a blind panic. "Brice and me, we're in that awkward more-than-friends stage, but not totally committed stage. Who knows how it's going to work out? Doom might be lurking out there somewhere, just waiting."

She had to be prepared for it, if it was.

"What doom? There's no doom." Aubrey went straight to the roses and inhaled deeply.

"A man doesn't send something like this unless he's trying to sweep you off your feet."

"Yes, well, it's working."

"So, you called him to thank him, right? What did he say? Is he taking you out soon?" Aubrey pulled a pint carton of strawberry milk out of the box, still cold from the grocery store. She opened the spout and held it out for Ava to take. "What? You're just standing there not saying anything. You've called him, right?"

She took the milk. "Uh, I haven't got there yet."

"And you're procrastinating because…?"

"Okay, I can admit it. I'm a big chicken. Babysitting with him at Danielle's went so great. I mean, he was really Mr. Perfect. What if I mess this up?"

"Ava, Ava, Ava." Aubrey was using her gentlest voice, the one that was filled with so much unconditional sisterly love. It just proved that Aubrey was blinded by flaws, too. "This romance with Brice is totally new for you. You've finally found yourself a perfect guy."

"And it's too good to be true, right? That's

what I'm afraid of." And much, much more, but could she admit that to Aubrey?

No.

"You are perfectly lovable. Mom was wrong to say that to you when she left. To blame you for her unhappiness. It wasn't true then."

"We're talking about men, not Mom."

"Okay." Aubrey's heart was showing. "Don't you think the crazy accusations would have scared him off if he was going to be?"

"I can't believe he helped me babysit. He said *my family is important to me, so it's important to him.*"

"See? How many signs do you need?"

"I don't know if there could be enough."

Aubrey traced the pattern of the tiny intricate roses carved into the trim of the gleaming, perfect case. "I really think his heart is true. I think he's the right man for you. Why don't you grab hold of this blessing the Lord is placing before you? Brice might be the happily-ever-after I've been praying for, for you. Just believe that God is in charge and embrace this chance."

"I'm scared I'm going to mess this up. That he's going to get a good look at me and see that I don't fit into the right image. That's what Brice is looking for. He wants someone from the same background and compatible lifestyle. Look at me, I'm not exactly mink-wearing, symphony-going material. You heard him talk about his fiancée."

"His ex-fiancée. Didn't you listen to him at all?"

"It's hard to hear really well with all this panic racing around inside my head."

"You're a nut." Aubrey rolled her eyes. "What am I going to do with you?"

"Not much. You're stuck with me."

"That's just my good luck." Aubrey smiled. "Call him. Take a deep breath and do it. Take the next step forward."

"Sure, what do I have to lose? It's only my heart at stake."

"Do you know what I think?" Aubrey knelt and began unpacking the box. "I think you're *more* scared this is going to work out."

"Uh, yeah."

"Go in the kitchen and call him. I'll watch the front. Oh, and I'll put up all this stuff I brought."

"Okey dokey. You're wonderful, you know that?"

"I do. Now go."

"Thanks, Aub."

Her cell was ringing as she streaked into the kitchen. Her heart jumped with jubilation when she saw Brice's name and number on her screen. Talk about perfect timing. Okay, she was scared, but this *had* to be a sign. She hit the talk button. "I love the flowers. Thank you."

"I know red roses are expected, but when I saw these in the florist's case, I thought of you. Bright yellow like the sunshine you are."

If he kept talking like that, he was going to scare her even more.

"What are you up to this morning?" he asked.

"No good, as usual. I just finished making a ballet shoe cake, it's for one of the construction dude's daughters."

"That was really nice of you, including certificates for a free birthday cake for everyone."

"It's the least I could do. My new kitchen is wonderful to work in. The question is, have you recovered from the trauma of babysitting?"

"No trauma to recover from. I'm made of tougher stuff than that. Remember how I said I had plans in place that we postponed?"

"You know I do." She heard a slight tinkle of chimes and peered through the open doorway. There was Aubrey hanging a beautiful ceramic bell over the door.

"I've been able to push those plans back a few weeks. I wanted to give you plenty of notice this time. I thought we could combine it with celebrations for the Fourth of July. You wouldn't be interested in spending that weekend with me would you?"

"Uh, did I hear you right? The entire weekend?"

"Now, before you start jumping to conclusions and questioning my morals, let me explain."

He was laughing, remembering their unforgettable first meeting when she'd told him to get some morals. At least he thought it was funny. That was a good sign, right?

"Okay, I'll wait for the explanation before I start firing insults."

"I have some property near Glacier National Park, and we won't be alone. I plan to invite my sister and her husband. My grandparents will be there, too. I was going to suggest that you invite Aubrey. We'll have a big cookout and watch fireworks over the lake. It'll be fun—and well chaperoned. What do you think?"

"Do you mean like going camping, or something? Because I try not to go too far out into the wilderness."

"Why? You're not a backcountry kind of girl?"

"If I tell you, then you'll stop dating me. Years from now you'll tell your friends it was a good thing you dumped me when you did."

"Not a chance, gorgeous."

She was in big trouble because her high hopes were rising higher than the galaxy. She was in bigger trouble because the logical part of her was drowned out by those rising hopes.

"Tell me about this story of yours, Ava. I gotta know."

"My dad loved to camp and he'd haul us all up to one of the national forests and we'd do the tent thing and the catch trout for supper thing and cook over an open campfire thing."

"Uh oh. I'm starting to see what might have been the problem here."

"I accidentally started a forest fire. It wasn't my fault. And it was only a little grass fire, but I never lived it down. Over the years the story has grown to gargantuan proportion and when Dad tells it now, you'd think I burned down half the western forests in the United States."

"And you started it how?"

"My marshmallow caught on fire. I was seven. I was afraid of flame, mostly, so I was sitting farther back than everyone else from the campfire. And Aubrey leaned over to say something to me and I forgot to watch the stick. It was sort of top heavy because I was holding the very end of it and it just sort of dipped into the fire.

"When I noticed that my marshmallow was turning black and spewing flame, I screamed and gave it a big shake. Blazing marshmallow fluff flew off the stick and onto Mom and Dad's tent. It caught fire, of course. It was a total disaster. Luckily, Dad followed the forestry rules of having so many buckets of water and dirt handy, whatever, and he got it put out with hardly any damage to anything but a piece of scorched earth where the tent had been."

"I'm beginning to see why your family calls you a disaster magnet."

"To this day, Spence will not let me be in charge of any fire-related thing. No barbecuing, no campfire, no lighting the Yule log in the hearth on Christmas Eve. It's embarrassing."

"You *are* a disaster."

"Don't I know it. You're going to hang up now, aren't you? You've changed your mind about me, about spending time with a big dope like me."

"Hey now, I don't think you're a dope."

It was his kindness that got her. His unending, constant kindness, even when he should be agreeing with her. Then it hit her. Duh. Could it be any more obvious? "Oh, no. I can't believe this. You have it, too."

"What do I have?"

"The flaw-blindness. Otherwise, you could see it."

"See what?"

He didn't know? That was only further proof. He was as fault-blind as she was. Unbelievable. "My faults? You can't see them, can you? All six hundred thousand of them."

"Nope. You look perfect to me."

"Then we're doomed. This is only a matter of time." She rolled her eyes, trying to make light of things. But that wasn't how she was feeling. Not at all. Suddenly it was so clear. His devotion, his kindness, his affection and his romantic gestures would last only as long as it took for him to realize the truth about her. "We might as well accept it now. One day you'll look at me and decide you can't take it anymore. Then the more-than-friends aspect of our relationship will be done. A great big crash and burn. Ka-blew-y."

"No crashing and burning. No ka-blew-y. I like you exactly the way you are, Ava. I like *who* you are. Or I wouldn't be inviting you to my birthday party either."

"What?"

"You know I'm turning thirty-one on Tuesday. I've finally talked my mom into just having a small family dinner at home. My grandparents are coming. I want you there, too."

This was such dangerous ground. This was like the camping trip. Everything was great and happy. Everything finally looked promising, like it really was going to work out.

And when you stopped expecting it, when you were sure it was smooth sailing ahead, *that's* when disaster struck. Like a category five tornado touching down right where you're the most vulnerable.

But what did she say? This sounded like the next step—a serious step. "Did I hear you right? You want me to come to your birthday dinner?"

"I'm asking you, right?" Brice adjusted his Bluetooth headset before he slowed his truck to pull into the left hand turn lane at the red light. Rex was in the backseat, panting extra loud, as if he were in agreement. See how Ava improved their lives? Just talking to her lifted their spirits. "You'll come?"

"As long as I get to bring the cake."

"I'd love the dump truck cake."

"Anything else you want with it?"

"Nope. As long as you're there, what else could I want in this world?"

"Oh, you are totally Mr. Irresistible, aren't you? You keep saying things like that, and I'm going to have to start liking you."

"*Start* liking me?" Brice chuckled. "I thought you were already in that pond with both feet."

"You must be mistaken. I *hardly* like you at all."

He could just imagine her rolling her eyes, looking so sweet and sparkling, the way she did when she smiled. In his opinion, they were right in that pond with both feet together. It was scary, but nice. "I'll pick you up Tuesday at six-thirty—" His call waiting beeped. His mom. "Can I put you on hold for a few minutes?"

"Okey dokey."

Ava. She put a smile into his heart and made everything better. The sun in his eyes was brighter than he'd ever noticed. The greens of the lawns and trees in his neighborhood more vibrant. Greener than he'd ever remembered.

He hit the garage door opener and switched over to answer the call. "Hi, Mom."

"Brice? Is that really you, or just my imagination. I can't believe I'm not getting your voice mail. *Again.*"

Uh-oh. She didn't sound happy. He racked his brain but he couldn't think of a thing he'd done. "I've been busy finishing up a project."

"Yes, your father mentioned that. For that baker. That friend of Chloe's."

He pulled his truck into the garage, not missing the disapproving tone in his mother's voice. "Ava McKaslin is a friend of mine, too."

"I know Chloe did her a favor by letting us overpay her for that wedding cake."

"Mom, you can't fool me." He cut the truck's engine and swung open the door. "Ava didn't charge Chloe—or you—for that cake."

"And how do you know this?"

He opened the door and waited while Rex leaped out. "I'm bringing Ava to my birthday dinner, and she's bringing the cake. You're going to be nice to her, right?"

There was silence. Frosty silence.

This was actually going better than he'd expected. That had to be a good sign, right? He unlocked the inside door and held it for Rex, who was yawning hugely and lumbered lazily inside. "Mom?"

"I'm carefully weighing my words and there doesn't appear to be anything I can say that you would deem appropriate."

"You have until Tuesday to work on that." He stepped around Rex who had collapsed in front of the nearest floor vent and opened the refrigerator. "I'm going to expect you to be on your best behavior."

"She's all wrong for you, you know that."

"It's not your decision who I date, Mom. Ava's important to me, and I want your word you'll be nice to her."

"I suppose I can try."

"Thank you. I'll call you and Dad later, okay? I've got her on the other line, so I need to go." He said goodbye, and he couldn't say exactly why there was a terrible sense of foreboding that settled dead center in his gut. He switched over to the waiting call. "Ava?"

"Yo. Danielle just walked in. She's taking the measurements for the shades she's making me. Hold on just a sec." There was a lot of cheerful talk in the background that grew fainter. "Brice? I've got a full house here. Spence just pulled up with the tables Aubrey refinished for me."

"Sounds exciting. I bet the place is looking more like you imagined."

"It is. I'm going to be officially open for business this weekend. There's a ton of stuff I still have do, and I'm totally excited *and* scared."

"I can understand that." Did he. "What can I do to help?"

"As if you haven't done enough with the woodwork. It still takes my breath away."

"Good. That's the idea."

Ava nearly stumbled at his words. Oh, she was so overwhelmed. So out of her realm of experience. Tender feelings for him just kept lifting through her, rising up until all she could feel was joy. Was it illusion? Could this possibly work out between them?

"I'll give you a call tomorrow," he said in that dependable, easy-going way of his. "See if you need any help hauling anything or helping with the set up. Okay?"

"Okay."

Ava leaned her forehead against the heel of her hand, listening to the click as he disconnected. Could this man be any more perfect?

It took her a second to realize that all the chatter in the front room had stopped. Her sisters were staring at her. Katherine's eyes were hopeful and sparkling. Aubrey looked as if she were going to start jumping up and down with glee.

This was another problem with a big

family. A girl had no privacy. Ever. Even when you were grown and gone from the nest, you could not get away from nosy sisters, bless them.

Danielle shifted little Madison on to her other hip. "Did we hear that correctly? Are you going to a family birthday party?"

"Oh, this is *big*. Huge," Katherine added. "He's taking you home to meet his parents."

"See? What did I say?" Aubrey steepled her hands, as if in prayer. "This is the next step."

"Don't psych me out, I'm trying to cope here." Ava spotted Spence and his big gray pickup parked against the curb. He was glaring in at them. "He obviously needs help. I'd better get out there—"

"Was it my imagination or did you tell Brice about the camping trip?" Katherine asked, using the box Aubrey brought to prop open the door. "And he *still* asked you out?"

"The story just popped out. It wasn't intentional." Ava shrugged. "I guess that old family stuff has been on my mind lately."

"I know how that goes, but you don't have to let the past affect your future. Good things happen to good people, and this is one of those times." Katherine grabbed a pair of sunglasses from the counter. “Take my advice. Leave the past behind where it belongs, and go live your future. You can do that, right?”

“Sure.” Easier said than done. She didn’t dare let herself believe it. Being with Brice was too important. She hoped that as long as she stayed right here, in this more-than-friends-only stage, then it wouldn’t get serious. She wouldn’t lose any more of her heart.

Chapter Thirteen

On Tuesday evening, as they headed up to Brice's parents' house in his red sports car, she felt as if they were driving heavenward. The foothills of the Bridger Mountains offered breathless views of the higher Rocky Mountain peaks and the deep, divine blue of the summer sky. As gorgeous as the view was, where were her eyes glued? On Brice, looking amazing in a black sports coat, shirt, tie and trousers.

Dazzled? Yeah, you could say that.

"We're almost there." Brice drove with confidence on the smooth, S-curving road that skirted private developments more upscale than the one he lived in. "You look a little pale. Are you okay?"

Okay? If she could survive the panic attack, she'd be just fine, thanks. There was a perfectly rational explanation for the panic. This couldn't be real. It was too nice to be real. Too wonderful. She tried to relax. Tried to pretend she wasn't terrified. She'd never felt like this, so vulnerable and so close to him.

Careful, Ava, she warned herself. Don't start to believe in the dream.

Brice pulled into a grand driveway that rivaled anything she'd seen on TV and that's when the nerves hit her. What had she been thinking? It was way too early in their relationship for her to meet his parents. Besides, she'd already met his mom. She'd been very dismissive of Chloe's choice of wedding cake designs.

"I don't suppose your mom is expecting a more fancy cake design?" She looked at the bakery box sitting on her lap.

"Does it matter?" He shrugged as if he couldn't imagine how she might even think it would.

Okay, maybe not. But as he pulled in front of a lavish Shakespearean-looking brick home with a turret and those diamond panel windows, she couldn't fight the strong feeling that her nifty dump truck cake might seem a little hokey by comparison. "You're sure about the cake?"

"Yep." He didn't look like he had a doubt in the world.

Okey dokey. Maybe it wasn't the cake she was worried about. Maybe Brice's family would take one look at her and think, not right for him. She smoothed the linen skirt of the dress she'd borrowed from Aubrey.

Okay, really, it was just her old insecurities flaring up like a big case of emotional warts.

He smoothly parked the car in front of a four-car garage and cut the engine. "You haven't changed your mind about coming in with me, have you?"

"Let me get back to you on that." Her voice wobbled.

"Don't be nervous. My family is going to love you."

"And if they don't?"

"They will learn to love you." He cupped her chin in his palm.

She focused her violet-blue gaze on his, her whole heart showing.

He got out of the car, noticing his grandparent's Land Rover was parked in the shade. Anticipation uplifted him as he circled around to open Ava's door. He couldn't wait for his grandparents to meet Ava. He knew they would love her. His parents might take more time to accept someone new, but he knew they would come to adore her, too. How could anyone not fall in love with Ava?

He took the boxed cake and offered his hand to help her from the low-slung car. The brush of her hand to his renewed him, more every time.

Having her at his side was like a gift. She swept beside him with that buoyant walk of hers. Everything about her was bubbly. This evening, she wore a light purple summer dress that shimmered as soft as a dream. Matching lavender sandals clicked on the brick walk, echoing slightly in the balmy, quiet grounds. The purple gift bag she carried made a pleasant crinkling sound as she walked. Her hair was pulled back in one of those fancy braids and stayed in place thanks to a few little purple butterfly barrettes.

Cute. Whimsical. She was like a spring

breeze and he could not get enough of her. Powerful affection filled him. He hesitated on the doorstep. "This is your last chance to bolt."

"How did you know that had crossed my mind?" She winked, and looked even more sweet and adorable. "I'm as ready as I'll ever be."

"Super-duper." He said that to make her smile, and it worked. He opened the front door. "Hello? Anyone home?"

Their steps echoed in a mammoth marble foyer.

Ava looked around, a little afraid to step on the very expensive looking marble beneath her shoes. "Is this a house or a museum?"

"It always felt like a museum when I was growing up. Come all the way in. Don't worry. We don't charge admission. Not on Tuesdays, anyway."

Her gaze went directly to an ornately framed watercolor, which was mounted on the wall directly ahead of her. It looked old. Ancient. Probably by some master—Aubrey would know which one. "That looks real."

"Mom likes to hang her expensive pieces

where she can impress everyone who walks through the door."

"Me, too. We have a cross-stitch welcome sign hanging in our entry. Aubrey did it last winter. It's a total classic. We've had offers."

What was it about her that made even visiting his mother fun? He set the cake on the antique table against the wall.

"Did you really grow up here?"

There was that little furrow between her eyes again, a sign she was puzzled. So, he hoped, did she see what he wanted her to see? Most people who walked through the door were impressed by Monet and the imported marble. There were no family pictures framed and hung on the walls. No cross-stitched sign welcoming guests. No hints of love or comfort anywhere.

A maid in a black uniform hurried discreetly toward them. "Master Brice. Happy birthday! Let me take your things. The family is in the rec room. Dinner will be served promptly at seven."

"Thanks, Wilma. This is Ava. And here is the cake."

"Oh, well done. I'll get this to the kitchen." The tidy lady hurried off with efficient speed.

Ava knew she was gaping. Okay, call her intimidated now. What she had already seen of Brice's life was a neon sign they weren't compatible; *this* was a billboard framed in blinking red lights. "She took my purse and your gift."

"She's supposed to." Brice looked amused as he guided her through a cavernous formal living room filled with rich polished woods and upholstered velvet and toward a slowly downward winding staircase.

No way was this a *home.* It was too perfect to relax in, and there was no feeling of love or life. From the expensive imported carpets to the vase that looked like it came from ancient China. Where did his parents put up their feet at the end of a long day and watch television? And there wasn't a book anywhere. Not even a Bible. The rooms, stuffed with expensive furniture, felt vacant and hollow. There was no heart. No warmth.

This was Brice's childhood home? No way could she imagine children growing up here. Well, not the way she would want to raise children, anyway. With noise and friendly chaos.

Their footsteps echoed in the coved

ceilings overhead, just like they would in a museum.

"Everyone's downstairs." Brice took her hand, his gaze and his touch were more than tender. It felt as if he cherished her. Being cherished by Brice Donovan was just about the best thing she could wish for, but with every step she took, she wondered how this could possibly last.

Voices grew in volume as they descended the grand staircase and arrived in a slightly less formal version of the living room. Four people rose from stiff, uncomfortable looking couches. Brice's parents and grandparents stopped in mid-conversation to stare at her.

During the few seconds of awkward silence, she felt Brice's hand tighten on hers. Tension rolled through her. The sudden silence felt uncomfortable. So did the hard way Brice's mother studied her.

Okay, she could see the mistake right away. She was wearing purple. Everyone else was dressed in sedate colors. Navy. Black. Beige. She stuck out like a grape Popsicle. Her dress wasn't floor length, her hair wasn't swept up and sedate. She wore her cross and not ten-thousand-dollar pearls—not that she had any or wanted to have any.

It was too late to rethink the wardrobe. The important question was whether Brice thought bringing her was a definite mistake?

"Everyone, this is Ava McKaslin," he said in that warm baritone of his.

Since her knees were a little wobbly, she took care stepping forward so she didn't trip as Brice introduced her to his parents.

"It's good to meet you." Brice's father, Roger, stuck out his hand.

She hoped her palm wasn't too damp. Oops. Nerves. She wanted her grip to be firm enough for him. She met his gaze, and she realized he had Brice's eyes. And they were warm and kind.

"I understand you designed our Chloe's wedding cake. That was beautiful. Everyone said so," Roger Donovan said stiffly, as if he were uncomfortable, too. "Chloe comes back from her honeymoon tomorrow. I'm sure she will tell you herself how happy she was with it."

"Thanks. It's very nice to meet you." Her voice hardly wobbled at all. Whew. That went pretty well. Considering.

"And this is my mom, Lynn. I know you've already met."

Lynn Donovan nodded once, a curt bob that was barely an acknowledgement. "I understand you're designing Carly Frost's wedding cake. Maxime and her oldest daughter were just telling me today how pleased she is so far."

"That's nice to hear. I'm glad they're happy."

"Hmm." The woman managed to make that sound seem judgmental, and said nothing more. She pursed her lips and stared hard at Ava, as if she didn't like what she was seeing.

Okay, this wasn't going as well. Ava took a rattling breath, feeling more and more unsure. Until Brice's hand engulfed hers, and his touch was a steady anchor of comfort and reassurance.

"Hello, to both of you." His grandmother looked elegant in her designer pantsuit. She crossed the length of the room, arms out, and pulled him into a quick hug. "Happy birthday, young man."

"I'm glad you could make it." Brice kissed her cheek. "How was your flight home?"

"The usual. Lines. Customs. Only one lost piece of luggage. An improvement from the trip over." Merriment twinkled in her eyes and she grasped Ava by the hands. "Ava, dear girl, how is your grandmother? Mary and I have been playing phone tag for the last few months."

"Gran is fine, or so I hear. I haven't spoken to her for the last few weeks, but she's scheduled to call soon. I'll tell her that you were asking after her."

"Tell her I demand she calls me."

"I'll tell her. It is good to see you again, Ann. And you, too, sir."

Brice couldn't believe it. He curled his hand around the nape of her neck, tenderly pulling her closer. "Okay, how do you know my grandparents?"

"We met at my Grandpop's funeral, although it's been a few years now," she explained. "I'm glad to see you are both well."

"As right as rain." Gram clasped her hands together as if in prayer. "How wonderful that you are with us here tonight, dear. To think you and Brice are dating."

"I'm afraid that's just a rumor. I suppose it will never stop if I keep hanging out with him."

"Oh, you have your grandmother's sense of humor." It was plain to see that Gram already adored Ava. "I hear you've brought the cake tonight. Something special for our Brice. Now, we'll know just how much she's fallen in love with him when the cake is unveiled. What fun."

"I'm afraid it's not what you're expecting." Ava rolled her eyes in that way he loved so much. "Brice requested the cake, so if you don't like it you have to blame him. I'm the completely innocent baker."

Ann and her husband Silas laughed pleasantly, as if they understood completely. Except for the fact that Brice's parents were staring at her as if she were their worst dream come true, the evening was going great.

The maid lady chose that moment to announce the salad was ready and to come to the table. She caught Lynn's coolly assessing gaze and thought, uh oh. But the minute his big hand enclosed over hers, she felt cherished all over again.

"See? They love you," he whispered in her ear.

She might not be so sure, but he looked happy and she wouldn't jeopardize that for anything.

"Did I tell you how beautiful you look?" he whispered again, hanging back to let the others head upstairs first.

"Not recently."

"On a scale of one to ten, you're a two hundred. A definite Miss Perfect."

Whatever you do, Ava, she warned herself, don't fall in love with him.

But it was too late.

Seated at his place at the mammoth dining room table, Brice couldn't believe how great dinner was going. Okay, Mom wasn't as warm to Ava as he would have wished for, but she was doing pretty well considering. There had been no comments, bold or veiled, that could hurt Ava's feelings. It mattered to him that his mom was keeping her promise.

His dad, he could tell, thought she had it together. He'd quizzed Ava about her business plan, while Granddad had added his advice, and they both pronounced her plans financially sensible and well done.

Ava smiled in that sweet way of hers, winning his heart all over again, thanking Wilma as the maid cleared her plate.

Powerful love for her hit him like a punch

to his chest. He couldn't breathe, couldn't feel his heart beating. He could see only her. Be aware of only her. Seconds stretched into eternity and it was scary, this all-consuming love for her. Scary, but right.

He knew she was the right woman for him. The real question was: Did she feel the same way about him?

"Excuse me," Ava said in her cheerful way, "but I'd better help set up the cake."

"Oh, the cake!" Gram clasped her hands together in anticipation. "This I have to see."

"I hope it's chocolate, like Chloe's wedding cake," Granddad commented.

His mother's lips pursed tight; but thank the Lord she kept her opinions to herself. Brice's heart swelled with love for his mom. He was proud of her. He knew how hard it was for her to keep her promise to him. Catching her gaze, he nodded his silent thanks, and some of the tension eased from around her mouth. He knew it was going to be okay.

"Yes, it's chocolate." Ava bounced up from her chair. "But this is a different recipe than I used with Chloe's cake. This is more like fudge. I call it my triple chocolate dream cake."

Granddad grinned. "I like the sound of that."

"He has a terrible sweet tooth." Gram shook her head, as if in great disapproval, but there was no mistaking the depth of love alight in her eyes. "What am I going to do with you, Silas?"

"Just love me for who I am, I guess," Granddad grinned at her.

Across the table, Brice recognized that loving glance his grandfather gave his grandmother and understood it for what it was truly, for the first time. Not merely love, but a breadth of love that happened to a man, if he was blessed, once in a lifetime. And he had to be brave enough to grab hold of that rare blessing and not let go, no matter how scary it was.

Opening himself up to love and hurt and rejection again was tough. But truly, Brice realized as Ava pushed in her chair, her purple skirt swirling, his heart had already made the choice.

Ava was his everything. He knew it, soul deep. He wanted to spend the rest of his life loving her, protecting her, cherishing her.

She took two steps and then turned to give him a death-ray glare. "From your chair, I think you can see part of the kitchen, and you are not supposed to see the cake until it's ready. No peeking. Got it?"

"Yes, ma'am."

"I see that twinkle in your eye. You're thinking about peeking."

"If I was, you've made me change my mind."

"Oh, *sure* I did." Was it so wrong that she wanted this to be a surprise? She'd worked really hard on his cake, just for him. She'd wanted him to be happy with it. As she headed to the kitchen, it occurred to her that making him happy was taking top priority on her list of the most important things in life, and how scary was that?

With every step she took through the magnificent house, she felt more and more out of place. Sure, his family had gone out of their way to extend their warmth to her, and she was grateful for that, but did that help all the bad feelings that kept wanting to bubble up like lava into a volcano's dome?

No. Not a bit. The pressure was building, and there was nothing she could do about it. She smiled at Wilma, who was busy setting down the cake plates in a totally fancy china pattern, and fetched the bakery box from its spot on the counter.

"Let me set out the cake," the maid lady said, as if possessive of her job.

"Oh, I want to make sure it's perfect. I'll just unbox it, then."

"Very well."

As Ava carefully picked up the box and moved it out of Brice's sight, she felt the tangible stroke of his gaze like a tender caress to her cheek. Pure sweetness filled her heart, and she did her best to hold back every feeling. Every caring emotion. Every piece of growing affection she had for this man.

She stood frozen, his loving glance holding her in place like a tractor beam.

Don't let yourself fall any more in love with him, Ava. She gulped hard and forced her foot forward. It took a few more steps and then she was safely out of his sight. But out of the tractor-pull of his feelings?

Of course not. She felt the pressure building in the center of her chest, like the rising dome of that volcano about to blow. She felt little and plain and very purple in her dress, in this enormous kitchen that was roughly the size of her apartment. She could see into the next room—some kind of solarium thingy, with rich-looking imported carpets and antiques and more paintings on the walls—probably from some master she knew nothing about.

This was Brice's life, she realized. This was where he grew up, this was his childhood home, he'd had maids and probably nannies and, as she heard the conversation drift in from the dining room, he was intelligently discussing the summer symphony series.

She felt the first crack in her heart as she lifted the lid of the box. Even so, there was no way to stop her love for him as it brightened in intensity. No way to hold it back. She didn't even know she could hold so much love inside her, but there it was, an infinite amount, welling up right along with the building pressure of the truth. The truth she could no longer deny.

Brice *was* Mr. Perfect. But not *her* Mr. Perfect.

The first stroke of agony burned like fiery lava licking at the edge of her heart. Who knew doom would fall so quietly? The only sounds were the muted clink of Wilma counting out the silver and gold-plated dessert forks and the pleasant murmur of voices discussing Beethoven from the next room.

All she had to do was to lean a little to the right, and she had a clear view of him. Of Brice, looking like a magazine cover model in his designer suit, the ivy league educated, successful son of one of the oldest and richest families in Montana. Mr. Eligible Bachelor, who looked comfortable in this museum of a house. This wasn't the Brice she'd come to know and, sadly, to love.

Ava felt another crack slice through her heart. She lifted the cake carefully onto the counter. She looked at it now through different eyes. She'd put her heart into doing her best job for Brice.

The big blue and red dump truck was parked in the middle of the cake board she'd decorated to look like a dirt and gravel road, made of sugar paste and crumbled chocolate cookies, tacked with sugar glue and sprinkled with edible gold sparkles, to jazz it up. A construction driver was tucked behind a steering wheel. D & M Construction was spelled out in silver script on the door. The bed of the truck was mounded high with gray boulders, which were individuals bites of iced cake.

Her best dump truck cake ever, and it didn't seem that way now. It wasn't right.

She wasn't right.

Brice's mother tapped into the kitchen and blinked, as if she were totally confused. "That's a cake?"

Yeah, just as she'd thought. Ava took a steadying breath and wished she was centered enough for a quick prayer, too, but she wasn't. "It's what Brice wanted."

"Yes, I can see that."

"I know, it looks really close to the real toy, doesn't it? But trust me, everything is edible."

"It's certainly…interesting." Lynn was apparently struggling for something complimentary to say.

But there was no denying the truth, not anymore. She lovingly slid the elegant white candle that had been laid out by Wilma into the center of the cab's roof. Just one candle, that was all, and it looked out of place on the cake.

She thought of the bright yellow number

three and one candles she'd brought for the cake, and decided to leave them where they were—in the back of the bakery box. Lynn Donovan didn't look as if she'd ever used novelty candles. Only classy all the way.

Which was probably why the woman had such a pained look on her face. "Brice will be pleased with this, I'm sure," she said stiffly.

Ava caught sight of Brice through the archway, leaning to speak with his grandfather. Her heart cracked a third and final time. She'd been right all along. There was no way this could work.

"You see it too, don't you?" Lynn said quietly. "He's really a good man. He deserves the very best of everything, don't you agree?"

Yes. Her entire soul moved with that word. She wanted the best of everything for Brice, too. But the man she watched could have been a stranger. Sure, he looked like the Brice she'd fallen for, but the man she knew was a craftsman. He made beauty with wood with skill, discipline and heart. He loved fast-food nachos and drank strawberry milk. He had a sometimes well-behaved dog, an easygoing manner that made her feel comfortable with him, and a sense of humor that made her feel lighter than air.

But *this* Brice, he was the real thing, honest hardworking guy and the most eligible bachelor all wrapped up into one. He was so perfect, that was his flaw. She'd finally found it. She'd known all along this relationship couldn't work, didn't she? But did she listen to her experience, to that little voice inside her head, to the iron-clad no-man, no-date policy that was supposed to keep her from being hurt like this again?

No. She was foolish to think that there could be a Mr. Perfect for her. She always fell in love with the wrong men, and there was no man more wrong for her than Brice Donovan.

She was vaguely aware of Lynn ordering Wilma around, of being herded back to the table, of seeing the anticipation on Brice's handsome face as she slipped into her chair. But her mind was in a fog. Her heart was a total mess. Somehow she had to hold it together.

Ann gasped when Wilma entered, carrying the cake. "Oh, that's delightful. Simply *adorable.*"

Her praise felt like a blow from a boxer's glove, as kind as those words were. Ava swallowed hard against the lump rising in her throat. She had to hold down her negative thoughts and keep them from blowing over.

"That looks like the real toy," Silas said in wonder. "I can't believe that's a cake. Is it really a cake?"

"It's a real cake, Granddad," Brice spoke up. "And I bet everything on it is delicious."

"That's not real dirt, is it?" Lynn asked in distress.

"It's crumbled chocolate cookies," Ava explained gently.

His beautiful, precious Ava. He saw all the love she'd put into his birthday cake. The D&M Construction logo on the door. The dog seated beside the driver inside the little cab. The detailing that had to have taken hours. She'd done this for him.

One look at her and he was hooked like a fish on a line. He loved her without condition, without end. She sat across from him, and the expanse of the table might separate them, but he could feel the connection of love strengthening between them.

"I've never seen anything like this," his

dad said from the head of the table. "You have a talent, Ava."

"It's not hard at all. You'd be surprised how easy it can be. And fun, too."

"Can you make other things, besides trucks?" Granddad asked.

Ava bit her lip, looking as sweet as sugar icing. "Well, I just did a ballet shoe the other day. That was a first for me, but I've done all sorts of things. Everything from football cakes to a medieval castle."

"I'll ask for the medieval castle for my next birthday," Brice told her.

She beamed her beautiful smile at him, the one that gleamed like a little dream.

I'm in big trouble, he thought. Just when he'd thought he was so in love with her, he'd fallen as far as he could go, he fell a little more in love with her. As his dad started the first notes of "Happy Birthday" and everyone joined in, he didn't have to wonder what he would wish for: Ava.

She was his dream come true.

Chapter Fourteen

Brice pulled the car to a stop in a spot marked for visitors, in the shade of tall poplars that lined the grassy lawn of her apartment complex. Ava knew he was going to ask her what was wrong, and what was she going to say? That she'd done it again. It was all her fault. She'd brought this misery down on herself.

"Thanks for coming," he said, breaking the silence between them. "I hope my mom wasn't too much. She comes across a little sharp, but she's a softy down deep. My grandparents love you. I think you've got lifelong customers. Granddad wants to order a cake for his birthday next month. You might want to start thinking up something with a golf theme."

"I'll get right on it." Her voice sounded strained, but it was harder than she thought to hold back so much pain. The thing was, when you'd been struck by misfortune as much as she'd been, you learned to cope. There was that first initial hit that hurt deep, but then shock set in and it didn't hurt so much. You could figure out how to cope until the shock wore off. And she was just about there. She could feel the press of hot, sharp emotions slicing through the defensive layers of her heart. The burn of tears gathered in her throat, rising up, too.

"Why do you look so unhappy?" He studied her, leaning closer, his gaze tender with concern.

"I'm not unhappy." That was the truth, she told herself stubbornly. She wasn't unhappy; it was much, much worse. She'd known better, but here she was with the wrong man. And here she was, exactly where she tried to avoid being, clutching every shard of her broken wishes. Why had she done this to herself? She'd known from the start this would happen. She should have listened to the fears inside her heart and resisted his kindness and his charm and his affection.

Then again, how would she have resisted caring for Brice? He was perfect. A thousand on a scale of ten.

"Did something happen I don't know about? My mother was unkind to you." He said it as if he'd expected her to be.

"No, she was fine. The problem is all me. It's me. Just like it always is."

"How could that be possible? You're perfect to me."

His words were the final blow, echoing around the damaged chambers of her heart. Agony clawed through her, so sharp and deep she squeezed her eyes shut against the physical tangible pain. How could a feeling hurt so much?

"Perfect? *That's* the problem. You just can't see it yet. You can't see me yet. And if tonight didn't do it, then I don't know what will."

"What are you talking about? Whatever it is, I can fix it. Just tell me."

Wouldn't you know it? She'd finally found a good man, a more-than-stellar man, and he was still the wrong man for her. How was he going to fix that? He couldn't see, yet, that this wouldn't work out. It couldn't. There was absolutely no way.

She was never going to be anyone other than someone who lost her keys, who liked the color purple, who liked cross-stitch on the wall instead of fine art. She didn't belong in his world.

She was doing them both a favor, cutting their losses now. Before they fell even more in love. Think how devastating that would be, right? Because every day she spent with him, she loved him more. So think what he would come to mean to her in a year. In two. How much more would it hurt her heart then, when it finally hit him that she wasn't the woman he'd made her out to be?

He deserved the right woman. The woman he thought she was. The woman he expected her to be. Since her vision was blurring, she released the seat belt while she could still see. The thunk of it sliding into place behind the seat hid the sob that caught in her throat.

"Are you crying?" Brice sounded distressed.

"Nope." If she could blink the tears away, then she *couldn't* be crying. Really. Even if the burning behind her eyes was getting worse.

"You look like you're crying."

"L-looks can be d-deceiving." She groped to find the door handle.

His hand caught her wrist, holding her in place. Why did the affection she felt in his touch feel like the final straw? The tears she'd held back so carefully leaked one by one down her face.

"Okay, I might not know what's going on," he said, "but this isn't right. Did I do something?"

She shook her head, more tears rolling down her face.

"Did I say something?" She shook her head again, leaving him at a total loss. He felt his chest crack with pain for her. "Ava, please tell me what's wrong. I can't fix it if I don't know what is broken."

"Oh, see how awesome you are?" She choked on a sob. "You just don't see it, do you? This just can't work. I mean, hello? I told you from the start. I'm a romantic disaster. I always pick the wrong man, and now there's you. What am I going to do about you?"

His thoughts were going in different directions, and his guts were telling him she was about to break up with him. It was his experience that women who were happy with you generally didn't sob like that. He could feel her emotionally pushing him away, although she hadn't moved a muscle. "Wait a minute. I'm not the wrong man. Why are you saying that?"

"B-because it's the truth."

"It can't be the truth." Tenderness filled him, and a love so deep that it couldn't be measured. "Because I *know* this is right."

Did she have any idea all the vulnerability he saw in her big violet-blue eyes? That he could feel the worry and fears in her heart? That he could hear the unspoken agony she hadn't spoken aloud? He thought not, so he said it for her: "I love you. Just the way you are. I love that you forget your keys and know how to make a dump truck cake and that you always make the sunshine seem brighter, the world better, *my* world better."

She didn't answer. It didn't look as if she could, her hand at her throat, her eyes bright with emotion. He knew what she needed to hear. He knew he'd been holding back the truth in his heart, and now was the time to lay it on the line. He knew how much his reassurance meant to her. They were linked emotionally, spiritually; he'd known she was special to him from the beginning. She was heaven sent.

It was hard to find just the right words, so he went with what was in his heart. "I love you, Ava. This is the real thing. I'm very serious about you. You have to know that I'm in this forever. That one day, I'm going to get down on one knee and ask you to be my wife."

Her eyes widened in unmistakable fear. Fear. He hurt for her. Yeah, he understood exactly how that felt to be so terrified, but he was taking the risk. "This is the only way to get past the panic. You have to take that leap, Ava. You have to look at the man I am, and the promises I've made and have already kept and believe that I will be that man for you. Forever."

Her lower lip trembled. "See, that's what scared me. And if I'm this scared, it has to be a sign, right? That this is never going to work. Love ends, and I have to be smart about this."

"No, you're being scared. I can feel it, Ava. I can feel your heart, and right now, I'm sure in a way I've never been. Because I can feel how much you love me and how terrified you are."

"Yeah. I'm afraid for a reason. This is all wrong, and my heart is going to be totally devastated when you figure out that I'm just me. Just Ava."

"Just Ava? See, that's where you're wrong. You are my everything. My dream come true."

"*That* is why it can't work." She pulled away from him, when everything within him longed to draw her closer. Misery marked her face and shadowed her eyes. Sobs tore apart her words. "But this is better than you deciding down the road that I'm not what you want. That's what happened to my parents, you know. I watched it happen. I m-made it happen. Love isn't always enough."

"But—"

"No, don't say it." She stumbled out of the seat to get away from him, but he was saying it anyway.

"I want *you*, Ava."

She truly believed that he loved her. She only had to look at him to know that his love for her was deep. She felt so close to him she could sense his soul as if it were her own, and she could feel his love for her there, a love without measure.

But without end? That was the question. And she feared it had a different answer. If only she could peek into the future and know for sure, then she could find a way to think clearly past the fear overtaking her.

Love wasn't always enough.

That's why she did what she had to do. To be smart about this. To be logical. To hold it together. She could keep calm, hold her heart still, and keep her emotions frozen. She *would.* Really. She just had to make it as far as her apartment—she was almost there—and *then* she could fall apart. Into a hundred thousand tiny pieces, but not here. Not now. Not in front of Brice.

How did she put all that he meant to her in a few parting words? She was clueless. Panic blinded her. Fear gathered like a hurricane in her stomach. It felt like disaster striking one more time as she took a step away from the car. How could the action meant to save her from pain—to save them both from terrible pain—feel like the worst mistake ever?

Because you're afraid, Ava. She took another step back, not at all sure if she could keep going. What she knew for sure was that she could not reach out to him. The hurricane of fear in her stomach began to gust, like the edge of the storm hitting shore.

The plea in Brice's dark eyes, the sadness settling into his handsome face, the sincerity of his good soul, felt like the summer heat on her skin. It just went to show the power of this bond—at least on her side—and how much she stood to lose, to be hurt.

Walking away was the best choice. There would be no happily-ever-after ending for her. True love didn't exist for a girl like her. And if it did, would she take the chance to find out?

That made her step falter. There was Brice, climbing out of his car, coming for her. And she could feel his love for her—he was sincere. He did love her. But how did she tell him she was afraid it wasn't enough? That one day he would look at her and see a disappointment.

Lord, please help me, here. Show me that I'm doing the right thing. Please, I'm begging You. She took another step back, she'd chosen a direction and she had to stay on it. She needed the strong safety net of her faith, of her stable life, of the path she'd stepped off of when Brice had walked into her life.

Her cell chirped and vibrated in her little pocketbook. Saved by her family. The Lord worked in mysterious ways. She dug the phone out and flipped it open without even looking at the screen. She could feel that it was one of her sisters. Hopefully not calling to ask how the dinner with Brice's parents went.

"Ava?"

She didn't recognize the woman's thin and strained voice. She glanced at the caller screen. It was her stepsister's cell number. That couldn't be right, could it? The woman did not sound like Danielle.

"I—I'm so glad I caught you." Danielle choked out a sob. "Katherine's up hiking in the mountains with Jack, and she's out of range. Aubrey isn't picking up. I know you're probably in the middle of dessert or something, but c-can you come?"

"Absolutely." Ava felt her strength kick in. Now she knew why she'd felt as if doom was about to strike. "Come where? What's wrong?"

"It's *J-Jonas.* He's been sh-shot."

"Shot?" Shock washed through her. Jonas was shot? That didn't seem possible. She thought of her tall, kindly brother-in-law who always seemed so invincible. "You mean he was working tonight?"

"Y-yes. He's c-covering for someone on vacation, and—" Another sob broke her voice. "I'm at the hospital and there's no one to t-take the k-kids."

"I'll do it. Is Jonas going to be okay?"

"They d-don't kn-ow. Please c-come."

"I'm on my way." She snapped shut the phone. Okay, talk about a sign. There was Brice, watching her with concern in his eyes. So big and strong, everything within her ached for his strong arms around her. She longed for the safe harbor of his love.

How did she know that his promises were real? That she wasn't letting her fears rule her life? How did you know if a love would last? Well, she'd asked for the Lord to show her the way, and this was it. Her family was what mattered, the people she'd been able to love and trust all of her life. Not some romantic dream.

For a breathless moment their gazes met and she felt his empathy, his concern for her never wavering, steadily pulling her closer like a tractor beam.

How did she give in? How did she walk away? Panic crashed like a storm, stealing her breath, leaving her ice cold in the brazen heat. As afraid as she was to walk away and lose him forever, she was more terrified of really leaning on him. Of really trusting him.

"This is for the best," she said. "Family is everything. I think that when you love someone, you truly love them. That it's like the Bible says: *'Love never gives up, never loses faith, is always hopeful, and endures through every circumstance.'* That's not what I think we have."

She watched the pain fill his eyes, and she hated that she was hurting him. But it was for the best. It was the right thing to do. You couldn't go into a serious relationship already knowing it couldn't work.

And if that was her fear talking, then maybe that was for the best, too. Because how could a man as truly wonderful as Brice love her that way?

"Did you say that Jonas was shot?"

Somewhere in the dim recesses of her brain she remembered Danielle saying Jonas and Brice had volunteered together once. So it was only normal human concern behind his question. Somehow, she made her voice answer. "Yes. He was covering someone's shift tonight, I guess, and that's all I know. I promised my sister. I have to go."

"I'll drive you." He held out his hand, palm up, looking as valiant as a knight of legend, one of good deeds and of good heart and she was hopeless.

Never in her life had she wanted something so much as to place her hand in his. To throw caution to the wind and trust that everything would be fine. That he was right—twenty years down the road they would be together and happy. That they could survive the rift of his mother's disapproval, unlike her own parents could have done.

But it wasn't logical. It wasn't smart. It wasn't safe. She took another step back. It will only end in heartache, that little voice within her said. And if there was a part of her that knew she was really afraid, she couldn't listen to it. "I'll drive myself. I can't be with you. You are great, you have made such a difference in my life, but I think real love is like a special kind of heaven on earth. It shouldn't hurt like this. It just shouldn't be this frightening."

"Ava, wait. You wanted to know if this was the real thing, if we had a shot at a real happiness together. I'm pretty sure we do. But we'll never really know if you walk away. Don't you want to find out?"

"I already know." She hauled her key ring out of her purse and the first deepening rays of the setting sun brushed her with a rare magenta light, that shone like heaven's light. "Goodbye, Brice."

He couldn't say anything. He stood there like he was made of granite, despair filling him, watching her hurry the rest of the short distance to the covered parking. She slipped from his sight, and he felt the first fall of grief. The hard ball of it burned in his throat. Was he really losing her? How could she be so sure?

There was no way. Because he could see a different path. A different outcome. As intimidating as it was to be given this singular blessing of true love, he was more afraid of spending his life without her as his wife. Without her sparkle and her life and her brightness lighting the rest of his days.

He couldn't believe he'd lost her.

Chapter Fifteen

After saying about ten prayers for Jonas on the drive over, Ava couldn't keep thoughts of Brice away. He might be out of sight, but not totally from her mind. His words kept troubling her. *You wanted to know if this was the real thing, if we had a shot at a real happiness together. I'm pretty sure we do. But we'll never really know if you walk away.*

Hey, it wasn't her fault, she thought as she drove up to the parking garage and snapped a ticket out of the automatic dispenser. She dropped the ticket on the dash and waited for the red and white striped arm to lift. If her vision was blurring again, it was just from being so tired. Really.

Not because she felt as if there was an

enormous void in the center of her ribcage, where her heart used to be. And as she pulled into the closest space by the doors and took the elevator to the main lobby, that void began to fill with bleak misery.

You did the right thing, she told herself as she took another bank of elevators to the intensive care floor. She wasn't going to set herself up for more doom. She wasn't the right girl for Brice. No matter how much she wanted to be.

As soon as the doors opened she popped out into the echoing corridor and headed down an endless hall with closed doors. She followed the directional signs, struggling to keep tight control of her feelings. She was here for Danielle, she was here for her family, where she belonged, where she was accepted, where she was safe.

Safe. That was the word that was haunting her. She felt the tangle of emotions ball up tight in her chest, growing tighter and tighter, sheer misery. Pain throbbed between her ribs, making it hard to breathe. Almost as if she were sobbing, which she wasn't, of course. Really.

She could do this, she could hold everything down, because if she didn't, she wasn't sure she was strong enough to hold back the tidal wave of sheer agony. How could she feel so alone without him? She'd been alone before, she'd managed just fine without Brice Donovan by her side. And if she needed him, then she'd learn to get past it.

Pain arched through her as if she'd broken a rib. It was only heartache. Although nothing like she'd ever known before. Because she'd never loved any man before the way she loved Brice. The way she still loved Brice. She didn't want to love him, she didn't think it was smart to love him. She didn't fit into his life, not really, and why start on a road you knew would end?

Okay, so she didn't *know* it would end. She was just terrified, but wasn't Brice right? If she could see through the blur of panic long enough to think clearly, she had to admit he was totally right. You didn't know unless you gave something a chance.

The truth? He terrified her. Absolutely. Positively. Without condition and without end. She was too chicken to hand over her heart to the one man who really wanted it. Because she was too terrified that he might get a really good look at her and stop loving her. That he'd see who she was deep down, at heart, at the bottom of her soul, he'd stop loving her.

Love ends, she knew it. Wasn't that the lesson of her childhood?

Yeah, that frustrating little voice inside her argued, but it's not the only lesson, right?

Right. She was afraid because she'd never been here before. Brice wasn't just Mr. Perfect, he was *her* Mr. Perfect. Exactly like a dream the angels had found in her heart and made real. She didn't have any reason at all to find fault with him and push him away. She was out of excuses. Out of options. Had she been picking boyfriends who weren't good enough so she didn't have to be right here, where it was so scary? Because the relationships had always ended, she'd be able to retreat back to her safe life, with her sisters and her lifelong job at the family bookstore. No risks. No failures. No pain.

Brice was different. That's why he made her feel all these things she hadn't had to experience before. Like being so vulnerable it was as if she were inching out onto a tiny little limb hanging way out over the Grand

Canyon. With every move she could feel the limb sinking downward, getting ready to snap beneath her weight.

And like the scared little seven-year-old inside her, she'd jumped right off that limb onto the safe earth. Brice was right. If she stayed here, she would never know if the limb would break beneath her weight or if it would support her across the void.

Then she saw Danielle in the intensive care waiting room, her elbows on her knees, her face buried in her hands, sobbing, and Ava forgot everything but comforting her sister. Her heart broke at the strangled sound of Danielle's muffled sobs. As she came closer, she noticed a smaller room off to the side, where a volunteer was trying to read to the munchkins.

Tyler saw her first. "Aunt Ava! I wanna go home."

"That's why I'm here, cutie." As heavy as he was, she scooped him up and gave him a hard hug. She didn't even want to think about what would happen to this little boy if his daddy wasn't okay. Madison was fussing in the volunteer's lap, a pleasant-looking grand-mother type who had a sad smile as she put the book away and stood, taking care with the miserable little girl.

"You go help the nice lady with your sister, okay?" Ava set Tyler back down and smoothed his hair. "I gotta talk to your mom for a sec. Then we'll go by and get pepperoni pizza because you know that helps to make anything a little better."

Tyler nodded, swiped at his eyes with his sleeve and bravely went to help his sister like the good big brother that he was.

Ava's heart broke when she knelt down beside Danielle. She'd never seen her stepsister like this, her hair was tousled and her face streaked with tears. She simply wrapped her in a hug, feeling her heartache and terror. She couldn't bear to think about what Dani's future would be like without her beloved Jonas. With her great love lost.

Okay, she wasn't going to *take* that as a sign from above, because it wasn't. Really. She released Dani and fetched a full box of tissues, since the box on the table beside her was empty. "Any word?"

Dani shook her head. "He's still in surgery."

"That's gotta be good, right? He's hanging in there. And he has you and the kids to fight for. I've been praying on the way over. Do you want to pray together now? You'll feel better."

"Praying is all I've been doing. I feel terrible interrupting you tonight. Where's Brice?"

That was Dani, always thinking about everyone but herself. "Don't worry about that. I want to know what I can do for you. To make this easier for you."

"Oh, Ava." Dani wiped at more tears. "Nothing but Jonas being just fine is going to make me okay. Do you know what I've been thinking about? I can't get out of my mind how I complained at him this morning. How he wasn't home enough, he wasn't supporting me with the kids enough, that I didn't feel as if he were really listening to me about the hedges needing trimming, and I was so *mad* at him. Just mad. How stupid was that?"

At the misery on Dani's face, Ava's heart broke even more, impossibly, as if there was enough of it to break again. "I know you. You weren't that bad. You couldn't have been. You adore Jonas."

"I do. But if he passes away, then the last thing I said to him was selfish and unkind. And I was just tired, that was all, but it doesn't change what I said. That when I should have reached out to him, when I should have asked how he was feeling, why he was preoccupied, if there was something I could do for him, I pushed him away. And—" a sob tore through her words "—I just can't bear it."

"Shh, he knows how much you really love him. Dani, don't cry harder. We'll put it in prayer, all right?" She took her sister's hands, so cold, and cradled them in hers. *"Dear heavenly Father, please—"*

Even in prayer, she could feel Brice's presence, washing over her like a sign from above. *"—Please watch over Jonas in surgery and let him know that we love him, especially Dani, who is hurting so much. Please ease her worries, and bring Jonas back safe to us. In Your name, Amen."*

Like grace, peace washed through her. She opened her eyes to see Brice, with Madison cradled in one strong arm and Tyler's hand tucked trustingly in his much larger one.

He was such a good man. At heart. Of character. Decent to the core. Seeing him again made every vulnerable piece of her spirit long for his love. She wished she could go back and find the clue that would show her this relationship between them would have worked out right.

That was the real issue, wasn't it? That she was terrified that she wasn't enough. That any man—even one as sincere and incredible as Brice—could love her enough to weather any storm to come. She'd watched her parents' marriage crumble, and she never wanted to feel like that again. But how was the pain of not being able to love him, of not ever having the chance to be his wife, any better than never being able to love him at all?

"If it would help you out, I can take charge of the kids," he said. "Get them home and some dinner in them. Ava, I know you were going to do this, but no one else is here to be with Danielle. You should stay with her and let me do this for you."

Was she capable of speech like a normal person? No-oo. She just stared at him, falling in love with him all over again. Was it smart?

No. Was it sensible?

No. But could she stop it?

No.

The strength of her love for him overwhelmed her, filled with the blazing light of a hundred galaxies, so bright that it changed how she saw him. She now looked at him in a way she'd been too afraid of before. Through the eyes of her heart, through her deepest dreams and into her future. Where there was only a love for him so strong, that it felt as if nothing could defeat it. Nothing could break it.

She could see that happily-ever-after dream of hers, and it was within her reach. All she had to do was to accept it. She'd never realized how terrifying it was to be so vulnerable and to have a dream come true. It was so much to accept. So much to treasure. So much to lose.

So much to lose.

She understood better Danielle's agony. From a deeper place. Life was uncertain; anything or everything could change in a moment. She'd spent her life being afraid of that moment, of losing everything, that she'd lived her life to protect herself from what Danielle was feeling at this moment.

But was that how she wanted to live? To spend her years protecting her heart and her life from loss? How could there be any goodness in that? There would be no love and no joy. What if Brice was right? His words came back to her, and she knew, when their gazes met and held, that he was thinking this, too.

If she walked away now, she would never know. Maybe never knowing would be a greater sorrow than finding out what could ever be.

"Thanks, Brice. That would be great."

He didn't need to say anything, she knew he understood. They had things to say to one another, but not here. Not now.

"Let me give you my house key." She pulled her ring out of the pocket and removed the key with trembling fingers.

When she handed it to him, their fingers touched and peace filled the empty places in her soul. It was love, his love, that made her believe.

"Thank you," she whispered, because she had no voice.

"Anything for you, sunshine."

She believed him. She watched him walk away, remembering the Scripture she'd quoted to him. *Love never gives up, never loses faith, is always hopeful and endures through every circumstance.* It was all him, she realized. He was the man who embodied that verse. Who had a heart big enough and a character true enough to never give up, never lose faith and endure through everything.

And then, she realized, so did she.

"Brice is such a good man," Danielle said on a sob. "Sometimes you just don't realize exactly how blessed you are."

"And sometimes you do," Ava said, and knelt down to stick with her sister through the wait ahead.

Brice headed down the hallway, finished checking on the sleeping kids. Although it was nearly six in the morning, he'd been pretty much up all night. He hadn't been able to get a wink of sleep with so much on his mind. With so much left unsaid.

Ava had called around two in the morning to say that Jonas was out of surgery and was touch and go in intensive care. She would be by as soon as she could leave Danielle.

He'd just put the tea water on when he heard the front door creak open. Ava was in the entryway, dropping her purse and keys on the little table there. Exhaustion haunted her face and bruised the delicate skin beneath her eyes, but not outright grief. "He's doing better. Danielle's still with him.

"Good. I've been keeping him in prayer."

"Thank you." She moved aside, and it was hard to read what was in her eyes, what she intended to say, and then he knew why. They weren't alone.

Aubrey stepped in, holding a grocery bag. "Hi, Brice."

"Good morning. Would you two like some tea?"

"That would great, thanks." Ava answered for both of them, taking the sack from Aubrey. The twins exchanged glances and without a word Aubrey slipped down the hallway to check on the kids. Or, more likely, to give them some privacy.

Ava came toward him. "Katherine is at the hospital now, and we're taking turns with Danielle. It was really great of you to do this. It meant she didn't have to worry about her kids, and she wasn't alone until the rest of the family could get there."

"It was my pleasure." Brice came towards her and took the grocery sack from her arms and set it on the counter, so there was nothing between them. Nothing to hide behind. Only the truth of their feelings. "Do you know how devoted to you I am? How sure of my love for you?"

"I'm starting to get the picture."

He would always be devoted to her. Always ten thousand percent committed. Love moved through him of a strength and breadth that knew no bounds. That would never know a limit or an end. "Here is something you should know about me, something I haven't told you yet, but I intend to spend the rest of my life proving this to you. I will never give up on you. I will never lose faith in you. I will never fail you. Even if you ever give up on me, I will still be here. On your side. Come what may. I love you, Ava."

Her heart took a long tumble. Could he be any more wonderful? And wasn't that the scariest thing of all? Because right here standing before her, was every kind of heaven she could dream of having on this earth. Every blessing of love and faith and commitment she could ever wish for, and she would spend the rest of her life cherishing.

Totally scared, and yet more scared of not reaching for him, she pressed her hand to his, trapping the big curve of his palm against the side of her face. "I love you, Brice. Forever and ever."

"Then you'll marry me, when I get around to asking you properly?"

"Consider it a guarantee. You are my Mr. Wish Come True."

"And you, you are perfect for me, just the way you are, and that is never going to change. Can't you see that?" He looked so vulnerable for such a big man. All heart. All honesty. "You are the sun come into my life. I was in the dark before you."

He smiled. Not the dazzling one she'd so fallen for. Not the one that made his goodness of spirit show in his eyes. But a better one, a deeper one. One she'd never seen before. It was serious, too, and sincere, soul-deep.

He leaned closer and then closer still until his mouth slanted over hers. Slowly, his lips brushed hers with a brief, tender reverence. She was so in love all she saw was him. He filled her every sense and every thought. He was the reason for the beat of her heart now and forever. Her Mr. Wish Come True.

Epilogue

The first customer to officially walk through the newly opened bakery door looked very familiar. Ava squinted through the fall of light from the cheerful windows to the broad-shouldered handsome man closing the door behind him. Was he Mr. Perfect or what? Her soul sighed. She closed the cash register drawer, and her engagement diamond glinted in the bright sunshine.

"May I help you?" she asked courteously.

"I sure hope so." Brice Donovan carried a vase of yellow and red rosebuds and placed them on the counter between them. "I've come to check on the progress of my cake."

"Lucky for you, Mr. Wonderful, I just finished boxing up your order."

"Say, you wouldn't want to go get a cup of coffee afterward all this, would you?"

Call her happy. Why wouldn't she be? She was engaged to the best man in the entire world. Okay, she might be just a little biased when it came to Brice, but only a tad, a dash, a smidgeon. "I'll have you know that I'm engaged to be married."

"Lucky guy."

"No, lucky me."

His kiss was the sweetest heaven. The way his love filled her was the best of blessings.

The bell on the door chimed, and more customers tumbled in. Aubrey and Katherine, dressed for work at the bookstore. "It's a little quiet in here," Aubrey said.

Katherine took a look at the two who'd quickly stepped apart and smiled. "And for a good reason. Ava, after you finish my wedding cake, you'd better start on your own."

"I know." They hadn't set a date yet, with Jonas still recovering in the hospital, but they weren't in a serious hurry. They had the rest of their lives together. How amazing was that? "Wait, does this mean you've decided on a design for your wedding cake?"

"Yes. Finally." Katherine beamed her own happiness.

Wasn't this a wonderful world? Okay, so it wasn't perfect, but look at the blessings the Lord gave every day. Love and families and sisters. Hope, dreams to come true and chocolate cake. Lots of chocolate cake.

"The climbing roses design, right? I knew it." Ava rolled her eyes. The door chime rang again.

More customers? Then she recognized Brice's grandmother, Ann, and his mother, Lynn, who was *almost* actually smiling.

"We thought we'd stop by and support your business," Ann explained, pausing to press a kiss to Brice's cheek. "And to pick up some treats for our garden club meeting this afternoon."

"You came to the right place." Delighted, Ava went to box up a chocolate dream cake, only to have Aubrey step in to do it.

"Go," her twin shooed her away. "Mr. Perfect needs you. I can help out until the teenager gets here."

"Cool. Thanks, Aub." Did she mention what a great blessings sister were? They were absolutely wonderful.

"Come with me," Brice said, taking her by the hand and pulling her into the kitchen. He wanted a moment with her all to himself. He waited until the door swung closed and they were alone before he pulled her into his embrace. It was a long day and would probably be a busy one, and he wanted to say this while he had the chance. "I'm proud of you, sunshine. You know how much I love you, right?"

"Sure, but a girl always likes to hear it on a daily basis."

"I do love you." He cradled her face with his hands, sheer tenderness.

She kissed him sweetly, so happy she was floating like a big helium balloon, but this time there was no doom in sight. How could there be? They were in this together, a team. Between the two of them and with the Lord's help, they could solve any problems that came their way.

"I love you, too," she told him, this man who was her idea of heaven in this imperfect world, and would always be.

Wow, was she turning into an optimist or what?

With joy in her heart, she thanked the good Lord before giving her husband-to-be another sweet kiss.

* * * * *

Don't miss Jillian Hart's next
inspirational romance
EVERYDAY BLESSINGS,
available June 2007.

Dear Reader,

Thank you so much for choosing *Every Kind of Heaven.* I hope you enjoyed Ava's story as much as I did writing it. Ava has learned to expect doom—she's dated a few too many less-than-stellar men. But when Brice walks into her life, his steadfast goodness and caring make her rise to the challenge of changing her view of herself and embracing the heavenly blessing of true love in her life. I hope Ava's story reminds you of how gracious God is and the wonderful gifts He sends into our lives with every day.

Wishing you heavenly blessings,

Jillian Hart

QUESTIONS FOR DISCUSSION

1. At the beginning of the book, Ava believes that the kind of man she needs, one perfect in every way, does not exist. What's a nice girl to do? Settle for Mr. So-so or Marginally Moral? Have you ever felt this way? What does it say about Ava's character that she refuses to settle for Mr. So-so?

2. What is Ava's first impression of Brice? How does her impression of him change after learning his real identity? How does this change her feelings toward him?

3. Brice is charmed by Ava's insults, when other men might be offended. Why isn't he offended? What does this say about his character?

4. Why is Brice truly the most eligible bachelor? What traits make him a good man?

5. What real fears are behind Ava's no-men, no-dating policy? Why does Ava look at Brice and decide only romantic disaster awaits her if she dates him? How does Brice convince Ava to amend her no-dating policy

6. As Ava and Brice get to know each other more, what aspects of their character does each come to admire?

7. What does the work that Brice does for Ava represent?

8. Why is Ava the perfect woman for Brice? Why is he the perfect man for her?
9. Ava's mother abandoned her family when Ava was seven years old. How does that affect her? How does that keep her from trusting others? What pattern is she afraid of repeating by falling in love with Brice?
10. How important are the values of family to Ava? How does her family help her through the hardships in life? How important are those values to Brice? How does this influence their growing relationship?

BETRAYED BY RITA HAYWORTH

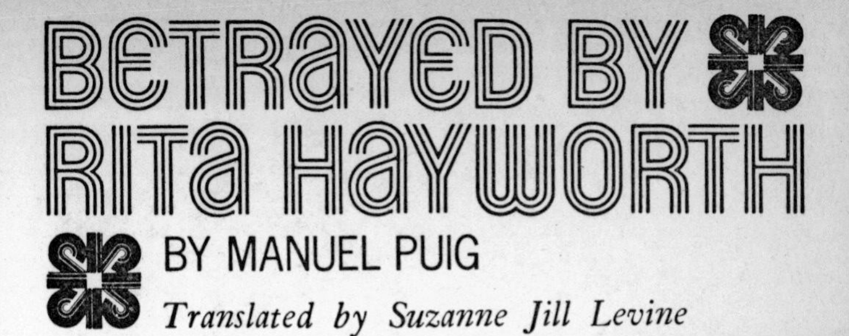

Vintage Books • A Division of Random House • New York

First Vintage Books Edition, February 1981

Published in the United States by Random House, Inc., New York, and in Canada by Random House of Canada Limited, Toronto. Originally published by E.P. Dutton & Co., Inc., New York, in September 1971. Assistance for the translation of this volume was given by the Center for Inter-American Relations.

Library of Congress Cataloging in Publication Data
Puig, Manuel.
Betrayed by Rita Hayworth.
Translation of La traición de Rita Hayworth.
Reprint of the ed. published by Dutton, New York.
I. Title.
[PQ7798.26.U4T713 1981] 863 80-6123
ISBN 0-394-74659-7

Manufactured in the United States of America

BETRAYED BY RITA HAYWORTH

I

Mita's Parents' Place, La Plata, 1933

—A brown cross-stitch over beige linen, that's why your tablecloth turned out so well.
—This tablecloth alone gave me more trouble than the whole set of doilies, a full eight pairs . . . if they paid more for needlework, I could hire a sleep-in maid and spend more time on embroidery, once I get my customers, don't you think?
—Embroidery doesn't seem tiring, but after a few hours your back begins to ache.
—But Mita wants me to make her a bedspread for the baby's crib, with bright colors since the bedrooms get so little light. Three rooms one after the other leading into a hallway with big windows, all covered with canvas curtains that you can pull open.
—If I had more time, I'd make myself a bedspread. You know what's really tiring? Typewriting on a high desk like the one I have in the office.
—If I lived in this house, I'd sit next to the window whenever I had a minute to work on Mita's bedspread—for the light.
—Is Mita's furniture nice?
—Mom feels terrible Mita can't take advantage of the house, now we've got all the modern conveniences, and she's right.
—I had a premonition when they gave Mita that job, it seemed the year would never end, imagine going away for a whole year, and now she's there to stay. You've got to face it, that's where she's going to live.
—She ought to come twice a year to La Plata instead of only once.
—Vacation days fly, the first day she's here doesn't seem so short, it seems like you're getting a lot done, but then the time is gone before you know it.

—Mom, don't think I get that much advantage out of the house either.
—I think your children got into the chicken coop.
—Clara, you should come every afternoon with the babies, they never touch the plants. But they drive grandfather crazy with the chickens.
—How much are you getting for the chickens?
—When you write to Mita, tell her to take her time getting furniture. I'm afraid if she buys her own furniture she's going to stay in that town forever. Write to your sister, she's always anxious to hear from us.
—Did you buy all new furniture for this house?
—If the house had been finished when Mita graduated, it wouldn't have been easy for her to go away all by herself, to work in that small town.
—Is Vallejos as ugly as Mita says?
—Not at all, Violeta. I liked it quite a bit, it's not so ugly, do you think so, Mom? When I got off the train, my first impression was awful, there's not a single tall building. They're always having droughts there, so you don't see many trees either. In the station there are no taxis, they still use the horse and buggy, and the center of town is just two and a half blocks away. You can find a few trees that are hardly growing, but what you don't see at all, anywhere, is real grass. Mita has already planted lawn grass twice, and at the right time of the year too, but no luck.
—But by watering the pots practically twenty times a day she finally managed to grow some beautiful plants in a kind of small patio behind the kitchen.
—Then it's not so bad?
—When I first saw Vallejos I didn't like it, but life there is very easy. Mita has a maid who cooks and cleans the house, and a girl who takes care of the baby while she works in the hospital. All the poor people in Vallejos love Mita since she isn't stingy with the cotton and antiseptics and bandages.
—Is it one of those beautiful, new hospitals?
—The man who was in charge of the laboratory before Mita came was so stingy—as if everything belonged to him and not the hospital.
—The other day I saw Carlos Palau's latest movie.
—Mita's sure to see it when it comes to Vallejos.

—How long was she engaged to Carlos Palau?
—We never really thought Carlos Palau would make it.
—She was never engaged to Carlos Palau, he would ask her to dance, but I always stayed to the very end to chaperone the girls home.
—He was only a stagehand in the local theater.
—He's the only real actor in Argentine movies.
—Mita's husband looks exactly like Carlos Palau, I always said.
—In a way, but not exactly.
—Some of the Palaus still live in the same slum.
—But I never thought Mita would get used to living in a small town.
—What the chickens eat first are the leftovers from dinner, even before they eat the corn.
—Grandpa, which one is the one you're going to kill for Sunday?
—Today I'm going to kill one for Violeta's father, but don't tell Grandma, she'll get mad.
—Grandma's in the kitchen with Mommy and Violeta, she can't see you.
—I'm going to kill this chicken for Violeta's father and send it to him for a surprise.
—Grandpa, who makes more money, you with the chickens or Violeta's father fixing shoes?
—Clara, while your mother was here I couldn't tell you about the office. He's the kind of man that grows on you. He proposed to me.
—How can you say he proposed? That's when a man wants to get married, a married man can't propose, Violeta, what he does is proposition you. Don't start twisting things around because then I'd rather not listen.
—He's not at all handsome. It's just that he grows on you.
—If you want to embroider a bedspread the best time of the year is now, days are longer and after work you still have an hour of light, it's not half as tiring if you embroider in daylight, if you're lucky and get out of work early.
—Poor Adela.
—Poor thing, she has to use artificial light in the office all day long.
—I'll have to go without getting to see her.

—Didn't you know that she worked late?
—Adela could have used a degree, then she wouldn't have to be a secretary.
—The one who got the degree doesn't need it.
—How's business going with Mita's husband?
—He sold a house and with the money he bought some cattle. Mom wants me to make a bedspread for Mita but I don't think I'll have the time. I'll send the patterns to her in Vallejos and she can make it herself. She has two maids. Don't tell anyone but Dad went to kill a chicken to surprise your father.
—It doesn't seem right to me that she got married in that town, instead of staying to help here after all the sacrifice your mother went through to give her a good education.
—Adela's new glasses are made out of genuine tortoise shell.
—I'm sorry, I'd help you kill the chicken but it really upsets me. Dad is going to be ever so grateful.
—Mita didn't want to look when I killed a chicken either, but she sure ate it up all right.
—Remember that classmate of Mita's at the university, the professor's daughter, the one who was always so finicky?
—Sofía Cabalús?
—Did she ever get married?
—Now Mita must miss the good times she had here.
—Sofía Cabalús never set foot in this house again after Mita went away. It's been months since I've seen her.
—They told me in the office that her father went crazy, he hardly ever makes it to class. And all they do at home is read. You never see Sofía because she's always locked up in the house reading.
—Don't go before Adela comes home.
—I'd love to see her new glasses.
—They cost her almost a half-month's salary.
—She'd get splitting headaches when she went without glasses.
—Grandma, why does Violeta put black around her eyes?
—She's already getting involved with her new boss.
—Her father's going to be happy with the chicken. Who knows how long it's been since they've had chicken?
—I really hate to scold her but it's even worse to keep quiet and let her mess up her life with that man.
—Her poor mother, if she could come back from her grave today.

—Violeta must know we don't take our shoes to her father anymore.
—Every time I went to pick up the shoes I had to come back empty handed. It's not right for him to promise they'll be ready Tuesday and then Tuesday they're not ready even if it's only a simple heel. That's how he's been losing customers, for daydreaming all the time.
—They're not rehearsing at the Italian Society anymore, it's useless, opera is very difficult, and if the voices are no good it's a disaster.
—One day one friend buys him a drink, the next day another. Even your father sometimes pays for the drinks, he won't admit it but I'm sure he does.
—Mita and Sofía Cabalús started giggling and had to leave the rehearsal.
—What should I make for supper tonight?
—You'd better start cutting the lettuce out back. The edges are turning purple.
—I can grill a few steaks and make a big salad. Your father can finish the stew from lunch if he's still hungry. Why did you have to give that shoemaker a chicken?
—Violeta's father gets more mail from Italy than we do.
—It's time for me to go home; tonight I'll make croquettes for supper, the kids like them, and if I put them on the table without a word, Lito will eat them too.
—I don't know why he doesn't see a doctor.
—Pop, I want you to kill me a chicken for Sunday.
—I always eat everything and I never have trouble.
—What a bull-headed man. Just because you can eat like an ox you think everybody else can. How bull-headed can you get?
—Lito's stomach is a mess, he has to be careful.
—And his brother is the same. They all have weak stomachs, it runs in the family.
—It doesn't run in the family. It was the sister-in-law who finished off Lito's stomach. Even when we were engaged he'd complain to me about his digestion. I'd ask him what he had to eat and it was always the same: spicy food.
—When Lito was living with his brother he already had stomach trouble.
—And my sister-in-law keeps making those horrible stews. She

spices the food by drowning it in hot pepper. The only thing that crosses her mind is to add more hot peppers.
—She's always out, that woman. When does she have time to cook?
—A good stew takes a long time, and watching over. Mom, you don't know what a help it is to grow your own greens, if you don't there're so many things you have to buy, all kinds of greens and seasonings that aren't spicy. You have to have basil and rosemary and lots of parsley. And she never has anything in the kitchen, so the last minute she throws hot peppers in the pot and any meal she makes comes out too rich, even if she pays a fortune for lean meat.
—I don't know how Mita does it because Berto has a very weak stomach too.
—If he eats calmly he digests everything. Mita says his problem is nerves, he doesn't have the weak stomach Lito has.
—Grandpa left to take the chicken to Violeta's father. Can I go with him, Mommy?
—He went out with that grey apron on again. If Mita saw him go out with that grey apron on she'd be furious.
—Clara, your father's one pleasure in life is to walk around with that apron on.
—Mita wouldn't stand up for Violeta any more if she knew what Violeta was saying about her.
—Mommy, grandpa already crossed the street so I couldn't follow him.
—But Adela couldn't have studied with such poor eyesight. Remember the headaches she'd get.
—Such long hours at that place, and besides which, she has to work with the light on.
—If Mita came to live in La Plata, would she still want to keep on with her career? Sofía's father could get her into the university as somebody's assistant.
—How I'd love to see Mita's baby.
—No, what Berto wants is for Mita not to work anymore, as soon as his affairs get straightened out a bit.
—I am completely worn out.
—Violeta thought you worked from nine to six, and she had to go make supper for her father. She says hello.
—Did she have anything to tell me?
—She began to tell Clara about a man at the office.

—I wanted to talk to Violeta, poor thing. Her father makes his own supper. Who knows where she went.
—She said she had to go make supper for her father, she left before seven.
—Mom, I'm completely worn out. What did you do today?
—I was planning to clean the stair rug but once Clara came we sat down to do a little sewing.
—Did you persuade her to make Mita's bedspread?
—She's going to send all the patterns. How I'd love to see Mita's baby!
—The tile floor looks so beautiful with the new wax. While I was waiting for you to open the door in the vestibule I could see how it shined all the way from the vestibule to the end of the hallway.
—Clara was right, but I'm not going to let her wax it for me again, she has enough to do with her house and the children and her husband. Because he likes croquettes and can't eat fried food. Clara takes the time to boil the meat for him, cut it up, season it with rosemary and cheese and pop it in the oven for a few minutes till the croquettes turn golden brown. They look like real croquettes; she fools the eye and doesn't upset the stomach.
—If it has to be waxed next Saturday, I can wax the whole thing for you in the afternoon.
—Violeta didn't know you had such long hours.
—There was a lot of work today.
—Violeta complained that her typewriter is on a high desk, and she gets tired.
—In her office there isn't half the work there is in mine.
—She had her eyes made up like a gypsy. She must have gone to meet that man.
—But if he's married he must be home eating supper at this hour.
—Then she must have gone to meet someone else.
—What do you expect her to do? If she goes home, all she'll find there is her father.
—I sometimes think what if all the mothers came back from their graves?
—First you have to sweep, then you go over it with a dry mop till the floor's clean enough to take the wax. Then you dip the mop in the wax, without soaking it, and you spread an even coat of wax over the whole floor. Then you let it dry a little and then

comes the most tiring part, which is walking over it with rags to bring out the shine.

—It wouldn't have turned out this way if her mother was alive.

—In the summer you'll be able to see more than the shiny tile of the vestibule and the hallway, the doors that go from the hallway to the patio will be opened and you'll be able to see the shiny tile right to the very end of the patio.

—Mita says she doesn't feel like decorating the house she's rented because it's so old.

—The worst is that in Vallejos it costs so much to have a garden.

—It's nice to have this big house but it's also a lot of work to keep it clean.

—Poor Mita can't take advantage of it.

—I don't want you ever to wear that apron outside the chicken coop.

—Pop, set the table. I'm tired. My back hurts.

—How long since there've been any letters from Italy?

—There was a letter from Mita yesterday but nothing else. I'd like to send a picture of the house to Italy.

—What was in the package Clara took?

—Stale bread for crumbs.

—Didn't you send any picture of the house to Italy? Send them one, they're always anxious to hear from us.

—I'll write them, even though they haven't written.

—They'll write when they finish cutting the alfalfa.

—Mita says she's afraid of spring beginning in Vallejos because that's when the wind and dust really blow around.

—Adela, write your sister, she's always anxious to hear from us. You don't know what it's like to be away from home.

—What should I tell her?

—Don't tell her I went out with the grey apron. Tell her to come see us soon, we want to see the baby.

—And many regards to Berto.

—Tell her if they come to live in La Plata they can live with us, the house is more than big enough. We could find a good job for Berto.

—Don't be bull-headed Pop. He already told you he doesn't want to work for anybody.

—Tell her you met Sofía Cabalús, lie to her.

—I always think of calling her on the phone and then I forget. I'll call her tomorrow from the office.
—Lie to Mita. Tell her Sofía Cabalús promised you her father could get her a job in the university, as assistant to some professor.
—Did Violeta have any new gossip?
—She started to talk about Mita, why she went through all the business of studying pharmacy instead of what she wanted, and then she went and got married and doesn't plan to practice anymore.
—I'm going to write Mita to tell her that if she's here in La Plata, and better still if she's working at the university, she can register at the School of Liberal Arts like she wanted to.
—Enough studying! When is it going to stop?
—Pop, if you eat any more you'll burst.
—Don't give Clara so much stale bread, I won't have enough for the chickens.
—I already grated a jar full of bread crumbs for veal cutlets, so all that's left over this week you can give to the chickens.
—You complain that there's no bread and you're the one who eats so much bread at the table, I don't know how it all fits in your stomach.
—Where are they showing the Carlos Palau movie?
—It's a first-run, at the Select.
—When it's cheaper, I want to see it.
—In the picture in the newspaper he looked just like Berto.
—Today all Violeta did was criticize Mita, because Mita was so crazy about the movies.
—You know, I think Violeta wrote Mita and Mita didn't answer back.
—That's why she's against Mita.
—In the last letter Mita put at the end: "This letter is for Violeta too."
—Violeta wanted a letter all for herself.
—What did she say?
—That Mita was movie-crazy and that she always gets her way and she married Berto who looks like a movie actor.
—If you don't eat you're going to get sick.
—I'm so tired I lost my appetite. Today my glasses fell on the ground, I almost died.

—Where?
—On the street. If they break on me again I'll die.
—When do you have to go back to the optometrist?
—It seems a pity to waste my eyes on the movies, otherwise I'd go see Carlos Palau.
—He looks like Berto, especially from the side.
—If Mita could get a job at the university we could meet in front of my office. When I go by the windows of the library I always think of Mita.
—To think that after all the hours she spent studying she still wanted to go there with Sofía.
—To read even more, Mita has eyes of steel.
—For reading novels.
—I always see the same faces there, there's so little light in that library. Those miserable lamps hanging from the ceiling are black with dirt, they each have white glass shades, like ballet tutus, but absolutely black with soot. With a rag soaked in turpentine they could be cleaned in a minute, the lights as well as the shades, and there would be more light in that library.

II

At Berto's, Vallejos, 1933

—Just because we're maids they think they can pull up our skirts and do anything they want to.
—I'm not a maid, I'm the baby's nurse.
—That's because you're still young. Later on you'll be a maid.
—Don't talk so loud, you'll wake up the baby.
—But never go home alone at night on those dirt streets.
—The nurses at the hospital who go home at night all live on those dirt streets, and they go home alone.
—Those nurses are all tramps.
—One of them had a bastard.
—You better be careful since they can see you're a maid and I'll bet you're on their list already, even if you are only twelve. One of those bums who live around your house might chase you.
—Their teeth are brown from salty well water.
—I'll bet you're on their list.
—You're who's on their list.
—You just be careful, they already know your father threw your sister out of the house for having a bastard.
—Sleep, Totie, sleep. Be good and go back to sleep. That's it, that's it . . . This shitty bitch thinks I'm one of her kind.
—You got to be more careful than ever now that you got your period. You've had it if they pull the wool over your eyes. They'll make you a baby in no time.
—Let her talk, the bitch. My Totie, when you're a big boy you're not going to say bad words, right, sweetie? You're lucky you're not like Ines, she's not lucky at all, poor little thing without a father. Where is my sister anyway? You think she's dead? I'm very young but I'm an aunt already, and tonight I'm letting Ines sleep in my bed, between me and Fuzzy, so Ines will keep warm and cozy between her two aunts. If your daddy came

home dead drunk and took off his belt you'd get scared for sure. He gave me the belt. Totie, I hope to God your daddy never gives you the belt when you get older. That silly Ines starts crying and all she gets is more of the belt. I wish you would marry her when you grow up, she's a little older than you but it doesn't matter, Ines already says Momma and Dadda. When are you going to learn to say Momma and Dadda?

—I have to make the cold cuts. Amparo, don't be lazy, wipe up the floor, you're such a slob, the missis already told you what the baby dirties up *you* have to clean.

—I'm not a slob. Whose apron is cleaner, yours or mine?

—Do they ever sweep the floors in your house? My house might be a hut but we sweep the floor. Even if there are no tiles we always sweep the dirt floor.

—My house has a dirt floor too and that doesn't stop us from sweeping it.

—The floor at home is so even it looks like cement. Every day, after sweeping, you have to throw a little water on to keep the dust down.

—At home Mom throws whitewash on the floor. Will you go to sleep, you little pest!

—Mister Berto can hear you.

—Amparo! Will you shut that kid up, I'm trying to work!

—Mister Berto is doing accounts in the dining room.

—You're lucky to have a warm bottle all the time, Totie. Poor Ines wakes up hungry and gets a cold bottle since it takes an hour for Mom to start the fire in the middle of the night, and Ines cries even more if Dad gives her the belt, Totie. It's a good thing your daddy didn't kill the head doctor at the hospital.

—Come here, Amparo!

—The boss!

—He wanted me to kill a spider that was going up the wall, but I couldn't reach it.

—A big spider? In my house there's a black widow hidden in the straw on the ceiling that I can never get at.

—When Mom is doing the wash outside in the tub I leave Ines with her and I take a pail of water into the room and throw it on the wall, and between the bricks there are lots of hidden spider webs, if you throw a little water on 'em the shitty spiders come out of hiding and I whack 'em with my shoe and squish 'em against the bricks.

—Does the floor look good when you throw whitewash on it?
—That was just a lie, what Mom threw was water with a disinfectant that Mrs. Mita gave her. She threw a whole pailful and it evened out the floor but left some white spots from the disinfectant.
—Amparo!
—He's asleep again, sir.
—Dress him up nice for six o'clock, we're going to pick up the missis at the hospital.
—I'm going to put on his panties and the little hood Miss Adela brought him from La Plata.
—Did Mister Berto scold you?
—He didn't take his nap, he's doing accounts in the dining room. It's a good thing he didn't kill the head doctor with that punch he gave him. He would have gone to jail.
—And he'd still be there. But the missis never said she was going to take you to La Plata, what are you complaining about?
—If she hadn't lost her vacation, she would have taken me to La Plata.
—Will you mop the floor once and for all.
—I'm glad Mister Berto didn't kill him.
—How many quarts of milk do you want me to leave?
—I already told you not to knock on the door in the afternoon; leave me three quarts.
—The bell doesn't work.
—We disconnected it so Mister Berto could take his nap. Come in without knocking.
—Today he didn't go to bed. If that noise woke him up, you would know what hollering is.
—Your boss got away with it more than once he just better not holler so much.
—You ought to know the drought killed off Mister Berto's steers. You were lucky but if you knock on the door again, I hope all your cows die too.
—That's because I got only four cows, and I take care of them myself. Those who had a lot screwed themselves good.
—Get out of this kitchen and go home, your cows are dying.
—I'm not talking to you. What a pretty apron you have there, Amparo!
—It was stolen. This little thief, after her first communion she didn't return the clothes the nuns lent her.
—Are you going to pay me the twenty quarts a week or not?

—Wait a minute, Amparo has to ask Mister Berto.
—I'll wait for you on the road. My horse is taking off.
—Mister Berto says he'll pay you next week.
—Amparo, be careful with Felisa, she's a tramp.
—Don't believe Felisa. When I received first communion the nuns gave me this outfit just like they do all the poor girls at the back of the procession. And Mrs. Mita told me to keep it, and anyway the bottom was all torn. She fixed it for me.
—Mrs. Mita told me that when you're older she's going to teach you to be a nurse at the hospital.
—I don't want to, they really are tramps.
—Felisa is worse.
—The nurses walk around with their uniforms all worn out and unstarched.
—But it's better than being a maid.
—What did Mister Berto get away with?
—With being killed by a jealous husband.
—But Mister Berto never goes out if it isn't with the missis.
—Yeah, but when he was a bachelor he missed being chopped up more than once. Be a nurse, Amparo.
—There's a nurse who had a bastard.
—Your sister also had a bastard. Who do you think you are, anyway?
—Why did you wake up so soon? You little brat, I'd give you the belt if I could. But I'm going to take care of you until you grow up. And when your mommy decides to buy the furniture I'm going to sleep here in your house. If there was a bed for me I'd stay over to take care of you all night. What cost more, a bed or a steer? If your daddy had a lot of money like Mora Ortega's father, I'd never have to leave this house, like Mora Ortega's nanny. . . . Don't cry, I'm going to change you right now, I'm going to take off this wet diaper and put on a dry one, if you'll stay still for just one minute, I'll give your diaper a little ironing, and then it'll be all soft and warm, for your poor little sore behind. And now Mora Ortega is grown up, she's a young lady, and her nanny still lives in the house and has a fiancé from the country who comes to visit her at the house in the living room. Mora doesn't have a fiancé yet but when she gets engaged, do you think she'll take the living room for herself and send the nanny to the kitchen?
—Amparo, you have to take this letter to the post office for me

afterwards. How's my little fella? Brush his hair nice, Amparo, so that we can take him to see his mother in a little while.
—I'll take the baby to the post office with me, sir.
—Amparo, remember you swore not to tell a soul.
—I haven't said a word to anybody, cross my heart and hope to die.
—Never tell Mita we have a secret.
—No sir. But the Missis asked me why I had a bruise on my arm.
—A bruise from what?
—From when you saw that I saw you were behind the door, listening to what they were saying.
—What bruised arm?
—When you, not meaning to, sir, held me real tight by my arm until I swore I wouldn't say a word to Mrs. Mita.
—And did Adela ask you anything?
—Yes, the missis and the young lady asked me why my arm was bruised. But I already swore to you I wouldn't say a word about seeing you listening behind the door to what they were saying.
—Swear it again. That you're not going to tell Mita or anybody.
—Yes, sir. I swear to you by the light that I see by, may I be stricken blind this very minute.
—God will punish you if you break your oath.
—No, in the catechism they told us it was a sin to swear, that you should never swear.
—And what did you say about your bruised arm?
—That it was the priest who had pinned me down in church. I told Mrs. Mita about what happened in church once. The priest hit the Roldán girl so hard she fell down, and the Roldán girl got up half dizzy and didn't know where she had to go and was going towards the vestry when the priest grabbed her by the arm and threw her against the wall because she didn't know how to swallow the Host and she began to chew it, it just wouldn't go down all stuck in her throat, in the dress rehearsal for first communion.
—Who's the Roldán girl?
—A girl who lives in a hut on the other side of the tracks. She walked with me at the back of the procession.
—And Mita believed you?

—Sir, I didn't know you were writing a letter, I thought you were doing accounts. Are you going to buy the furniture?
—Amparo, you dirty slob, I had to clean the floor myself.
—I don't have to go to the post office because Mister Berto tore up the letter he was writing.
—Get me some bread crumbs from the bakery. Guess what? For supper I'm making v-e-a-l c-u-t-l-e-t-s, but in your house you only get the leftovers from the stew your mother made at lunchtime.
—You're lucky, Totie, not like Ines. Ines isn't my sister, did you know? If you only knew, poor Ines is the daughter of my big sister who's single, that makes me Ines's aunt, so when she's older I can hit her. . . . And Fuzzy, she is my sister, but younger and if I pull her hair she scratches 'cause she has nails like a cat. I can't hit you because your daddy has money and he pays me to take care of you, but if you don't lie still I'm going to give you a good pinch when nobody's looking, pest! keep still, I said! If you only knew that poor Fuzzy has never once had veal cutlets and the night it rained so hard I couldn't go home and Felisa made veal cutlets, and afterwards when Mister Berto took me home in the car after dinner, I went to bed with Fuzzy and told her about the cutlets. Fuzzy uncovered my tummy and ran her cold hand along my tummy to see if she could touch the cutlets. I hope to God your father makes a lot of money and buys the furniture. How lucky Mora's nanny is . . . her fiancé rings the bell and she opens the door, and doesn't have to wear an apron. . . . It's a good thing your daddy isn't in jail, your poor mommy all of a sudden the head doctor took away her vacation and she couldn't go to La Plata, but Mister Berto left him half dead on the floor.
—What did you buy?
—Two pounds of breadcrumbs for veal cutlets.
—Breadcrumbs cost five cents more a bag now, how come you have five cents left?
—I told the baker not to charge me more because Mrs. Mita gave him salve for his pimples at the hospital.
—Why are you taking such good care of your boss's money?
—Why did they want to kill Mister Berto?
—They shot at him once, and another time too, I've been told.
—They all fell in love with Mister Berto?
—Can't you see he's as handsome as a movie star?

—O.K., Toto, now I'll brush your hair and your daddy will take us in the car to pick up your mommy. Keep that arm still! My poor side, stop hitting it! it's sore, when Fuzzy sleeps she stabs me all night long with those broomstick arms of hers, so skinny and she wouldn't eat more stew. If you people have a left-over cutlet tonight, I'll ask your mommy and she'll give it to me tomorrow. Fuzzy never ate one cutlet. You're still too young to ask for veal cutlets, but you ought to ask for one tonight at supper. But you're too young, if not you could hide it and I'd take it to Fuzzy tomorrow. But you shitty little bedbug, you don't even know how to talk yet.
—Amparo, how nice you brushed his hair, but put away the dirty diapers, and don't leave the baby's things around, you're the one who has to keep them in place, not me.
—Felisa, yesterday I saw the missis crying.
—Don't say that in front of Mister Berto, the missis cries when he's not looking.
—Toto, don't mess up your hair! Keep your hands still. And that miserable thief of a baker wanted to raise the price, we have to save, Totie, so your daddy will buy the furniture and I'll stay to sleep in the new bed. When it rains the grass is going to grow for the steers to eat, but my shitty luck, no matter how much it rains it's not going to bring back your daddy's dead steers. I'm going to take care of you until you grow up.

III

Toto, 1939

There are three little boy dolls, and the queen of France, her hair is done in an upsweep and her skirt is as full as can be, the three little boy dolls in white stockings all the way up to their bloomers, the girl dolls in silk costumes and the boy dolls in silk costumes too, Mommy, and the men in white dickeys same as you, tiny lacing, white wigs, they're porcelain and stand on a shelf, of the mother of the boy next door, and they're hard, you can't eat them, dressed the same as the silly face dolls, they are kind, and look at a girl doll sitting in a hammock, painted on the cover of your box of spools, in the drawer next to the tablecloth and napkins, the box that had candy before. They were dressed up in the same costumes in the Charity Show at P.S. 3, the biggest kids dressed like the dolls for the gavotte, the best dance at P.S. 3 Mommy! why didn't you come? with Daddy, because Mommy on duty at the drugstore missed all the dances the kids did at P.S. 3. It was a little boy doll and a little girl doll, and a little tree and a little house, all ending with toothpicks stuck on top of the nutcake, right? Or was it a custard cake? You ate a little doll Mommy, I ate another with a green hat, did I eat his head? does it hurt the dolls? and Felisa had the little tree that was made of sugar too, painted many colors. Daddy doesn't like sweet things but the boy next door is in second grade and has no more canary, let me change its water, "No, no" the boy next door because I went to kindergarten one week only, right? in the Charity Show the other kids who went to kindergarten a whole year did the little dwarf number that I didn't like. One day I practiced, all the other little kids go one after the other on line and the teacher at the piano sang si fa sol-sol-sol la and all the kids walking one leg lame and at the same time bending over on the same side, I did the wrong leg and didn't want to go to kindergarten any more:

can't I borrow it? "When the canary sings it's because he's happy" because it's his birthday? did the mother of the boy next door put a sponge cake in the oven? Mommy, it's not baked yet, I'll stick a toothpick in it and if the toothpick comes out all clean the cake is all finished baking but no, until it cools off you can't cut it and put in the custard, what scrumptious smoke comes out of the oven and goes all around the house and gets to the canary, right? it touches his little beak and that's why he sings until the boy next door had no more canary. The boy told me and his mother told me: it's the cat's fault. Does the cat know how to cook? with potatoes? and garlic and parsley? the boy next door "I went to look for the bag of birdseed and forgot to close the cage, to make a long story short I heard a noise, the cat had jumped from the table to the cage and with one paw he popped the canary into his mouth and when I turned around the canary wasn't there any more," in one piece? did he swallow him in one piece? "the cat swallowed him in one piece and it went right down to his tummy, that's why he's so fat, touch his tummy" Mommy! don't look at him! me neither, I look at him from far-away, and didn't you call the police? in the boy's house they let the cat sleep in the hall. But in kindergarten I stayed only three days, that's all, the boy next door "In first grade you have adding and subtraction, if you're stupid the teacher'll break your back with the pointer if you don't learn": the march of the little dwarfs was the ugliest dance in the Charity Show at P.S. 3, at the Town Hall and Daddy "Waiter, what's for dinner?" before the dances they serve smooth yellow mayonnaise, Daddy's plate was decorated with a little sardine, right? But I'm stuck with the green and black olives! I don't like them! Daddy, you're not eat-ing the sardine? let me have it Daddy, have to go weewee! "You can go by yourself", I can't reach the light! but Mommy at the movires at intermission all the lights go on "Let's take advantage and go weewee now" to the ladies' room "because women can't go into the men's". A big girl. With a hard starched dress that scratches, she scratches with her dress, the Witch of Snow White scratches with her beak nose, sitting at the next table, no, don't ask her! "Honey, can you take my little boy to the bathroom?" Daddy, she can't take me to the men's room "It doesn't matter, take him to the ladies' room" no, you come! "What bathroom does Mommy take you to in the movies?" through a hallway in the Town Hall there's a locked door and if it were open I would escape to the drugstore where you were Mommy, right across the square, right, Felisa? "A bad gypsy with a face made of coal and hairy arms steals little boys who are well dressed and have run away," because once I ran out by myself to the square. An open door in the hallway but it wasn't the bathroom the biggest kids are dressing up for the gavotte and on the hook a pink mask I can't reach, which of the kids will put it on? a boy or a girl? The light is on in the ladies' bathroom like our bathroom except there's no bathtub and can the big girl reach the light? "Aren't you ashamed to be in the ladies' room, sissy?" the light is already on and the girl didn't close the door, I can escape, Felisa, is he behind the door? the gypsy puts the little boy in his bag and on the street nobody realizes it but a policeman puts him in jail because he knows he's a gypsy, yes, but the gypsy puts on the pink mask and says "I'm carrying a cat with rabies and scabs in my bag" and if the boy shouted at that very moment when the gypsy unties him afterwards where are the gypsies' tents? "They already left Vallejos, but one stayed behind and steals little boys" where is he hiding, Felisa? "On the other side of the park pond, where the horse corral is, his face looks black like coal" and he hits little boys with his whip, just like horses. The teachers hit with their pointers, but not the kids in kindergarten, and the girl can reach up and turn off the light before I finish going weewee and Daddy "Thank you for taking him, honey" and he patted her on the cheek without getting scratched by her dress. And what's for dessert? A whipped cream cake with a cherry on top "No, waiter, I don't want cake" Daddy! let me have it! I'll eat your cake and mine, Mommy gives me her cake, so she doesn't get fat, in the Vallejos-La Plata sleeping car "You better behave, this is not home," Daddy I asked for your cake since mine didn't have a cherry "Don't tell lies, you know what happens to little boys who tell lies, they grow a tail and look like monkeys" and now they're turning the lights off "If you don't behave we're going to go right home without seeing the dances" and if I tell Daddy the truth that I came back from the bathroom without going weewee he'll take me home before the dances begin and the big painted curtain rises, the national emblem on the stage because "Our pupil Joaquín Rossi will recite for us the beautiful poem 'Our Country' by Francisco Rafael Caivano" but don't ask the girl, Daddy, the light is on in the ladies' room and I can go alone, nobody is in the other room where all the clothes are hanging, on top of the chair I can reach the pink mask and if at that very minute the kindergarten teacher comes in I'll tell her a dog came by and I climbed on the chair so he couldn't bite me and should I go to the bathroom with the pink mask on? so the gypsy will think I'm somebody else, I climb on the chair "What are you doing here? what are you messing around with?" A big boy disguised as a chinaman! He wasn't dressed up for the gavotte which is only for the kindest big boys! did you really see a dog? since smaller boys shouldn't tell lies because a long tail grows behind them like monkeys and then it's easy for the gypsy to get me, he grabs me by the tail and that's that, "What are you messing around with?" and I couldn't tell him the lie about the dog; I told him I had gone to the bathroom where men are supposed to go. Kindergarten wasn't a garden, just a room with a table full of wet sand, but Daddy didn't want the cake I missed getting with a cherry; the wine jug at home has a yummy red top like a cherry, too bad it's made of glass. Mommy, after the movie let's go see the store windows, will you promise to take me? a long stop in front of the toy store window with the painted wooden cow and a wire tree, the cheapest ugly cardboard houses because Felisa is going to be late with supper and can we take advantage and look at the funny faces? all the wedding pictures in the photographer's window and Mommy doesn't it make your mouth water? the pastry shop man changes his window every day: for my birthday we ate the chocolate one, the cake roll you know how to make, but the one with whipped cream makes you sick, right? and the more expensive one filled with ice cream and glazed fruit; a big green fruit in the middle like the stone on your brooch. Where are you going? Is it naptime already? Where? you don't have to work in the hospital today, where are you going? to bake a cake? Mommy! don't leave me alone, I want to play some more! why don't you bake me a cake? Mommy's not going into the kitchen, is she going into the bedroom to look for the recipe book? Daddy called her and Mommy had to go in to take a nap. And the only thing I'm going to cover is my mouth, I don't want to cover my nose with the scarf, I won't obey and Daddy isn't cold, he put on the poncho, it was Uncle Perico's who died, at the end of the Charity Show it's very cold out since it's so late, much further if we go by the toy store but Mommy always takes me home but first we go by the toy store: on that corner the one under the light there must be a policeman, it's not the gypsy, I don't want to go that way! Let's go look at the window! "People don't make so much noise at one o'clock in the morning" and the light in the window is off, "I told you the light wasn't on, because of your silly notion we have to go three blocks out of the way" did they change yesterday's toys? can't see a thing, the ones that are hanging up look to me like yesterday's, it's so dark, the only thing you can really see in the glass are the houses on the other side of the street and the trees along the sidewalk like in a mirror, all black because the trees on the sidewalk and the face in the glass are black like coal and the cherry top is glass, if not I would eat it up. Who's looking at himself in the glass? it's not him because that ugly poncho is Uncle Perico's, and it's a good thing Mommy and Felisa waited with all the lights on because Mommy is afraid of the night until Daddy and I got back from the Charity Show. But now she's taking a nap, Amparo went to Buenos Aires and she's not coming back any more and Héctor went to play with the big boys. The boy next door "Is Héctor your brother?" Mommy slaps me but it doesn't hurt much and Héctor too but he's bigger than me, he runs faster, Mommy can't catch him and the boy next door "Your Daddy is the goodest of all, gooder than mine" because he never spanks me, and he never spanks Héctor either and once I woke Mommy up during naptime because I'm bored and Daddy "I never slapped you but the day I put my hands on you I'll break you in two" and I'm going to think about the movie I like the best because Mommy told me to think about a movie so I wouldn't get bored at naptime. *Romeo and Juliet* is about love, it has a sad ending when they die, one of the movies I liked the best. Norma Shearer is an actress who's never naughty. Mommy slaps me but it doesn't hurt much but when Daddy slaps you he breaks you in two. In Héctor's communion book there was a saint just like Norma Shearer; a nun with a white costume and some white flowers in her hand. I have pictures of her serious, laughing and in profile cut out of every magazine, in lots of movies I have never seen. And Felisa "Tell me what happens in the musical" and I told her lies not that the two of them danced alone and the wind lifted up her dress and his coattails, but that some birdies came flying along slowly and lifted her dress and his coattails because Ginger Rogers and Fred Astaire rise in the air to music, and the air carries them high with the birdies who help them twirl faster and faster, what a pretty flower! I think Ginger wants it, a white flower high up in a tree and does she ask a birdie to get it? and the birdie makes believe he doesn't hear her, when I want to give them breadcrumbs they get frightened and I have to go far away. Are they afraid of me? and of Mommy too? but there's a birdie who's the kindest of all and when Ginger is not looking . . . he flies over and cuts the flower from the tree and puts it in her blond hair and then Fred Astaire sings to her that she looks pretty with the flower and she looks at herself in the mirror and has the flower that she wanted in her hair, like a barrette, and she calls to the good birdie to come to her hand and pets him a lot. Felisa believes every bit of it and it's a lie, just in *Snow White* all the birdies are friendly, because it's an animated cartoon, when it isn't an animated cartoon they can't make the birdies come to their hands since they're afraid, Choli's pigeon is not afraid, but the birdies are prettier. The pigeon goes to the pear tree and back and does some twirls like in *Snow White* because Choli couldn't take it on the train, she went away forever to Buenos Aires "The only friend I have in Vallejos" and she went away. Mommy doesn't have any other friend, I'm close by and the pigeon eats, sleeps at night in the garden in a high little house without a door. The birdies come down to eat the bread and milk that Felisa makes for them and a lot of them go up to the roof and the trees all together and come back down, and each time they take a little bread, but I have to look from far away. Felisa, can't the cats get up to the pigeon's little house? "Nobody can reach this pigeon, cats or buzzards" Mommy has to promise me they can't, what are buzzards, Felisa? "They are big ugly birds" What do they look like? "They're big, black, with hooked beaks" how big are they? no, they're not as big as cats "Like cats more or less." Mommy! the little pigeon has to sleep with me! in the garden at night the little house doesn't have a door, cats have big mouths, but does he pull out the feathers with his hooked beak before he eats the little pigeon? No, pigeons don't let themselves get caught, they fly fast, much faster than the bad birds that are heavier with their bellies stuffed from eating . . . canaries? When Mommy gets up from her nap she has to promise me that nobody can get the little pigeon, it twirls here and there, Mommy throws streamers better than anybody untwisting and making more twirls than a birdie until they hit the ground, Ginger Rogers twirls all around a big house and they had to take all the furniture out so that Ginger wouldn't bump into anything, she knows how to tap dance without scratching the floor. Before, all her movies were funny, Saturday we saw the best Ginger Rogers film because it's a musical and has a sad ending, that Fred Astaire dies in the war in the crashed airplane and she's waiting for him but he doesn't come. And there's trouble because they're waiting for them since they have to dance together in a Charity Show, and then she sees that his fat friend comes to bring bad news and he looks at her very sad almost crying and she realizes, then tears fall down her cheek and she looks toward the stage where nobody's there because Fred Astaire isn't coming back any more because he died, and then she sees her and him come out transparent, 'cause she imagines that after dying they keep dancing and they go further and further away and get smaller and smaller and out there they twirl around some trees and then you don't see them any more. Where are they going, Mommy? "You can see through them, they're transparent, it means she will love him forever the same as when they danced together, even though he's dead now" is Ginger sad? "No, because it's like they were together, now nothing can keep them apart, war or no war." Héctor isn't my brother, Mommy says Héctor is my cousin but his mother is sick and Héctor lives in my house but he doesn't play with me and the picture cards. I have all of *Romeo and Juliet* drawn on picture cards, first the black crayon for sketching and then all the colored ones for coloring in the movies that Mommy drew Romeo on one card, Juliet on another, then the balcony and Romeo, who is climbing up the rope ladder and Juliet who's waiting for him, and yesterday she finished drawing a whole other movie, the one of Ginger Rogers and the guy who dies, and Mommy told me if I behaved well and didn't make any noise at naptime she's going to draw me another movie, it's playing this Thursday and it's the most beautiful musical and Mommy says she saw some pictures of it and it's as fancy as can be. It's called *The Great Ziegfeld* and it's lucky Mommy can go to the movies this Thursday, she doesn't have to be on duty at the drugstore. Héctor doesn't want to play with me, only with big boys like him. Pocha Perez too, she's twelve years old "Come around at naptime and I'll let you play with the manger" at the end of *Romeo and Juliet* Pocha, her mother and her aunt were in the row in back and Mommy "I saw *Romeo and Juliet* on stage in Buenos Aires" and she's going to let me go back alone one day at naptime to play with Pocha because she lives on the corner and I don't have to cross the street "Pocha, play with the little boy so we can talk a while with Mita" and at the end of *Romeo and Juliet* Pocha showed me the manger that she has all set up in the dining room "Don't touch!" can't I touch the little cow? and since I don't have to cross the street I went to Pocha's house one day at naptime; she has black paper curls and a dress with little green flowers, she has two of the same kind one with green flowers and one with blue flowers, her aunt is sitting at the sewing machine. "Know something, Pocha? In the row in front of us at the movies there was a little old lady who was crying" and naughty Pocha laughed. "How that poor little old lady cried" because I cried when Romeo and Juliet die and I went to play with the manger: it's all set up in the dining room and the piano's in the hall and she's going to let me play "We can't play with the manger or piano because they're taking their nap, let's make believe you're the boy and I'm the teacher" no! "that's the way you learn to count," no Pocha, when you going to lend me the manger? "You can't take it apart" after naptime it's too late and I have to go to the movies with Mommy "You're too young, we can't play because you don't know anything," I know every game there is "You're too young" no I'm not, I play drawing movies with Mommy "Let's play taking a nap" how do we do it? "We make believe I'm sleeping on the roof and I'm asleep covered up with a blanket but I don't have any underpants on. And you are a big boy, and you come . . . and do something to me" do what? "That's the game, you have to guess" if I guess can we play with the manger afterwards but what does the boy who comes on the roof do? Mommy didn't look, the murder movie is scary and somebody comes into a dark room and the murderer's behind the door and Mommy and me we didn't look because it's a scary movie and before the long movie once they showed a short movie about the bottom of the sea and it has hairs that wave like streamers but "Don't look" and I looked, I was naughty when the little fishes with many colors came close and went right next to the carnivorous plants at the bottom of the sea. "Swear by your mother you don't know what big boys do" I swear it I don't "When the boy climbs up to the roof while I'm sleeping he takes off my blanket and fucks me." What does "fucks" mean? "It's a bad thing that you can't do, you can only make believe, because if a girl does it she's lost, finished forever." Instead of not looking I looked because in the nice clear water at the bottom of the sea those hairs like streamers that wave come together all of a sudden and the fishies coming in between the hairs get caught. "Don't ask any more, I'm not going to tell you" naughty Pocha doesn't want to tell me what the boy with the hairs did "If you don't know it means we can't play, you're too young" Pocha tell me what "fucks" means "We can't play that, you have to be a big boy with hairs on your weeny" and I didn't tell Pocha I had seen a movie about the bottom of the sea with the plant full of hairs that eats the colored fishies, Pocha, then we can play that I'm the girl and you're the boy, because I don't know how to do it, and that's how I can learn, and Pocha "O.K." I lie down on the rug as if I'm sleeping on the roof and Pocha that day had on the dress with little green flowers, comes tiptoeing from behind and who's spying through the door that's a tiny bit opened? Pocha's aunt! laughing at me, with her paper curls too and I asked her what "fucks" means. "Pocha, you're disgusting" and her aunt went back to the kitchen. "You're too young to play with me" and I can't hit Pocha because I'm smaller, and if not, I'd cut off her curls with the scissors for cutting out stars and then I'd stick the hard curls in her mouth and make her eat them. And then I'd say to her "Pocha, have a candy" and what I'd give her would be hard dog doodoo that I found in the street. It's because of her that Felisa hit me. If it wasn't naptime now I could go play with the manger but Pocha's there, she didn't want to tell me what "fucks" was. What did he do to her with the hairs? "The boy puts his weeny in the little hole of my tail and he doesn't let me go, I can't move at all and he takes advantage and fucks me." And she won't tell me what "fucks" means. The hairs are what eat the fishies in the movie about the bottom of the sea. First the long hairs move all soft and the water and the fishies came near, right? "Toto, don't look!" now you don't see them any more! because the hairy plant swallowed them. The girl who does it is lost, finished forever, the big boy comes along, gets real close, sees that Pocha is sleeping, very slowly picks up her dress with little green flowers, and Pocha forgot to put her underpants on! and so that she doesn't move the boy puts his weeny in the little hole in her tail and he moves his hairs all over her, and if Pocha stays still like a fishie the boy's hairs start eating her behind, and then her tummy, and the heart, and the ears, and little by little he eats her all up. The little gold chain, paper curls, shoes and socks, the dress with little green flowers and her undershirt are all left on the floor with nothing inside. Pocha is lost, finished forever, she's never seen again. The other dress with little blue flowers stays hanging in the closet. Wham! the slap Felisa gave me, and she never hits me. In the kitchen stove the wood is burning into pieces of pumpkin pie and I feel like eating them and they become fire when I swish the candy coals around with a knife they break into smaller pieces and sparks come out "You're going to burn yourself!" Felisa doesn't want me to swish the wood around in the stove "Keep still I said!" and Mommy was on duty at the drugstore and Daddy was doing accounts at his desk and Felisa took my knife away. "Felisa fucksface!" and Felisa slapped me. Mommy! "Who taught you that word?", "Missis, this child is behaving worse every day," "I'm not going to say anything to Pocha's mother, but I'm going to give Pocha a good scolding. You know Berto, this child is very naughty," "Yes, well then this Sunday he starts Baby-Soccer" I don't want to go! "This child is very naughty, I'm going to put him down for Baby-Soccer so he can play with the other boys," "He's driving us out of our minds every minute of the day," "He doesn't obey when you tell him something" because Uncle Perico died. I didn't want to go to kindergarten any more and I began to play with the picture cards, but I wasn't playing the movie about the bottom of the sea where the fishies died the day Uncle Perico died "Toto, stop playing, Uncle Perico just died a while ago" with the prettiest picture cards of Romeo and Juliet all lined up along the tiles in the hall but Daddy "Poor Uncle Perico died, come and get dressed, and remember you have to be quiet and not talk loud or sing" because Mommy can't draw the movie about the bottom of the sea when she wasn't looking. Uncle Perico, always in the bar with country people, after the cattle fair they go to play billiards, they never go to the movies and it's a pity the bushes on the bottom of the sea eat the pretty fishies in many colors, they should eat the bad fishes and the old fishes that look like octopuses and sharks but in the picture cards Mommy says the movie that's going to turn out the fanciest is *The Great Ziegfeld* which they're finally showing this Thursday. "I told you to stop playing! aren't you sad that Uncle Perico died? you are naughty and spoiled, and worst of all is that I can see you don't love anybody!" They didn't spank me, if Daddy puts his hands on me he'd really break me in two and the mother of the boy next door pulls his pants down and spanks him on his behind but I didn't cry when Uncle Perico died. Shirley Temple is very young but she's an actress and she's always good, everybody loves her a lot and she has a bad grandfather with long white hair, in a movie, and he smokes a pipe and in the beginning he doesn't even look at her but afterwards he begins to love her because she's so good. And she didn't tell lies. Donkey ears don't grow on a kid who's naughty, a little tail grows from telling lies. If the boy next door's uncle dies I don't think he's going to grow donkey ears. But if the gypsies get hold of a boy his mother doesn't recognize him anymore because they rub coal all over him. In school the teacher with the pointer hits whoever doesn't know how to count up to a hundred in both ears with the pointer and the boy looks at himself in the mirror to watch his ears grow until they are donkey ears and if I say to her "Teacher, fucksface" she'll pick up the pointer again but this time to kill me and I jump through the window but I'm tangled up with the teacher's leg. The long tail grew when I said I'd gone to the men's room in Town Hall! Now the tail is longer than ever and I can't jump and the teacher's getting closer and closer with the pointer in her hand! If Felisa comes into the kitchen to give me another slap I'll jump out and get away because she doesn't have a pointer and I'll try so hard to make a giant jump out the window, so's not to fall into the park pond and you have to watch out since there may be fucks bushes at the bottom. And I jump . . . and I'm almost flying . . . the gypsy's corral is on the other side of the pond and do I land inside? Then I say I am a fishie and I'm going to fall into the fishbowl, glub, glub, glub I shout out loud and Mommy is looking for me because it's time to go to the movies, right? Mommy looks for me and can't find me and goes to look for me in the bathroom at the moviehouse, but I'm not in the ladies' room and she can't go into the men's room! but they're showing a beautiful movie and she sits down to see it and a fishie's shouting is heard from faraway and Mommy "How badly that fishie behaves, he doesn't love anybody, since his uncle died and the fishie didn't even cry, he just went on playing." And I stop shouting because a door opens; the gypsy comes in, on tiptoes, he's holding a kidnapped girl, and he hits her, right? he takes down her panties and gives her a spanking on her behind, right? no, the gypsy is bad, he pulls down his pants and his underpants, he puts his weeny in the little girl's tail and when the poor little girl can't move any more he moves his hairs all over her and little by little he eats her all up, first her leg, then her hand and the other leg and her fat little behind. And Shirley Temple is tied to a wagon near the horses. But I am not a bad fishie, I'm a good fishie and I untie the rope and Shirley Temple escapes. Because I'm going to be good like Shirley. The windows at school are very high but I'm going to tell Mommy that when she goes shopping to stand on tiptoes so she can see me in class, she has to come by every day, I'm going to make Mommy promise, and I'll promise to behave, and after school she has to come get me. For my birthday we're buying a cake and afterwards we're going to a movie to see a musical and if I feel like going weewee she'll take me to the ladies' room. And I already told a lie: that I went to the men's room, because then I'll grow a little tail and it's lucky the boys can go weewee in the backyard of the moviehouse and nobody says anything, even though the little stream of weewee makes a hole in the ground and the yard ends up full of mud puddles and Mommy watches out where she walks and she makes sure she doesn't put her feet in the mud and I go weewee . . . if the big girl with the dress that scratches isn't there . . . and she's naughty . . . and she might pick up mud from the little puddles and rub it all over my face and make it black . . . but I hide in the ladies' room and the big girl catches me and for punishment she puts a little skirt on me for going into the ladies' room. . . . Mommy! did the movie begin already and is it dark inside the moviehouse? Mommy must be waiting for me in her seat but I'll shout and she'll come and save me! "Who's the little black girl who's shouting? Yesterday there was a fishie who shouted and ran away and its owner came and put it back into the fishbowl, and now they got the little black girl who ran away and she has to take care of the fishie and they're both going to cry all night so I better close the window since they'll wake up Berto, noises make him nervous." The little black girl and the fishie are in the gypsy's corral. They're black with dirt and mud and hairs from the horses' tails. The gates are locked with a key and a latch. And the musical is already beginning and Mommy is sad because I'm going to miss it, the first number isn't the prettiest, it's only a tap dance, the fanciest number is at the end, what could the fanciest number be like? The curtain rises and there's another shiny curtain behind and this curtain rises and then there is the last curtain which means they're going to begin the fanciest dance of all and I can't miss it: what a strong wind! it's such a strong wind it opens the gate and the little black girl and the fishie get away, how lucky, they run as fast as they can because the gypsy is following them and the little black girl and the fishie have to jump over the park pond wide with black dirty water and they jump but they're very little and they fall in and the gypsy doesn't see them because they fell under the black water and the gypsy keeps running running and he is never seen again. When the dancers are all on line it's the beginning of the last number, it's all set to be drawn on the picture cards: the fanciest movie of the whole collection, but Mommy comes out of the moviehouse sad because I'm not there. Mommy cried once when we were walking along the street but I don't remember why. When? Why are you crying, Mommy? she doesn't tell me, but the little black girl and the fishie are dead floating in the pond, and luckily after the airplane crashed Ginger Rogers and Fred Astaire dance transparent in the memory, since nobody can keep them apart any more: war or no war, when Mommy wakes up after naptime I'm going to tell her I didn't make any noise and I behaved like a good boy. The fishie and the little black girl are going to be transparent in heaven after death but I don't want Mommy to draw them on the picture cards, they're so dirty they'd come out ugly transparent. Isn't a birdie prettier? did some birdie die? the boy next door's canary? no! Mommy's not going to draw him! another one, in the memory, that's also transparent in heaven, then Mommy realizes that he's dead and every day when we come home from the movies we look up at the pear trees and we tell him what happened in the movie, who was acting, the musical numbers, just as if he were seeing them so he doesn't feel sorry he missed it all: from high up in the clouds everything looks little in Vallejos, and the gypsy is not in the corral any more. The nicest thing is to be on top of the little clouds with Ginger's other birdies and we play every day, the teacher with the pointer is tiny down below in school, and Pocha in her aunt's kitchen. Nothing but the birdies can get up to the clouds, they eat big cake crumbs that Felisa sends them and nothing else, right? right, because there are no black birds big like cats with hooked beaks, I'm going to make Mommy promise.

IV

Choli's Conversation with Mita, 1941

—Mita, you should be happy with this child of yours. He couldn't be sweeter.

—

—No, that's not true, believe me. I was sure he would have lost his looks by now, I figured his features would have become coarser, like a man's.

—

—I was afraid too! he couldn't go on being so handsome, he's going to be eight, and he's simply adorable. "Mommy, take me to see Choli in the house with the staircases," in this dirty town my staircase must have looked like a palace to him.

—

—Like his grandmother's house! he thought he was *there*, with his grandmother and aunts in La Plata. But I'm not as old as your grandmother, or am I? These children look so big to me I can't stop thinking about age.

—

—About ten years younger, because I take care of myself.

—

—You're right, that's not why. He never thought he was going to die so soon.

—

—He'd sure be mad, I make up my eyes now and wear my hair down. They all stink.

—

—You were lucky to find the one good man in a thousand.

—

—Because you say "yes" to everything. When I think of the twelve years, twelve! that I lived with that dog I get furious.

—

—For my baby's sake, otherwise, twelve years down the drain.

—

—And what's so bad about starting the day off talking? Jáuregui was the kind of man that if he didn't want to listen to you, he wouldn't.

—

—A whole hour telling him I ruined his jacket. You see I made a hole in it, trying to take a stain out; then he comes and asks me for it and puts it on because he didn't know I'd made the hole.

—

—How could you stand such jealousy? Having to wear long sleeves in the heat of the summer, of course he's not the kind to look at another woman, and Jáuregui looked at all of them. It was disgusting towards the end, him pushing fifty.

—

—All day in rags, but in the evening, once I had the kid busy at his homework, I never once missed taking a bath and changing my clothes, so at least I could go out on the balcony for a while.

—

—Being dressed up doesn't matter to you because Berto doesn't want you to look sexy.

—

—Because you know all he lives for is his home, he's two steps from the store and once there he doesn't move, but where can he go in Vallejos anyway?

—

—No, I was unhappier in Buenos Aires, at the beginning. I don't care how classy that store was, it's tough being a saleslady.

—

—How long since you were there last?

—

—And your mother?

—

—But he doesn't like the movies, does he? He could at least take you to the movies once in a while.

—

—Sleeping pills! You went to college, you ought to know better. Staying up late reading the newspaper, maybe that's what makes him so nervous, why do you spoil him so much? don't read him the newspaper! he should stop bothering you with his money-grubbing.

—But on the street nobody's ever seen me in rags, of course here there aren't any interesting people to talk to. And then I'd always change before going into the kitchen, or put on an apron and a cloth around my head, because otherwise I'd get spots on my clothes and smell of cooking. When I dressed up a little he'd laugh at me, as if to say "what for?"

—

—But on my sales trips there wasn't a soul who didn't say, "You're an interesting one, Choli."

—

—Interesting, the type that makes people wonder "who can she be?"

—

—It's the eye shadow, don't you agree?

—

—For a man they do crazy things, they rob, they work as jewel thieves, frontier adventuresses, smugglers, and the spies? I don't think it's all for money, they get involved because a man asks them to.

—

—The turban. The dark turban makes me look exotic. Of course now that I've got all a Hollywood Cosmetics supervisor gets for nothing, with the tons of free samples I carry around, I can find out which is best for me.

—

—The kind of woman that can put on makeup and still look refined.

—

—With a simple suit you can't wear too much makeup, the college-girl type. To each her own style.

—

—No, but if you told me you were the most striking woman in Vallejos then I'd stop believing you.

—

—But it's just as well, I'm only passing through Vallejos this time.

—

—It makes them furious. They'd prefer me to lock myself up in the house in mourning.

—

—Really? It's just that I learned what elegance is. And I know how to carry on a conversation too, don't I? Even if I didn't go to college, right? Mita, I get along with you because you're not envious, all you put on is a little lipstick and a touch of rouge, but you know the women around here never liked us, we weren't born here.

—

—You have your own home. And Berto is two steps away in the store; the only time you don't see him is when you go to the movies, from six to eight, but just come back one day in the middle of the movie, that's enough, if you have any suspicions, but I don't think Berto would do it to you.

—

—What? he'd only have to snap his fingers to get back with one of his old flames, you don't know what these country mice are like.

—

—Because I argued with him. You went through college and he should listen to you, I wish I'd gone to college.

—

—Why can't anybody say that to him?

—

—He was already set against me when I spoke up for women who wear makeup.

—

—The kid? the last Sunday I was in Buenos Aires. He took a book home from school to go over geography, and you should see how well he knows the map of Europe.

—

—And I look good in it, maybe it's because I'm tall, I'm the American woman type.

—

—On my sales trips.

—

—White-framed sunglasses with my hair straightened and dyed auburn.

—

—The head of Hollywood Cosmetics. I should talk very little, command a lot of authority, dress very stylishly and not pay too much attention to the customers.

—

—"Do like the American supervisor who came last year, she

didn't get friendly with anybody," and of course she didn't talk because she knew very little Spanish. So since I already look American, I took advantage of it not to pay attention to anybody.

—

—Comfortable sport suits, with a tight belt to show off my waist, and I brush my hair till it looks like silk, so dancing in a nightclub you can throw your head back and it's sexy falling down your shoulders, and if there's a goodby at the airport it waves in the wind and looks really romantic. The trick is to know how to keep it silky. If you never wash it, it gets sticky, and if you wash it too much it becomes feathery and dry.

—

—A good base of pancake on the face and almost no rouge (it's better pale, more interesting) and then a lot of eye shadow which gives you the mysterious look, and of course mascara for the lashes. You know something? all of Mecha Ortiz's hairdos look good on me. There isn't an actress I like better in Argentine movies.

—

—And besides, no matter what she does with her hair it always looks good. Who knows what kind of a bum her husband was, because she's a widow, you know.

—

—She's gorgeous with long hair, real long and that high wave over the forehead. What an interesting woman!

—

—From having suffered so because to do such strong dramatic roles she must have had a terrible life, you can see she feels them. She just started working as an actress after she became a widow.

—

—And when she falls in love in a movie you feel that she's dying for that man, nothing else matters to her, she's ready to sacrifice everything to go after him.

—

—In Buenos Aires, tons of them, to talk awhile, nothing else. I don't know if I'd do the same as her, for that you have to really be in love, madly in love. Now I don't expect anything anymore, you know what I mean? nothing.

—

—I can't.

—

—He was always handsome, a regular movie actor.

—

—From country to town and from town to country, but you would never see him with a girl, he'd always be alone with some friend, never with girls. But just the same, from time to time you'd hear that some girl was mad for him, that she wanted to kill herself or become a nun, and even girls with fiancés . . .

—

—That you keep him locked up, because he never goes anywhere and seems completely taken up by his business.

—

—If you don't want to know who they were, I won't say a word. It was so many years ago; I still had some illusions when I was engaged to Jáuregui.

—

—The difference in age. But he would always let me have my own way; when he'd come to visit me at Bragado there wasn't a day when we didn't go out for a drink at the café. I'd ask for a beer because my brothers didn't like me to drink vermouth. And Jáuregui was the silent type.

—

—That he'd begin to tell me about his things when we got married and we would be closer.

—

—I hardly wore lipstick then, you know what I mean?

—

—In the winter. When we got to Vallejos it was freezing cold, we had a tiny heater that hardly warmed up the room. How cold it was getting undressed! And Jáuregui took advantage, all right. Me, I didn't know a thing, just like an angel.

—

—Did you undress in front of your sisters?

—

—Me, never!

—

—When we were fiancés he touched me all over the place but only with his hands under the clothes, which is not the same as touching you with nothing on. It's so ugly to be naked, they can see all your defects.

—

—With the light off. But I'm so white you can see all of me, and once when he pulled the sheets off I covered myself with my hands and then he caught my hands and I couldn't do a thing, having to get undressed in the same room with a man, and nothing could calm him down, I'd never seen a person lose his control like that. When we were fiancés I would kiss Jáuregui but that was all I'd do. Have you seen cats when you throw water on them, they look like they're going crazy and their hair's standing on end? Jáuregui wasn't the same person, his hair was all messy.

—

—You'd say "yes" to everything, because he'd promise to let you go to La Plata.

—

—And for your sister's wedding?

—

—That time it might have been because they wouldn't give you leave at the hospital, but all the other times you didn't travel because of Berto, because of Mr. Berto's moods.

—

—Because of the trouble I had with Jáuregui's probate.

—

—And he died, and if they asked me things about him I couldn't answer, all I know is that he'd always two-time me and each time I'd find out about what was going on . . . I'd thank my lucky stars. How could I answer all those questions the lawyer asked me?

—

—Asking my sister-in-law for all the details by letter and she got it all wrong anyway, and listen, how could I ignore his carrying on with the cashier? since when do you need a whole hour every night to balance the accounts?

—

—Even so, I used to eat with my boy and then warm up his supper, even though he'd screw up his puss and complain the food was overcooked.

—

—No, you would have died.

—

—Mr. Berto, you have to put up with that bad temper of his. Even so, I didn't stop dressing up, I'd take the cloth off my head and the apron and if it was in the afternoon I'd go have *mate* with you, impeccably dressed, flawless; I can still see you now, getting up from your nap with your eyes swollen from sleep and full of hope.

—

—Because Berto had just said you could go to La Plata that winter!

—

—I started trembling before you did, believe me.

—

—If you're like that you'll never be able to fight for your rights. I never kept my mouth shut with Jáuregui, I'd always answer him back.

—

—Did you make more money in the hospital than in the drugstore?

—

—They always went to me for everything because they knew I could find a way, the ones with no forehead or long faces, to find a turban that would look good on them.

—

—How old are you?

—

—What did he give you for a present?

—

—Why not?

—

—No, very few men came to the store, only Ramos the sales representative, what a darling. And his assistant who carried the yard goods in, a regular roughneck, he reminded me of Jáuregui.

—

—Because he wouldn't talk.

—

—Mita, so many hopes I had about Ramos. . . .

—

—A little young for me, but so sensitive, and refined, such manners! . . . And he knew everything! he knew more about fashion than the girls at the store, he would bring us the latest news.

—

—Right from the start. He would tell me about the things he saw at the Opera House, marvelous classical dances.

—

—I didn't go, because I'm a fool, I wanted to wear a new black velvet dress, which I finally didn't make. He said he found me so interesting that he wanted me to tell him all about myself.

—

—About Jáuregui and everything, every little detail.

—

—From the first night on. And about Jáuregui's ways. You could see he wanted to arouse me because a few days later he asked me to repeat it all over again. . . . Then and there I thought he wanted to take advantage and make some proposition, I was already disgusted . . . but nothing, I don't know what could have come over him. I had never talked to a man about those things.

—

—Me, once in the store. I took his hand. And velvet dress or no, I should have gone to the Opera House, I could have worn something simple.

—

—He didn't move it away, but he didn't press mine. His assistant always reminded me of Jáuregui, the woman in charge of the store caught it and trying to be funny one morning when his roughneck assistant was bringing in some bolts of cloth she started to blab about me liking Ramos.

—

—But he was a man you could talk to.

—

—My legs would practically collapse from exhaustion.

—

—Mid-afternoon. The girls in the workshop make *mate* with hot milk, and when I could I'd join them, the girls drink it as soon as it's ready because they can quit sewing when they want, but if I was in front with customers I had to be patient. At the beginning I'd tell my problems to the girls in the workshop, but afterwards no. Around six your legs start collapsing from standing and the day drags, that cup in my hand, sitting on a stool in the shop. Sewing always bothers your back, but then too the girls only had stools and nothing to lean back on, I who had a house . . . you think the owner couldn't afford real chairs? and in the winter at that hour it's already dark. It's OK in the summer because you come out in daylight and there still seems to be time to do something worthwhile, but in the winter at *mate* time it's already night and coming out in the freezing cold, no money to spend, where are you going to go? At the beginning I'd tell the girls in the workshop about my problems, I was such a fool.

—

—The youngest ones, and on top of that, uneducated, they think they're gorgeous and they see us older ones as worn-out rags. But I've done a lot of good things in life, and no sooner do I start talking about my life people sit up and listen.

—

—I hear myself talking and it sounds like a movie to me, Mita, not every woman takes care of her son the way I do, so that he won't miss a thing.

—

—That he was in kindergarten, if they knew he was in high school, they'd take me for forty, at least.

—

—Nobody knows Jáuregui's business was a hardware store, they assumed I worked behind the counter: I never worked until I walked into that clothing store.

—

—That my husband had a ranch and then died and the lawyers ate it up.

—

—They'll lose their youth soon enough. After that I'd have my *mate* and keep quiet. "They belong on those stools, don't stand up for them" the owner said to me one day "they're tramps, they call you the ranch lady behind your back and they laugh their heads off." Not every mother can send her son to a good school on a modest salary.

—

—My whole paycheck went to the school. The boardinghouse didn't cost much anyway, and I could take it out of my savings.

—

—No, Mita, my troubles are over, luckily it's different now at Hollywood Cosmetics, with the freedom I have.

—

—A sensitive man, who talks well, and if she gives in he should make her feel like a lady and receive her properly.

—

—A silk bathrobe, in a perfumed room, or something like that.

—

—You're right, he's very intelligent, he didn't have a cent and now he's making a place for himself. At my house there were a lot of us but his case is different. It was a pity they didn't send him to college, his older brother was making tons of money.

—

—Yes, but you got an education, he didn't. I almost died when I saw how far the United States was from England. I thought London was the chic part, but closer.

—

—If I say white, he's already thinking black, so suspicious, he thinks I do hanky-panky on my sales trips, and now that he's doing well, why is he so nervous? . . .

—

—They would take the car apart and then put it back together again. My baby didn't drive because he couldn't reach the pedals, but Jáuregui taught him how anyway.

—

—He was the only one Jáuregui got along with.

—

—Jáuregui taught him to take the car apart and they would put it back together and take it apart over and over again.

—

—He's not going to have a car when he's older.

—

—How can I afford to buy him one? If Jáuregui were alive he'd lend it to him. They would take the motor apart and put it together again but they'd still have to take it to the garage.

—

—Boys are like that, Jáuregui's sister always brought the baby toys but he never got close to her, but he was nuts about his father and the boy at the garage. And the boy at the garage would let him touch everything, the tool box, the pump, like you let Toto have the magazines and spools of thread. How he'd get dirty from the car grease!

—

—Of course he never has any time, always at his desk, talking with the employees, you don't think they talk about women all day? what else could they be talking about?

—

—Traveling all over the country, although yes, it is a bit lonely, always traveling, alone.

—

—Just when I'd feel like chatting a little. In Mendoza at that hour it always gets cold, no matter how sunny it was during the day, it's the mountain weather.

—

—Any jacket is fine. The work keeps you moving and besides, there's always a strong sun to keep you warm. But as it gets late you have to bundle up good and you don't see a soul on the street.

—

—A good thing there's central heating in the school in Buenos Aires, it's the first thing a top-notch school should have because of all the time he's sitting still doing his homework; now I don't have to shout at him, there he's learning what discipline is.

—

—Always in the best hotels. It's the policy of Hollywood Cosmetics.

—

—They're hand embroidered. And you can see yourself in the waxed floors. Sometimes I talk to myself, they must think I'm crazy, or I talk to you, about anything: "Mita, smell the fragrance of this wax" or I ask you "do you like starched sheets?"

—

—They always invite you for a drink, I'm sick and tired of the same tricks over and over again.

—

—Marriage, no. I'd have to know the man real well, somebody very intelligent, like Ramos, who can teach me, and about classical dances too, because I don't want to die an ignoramus. A man who knows about everything.

—

—I almost left. When Toto came to open up I was getting sick of ringing the bell, and as soon as I knocked on the window Toto appeared, white with fear, and I thought, "Good God, someone must be very sick!" but it was nothing, he came to tell me on tiptoes that Berto was taking his nap and that I shouldn't make any noise.

—

—What if a telegram comes when the bell is disconnected?

—

—Is he scared of him? And I stayed with him until you got up, he was very quiet, building little houses, because the kind of toys Toto has no other boy in Vallejos has, and in Buenos Aires I've seen how much those toys cost.

—

—Very expensive. I don't know if Berto would tell you how much they cost.

—

—Jáuregui would never tell me anything about anything.

—

—In Tucumán, on my last sales trip.

—

—Scary, a rare breed, always busy, the silent type, plagued with headaches, the kind of man who likes to sit quietly by your side holding hands.

—

—No, he knows the best of Tucumán, when we were at a café he'd get up a thousand times to make a telephone call or say hello to somebody on the sidewalk.

—

—"Crazy about me," he'd say. He said he never saw a figure like mine.

—

—A den in the suburbs. He begged me on his knees, I wouldn't have gone for the world.

—

—Would I look bad in red?

—

—Determined that you should buy the turquoise, he didn't even let the salesman talk!

—

—It's a good thing you didn't, because he'd get you so excited you'd buy anything in any color, even dark brown! You know how salesmen are.

—

—In the kitchen making my pancakes I could hear the storm coming on: "Mommy, buy the turquoise, it was the prettiest one there" and Berto saying "no" and "definitely not," what a tense man!

—

—And this one didn't give up! "Daddy: Mommy has to buy the turquoise" and Berto, of course, exploded.

—I'm telling you, it wasn't my fault, he was a good catch and he got away; but in the end he turned out to be a heel. He has a bad name in Tucumán.

—

—No, because he behaved like a heel to some woman.

—

—No, a gorgeous woman, extremely interesting, much better than him.

—

—For having a soft spot, and on the third day . . . she gave in.

—

—Exactly, a very pretty little lodge in the suburbs. So he offered her brandy and they hadn't exchanged but two words when he had his hands all over the place, he didn't even put on a silk robe, or anything for that matter.

—

—I don't know, it gives you a feeling of respect. I saw some in a store in exquisite brocade. . . . So she told me that a half hour later he woke up—he'd gone to sleep like they do—he got up, all set to go, after all he's a busy man and so on and so forth.

—

—Because she felt like staying! overnight so she wouldn't have to go back to the hotel (she was on a sales trip too), she wanted to have time to look at the curtains, hand embroidered by the Indians from up north and simply exquisite, and stay there like in her own home, she told me so herself.

—

—Every little detail, but he didn't let her. And she kept insisting until finally he became rather unpleasant, he went and told her the lodge wasn't his, it belonged to a friend.

—

—Because he didn't say hello to her any more on the street. But, Mita, I wouldn't have let Jáuregui do that, bang his fist on the table and make the child cry just because he insisted you buy that material, it's the latest fashion and anyway, why do you always have to wear those old-lady dresses, excuse me for saying so, but they're so dull. And old-fashioned.

—

—That shouting, and the fist-banging, and the broken plate, it frightens children.

—

—I'm not saying you should wear bright red or the famous turquoise, that's not your style, but just the same if I had been at the table I would have defended Toto, all he wanted was to see his mother well dressed, like a movie actress.

—

—I shouldn't act so dumb on the street.

—

—Because talking you can get to understand each other, and even get to like each other. Sometimes you have to be shrewd and make them believe you might accept.

—

—And then you don't have to go back to the hotel so early.

—

—Don't you go and think I was ever such a fool.

—

—Didn't you think so? Admit it.

—

—They lose interest right after and they don't want to talk anymore; once they've seen you with no clothes on they think they already know everything about you, you're not worth a thing, you're like last year's fashion.

—

—Exactly: empty-handed and more alone than ever.

—

—Yes, and afterwards you're back at the hotel room, alone again, and not a soul to speak to.

—

—I always answered back to Jáuregui, and when he'd get angry at the child for no reason, I could have pulled his eyes out, father or no father. But Jáuregui had won the child over.

—

—But don't worry, on a sales trip there's always something to do.

—

—The clothes get creased in the suitcase. Going back to the hotel every night there's always something to fix or iron, and at least you're relaxing.

—

—One of the things I enjoy most is to try on all my clothes in the hotel and study myself in the mirror.

—

—To find matching kerchiefs and shoes and handbags for the dresses and suits. First the morning outfits, with a scarf on my head, and then the afternoon change with my hair in a band or loose. I spend hours changing, it's so much fun, a pity I can't take pictures of myself. And so I pass the time.

—

—No, I have them bring up coffee and buns, I don't eat supper, which is good for the figure and the pocketbook. And when I feel like looking pretty, I try on the evening wear, in an upsweep, like Mecha Ortiz in *The Women* when at the end she's going to meet that man she loves so much.

—

—I don't remember.

—

—Was it the husband? She was absolutely stunning, a slim figure, a fitted black dress and the face of a woman in love, happy to go to him, since it was such a long time that she hadn't been with him; a sensitive man, intelligent, refined. And there's nothing like being well dressed, you look like somebody else entirely. Because you are what you are, whether it's sagging breasts or a potbelly, which I don't have at all, the thing is that with a well-made dress, that covers the faults, a woman can be gorgeous, and she's no longer just any woman.

—

—No, that's not the main thing, I don't agree with you Mita, pardon me. She has to be interesting! and you mustn't forget the eye shadow.

—

—No, but it's more interesting as if she were hiding a past. Where do those women get the courage to lead that kind of life? The jewel thieves, or the spies. Or even the smugglers. But they have another kind of life. More interesting. Because that's the main thing, that people see her pass by and say "what an interesting woman . . . who can she be . . . ?"

V

Toto, 1942

Without a model I can't draw, without a model Mom can draw, with a model I can draw better than her. What can I draw until three o'clock? Naptime is the biggest bore and if a plane flies over Dad wakes up, the shouting starts and it's Mom's chance to get up. This time tomorrow getting dressed, the González girl's birthday, the popeyed González girl. Tiny-eyed, and still tinier-eyed from sleep, Alicita's father doesn't get undressed to take his nap, and everybody in line, me, Alicita and the González girl, no more selling, making so much money playing store at Alicita's, and everybody in line! only a half-hour and her father's already up from his nap: I didn't make any noise, they did . . . and no breaking things, scary running to get in line, and her father took his hand out of his pocket and . . . one, two, three candies, Alicita's father is a father of girls. Put my fingers down hard, I can rub out the colors of a butterfly, you have to touch it ever so gently, color dust on the wings: a kiss on my forehead "see you tomorrow" Mom says to me every night, soft and gentle it feels almost like a butterfly when she touches my cheek, Alicita's father touched me the same way, he's a father of girls. The González girl's father is the González girl's father but he also has two boys and he mustn't touch like that. Or is it because he has a store and he's nervous? no, because he's the manager of the hardware store but not the owner. And at night before bedtime, Alicita's lying I'll bet, they play putting the doll to sleep, and he's the doctor if the doll is sick, so many dolls! there's always one who has the flu in Alicita's room, and Alicita and her mother and her father and all the dolls turn off the lights at the same time, store owner's nerves, they have to read before going to sleep and it's better to see the light on if a storm comes, should I call Mom? what if Dad is just falling asleep? The storm last night was over right away, then I went to sleep. Some thunder without lightning. At school in the morning it began again but just a little and without lightning. It's cloudy now but it isn't raining any more and I'll go to the store to draw posters till three when I have a piano lesson since nobody's there now, I'll write Alice Faye in (with fancy letters) *In Old Chicago*, and then I'll trace Alice Faye's big face on the glass part of the door. There's mud all over the backyard, and the store people don't come till three, what can I do? A good thing the birthday's tomorrow, Dad's shouting scared my class partner and he doesn't want to come and play in the vestibule, he rang the bell at naptime because I forgot to disconnect it, Dad bellowed like thunder from the bedroom. And the clock won't move an inch until three o'clock comes along. Mom doesn't get up until three-thirty. Tomorrow she won't take a nap, she has to dress me. Let's see if I can make Chinese letters. Alicita can't play today, she's being punished, they're not going to punish me, who do they think they are. I got A in Art and Science too, A– in Math and A– in Dictation and A in Reading. The English teacher told Mom I learned everything she taught me. Today after piano I have English and at five I'm all finished and I come in for my milk, and the store people are already back so I can go and play a little with Lalo who's big and wears long pants and lets me help him stick labels on the bottles, he's nice, but Dad once said he's a troublemaker and Dad bets they're going to get rid of him before the month's over. Lalo is the nicest looking, he's not a dirty Indian like the others even though he lives on the dirt streets too he doesn't have an Indian face and brown teeth from that salty well water, he looks like an actor, like in the serial about the boy who escapes from reform school who is really good but in a moment of anger he knifes a policeman. But he doesn't come to play until it's time to open the store, if Mom invited him to stay for lunch after work at one o'clock maybe he would stay, since every time he brings in the wood he stares at the food Felisa's making, and once I was going to save him a cream caramel meringue but Mom won't ever have him. The bicycle I like is the smallest one, with little wheels on the side so I won't fall, Dad doesn't like it, but I do. And after English I play with Lalo a little and then I go back to do my homework because I want to draw a windmill, the teacher didn't ask for a drawing but I want to draw the windmill I saw in a magazine but the rule of three example is about a waterwheel.

And I want to color it in nicely with a perfect outline in black, and when I had to draw the digestive system of the bird I didn't do it from our textbook, I copied it out of Héctor's zoology book, which was harder and the teacher saw it and I thought she was going to like it and she said it was more than the digestive system since the reproductive system was there too and she said "Come and see me at recess." And I went at recess and she got hold of me and explained everything "Toto, I should make you tear out the page but since you did such a good job I'm going to explain everything to you because the superintendent may come and say you drew that just like a parrot talks without understanding what he's saying." And she began to explain what ovaries and genitals and male's fluid are and all about birth because some yellow bunches and a mess of little pipes going every which way were in the drawing and a kind of green cup upside down with hard names and the drawing was nicely colored-in but real icky with all those tangled-up lines it looked like the body of a poisonous spider and on top of everything was the bird's head with a couple of feathers. And the teacher said "Do you understand what I'm saying?" and me "Yes" and I didn't understand a thing because I was thinking about something else on purpose and I didn't even hear what she was saying, that the rooster, and that the male's fluid, that she was boring me to tears, and let her ask if I understand I'll say "yes, yes" and to myself I'll say to her "pest" that it was bursting my brains making so much effort to think about other things. Alicita doesn't make very pretty drawings, she says she has no time, she has to go visit her aunt and the little baby. I have time to draw because if I don't go to English and then I go to the movies at six, I do it at English time, and if I have English I do it at movie time, but if they're playing a good movie and I have English I do my homework quick quick after milk and I don't play with Lalo, I don't think they're going to get rid of him. But if Lalo wants to play with the bottles at six and they're playing a good movie I'm not going to help him stick labels on, the movies are more fun. And if the piano teacher gives me the two o'clock I don't have to wait till three. But if Alicita is not being punished I end up not playing with her until three anyway. Alicita is always saying she's being punished and that's why she can't play, but one day it was a lie because her mother winked at her. Alicita is the prettiest girl in our grade. I sit next to my partner. Alicita sits next to that blond, the González girl.

Alicita is a brunette, but not black hair, it's clean brown that you feel like touching, and the wide white silk band, too. Her hair band shines and her hair shines. Her hair band shines brightly, the well water is hardly moving when I lift up the cover, I lean over to throw the pail in and splash! the sun comes shining in at the same time and what a great splash all those sparkling little drops, and I bring the pail back up and splash! the drops jump again, all the little lighted lamps that go off, because the well has to be closed so dirt won't get in. I saw Alicita comb her own hair, she knows how, she makes a part all by herself, first she pushes it all in front, all that long, pretty hair that should be called tresses, hair is for men, or animals that aren't very dirty, Pirucha has dirty hairs, but Alicita has tresses, because her hair is smooth and not curly, which is prettier, it falls softly with the bottoms pointed up so that they're pointing at me and if I come near to twist it around my finger Alicita says to me "Don't mess it up." And her hair shines and it should be called tresses because it's so pretty, they're like threads that grow out of her white head. I looked at Alicita's head one day because we were playing lice, she invented the game on purpose to see the head of the Chávez girl who they say has lice, she lives in a hut on the unpaved streets. And the Chávez girl had such a dirty head that you couldn't see anything, and finally it was my turn to look at Alicita's head and it was so so white, whiter than her face, and shiny, all her little hairs were growing like threads, sewing threads, but not the kind for mending socks, those others, which Mom used to embroider the red flowers on the bedspread, which came out the best, and when I went into the room it looked like the bed was on fire. And not all the little hairs in Alicita's tresses are the same, because one shines, another doesn't, another a little, another not at all, and if she moves, the one that shined before doesn't now, and the other one does and the one to the side even more, and less, and it's always changing. Her apron is all plaited like the teacher's and so short that when Alicita sits down you can see her vaccination. Her and the González girl they always play drawing daisies and then, since all they think about is boyfriends, they cross out a petal, and then the next, and the next and they say "he loves me he loves me not." I want to be Alicita's boyfriend, Alicita's hair is the best for playing he loves me or not since I can count the hairs in a bunch and the hair is close to the head where people think and secrets are, with the González girl she's full of secrets, they give each a look and they laugh right away because they guess what the other one's thinking, if the boyfriend is a third grader, like me, or a fourth or fifth grader. Héctor's a junior in high school, at the boardinghouse with his father in Buenos Aires. And after finishing the example, since I beat all of them because I'm the best in the class, I began to look at Alicita, and she had a little bunch that was half outside the hair band and I began to look at a little hair that shined, another that didn't, another that did a little less, "she loves me she loves me not." But she moved her head and all the glitters changed places and you couldn't see now. Afterwards I thought I could tell her not to move, who knows, anything, that I was drawing her, but I couldn't find out a thing. The González girl looks at me catching flies with her mouth and won't say a word. Alicita talks and laughs at everybody and tells me about her big cousin who's at Lincoln and plays tricks on the nuns, she gets up barefoot in the middle of the night with some of the others and some of the girls go to the bathroom to read novels and they get into the kitchen to steal cookies, but she doesn't know Teté, who's also with the nuns at Lincoln. Teté is my half-cousin. Alicita's not afraid to get up in the middle of the night and she wants to go to Lincoln. It's lucky Teté is coming to Vallejos, we can play at naptime when I'm so bored because Mom sleeps at naptime. If only Alicita would come, but she doesn't because her mother is a friend of Luisito Castro's mother, they take her there and Alicita plays with Luisito, big bully one day I saw him hit a boy smaller than him, he's tall and much bigger than me since he's in fourth, he's ten and I'm nine, he talks like a jerk with marbles in his mouth Mom says he has his mother's dumb face and talks like a three-year-old. Alicita once said Luisito asked her if she wanted to be his girlfriend, the dumbbell, with that stupid face. He really kicked that small boy, once he saw me in the movies when I came over to where Alicita was sitting to give her some candy and he looked at me, his shoes have thick soles "Don't be afraid of him, just give him a good punch" Dad said and how did he know? I only told Mom, the punch should be when Luisito is looking the other way, in the stomach, and the door all set for running and what when he sees me again after English? The teacher likes Alicita better than all the other girls, better than everybody, since the teacher goes to her house and is a friend of her aunt who has a pretty face with no makeup, a churchgoer's face, so thin, Mom says she's very frail because she gets sick from nothing, and I don't have an aunt who's a teacher. And one day the teacher asked Alicita how her aunt was, because if she was sick when the baby came she wouldn't be able to breastfeed him, since her aunt is skinny and doesn't have hardly any tits, that's why. And one day Alicita came in all smiles and told her that her aunt had a baby and was fine, so she was probably breastfeeding him, and she married the guy from the bank with the handsome face, always dressed in a good suit that Dad never uses and a white shirt with the little tiny knot tie, like in Harrod's catalog, so nice, he looks like he never gets angry, and he's at the Banco de la Nacion with the marble floor that Felisa's mother waxes, so big that you can dance there, and the golden bars on the windows and behind them the guy who married Alicita's aunt does accounts, with a movie actor's face. And the new baby when he learns to talk he's going to kiss him and say "I love you, Daddy" and won't he scratch the little baby with his beard? no, never, cause he shaves every day, he's behind the bars that shine cause they're gold, the floor shines cause it's marble and the face shines cause it's shaved. Dad has a beard that scratches because he's nervous, the barrels in the store are sticky with purple streaks of wine, and he's always wearing Uncle Perico's poncho who died. Brown like dirt the poncho, the sand dunes move if a strong wind blows and you have to cover the barrels since I pull off the cork to look inside. I drew the guy who married Alicita's aunt and he came out exactly just like in real life, I made the two eyes the same, big and wide opened with eyelashes and a small nose and a small mouth with a thin mustache and his hair with the point in front and no part like Robert Taylor, and if Alicita's uncle were an actor I'd have him marry Luise Rainer in *The Great Ziegfeld* instead of having her die, when she's sick and about to die and she makes a telephone call to her ex-husband Ziegfeld who left her for another woman and she tells him she's not sick any more so Ziegfeld won't get sad, and it's only the middle of the movie but you don't see her any more because she dies right away, and it would bc much better if at that moment the doorbell rings and Luise Rainer goes to open it and it's a guy who came to the wrong door, and it's Alicita's uncle, but Luise Rainer is so tired after getting up to talk on the telephone that she faints right there at the door, and he comes in and picks her up and calls the bellboy right away, because they're in a first class hotel, he's a boy without a father and his stepfather hits him. And he sends him to the drugstore for medicine and meantime he puts Luise Rainer on the sofa and lights the fire, he covers her with her white ermine bedspread, to keep Luise Rainer warm since she's freezing, and he realizes she's about to die. But thanks to the help of the bellboy who brings a whole lot of medicine. And in *The Great Ziegfeld* she really dies for good in the middle of the picture, and you don't see her any more, and she's an actress that I like, and then Myrna Loy who I don't like much at all comes out, she's tall and she never dies in any picture, I like Luise Rainer much better who's always playing the good one who everybody's always cheating, and sometimes she dies, but at the end it's nice when they die but when they die in the middle you don't see them anymore. Then it would be nice if the movie continued with the guy who married Alicita's aunt, with the help of the little bellboy, he starts taking care of Luise Rainer and the little bellboy goes to the hotel kitchen and steals ravioli, a partridge and pieces of jelly roll, no, better, a meringue cream cake, and brings them up and at first she says she's not hungry but Alicita's uncle tells her that with the snow that's starting to fall they're going to make snowmen and they're going to go sleigh riding at naptime and the little bellboy looks sad because he doesn't say anything about taking him, but at least telling these things to Luise Rainer makes her start eating some raviolis, and a little partridge and a good piece of cake, because nobody had ever brought her anything to eat before. And the man sees the piano and starts playing and the little bellboy does a tap dance and Luise Rainer starts singing like in the beginning of the movie and he starts staring with his mouth open and he and the bellboy give each other a look and the bellboy eats a little cake and Alicita's uncle doesn't scold him. And every day after work he comes to take care of Luise Rainer and the little bellboy tells him whether or not she ate, and now she has more than enough food in her room. And one day the uncle kisses her on the mouth and tells her he loves her and from the hotel kitchen I throw a coin at the organ grinder who's on the street so he'll play a song and Luise Rainer gets up little by little and realizes she's getting better and he asks her for a dance. And she's happy, now she thinks they're going to go steady and they're going to get married, but he's sad. And the little bellboy comes and sees them dancing and thinks they're going to get married and take him home with them. And he runs and hugs the man and gives him a big kiss on each cheek, that handsome nicely shaved good guy's face, his hair nicely brushed with pomade and says to him "I'm not going back to my stepfather any more!" and the boy turns around to tell Luise Rainer that they're going to live in a cabin in the snowy forest and he sees that Luise Rainer's eyes are full of tears: it's because Alicita's uncle has gone away, and he's not coming back anymore, because now Alicita's aunt had a baby and he can't go to Luise Rainer's any more after work because he's married. And that would be the end and I don't know if Luise Rainer dies or not, it doesn't matter because it's the end and she can't appear in the movie anymore, but the little bellboy cried every night, very softly so his nervous stepfather won't wake up and shout at him. That was some slap the teacher gave the Chávez girl!, the poor Chávez girl is nice and she's one of the short kids, shorter than me in line, I'm the one who draws the best, Alicita too but not as good as me, I'm the best pupil and she comes next. Last year I didn't go to piano but I had catechism and I had to go to the nuns I don't know for how long. And tomorrow the González girl's birthday and big Paquí from fifth grade is coming, "it takes hard work to make a man" says Dad since he wants to buy me the big bicycle that I'm sure to fall off, Paquí's a big fifth-grader, she doesn't fall off, she's nice, sort of pretty but her face is skinny. Alicita pretty fat face, pretty teeth but the corner ones long like dogs' and Chinese Japanese eyes when she laughs. Sister Clara is the one I liked best, sweet and young, Mom never saw her, she never believed she was so pretty, just like Santa Teresita in the prayer book. The goody goody face she gave me from the first day of catechism, but after, when she saw I learned all the prayers and the commandments and everything but everything, she began to love me, she'd call me "the little priest," since I was going to be a priest and belong to the Church. We saw the priest very little and we didn't see serious Sister Mercedes until we finished the first little book of prayers: every single day at the nuns' school for catechism and I sure got my fill of the inside of that school, which is only for girls. Unplaited black drapery just like the nuns' habits, all the same black material. Sister Clara didn't scare me, in the first little book there were the commandments and the infant Jesus and the Kings, but in the second book they began with the end of the world. The end of the world begins with a storm. It can come any night. And you have to pray before going to sleep so's to be ready. And you have to pray even if it isn't the end of the world, because in the morning Mom and Dad might be dead, they die sleeping. The end of the world begins with a storm, while everybody's sleeping and you hear some faraway thunder. And there's a flash of lightning but nobody sees it because all the windows are closed. Then rain begins to fall. And the thunder is a little louder, like a storm, but nothing else. Until it gets really worse, and Mom gets up to close the water ducts so the flowerbeds won't overflow, and she looks because there are bolts of lightning, a lot, one after the other, and suddenly it looks like day and you see everything in the backyard, even the chickens stiff out back, standing up watching from the chicken coop. And the thunder getting louder and louder until one is like a cannon boom and it's already too late to do anything: a lightning bolt full of electricity comes down and sinks right into the middle of the square and the earth splits like a piece of coal. And one boy asked Sister Mercedes if the rain didn't put out the fire and she answered "It would make it worse," because "It would be raining drops of fire," and then who knows where we could go, because the houses would be burning like sandwiches from the rain on top and the burning earth underneath and everything falls down. And the González girl asked if the people couldn't go into the church and the nuns' school and she said no, "They would be doublelocked with key and latch, and the Father and the Sisters would be the first to stand before God on Judgment Day." Then they'll be the first to get the drops of fire which'll make holes in the nuns' black habits and the priests' black cassocks, and it's going to make holes in them, and through the holes you're going to see all the ugly stuff, the bunches, and the tangled up pipes, and the upside down green cup, in the digestive-reproductive system. But it's a sin to think like that about the nuns and the priest because they're God's servants, I think a different rain will fall on them, black drops of boiling tar which make holes but at the same time cover everything with black like when the streets are paved. Pity Sister Clara, she's pretty but green a goody goody face like Olivia de Havilland and I told her she was nice like Santa Teresita, she didn't scare me with the end of the world. At night it's better not to eat too much it gives you bad dreams and Mom didn't give me any more fried eggs at night, not even boiled. I can't sleep and then scary dreams, Mom and Dad turn off the light because they already read the newspaper, and sometimes I hear Mom read the newspaper out loud to Dad since Dad is spoiled, all the time about Tobruk and Rommel and Pantellería and I'm sick of it already. Paquita isn't afraid of storms. She comes every Saturday at naptime to play with me and my class partner. The best game is jungle. And now it's too bad the pear trees that looked like the jungle aren't there any more, early in the morning they cut them and when I got up I knew right away the trees had been cut, almost from the root and only a little bit of trunk left, you had to go all around the store so as not to go through the backyard and see them. I didn't come near to see the stumps, but all that axing must have hurt the tree, that whitish wood inside must be very soft, Dad, can you chew that soft wood? "No, don't do that" and Dad, do the trees feel anything? "No, they don't feel a thing" but they had to make the store bigger and Dad didn't want the trees cut and me neither. I'm going to try hard not to think about it anymore. And he didn't go by either to see the cut-down pear trees, he went all around the store so he wouldn't see, and I asked him if he cried since his eyes were red and he said that men don't cry, it was from sleeping. But I'd seen him when he just woke up and his eyes weren't like that, his hair all messy and his scratchy beard. Mom did the same as me, she covered her eyes and now the jungle is the barrels, all in rows, a board goes from one row to the next because it's the Amazon river. The crocodiles are hiding under the boards, the girl has to walk over and she falls from the board right into the river. She has to run so the crocodiles won't catch her, they can swallow her with their big mouths. And if they catch her, the good guys have to come and save the girl from the crocodile, but if the girl gets eaten up the game ends and all of a sudden everybody changes places, and the girl becomes the crocodile who's holding her but he lets go and runs with the good guys because the girl who was so good before will eat him now but I shouted "Let's change places so the girl's the crocodile" and she became a crocodile, they have those mouths that swallow a man in one piece and are scarier than lions, but even scarier are the carnivorous plants at the bottom of the sea. I thought Alicita was good but she's always winking her eye at her mother, or the González girl, "Let's change places!" I shout to Paquí and she becomes a crocodile, all of a sudden Alicita pretends she won't show me the drawing she did, and she doesn't answer me if I speak to her, and she tells me lies winking her eyes, and always with those pretty little Chinese eyes, and she laughs, and the pretty teeth Alicita has though the ones on the side are long like dogs' . . . but maybe they're not dogs', they're already more like crocodiles', and the nice smooth socks on her legs . . . but maybe if at that moment I touch them . . . they won't feel so nice and smooth as they look, they'll have sharp scales like crocodiles, hard and sticky so you can't stick a knife in it, the guys who fall in the water waste their strength trying to knife them in the back but they can't and that's how the crocodile gains time and eats them. You can only see the white yellowish part when you turn them over and that's where you can knife them. But I'm not going to think about that any more, it's awful. I know a poem in English. But the teacher doesn't know what John Payne sings in *Weekend in Havana*, and I wanted to learn it in English. Rita Hayworth sings in Spanish in *Blood and Sand* and Dad liked it, since it was a benefit for the Spanish Society that day: the Spaniard Fernandez came to our house to sell tickets and Dad bought one for himself too. Dad's not going to like it, oo how scary, he's not going to like it, and yes! a lot, he walked out glad that he had come "Now I'm going to the movies with you all the time," since he had forgotten all about his store bills watching the movie, and we were walking out of the moviehouse and Dad said he liked Rita Hayworth better than any other actress, and I'm starting to like her better than any other too, Dad likes when she did "toro, toro" to Tyrone Power, him kneeling like an idiot and her with a transparent dress that you could see her bra through and she came right up close to him to play toro, but she was laughing at him, and in the end she leaves him. And sometimes she looks wicked, she's a pretty actress but she's always betraying somebody. And Dad, tell me about the other parts you liked, which actress you liked the best, Rita Hayworth? in this way we could talk all during supper about the movie, and isn't that like seeing it again? and it would have been even better if we'd gone to the café La Union having beer and sandwiches, so if Alicita and her mother walked by I wanted them to see Dad all dressed up with his white shirt and navy blue suit that he never wears, and his face handsome without a beard and pomade on his hair. And I was about to ask him if we could go to the café but his employees from the store were on the corner of the moviehouse and I began to pull Dad away but he went over to them to tell them to see the movie and the boxing championship was on radio, and the championship and the championship, and I told Mom we should go to the café and Mom gave me a look to keep quiet, if we went we'd have to invite everybody and pay for them and I was about to say the same to Dad without the others hearing me but Dad told them to come home to have something to eat, a little sausage and wine and listen to the fight and talk talk talk about the fight and because of the fight those jerks didn't see *Blood and Sand* and if we had gone with Dad to the café, it would have been so great, eating white bread sandwiches, which are the most expensive. And he never went to the movies again, because he says even if he goes the store bills and IOUs and deadlines are staring him in the face and he can't see the movie. But *Blood and Sand* he got to see. Did the first grade teacher like *Blood and Sand?* I wanted to offer her candy but Mom didn't let me. In the back seats with her twisted-nose husband. I got to class late the first day of school when till the very end I thought I had to go ahah, the first-grade teacher had a real tight uniform like a corset around her narrow waist like in *Gone with the Wind* and high-heel shoes and curls and a pretty face like the dancers that dance in a row, not the betrayer face Rita Hayworth has: Dad says she's the most beautiful of all. I'm going to write in big letters the R of Rita and H in big letters, for background I'll draw a mantilla comb and some castanets. But in *Blood and Sand* she betrays the good boy. I don't want to draw R.H. in big letters. And school had already begun "Toto, go to the blackboard" which looked smooth from faraway but up close it was full of holes. The teacher moved my hand with her hand and the letters got drawn on the blackboard, and then she let go of my hand and there was such a big ring on her hand and I saw her teeth because she was smiling and another row of letters was on the blackboard. Mom never wants to put on high heels like her and I didn't turn around to fool around with the other kids, you have to always look at the teacher, makeup on her eyes and thin eyebrows and black curls on her forehead with a fancy comb full of little jewels and all the drapes of her uniform and on tiptoes with her high heels, and the shining earrings since they're gold and her ring, the shining on her comb from the little jewels, and shining so much you want to eat plum jam just the color of her painted toenails. And in the movies but always from faraway I say hello to her and she gives me a sweet little smile, Mom never wants to get near so we can stand there talking a while with the first-grade teacher. And I stood there talking on Raul García's path, for the second time; the first time walking on top of the wall I looked and there was Raul García chopping wood behind his house, he looked at where I was and we started talking, I asked him if he was from Buenos Aires so I could tell him I'd been to Buenos Aires and that I'd seen plays and I felt like asking him if he loved the Millan girl. The Millan girl is in mourning and she looks half-dead and Raul García is always with her since he doesn't work and doesn't have a mother, and the two brothers live with their father and wash their own clothes, the old man does the cooking and none of them work. When me and Mom go to the movies we always see one of them sitting in front of the door. Mom says Raul García spends an hour in front of the mirror combing every single one of his little curls, longer hair than anybody in Vallejos, when they first came everybody laughed, I thought he was from some circus that had just come to town, the thin brother with a green face like Sister Clara's, the father with popping eyes and Raul García when he dances at the club with the Millan girl he puts on a half-asleep look with his eyes closed because he's dreaming that he's dancing who knows where that it makes him look so happy in the court of Marie Antoinette with Norma Shearer who's wearing the highest wig in the world. And some boys go with girls for a while and then they leave them and sometimes they never leave them and they get married, if not with the trampy teachers that go with traveling salesmen, not the Millan girl. But she has fat legs and when she dances she leans forward so much she looks like she's fainting and I felt like asking Raul García, when I was on top of the wall, if he wanted to marry her, I don't want him to get married, he's more handsome than her, but he was chopping wood without a shirt on and you could see his boxer arms and strong chest like those bad gangsters, you felt like sticking the hard muscle of his arm with a sewing needle, or a safety pin, or a weaving needle for making rugs. I'll bet he doesn't bleed though, bodies with strong muscles are different. But when you look at his face, he looks like a good man who dies in the war. And all the Garcías get up at twelve and the nasty old man and the two bad-tempered brothers never talk to each other and chopping wood in the afternoon and I told him I'd been to Buenos Aires and he's never been there, I felt ashamed for asking him, "in Buenos Aires I went to the theater at night" and "I saw *The Merchant of Venice*" which we didn't see because it was the best play in town and there was never any tickets left. Mom told me the story. And he said how did such a little boy know everything so well and I almost told him I was afraid of storms, I'll bet he isn't afraid of thunder or lightning like the lumberjacks or the Royal Canadian mounties, how nice it would be to live in a cabin, because with all his strength he can kill the bears and if I faint on the sled in the snow he can come and save me and have a glass of beer ready for me in the cabin with white bread sandwiches that we brought from town, and I'd tell him all about Buenos Aires and then every night I'd tell him the plot of a different play and then I'd start telling him the stories in the movies and we'd play the game which movie is the best and we'd make a list, and then we'd play which actress is the most beautiful and which acts the best and which is the musical number he liked the best of the ones I told him about since he's seen very few: mostly gangster movies. Raul García should take the first-grade teacher out to dance, but she's married, if not that would be the best, because she doesn't have the piano legs the Millan girl has, and she's always wearing the highest high heels, and she's pretty and she's one of those who are poor in the beginning and have to start off as chorus girls and a gangster bosses her around and a boy in the gang falls in love with her, he's Raul García, and they decide to escape together and go through a thousand dangers, until they stow away in a ship that's going to Japan, in the cabin of a very old drunken sailor who doesn't realize it, and they have to get undressed, at first she doesn't want to but he starts kissing her and they decide to marry secretly before God in the middle of the sea, and during the day they hide in a lifeboat, and at night when the drunken sailor is the watchman at the helm they go to the cabin, then they get undressed and go to bed and go to sleep kissing each other holding each other tight, and she's not ashamed of being naked any more because they got married. And they give each other long, very long kisses for loving each other so much, and she's happy with Raul García since he's so good and not afraid of anything, while the gangster all he wanted to do was hurt her with his weeny, he was very bad. And they ask for a baby, she prays to Santa Teresita to make her have a baby, and she doesn't know if he's going to come or not, and the trip is so long it seems like it's never going to end, and then her tummy starts getting bigger since it's getting filled up with the milk she's going to give the baby, one morning she feels sick from so much tummy and she gets seasick and Raul takes care of her and tries to comfort her since she can't stand the trip any longer it's so long, in that lifeboat all the time, and they're in the middle of this when they hear a baby crying, they look at each other and before she was as green as Sister Clara but then she turns pretty, pretty from all that joy and she sends him to look for the baby, that God has left cozily hidden inside a coiled rope, and his father finds him and kisses him and takes him to his mother who begins to breast-feed him right away and the next day they come to an island of palm trees and she gets a *lai* and the police never find them again. Now I'm going to draw the posters of a detective movie and naptime never ends, tomorrow it's lucky it doesn't matter the backyard is muddy and we can't play because it's the González girl's birthday at four and all of us kids that can dress up nice are going. Mom promised she wouldn't sleep today and Dad didn't let her, till three today when I'll go to piano, those crummy sharps, and then English and then I'll play with Lalo a little and then I'll make a neat copy of the rule of three problem with the windmill example, not like the mill at the back of the store, a Dutch windmill is more like it, and the four big yellow crisscrossed wings and the landscape with little hills almost completely covered with tulips of all colors, Alicita said that's the flower she likes the best and she said she was being punished "Toto, you can't come to play" and I told-and-I-told Mom let's go to La Plata where they're showing new movies and the layer cakes are bigger than in Vallejos and there are toy stores I can stand in front of for a whole hour, and grandma's two-story house, the only thing they don't have are *lai*, like in the Hawaiian movies, and there aren't any tulips which you can only find in Holland and they can't send them because of the war. If Alicita starts crying her heart out one day because she wants tulips she won't be able to buy them because there aren't any there aren't any there aren't any. What you could do is draw one or even better, buy good colored paper and cut out red, orange, cream-colored, yellow, sky blue, violet, lilac, blue, pink, white tulips and perfume them and then she'll I don't know what she'll do, stick them on the wall, or keep them in her notebook or the best thing is that if all of them came out very pretty she could put them on with a bobby pin, a pink tulip one day, a sky-blue the next, in her hair, such pretty tresses, like threads of the shiny embroidered flowers in Mom's bedspread.

Seven, seven o'clock and the party's still going on, dark like twelve o'clock midnight nobody lives in this foyer, I'll stick flat against the wall and if Dad comes by he won't see me. Mom . . . don't tell a soul! Mom is at the movies . . . a lightning bolt is going to fall right in the middle of the party, into the González's backyard; if it had only fallen before the rumba "María de Bahía," the lightning bolt should have already fallen at the beginning of "María de Bahía." Mom . . . don't say a word to anybody! if I only knew where I'm not going to find him . . . at home or at the movies? the kids still at the birthday party, at the end they serve more cake, nobody's in the street at this hour, they could murder anybody on this road and there wouldn't be any witnesses, and all the appetizers at the grown-ups' cocktail, there's going to be a lot left over and is he home or not? or did he go to the movies with Mom? would he let her go to the movies alone? Dad. I can hide in this foyer like in disgusting Paquí's and Raul García's backyard, he wouldn't let Mom go to the movies alone, would he? maybe Mom's at the movies with Felisa and Dad's at home, so I can get into the moviehouse because Dad's not going to be sitting with Mom and find out what happened, it's a sin to lie and I'll have to tell Dad everything, no, Dad's at the movies, today he's at the movies, I'll get into the house and wash up and Dad won't find out that I cried, I'll walk into the bathroom, I'll go to the sink . . . and Dad is going weewee and I didn't see him! he'll find out that I cried at the González girl's party! and if he's not there? but he's always there after the movies . . . but maybe he went someplace else, maybe they called him for a game at the handball court, and what happens is that they began playing and they got so wound up that they challenged another town to play and then after they went on to another . . . and another . . . and tomorrow Sunday there won't be a bus to come back on. Alicita turned around with her paper hat and fringes and said to me (she had already gotten her cake) that it was gooey, it had so much butter, I sat next to her with the same hat, to have more hot chocolate and all the kids ran out to the backyard, Paquí acted like a grown-up and stayed with the grown-ups talking in the dining room. Running and bumping into each other and falling down so much that the González girl's youngest fat brother couldn't get up. And what will they do now? the party lasts till eight, I brought her *Robinson Crusoe* for a present. And the González girl's father came out to say the games were too rough and that it was getting a little cold, drops of sweat under their arms and he made us all come inside again: the one who made the most trouble and noise was that idiot Luisito Castro raising a lot of dust and what are we going to do inside? the grown-ups dance so why not the kids and I asked Alicita to dance following the rhythm and we did it fine not even knowing how, one song ended, another began and Alicita next to me saying who had the ugliest dress of all, and Alicita didn't get away to whisper with the González girl next to me waiting for another conga, and you twirl around for the waltz and in line for the conga, the rumba you swing and then Alicita went to the bathroom. The grown-ups' table! a pitcher full of cocktail and they gave me a sip: a pitcher full of lemon-colored water that burns the throat. And this is another rumba, "María de Bahía," the prettiest song for dancing! and just this minute Alicita had to go to the bathroom? nobody answers but there isn't anybody in the bathroom and the door is closed in the room upstairs: can you open a door in somebody else's house? and inside there was a girl who looked like Alicita, who had put on Alicita's dress, who hàd grabbed her in the bathroom and taken off her dress. But it was Alicita. Playing dominoes, sitting next to Luisito Castro. Those horses' feet. And she looked at me with those little eyes that always laugh. The four of them playing dominoes, the González girl and some kid from Castro's grade, with those little Chinese eyes she tells me she's playing secrets and that I had to go. I grabbed her by the arm, pulling her away to come and dance. And Luisito told me he'd break my leg and that I'd better scram, but how could that kid be so bad. Dad? Dad, Luisito says he's going to break my leg, but he only talks like that, but he's not going to be bad, he's not going to do anything to me should I have hit him before? would he have broken my leg? needles, Luisito Castro's kick is like hammering in a thousand needles all at once, he rammed his foot as hard as he could with his shoe on. And I remembered right away that I didn't have to cry, Daddy, Daddy, I didn't cry hard, the softest I could: if Alicita had turned around to look out the window at a band of some circus musicians she wouldn't have realized that it hurt so much I couldn't keep the tears back and she didn't turn around, right? Should I climb a palm tree? . . . and jump from one roof to another and give myself a big push with the bell-tower rope and fly like a breeze right into La Plata to see the store window where there are toys with lights, silly Paquí doesn't believe there are toys like that, and rubber ducks for playing in the swimming pool, and all different kinds, but there were no crocodiles so scary to see one in the swimming pool with those teeth, and if the same teeth grow on Alicita and Luisito Castro is around he's going to have to knife her, but I wish the knife would go into its hard, scaly back, which is the ugliest and ickiest part of the crocodiles, and you must knife them in the soft smooth yellow part underneath, too bad because after all the knifing the whole thing is a mess and it loses the smooth part, which is the only part of the crocodile that isn't disgusting or scary. I'm not going to play at Alicita's house again, when Luisito Castro's back is turned so he doesn't see me I'm going to knife him in the face on the side of his nose, and I was sure stupid to miss movietime, playing sometimes, forgetting, looking at Alicita brush her hair, the buckle, lots of caramel spread on a slice of bread, she tells me things, she laughs, she jumps up and down with her white socks, those little shining Chinese eyes glittering sparkling shining Chinese lanterns, but I can't go there any more, I'm going to try very hard and think about something else but Alicita plays store, makes scones, swings on the swing, swings her doll, there's always something to look at her for, the buckle, the plaited uniform, the smooth little legs, the Chinese lanterns, the vaccination, and I can't go any more and when I have to ask her for some homework because I was sick and missed school, well I don't care, Teté is coming, luscious Teté to play with every day at naptime, when she comes to Vallejos she's going to stay at my house and I'll give her everything I robbed from Paquí. Let's go Paquí, let's go if you're bored, let's get away from this awful birthday party, bored Paquí they didn't ask her to dance because she's too little for the grown-ups, let her get into trouble, bad awful bitch, so dark on the street coming back, and how do you like that, she didn't believe there are toys that run on electricity in La Plata, a while ago it was just as dark as it is now, Paquí's father is Paquí's father only and how come he isn't nice? he's a father of girls, or is it because he's nervous about his taylor's shop? And Mom is seeing *Her Cardboard Lover*, how nice and pretty those posters with rich people's houses and fancy parties is Mom alone at the movies? when are they going to show *Her Cardboard Lover* again? I'm not going into the house with my eyes all red from the kick "Why did you let yourself get hit?" Dad, "Why did he let himself get hit?" Mom, why did I let myself get hit, Mom? and if Dad would come by right this minute I'd close the doors of this foyer and how long does it take the redness in the eyes to go away? and there where the street light doesn't reach I already saw Raul García's shadow in front of his house half a block away, "How's things, Paquí, still the prettiest girl in town?" and he makes some faces and closes his eyes half way "Coming from a birthday party? and you didn't save me a thing?" and "Kid, what a pretty little friend you have" holding Paquí's chin, but I don't know when they met because Paquí's house is around the corner but there's no wall in between like his house and the backyard behind the store, and Paquí "Why don't we show Raul the backyard where we play?" but it was all dark but the best time to play boo is at night coming in the back door the three of us and it was so dark you couldn't see the stones on the ground and we tripped every few minutes and we came in near the barrels and Raul García told me to hide that they would look for me and he had brilliantine all over his little curls and his face wasn't the same, like the robbers in the movies, and just the same I went to hide, all the way back behind the boxes and the jugs. And you can't hear them looking for me and suddenly I realized they wanted to give me a big scare, tiptoe near and say boo! and I went running out and got to the barrels, can't see them so I climb on top of a barrel and then I saw shadows that went behind the old truck without wheels. And getting close to give them a scare, but instead of being quiet they're whispering, how icky in the old truck there might be a cat inside who wakes up and bites us and the screaming wakes up the mice and snakes and they all come out to get us, and Paquí and Raul García . . . they're saying the worst things, pure garbage, kissing noises and Paquí telling him she's afraid since he's big and she was already a young lady but still very young, and he says to her that she's afraid because she never saw what a man was like and that she should hold him to see how it was, and Paquí says she's afraid she would bleed and that afterwards he wouldn't love her any more and he would jilt her, and he says he wouldn't leave her because she's the prettiest girl in town (a lie, the first-grade teacher is prettier) and Paquí grabs his weeny and says she's afraid, and she didn't know that maybe it would only be a minute before all the organs of his digestive-reproductive system burst out from inside, and he asks her to let him put his weeny between her legs and right then I felt like shouting to Paquí to save herself, she didn't draw the digestive system of the bird and she doesn't know all the junk there is inside, what with those little bunches and that sort of upside-down green cup with the hard name "transversal section" of the bladder, and that mess of twisting pipes like a poisonous spider's body and Raul García with those circus curls is the bird, that half-plucked bird's head, and I was going to shout but all of a sudden I felt like having another piece of that awful icky cake with too much butter and all of a sudden I felt like listening too, and when I asked for more cake Alicita stuck her tongue out and they gave me another piece but I felt like listening some more that he wanted to put his weeny in her so that she couldn't move and right then and there take advantage and hit her and tear off her clothes to see her tits, and make streaks all over her with a knife and pinch so hard it hurts even more and make black and blue marks all over her body . . . until the worst moment comes when you see things inside men's bodies, the green cup that can spring out and bite, and the knot of pipes that twine around your neck and press harder and harder like when you get hanged, and that poisonous spider's body whose touch must make you want to scream louder than anybody, even louder than the girl who goes crazy in *King's Row*, and women can't scream because if someone comes they'll see he put his weeny in her and Paquí is a whore. And in the end that's what they are, Paquí's a whore and Raul García a bum, and I thought he was so nice, I could never play with him, and Paquí tells him she won't even let him put his weeny between her legs, only the day she gets married and he I don't know what he's doing, as if somebody had kicked him in the stomach he began to say ah-ah-ah-ah, as if he was drowning and Paquí was trying to break away saying he was dirtying her, that he's splashing all over her legs and whoops! she saw me spying and grabbed me and shook me back and forth and bullied me saying I was a tattletale and that I had to swear to God I wouldn't say a word, and she ran off Paquí, Paquita, I want to wait in your house, till I don't look like I was crying any more! Paquí! Paquí! who could tell me if Dad's at the movies? who would know if Dad's home or not and Raul

García came and grabbed me by the arm and said if I went and told anybody he would break my head, his face like a bad guy's without shouting so the neighbors wouldn't hear and cats with scabs in the backyard could come and touch him, because if you step on their tails they get angry and the mice come out of their caves, the mice that go into garbage heaps and eat the most disgusting things, like dead cats run over by cars, and the snakes can hear and come crawling among the stones, and there could even be big birds in the backyard that make a complete circle in mid air at top speed and come down on kids to peck them as hard as they can. In Raul García's bad-guy face, covered with such hard scales and Paquí's thin no-makeup nun face, they can't peck into the scales, that's the hardest part of all, the scales of the most evil animals in the world. And in the end of the world they're going to burn, Paquí's going to die crushed between the barrels and afterwards the mice will eat her, Raul García cut in two when one of the guys from the store chop him with an axe when they find out he got into the backyard, and Luisito Castro will sink into a boiling well of plaster, and the raindrops of fire will come down and burn only the bad guys, the good guys are in fields of gentle rolling hills in Holland waiting for the Last Judgment, and there's no more dangers there; and where the guy who married Alicita's aunt goes the drops of fire don't burn, they become silvery and light like confetti, and I jump out of this foyer that's so dark and he lifts me up in his arms, I tell him the red eyes are from conjunctivitis, he'll never know I let somebody hit me, because high up from where we are we begin to look at all the thunder and lightning that's falling on the bad guys and I'm not going to be afraid any more because nothing's going to happen to us and Mom waves to me that she's safe too, nearby, on top of another hill with the people of La Plata . . . and I hope to God Teté gets to Vallejos in time, before the end of the world so she'll be saved too, and the first-grade teacher, and Lalo, and at school we always draw and do a few dictations and after that I go to piano and then English and I have my milk and go the movies with Mom and we go by the little rolling fields of Holland and from there I can see if Dad's at home or if he went to the movies, and I look at Alicita's uncle whose face is as smooth and shaven as always and shinier than ever, like dolls, and his eyes are no longer a man's eyes but precious stones which cost so much to buy, and he holds me in his arms against his chest and holds me real firm so nobody can pull me away with a yank, and it would be even better if we were stuck together, because then nobody could pull me away from the other side: I'll be stuck to his chest then, and without him knowing I'll slip inside the chest of Alicita's uncle, and from now on nobody can keep us apart, because I'm going to be inside of him like the soul is inside the body, I'm going to be next to his soul, wrapped up in his soul. And you can see the hilly fields covered with tulips of all colors, which are beginning to shine under the silver-lined rain of confetti, shining like the plants Mom embroidered on the bedspread. And if God forgives Alicita, she's going to come to the little hills, and she's going to be happier than ever to find the tulips, she's going to pet them, and kiss them, and then she's going to run and give her uncle a kiss with a perfumed mouth from kissing so many tulips, and she'll kiss and kiss her uncle, and I'm going to be laughing to myself, but softly, because Alicita, not that smart after all, isn't going to realize she's kissing me.

VI

Teté, Winter, 1942

Tonight I'm going to be a good girl and not ask for an orange. Toto already turned off the light and Daddy waits to turn off the light until I finish saying my prayers because I don't like to live in Toto's house, it's not like Grandma's farm far away, horses in the yard and the fieldhands saddle them any time I want. I can't ride any more with the riding pants I have on in the picture, they're too small on me, and Sister Anta told me I should never ride like men, but in a riding skirt, sideways like women, although it's much harder and if the horse bucks he throws me off, and afterwards I'm in critical condition. Mom is in critical condition and if Mom dies she'll go to heaven and I'm going to pray all day long so she'll hear me and see that I'm a good girl and as soon as I'm in critical condition and die, I'm going to heaven also, to be with her. Toto received first communion last year and this year he almost never goes to communion, and Mita never goes to church since "I can't stand priests and nuns," she says. Mita's all right but she never goes to mass and I prayed for her to give me an orange, but I prayed for her to go to mass all the time, to pray for Jesus Christ who suffers on the cross, so that the thorns on his crown that are so sharp and stick him in his head won't hurt so much, poor Jesus is so good and the thorns keep sticking him harder and harder. If Mita prayed it wouldn't hurt so much, and the gall they gave him wouldn't burn his mouth, poor Jesus! I pray for Mom, so maybe I'm the one who makes her feel better, Mom has been in critical condition for a long time, and sometimes she says "I'm feeling fine" and she goes out with Dad and they walk all during naptime under the sun when it's strong, afterwards no, because if the sun goes away it's so cold that it freezes all the puddles and the next morning I like to jump on the hard puddles that go crackle, crackle, they all crack and it looks like broken glass, such pretty shapes, I picked up a little pointy piece and began to suck it like ice, and Mita said it was bad for me, that I could get sick and I said to her that if I got sick I would go to heaven with Mommy and Mita "nothing's wrong with your mommy, don't be scared, nothing's wrong with her, the only thing wrong is that she's afraid of dying, because they operated on her once and she got scared, now she has to take care of herself a little and that's all, your mom will bury us all yet." Does Mommy tell God that Mita doesn't go to mass and that I'm a bad girl, and that Toto is naughty and all three of us fall into a pit? and instead of learning how to ride on the new bicycle that's too big for him he cuts out actresses from the newspaper and colors them in with crayons. And Mommy tells God everything and God punishes us. A pit all filled with dirt. Because Mom is sick and she's good just the same and always goes to mass, it's a good thing she's going to heaven when she dies. If I prayed everyday like the Sisters at Lincoln maybe Mommy would be fine all the time, when I don't pray she's sick and stays in bed all day, and she complains of rheumatism, and she calls to me and hugs me. She's going to take a walk with Daddy to the park, real far, a whole half mile away Daddy says, Mommy's face has a little color from the sun, she doesn't wear rouge or lipsticks because she made a vow when they operated on her kidneys, but Mita wears lipstick and complains that Berto makes her go to bed at naptime so she can't go out for a little sun, her face is an ugly pale and she wears rouge. The Sisters at Lincoln can't wear rouge and can't go out and they're an ugly white, like Mita when she gets up from her nap. It's a sin to hang decorations on the white walls, at Lincoln I couldn't hang up the set of fans that Grandma gave me, but getting into the freezing bed at night I put an embroidered cover on the hot brick without asking permission. The other pupils use the coarse woolen school cover, their feet are frozen after kneeling and praying against their beds, finally they turn off the light and there's no more praying. Sister Anta had a grudge against me and all the time "Naughty girl, what are you thinking about?" and I wasn't thinking about anything, I was thinking about the white uniform and the white bedspreads and that in Mom's room at the sanatorium there were some paintings of yellow and green boats. The paintings are pretty but it's better without paintings, it's a sin to have decorations at school and it should be the same at the sanatorium. And Mommy didn't get completely better and Grandpa would never come to visit her because they almost never see each other since Mom got married, but me he does. And then Grandpa had the attack. Her bedspread is white too and I wasn't thinking about anything bad, why was Sister Anta suspicious? now she's right, now that Paquí told me the stork is make-believe and when we're big, men are going to grab us and put what males have into our tails, to have children, which you can have even if you're single, and Paquí and me we'll never go out alone, we'll hold each other's hand all the time. And I had to confess to the priest in Vallejos that they'd told me everything and he said only married women can do that, when they want to get a baby from the stork, which is make-believe. It's the biggest sin, he said. And I asked him if the biggest sin wasn't to kill, to let somebody die, and he told me that for a twelve-year-old girl it's more of a sin to let boys "fornicate" her, because to kill you need a knife or a gun, while to sin with boys you only have to think about it and it's already a sin. Paquita and me began to talk to Toto to see if he knew anything but Toto doesn't know a thing since he's a little younger than us but all the boys know these things, even the ones in first grade, and Toto is nine years old and still believes in the stork, he doesn't say a word but he keeps quiet. And Paquita began to rub one finger in her other hand making her fist into an ice cream cone and she said to Toto "Look what I'm doing, I'm putting my finger into my cun . . . guess the word." And Toto didn't know and it seemed to me he realized something because he ran away and didn't want to play with us any more, and he sure is always hanging around. But I was a bad girl again last night and asked for an orange. And it would've been better if Paquita hadn't said anything to him because once the girl on the corner wanted to wise him up and he told his mother. What an ass, when Paquita told me about men, I was glad. I'm not going to pray for the gardener or the milkman not to run after Sister Anta because then they'll lift up her habit and make her have a baby, afterwards nobody will know that it was my fault because I didn't pray, and it'll be all hush-hush, and she'll have to leave the convent, and if I come back again next year she won't be there any more since she's the only one that doesn't like me, all the Sisters love me and Grandma gives them the biggest donations for the new church. And I leave all the food on the Plate but I never talk during rosary since I pray for Mommy not to die. And it wasn't true that when the stork brought me to Mommy it pecked her and that's why she got sick, because Paquí said the stork is make-believe and that's true, because before Kuki was born in the country, Aunt Emilia had a big tummy and she sent to Buenos Aires for a loose dress that's called "maternity" in the catalog. So it wasn't my fault, and Grandma's always grumbling to the fieldhands "My daughter isn't well, she got sick after she had Teté" and I asked Aunt Emilia and she told me about the pecking. Then it's not true that since she had me she's been sick, but Grandma doesn't tell lies, I don't know why Mommy's sick . . . poor Mommy, this morning she was crying because Daddy has to go on the road again to look for wine customers, she's always crying for fear she's going to die and we're going to be left alone Daddy and I, I prayed all last week but she kept being sick and she gets tired just from brushing her hair, that's so long and beautiful, and she feels bad for the rest of the morning, afterwards she eats a little pudding and steak, nothing else because everything makes her sick, and Mita says you shouldn't be afraid of germs and Mita doesn't wash the salad in boiling water and doesn't boil the cups and the unbreakable glasses either. Doesn't even put the mattresses out in the sun every morning and beat them and wash the floors with the disinfectant they used in the sanatorium, and she lets Toto eat apples with their skin on. But every night I'm a bad girl, for wanting to eat an orange. And Mommy wanted the spray that was in Grandma's house for killing germs on the walls, that they bought after Aunt Emilia's sister died and left the whole room infected with TB. Grandma had a grudge, since she wasn't a close relative, she was a distant relative. Kuki and I saw her, it was strictly forbidden, she was in the back room next to the horse's yard, I was playing with the colt one day and I heard screams I thought it was some animal. It was Aunt Emilia's sister, stiff in bed, she was pushing her head against the pillow trying hard to breathe because she was choking, was she blue, she stared at the ceiling and it looked like she wanted to stick her nails into the sheets. A blue blue face. And I prayed every night since we're in Toto's house, four AVE MARIAS and three Lord's Prayers every night and Mom is still sick, "You have to pray with your heart in pain, Jesus Christ's pain on the cross" Sister Anta would say and last night I was ready to pray till I fell asleep, to pray more than ever with my heart in pain . . . but I fell asleep, and I prayed less than ever and now I have to pray since maybe Mommy's going to die from the pain in her arms and instead of praying all day from sunrise on like the nuns at Lincoln, I want to play with Paquita: at Grandma's the field-hands get up at sunrise, when the sun first comes out it's bigger than ever and now it's already dark and time to sleep but I'm not going to fall asleep; I should have been praying since they made me go to bed, as soon as Daddy turns off the light there's no more praying, Daddy wrote me a poem "My little girl is the sun" and instead of more praying I'm thinking about playing. The heart in pain hurts more and more as you pray. As soon as the sun rises the nuns pray and don't sleep any more, Mommy can't sleep but me yes I may fall asleep . . . oh, what shooting pains in my chest . . . I'm sick too, I'm sick, oh Mommy, please, I can't breathe, I'm dying, I'm dying, no, no. . . . No, Mommy, don't look at my throat, no, no doctor, no. I don't have white spots, I'm dying because I can't breathe, I'm already dying, afterwards in heaven we're going to be together, but now I'm dying because I can't breathe, and if they take me to the sanatorium the doctors are going to put a white kerchief on my head and take me on the stretcher to give me oxygen, but I'm going to die in the corridor and all the nurses will look at me, a sick little twelve-year-old girl never died on them, only old ladies, and they'll cry because such a little girl died on them, and they'll say I'm an angel, wrapped up in those white sheets, my hands will fall from the stretcher all stiff, and even if I can't breathe I'm going to keep praying for you, Mommy, because you're like that since you had me, ooh I'm crying because I love you, Mommy Mommy no, don't call the doctor, I'm already dying because I can't breathe and on the stretcher at the sanatorium I'm in even more critical condition than you, much worse than you. And if they come to give me those injections they gave you that I thought were for the stork pecking, don't let them do it, I'll die just the same because I can't breathe and first I grab the sheets because I'm choking and then when I'm about to die I grab you and squeeze very, very hard, and you die with me, God will want us to die together, God is good . . . yes, an orange, oh yes Mita, I sure do want an orange from the tree, Mita's going to pull an orange off the tree for me, oh yes . . . this one's good, I'll suck it, make a little hole in it and I'll suck it . . . yum it's good, now I can go to sleep and I'll be a good girl, Mommy, I won't make you angry. . . . Mita reaches up and gets one of the low oranges, and the tree is full of high oranges. Now I'll go to sleep, if the choking goes away I fall asleep like a good girl and sleep with the little orange and I won't be a bad girl . . . I'm not choking any more, in the morning Mita grabbed a big pole and knocked down a high orange, a lot of very high ones and some other low ones she can reach with her hand . . . Mita picks one for me every night. . . .

Toto, don't come, I have to go alone with Paquita, it's nothing to do with boyfriends, no, we're not going to look for boyfriends, go and practice on your bicycle, you still haven't learned and you've had it for three months already. He's always hanging around, that's all he wants to do, and collect movie ads and put them in order and one day his class partner got back at him because Toto didn't want to tell him where the gun was hidden, the boy threw all the ads, which are about a thousand, on the floor, that Toto'd been collecting since first grade, and he swished them all around. And I was afraid Toto was going to grab the broken bottle for watercoloring and stick it in the boy, but he didn't care because he remembered which of the ads came first and second and third so he put them in order again. And Daddy said that Toto had a good memory, better than mine, but I'm not going to be playing with those ads and coloring in the pictures of actresses in the newspaper. He'll never learn to ride the bicycle, Berto bought it for him and he can't even climb on without falling off because it's too high for him, but his partner doesn't even have a toy, only some hand-me-downs from Toto, and he comes from his house half a mile away, takes a running jump and gets right on top of the bicycle. Daddy says that drawing doesn't come easy to me but I get bored drawing all afternoon. Paquita gets bored too and every day she goes real far to get the homework at the Pardo girl's house, almost near the railroad tracks, she has to walk like seven long blocks but the Pardo girl calls to the Cataldi boy from the backyard and he comes and tells them everything he does with the maid and Paquita wants to take me but I don't want to see him since then I have to confess and if Mommy finds out it'll make her sicker and she stays in bed and can't go out to get some sun which she likes so much. And from her bed she tells me to do my homework and make drawings like Toto. The Cataldi boy's in sixth. Paquita likes the swimming instructor who spends every afternoon in the bar where the traveling salesmen and bank employees go, and they look at me with kissing faces, but I'm too young. One of Grandma's maids had a baby at fourteen, I'm twelve and when I'm thirteen if I let somebody do that to me and I have a baby when I'm just fourteen Daddy'll give me a beating and send me to Lincoln and Sister Anta will put me in a corner all day long. Paquita kissed the Cataldi boy. But at naptime it's still light out. I don't like him, he's not any taller than me, still wears short pants and already has hairy legs. But Paquita didn't wait to confess since there were too many people and she went for a walk and passed by the bar to see the instructor, I'm tired of hearing her say he loves her too, a big man like that. Paquí prays for the poor and the war dead, and that's all. Cataldi asked Paquí for a kiss and she said "yes," only if they were in front of the Pardo girl. And they always talk for a while over there, Cataldi tells them about big boys and what they do with the maids, he tells them everything if Paquí shows him her tail, the Pardo girl always shows him hers and she wants Cataldi to show Paquí what boys have so she'll see how water comes out when he rubs himself. They already saw it many times: I don't want to go, after lunch me and Daddy go to the center for a while to make Toto practice with his bicycle. Then we go back for a nap. Toto doesn't go to bed, he colors in actresses. And if his father would see him now he scolds him, but Toto hides and Mita doesn't see him either, maybe she'd tell Berto. Daddy does see him because he doesn't take a nap, he tests Toto on the order of the movie ads and meanwhile naptime ends, since if Mommy doesn't want to take a walk to the park Daddy doesn't know what to do, he doesn't go to the coffee shop because if Mommy needs him for something he's always close by, Mommy talks to him softly from the room, so that Berto won't wake up since he's sleeping with Mita in the next room, and if she needs an aspirin Daddy takes it to her and when she's not calling him he tests Toto about which movie came before the other. And at Grandma's in the country I never take a nap because I don't go to school and I get up late and at naptime the fieldhands take me on horseback with Kuki, around in circles in the backyard. Because Grandma's house has a yard that's like the whole square in Vallejos. And we have the manger of the cows and calves and little new-born horses, Kuki's colts and one that's mine, Grandma wants us to go see him now that he's big. But Daddy doesn't want to go because he argues with Grandpa. Daddy worked in a printing press in this town and published a newspaper and wrote long articles and sometimes poems with another name, sometimes they bought part of those pages for big-town newspapers because they said he wrote better than them all. When Daddy was a bachelor. And Toto never goes to mass "Your dad sold the printing press because of your mom" how does he know? I pray a lot every Sunday in mass and Mita lets him skip mass, he's very young to know grown-ups' things "Your grandfather didn't want your mom to marry your dad, because he was poor" and two years ago Grandpa became paralyzed. Grandpa can hardly talk because he has paralysis, he walks with a cane, and Mommy says he used to break in the stallions before the attack. The fieldhands made him very angry and he got the attack. Mommy always prays for Grandpa and not herself, she doesn't ask anything for herself, everything for Grandpa so he'll get better. Why did the fieldhands make him angry? And I have to pray for Mommy, so Mommy won't die because every morning when she wakes up she's sick, and she cries to Daddy that she's going to die and leave a little child all alone, that's me. Toto should pray for the infant Jesus in the manger, so he won't get cold poor little thing, his parents were poor and they didn't have a house and couldn't buy anything to cover him with. I prayed a Lord's Prayer for the baby but I have to pray more for Mommy, if Toto prayed for the baby it wouldn't be so cold until the Three Kings arrive because the infant Jesus goes through twelve days in the cold without anything to keep him warm. "It's worse to be a little parrot" naughty Toto said to me. They call them little parrots because they're like parrots, but smaller than mosquitos, like new-born green mosquitos, and last night when I had the night lamp on going over the multiplication tables, it got full of little parrots, the little light bugs that only live one night. And tic-tac they bumped against my notebook and sometimes pic-pac when they bump against the wall, since they don't look where they're flying. Toto "They only live one night," and I couldn't believe it, while the light is on they go around in circles, but then they have to die. Around the night lamp and when I turn it off, I start praying but Toto "I'm thinking about the end of the world" and doesn't he pray? When I turn the light off the little parrots rise right up to the ceiling and stay there together and afterwards in the morning they're all dead on the floor, Felisa sweeps them up and the pan is full of little green bugs. I didn't scare them away, let them have a little fun poor little things, because tomorrow they'll be dead, Toto "Did you see the little parrots pic-pac against the wall, it's because they don't see, like they're blind" and I don't know how they figure out who's the mother, and Toto "They must fly together and never separate so they'll know which one's the mother and which is the baby" while the light lasts and then they go to the ceiling and stay together until they fall dead, but it's lucky they all die at the same time, the mother doesn't die one day and the next day the baby who's left alone, you see, it's not worse to be a little parrot, stinker! it's worse for poor Jesus who suffers with the nails and see Holy Mary suffer at the foot of the cross crying for him, how dopey you are, every day there are new bugs, at night they lay their eggs and all of them die, and the next day new little parrots come out . . . but the one who laid the egg is the mother and she died, "See, Teté, the baby parrots are left alone, without anybody to take care of them." Is that why they're so silly and let themselves be caught right away? they're not like mosquitos who escape so well, and Toto "Now do you see that it's worse to be a little parrot . . . ?" they don't know how to fly, they bump into my notebook, but they're animals, Toto's an animal too, he doesn't care a fig about the infant Jesus freezing in the manger and the only thing that bothers Toto is the end of the world. I wonder how big the dogs are in Grandma's house now, the puppies must be big. But last night I was a bad girl. I asked for an orange again. Grandpa would get up when the sun rose, and sometimes when it was still night, so he would see the sun rise. Daddy made a poem for me that said I was the sun, now he doesn't write any more for the newspapers, but sometimes he writes a poem for me. Daddy loves me so much, when Mommy dies and then me poor Daddy is going to be left alone, he said that when he goes as a traveling wine salesman and doesn't see me for many days he's going to disguise himself as a saint, like the cover of the book *Saint Francis of Assisi*, so God will believe he's a good man. Daddy doesn't say that seriously because God realizes everything but when he's disguised he'll talk to the other saints and ask them who's the prettiest little girl in the world and if she's a good girl, and the saints can see everything they want to. The saints can see Grandma's stable, and how the little colt grew, they see Toto hiding to color in the faces and dresses of the actresses, and they can see Paquí: God doesn't look at bad things, when Paquí goes to the Pardo girl's house and Cataldi comes I'm not going to look, because

God will push me off heaven and I'll fall faster then the parachute jumpers, I'll make a hole through a volcano and sink right to hell. And there I stay forever and now if I go one day with Paquí and listen when Cataldi tells everything and afterwards I confess, I can still go to heaven or purgatory, because I have time to confess before I die, but if I look after death, no, like the good angel Luzbel who turned into Lucifer. Toto always wants Daddy to be with him at naptime, if Daddy doesn't take Mommy out for a walk, Daddy takes me to school every morning, and on his way back he spends some time at the coffee shop, then he goes home to be with Mom, and then he goes to wait for me when school's out, then lunch, and then he's with Toto, and sometimes he makes Toto mad "Which actress do you like the best? the good one in *Blood and Sand?*" and Daddy answers "I'll take her" and then Toto "Rita Hayworth, the bad one?" and Daddy says he'll take her, and Toto gets mad and says that he has to say if he likes one or the other, and Daddy just says "I'll take her" and never answers the way Toto wants. Toto likes Norma Shearer. And in the afternoon I do my homework with Daddy, then he takes me to the piano lesson, and he talks with the teacher's father and they always argue about religion, because Daddy doesn't believe in priests and the teacher's father doesn't even believe in God. And Daddy stays up at night because he can't sleep and when I believed in the Kings he'd tell me he saw the Kings arrive, since it's nighttime and he can't sleep from his nerves. But he doesn't want to work in the printing press since it doesn't belong to him any more and for that he has fights with Grandpa, or why else? Daddy doesn't have a father or a mother, he told Mita that Toto was too attached to her, and Mommy lay down in the bedroom, me and Toto played store the day we came to Vallejos and right away Toto wanted to play, all he wanted was to play, and he doesn't have Paquí all day, now Paquí always goes to the Pardo girl's house, Toto always hangs around the bigger kids, he doesn't want to be with the little ones like him. Playing store, and Toto would make a list of clothes to sell and he put I don't know how many things down, he wouldn't let me do anything, he wrote down everything, and I didn't want to go on playing since I got bored, and I went to call Daddy, Toto gave me a pencil and paper, and he had another pencil and each one had to make a list, but he filled his paper up right away and I didn't know what to put, and Daddy got a little angry and told me to hurry up; because he saw Toto's list. Toto had put little linen dresses for dolls on sale, and frilly laces for infants too, I went to the bedroom to ask Mommy for a handkerchief to blow my nose and Daddy was telling Mita and Mommy that Toto only wanted to play with little girls and only wanted to go to the movies with its stuffy air, and Mita said he was right because Berto had already said the same thing: boys have to play with boys. And when I came back from the bedroom Toto had a surprise, a little box full of . . . things he'd robbed from Paquí's dolls, and that he'd give me for a present if I played with him every day. And at the best part Mita came in, she had to wash Toto, she always washes him later but that day no, and Toto didn't want to because he'd been waiting for me ever since he knew I was coming to Vallejos, he didn't want to take a bath, but then he did if we could play in the bathtub together but Daddy didn't want that because Toto is a boy. And while Mita was washing him in the bathtub, I spied through the little key hole, but I couldn't see anything because the bathtub is on the side and with the noise of the faucet Mita was saying to Toto that she forbids him to play store any more with Paquí's stolen things and also color in actresses because those are not boys' things and if she saw it again she was going to punish him and he would have no more movies. And Toto didn't cry, he didn't say anything, didn't stamp his feet like when Daddy makes him angry but it seemed to me that Toto wasn't there any more because only Mita was talking, and I thought Toto had escaped from her and she didn't realize it, because she kept talking alone, but then when she opened the door the two came out and I don't know how Mita washed his face with what soap because Toto was so white he looked like the face of the actresses when he colors them in with the white crayon and hears Mita and Berto getting up from their nap and doesn't have time to color them with rouge and they look dead. I saw Aunt Emilia's sister dead, she was grey-white, she died of choking from TB, after two years in bed. I don't know, maybe Mita dunked his head under the water while she was washing it and that's why I couldn't hear Toto talking, he was choking to death and becoming grey-white. Toto'd try hard to come up to breathe but Mita'd push him under, she's stronger because she's bigger, right to the white bottom of the bathtub, Toto looking up at his mother with his eyes opened, and goggling blue from choking, his face bluer and bluer and his hands trying to stick their nails in the water, it's better to stick your nails on the sheets, it gives more relief; until he is dead for once and for all and no longer tries to save himself and ends up looking grey-white. He's always trying to make as if he's perfect because he gets all As in school. But he stopped having his way. God punishes those who don't pray. And afterwards he didn't want milk or soda, and Mita made scones that day since it was the first day we were there, but Toto who always eats it all up didn't even want one, he came to tell me we couldn't play in front of anybody and that we should go to the chicken house but I didn't want to, and he took everything and went alone, the chicken house was already full of the chickens who come in at five to go to sleep when it gets dark, and the chickens and the rooster were already settled down on the racks, and Toto began to scare them away, so he could play and hang up the dresses like in the store, and he hung them from the racks where the chickens were sleeping, and the maid heard the squawking and thought there was a thief and called Mita and Mita called Berto because she was afraid and she went with Berto and they found Toto in the dark hanging many things from the racks, he had already hung ribbons from Alicita's hair, a little old Tirolese hat of Paquí's, and some brand-new tulle dresses from Paquí's best doll. And they didn't spank him because Berto didn't let Mita spank him, but he said that he was punishing him for disobedience, and he couldn't go to the movies. And he gave him a good lecture, Paquí told me they never never scolded Toto because he's the best in the whole school, he doesn't break anything and he eats everything, he's never sick and never gets dirty and they never scolded him and they always let him play what he wanted to because he never broke anything anyway, but that was a scolding, and Berto told him he wasn't going to play store any more and color in dresses and faces . . . because otherwise . . . he would put little skirts on him and send him faraway from his mother to go to nuns' school. He had to get everything together right away and in the dark he didn't see a little pink-tea tulle dress and he left it there, the next day I found it nice and clean without chicken doodoo and I kept it. And they forbid him to go to the movies for a whole week, for disobedience. But the punishment didn't do anything to him because the next day he woke up with temperature and didn't go to school and stayed in bed, and he couldn't go to the movies anyway even if he wasn't being punished, because when you have temperature you can't go out; and he didn't have white spots in his throat or indigestion because he didn't have a white tongue, he didn't have anything but the doctor said sometimes you need temperature to grow. But he didn't grow at all, Mita's frightened because he doesn't grow and after the temperature he didn't grow, the squirt. And the only thing he wanted in bed was that they tell him the story of *Intermezzo*, and the only one who entertained him a little was Paquí, but she had to go. They should tie a long rope on Toto's head and another one on his feet and pull from side to side to make him grow. From one side the helper at the store could pull like when they played at pulling out a tree by its roots, and other strong men could pull from the other side even though he'd scream and cry. And if Paquí wasn't there the only thing he wanted was for them to tell him the story of *Intermezzo*, the movie that was being shown and he couldn't go see it because of his temperature and anyway he was in a fix because he was being punished, he wanted to see the new actress who was in the movie and who he'd cut out in many pictures, and Mommy told him the story, she liked it, and Daddy told him the story, and then he asked Mommy to tell it again, the part of the kiss at the concert that he'd cut out, when the actress wore a long sleeveless dress. Toto doesn't want to play with me any more, if Paquí's there yes, if not no. Daddy doesn't like night either because he goes around and around in circles and can't lie down to go to sleep. Toto goes to sleep almost right away, if there isn't any storm. Paquí isn't afraid of the end of the world. I am a little, but during the day not one bit. Toto is. His class partner isn't at all. Mommy no, she says she hopes to God it comes soon. Mita doesn't believe in the end of the world. Daddy does, but he says that me and Mommy will go to heaven and that maybe he'll be saved from going to hell, he'll go to purgatory for a while and then he'll come to us. Mommy prays for Grandpa, so that he'll get better. And if Mommy dies I'll keep on praying for her, and who will pray for Grandpa? No, I'll pray for Grandpa because Mommy is going to be in heaven, she doesn't have any sins, but if she went to heaven because she forgot to confess something, how will I know? because then she'll be waiting for nothing in purgatory. It would be better if Grandpa died so then Mommy will pray for herself, because she doesn't have to pray for Grandpa to get better anymore, and I'll pray for myself and I'll see Cataldi and that's it, so then I'll know how it is and afterwards I'll confess and there isn't any danger that afterwards I'll look down from heaven, and I'll pray a little for the infant Jesus, and if Toto receives communion once in a while he's going to pray a little too so that the little baby won't be so cold in the manger, and so Jesus won't suffer on the cross . . . because the pain of thorns is the strongest pain, it must be something to have nails stuck in your hands and feet, must be bad enough to scream and cry real loud, like when my finger got caught in the door. Mommy . . . are you sick, Mommy? . . . she's complaining, poor Mommy, all day long, she walked too much, and now she's in pain, and I prayed, but Sister Anta said it doesn't matter how much you pray if you don't pray with your heart and feeling in your heart the pain Jesus felt on the cross, and maybe I wasn't feeling the pain and all that I prayed was wasted . . . and that's why Mommy's sick again, Mommy, Mommy . . . oh Mommy, let's go to Grandma's because there they eat supper when it's still light out, Mommy, here in Vallejos we eat supper at night and after supper it's dark out and you have to go to bed, and if I don't pray with pain in my heart my mother will die, because I'm a bad bad girl and I don't have a heart like in the little picture, the heart with the torch and inside the Virgin Mary sits on a throne, dressed in green, with the little baby among red and yellow flames, inside a dark red heart. In the backyard it's all dark now, if I don't pray at night and God sees me . . . and Daddy is about to turn off the light to sleep and you can't pray any more, then I'm sick, so so sick, I can't breathe, I'm choking, the angels are already coming to get me, only me? and now Mommy is praying and I hope to God Mommy dies soon so she'll come with me to heaven and from up there we'll pray for Grandpa, so he'll get better, then I'm going to play again with the mother dogs and the little puppies that are already big, anyway there are lots of them, I can give one to Kuki, and I'm going to have all the puppies I want and we can eat in the afternoons when there's still light, and if I pray, but I'm going to be dead already, if not Grandpa won't get better . . . and I have the choking, ooh, like Kuki's aunt who died of TB, I saw her choke to death, oh how ugly it is, when I can't breathe like that, and I won't be able to see the puppies that grew, oh well, the only thing I ask you Daddy is that you don't turn off the light, not yet, wait a minute . . . wait! . . . just a minute! . . . I'll promise to give Kuki the little colt and Paquí the set of fans if you don't turn off the light . . . because if you do turn it off, all the little parrots will die, they'll knock their heads against the wall, don't you see, Daddy? don't you see I didn't get to pray with a pain in my heart? Jesus Christ's pain on the cross! . . . and Mommy might die, yes, really . . . and I'll give Paquí all my dolls if you don't turn off the light. . . . No, no, you say you won't but I know you're going to turn it off . . . you say "no" but you're going to turn it off . . . and in heaven they know everything, so Mommy's going to learn the truth about everything; that it was because of me she died and she won't love me anymore. . . . Don't turn it off!!!! . . . the choking comes from inside and I stick my head in the pillow and I turn blue, completely blue!! . . . Mita? oh yes, yes an orange and I won't be a bad girl anymore, I'll be a good girl and I'll go to sleep, has she already gone? don't let her go! what is it like, Jesus Christ's pain on the cross? is it stronger than choking? . . . Mita is good, she went to pick off an orange from the tree so I won't choke . . . the reddest orange, higher than last night's, from the top of the tree, make a little hole in it and I'll suck it, it's full of juice, and then I'll throw it away . . . how painful is choking? . . . until I suck out all the juice, and now I'll be a good girl and go to sleep, Daddy wants to see me healthy, he says to me like a little sun is my healthy Teté "My little girl is the sun," and I wake up with color in my cheeks? Those clean, shiny, almost red oranges that are on the tree in the backyard, next to the well, if it isn't from the tree I don't want it, so I won't turn grey-white like Aunt Emilia's sister, or blue like when she choked . . . maybe Aunt Emilia's sister prays for Mommy in heaven oh! if Aunt Emilia's sister would only realize and pray for Mommy! Mommy would be fine then, she'd pray for grandpa, and go to sleep, because now it's time to go to sleep, yes, I'll be a good girl, and tomorrow I have to go to school . . . I did my homework well, and Toto did the drawing of a little dog for me, and how silly, he colored it blue. . . .

VII

Delia, Summer, 1943

If they told me it's because she loves him, well . . . But she don't love him, that bald-headed potbelly. Doctor Garófalo, a holy name around that house, the old lady is peeing in her pants she's so proud her baby daughter married a doctor, not in a million years did she dream Laurita would marry a doctor. Every few minutes over the backyard fence it's "a cup of oil," "three potatoes for the soup," "an onion," and give it back when the moon turns blue. Laurita has a good figure all right, but such a plain face, and after her first kid I guarantee she'll get so fat it'll turn your stomach. She borrowed window shades from Mita, for that set of diamondpanes in the hall so the sun wouldn't beat down on the lunch guests after the civil ceremony. On a Saturday, what a pity. The bank clerks come out every evening around eight, when everybody's already left the promenade, on Saturday of course they're through at three and at six I cross the promenade to the store and you can see them at the bar, it's the only day. The upsweep makes you look older and I wanted to have one myself, it looked good on Choli, the whole afternoon with paper curls missing my Saturday stroll because of that lucky bitch's wedding. Poor Turk, Yamil is so goodhearted, Mita says I shouldn't let him go. Yamil always sees her at the drugstore, "What a refined lady," he's always harping on that, "a better neighbor you'd never find," of course she's a better neighbor than Laurita, and when there was trouble Mita was the only one the Turk would go to for advice. "Yamil, if you love the girl hold your ground, tell them religion is for comforting people, not for making them miserable. Say you met Delia, a good girl, and you love her and now you can't bear to lose her, and that's that." Dirty old Turks, how they teach a Turkish girl to keep a clean house, I don't know. But if the Turk could see what a foul-mouth Mita is at home . . . A serving dish full of such delicious canelloni, she makes it with white sauce, and expensive really expensive meat for the filling. People who spend money on food like Mita, I'm telling you . . . once they had vegetable canelloni too but Berto doesn't like it, without meat nothing doing, he's got to chew hard and sink his teeth into a chunk of meat, not like eating soft meat stew all the time or veal cutlets so thin you can't see them, at home the same old story, Mom, Dad half-filled with coffee and glasses of water at the bar, common stew wouldn't do for the Turk, he takes good care of his gut. One price at the hotel, no matter how much you eat. Bank clerks don't exercise either, but López didn't get fat in the hotel, now even less at home with that bitch playing the little girl with the lace collar and all, the old cow. No waist whatsoever and stumps for legs. Younger than López she can't be, I'm nine years younger, he was twenty-six when I was seventeen. The Turk is twenty-five and I'm twenty-one. Big-nosed Turkish agronomer, hairy, potbellied, eyes like fried eggs, if I love him it's because he's good. Good and dumb, no, not dumb, he makes like he's dumb, but I'm sure he wasn't dumb with the Antunez girl. Dumb with the smart ones, smart with the dumb ones. López is smart with the smart ones, dumb with that dumb wife he got himself. Laurita is smart with a doctor, doctors are the smartest of all, but doctor Garófalo looks dumber than the dumbest grocer. With a grocer for a husband I would dip my hands into the nuts and prunes and open myself some cans of juicy peaches and take everything I needed for paella, canned mussels and squid, what I should have done that day was come in the middle of lunch and for sure Mita'd make me taste it because they make a lot, the maid serves out huge platefuls, twice as much as at home, and you can eat still another plateful from what's left over on the table, and I didn't think of going, in a cloud thinking about López maybe, no, that's over, who needs him, that jerk of a wife he brought home. You can't do any shopping with a *peso* . . . I can't spend more than a *peso* today, some greens for a salad, a bone for the soup. I still have some thin noodles and a little chopped meat for meatballs, Dad gets one, Mom three and three for me. Fifty cents worth of chopped meat is enough. If I could only get Laurita's mother to give me back everything she "borrowed" ha, from those hectic days before the wedding "Oh, excuse me, Delita, I simply can't think straight these days." I'd get a free supper out of it, one whole *peso*, and with the thirty cents more that I can add on I've got 1.30, the price of a pair of stockings. One pair a month! And nothing was left over from lunch, otherwise a little fruit and we could have a better supper, grapes are still expensive. But I had to take my picture, the old Turk wanted one, now that they lost out they try to be nice. "Mr. and Mrs. Mansur: If I dare to address these lines to you it's because I love Yamil very much and I can't stand to see him sad and without energy for anything. I know that you oppose him marrying someone from another religion, but I can't do a thing about that, I was born Catholic and even if I embraced another religion, deep down I would continue feeling as I am, a Christian. Surely you wouldn't want Yamil's wife to begin her married life with an act of hypocrisy. That's why I want to make my position clear, hoping that you will soon arrive at a solution, even though it may be adverse for me. Yamil cannot be at the mercy of our whims one day longer, he does not deserve to have anyone play with his feelings." Mita's letter would convince anybody, I copied it over neatly with my own writing, you can hardly understand Mita's writing, like a doctor's. "Moreover, I beg you to consider this matter with sincerity; Yamil has never deeply felt the Moslem religion and I'm sure he wouldn't mind being baptized as a Christian, so we could have a Church wedding. And doubtlessly nothing would favor his career more in the Ministry." And if his old folks didn't give in? who else would be left in Vallejos? Forget the bank clerks, for every one who marries a girl here, twenty don't. Sampietro, Burgos, Nastroni, García, all of them married girls from their home towns, the jerks, nobody's good enough for them here and then when they come back from the honeymoon the wife is always some creep, here they play around with the young kids and then they show up with some godawful old battle ax . . . López's is the worst, and how Mom believed the lie, that he already had a son back in his home town and had to marry the woman, now Mom says she didn't believe it, "I didn't believe it, honey, but what could you do if he didn't love you?", but thank goodness the Turk came along. Now I know, the worst thing is to let them put their hands below your waist and above your knee, on the neck, face and arms it's OK, or the legs from your knees down. Otherwise, it's easy to lose your head, once is enough to know what they are. I could eat a good bowl of ravioli tonight, homemade ravioli filled with calf's brains and spinach, sprinkled all over with a fistful of grated cheese. That's the way to fill your belly, and two glasses of wine and wash the dishes right away, I'm already falling asleep, and drop into bed with a heavy stomach, in a daze, and in two minutes flat I'm snoring away. Every evening after López left I stayed a while longer alone in the vestibule, in a daze, eleven o'clock at night, and right to bed and I'd be snoring away in two minutes flat. We're only three people and spending more than a *peso* for supper is too much, this month with the cost of the photograph. That damn stationery store, in the new spot, big as hell, prettiest stationery store in Vallejos and always empty, not a soul comes in, Mom stuck there all day behind the counter, she could just as well stay home. The dress for Estela's wedding next month, I have to get one . . . then I can use it for the club dances, a pretty taffeta dress. So the Turk won't cool off. According to Mita it was a stroke of luck to find the Turk, how could she know? unless Mom told her, maybe Mom asked her advice about the stitches, maybe she thought Mita, being a druggist, knew how to do the stitches, it seems Mita knew about López because she said I was so lucky to find Yamil, because he's so good and not at all tense, according to her beauty doesn't count, the main thing is good character. "Yamil is so goodhearted," she always says, but when good heart starts with the rough hands all over the place you'd change your mind, he doesn't know the first thing about caressing, but before he knew even less. I caress him. "Caress me like I caress you," and now he caresses better. I caress him like López used to caress me. Taffetan is softer than taffeta, it's a mixture of rayon and taffeta, I'll make it tight, I tried on Estela's last year, a fresh feel like silk and it costs less than taffeta; when you cross your leg the skirt gently caresses you all the way up from knee to hip, no man has such a big hand it stretches from knee to hip, what you shouldn't let them do is put their hand above the knee and below the waist, the hand rising underneath the skirt, how dumb you are when you're young. Mita always complains that Toto doesn't grow, "Stinker why don't you grow?" she said to the child right to his face, and he went to his piano lesson and she says to me "This son of a bitch doesn't grow." Mita with the belly that sure grows all right and you can notice the load, I tell her "Mita, you're only hurting yourself" and she "so I let it come out once in a while, after all the aggravation these shits give me." One four-letter word after the next. If I tell Yamil he won't believe me, and Estela who says to me "Let's go to the Model drugstore, I really like to talk to Mrs. Mita, she's so refined," before, not now . . . I didn't recognize Héctor when he came back this summer, Mita had to buy him everything new, nothing fit him, still a boy when he went away in the fall, but when classes were over he failed every course, Mita was so angry she didn't want to buy him a thing. But when they got off the train Héctor looked like a model, his face was even handsomer than López's, a big guy like the Turk. And the tongue of a truckdriver, hanging around that boardinghouse all day with his father in Buenos Aires. Coming off the train if it wasn't for Mita and Toto I wouldn't have recognized him, Mita bought hardly any clothes this trip, she came back with the same two-piece suit she went with, but she left a lady and came back a foul-mouth, she's already in her fifth month. Héctor infected everybody, he said to Mita "Iron the pipes of my new threads good so I won't go out looking like a yokel." And Mita understands every word and I told her he's a truck driver and she says to me "Don't be a yokel" and laughed, and Berto in a bad mood since he just woke up from his nap couldn't help laughing either. Héctor infected everybody, he says Yamil is a wet blanket. Toto didn't catch it though, "What a nice pair of jugs" Héctor says to me, and I didn't even look at him as if he hadn't said a word, and then I asked Toto if jugs were the chest or behind and Toto made me swear not to tell anyone "It's something to do with the reproductive system, Héctor must have seen while . . . the maid next door, and at night they meet when everybody's sleeping, and then he comes back to wash himself and shows me and asks me if it grew because the more you . . . the more it should grow" and I "Don't be a slob and tell me once and for all what jugs are." And instead of answering Toto says "I don't tell Mom anything about Héctor. If the maid died, Héctor would go to jail, but if she didn't bleed to death the first time she won't any more." Is that boy crazy? That's why what happened the day before yesterday didn't surprise me. And I kept still, and he "Héctor told me he wanted to eat your cherry but you don't know what the cherry is" and I didn't know if it was the one in front or back and asked him and Toto "The cherry must be the back of your tail what covers you up so grown-ups' weenies don't keep getting into your body when that sort of poisonous spider shows up" and I went along with him "Why does Héctor want to do that to me?" and Toto "It must be because he's angry at you since you're the fiancée of the agronomer Turk who at first you said was a bullfrog." But

"Toto, are you crazy? where'd you get all that from? you must be lying" and looking away all red in the face "I told you that to see if you'd believe it." All fibs so as not to let on he didn't know what jugs or cherry meant, what does it mean? I'd be embarrassed to ask the Turk. After that what happened the day before yesterday didn't surprise me. He didn't learn one of Héctor's words that Toto. With his agronomy friends Yamil always talks like that, he told me. "What does yokel mean?" I asked him the two of us alone in the vestibule, "What you want me to be" and he grabs my hand and puts it where he shouldn't, dirty Turk. What do I care, if that keeps him happy. As long as he doesn't use that oily brilliantine, I took care of that. If he doesn't touch me where he shouldn't let him enjoy himself, I can touch him all he wants, it doesn't do me any harm, that doesn't make you lose your head. Pomade is better for his hair, curly and on top of that greasy, strictly lower class. I'm safe until they come back from surveying in Los Toldos. Let him bring candy, not earrings. I spent too much on lunch today, squash isn't filling, so far to walk, more than nine blocks to that farm to save five cents, and I finished off the heel of my open-toe shoes, the leather was already worn, now I can't get away with the half-sole, one and a half *pesos*, yokel that I was. I didn't remember to check the sole. A white dress never again, wash it every four times if Yamil's not here and if he is every two times it gets so dirty with hand marks all over the place, in summer his hands sweat soot. And with each washing it gets more and more worn out, and soap doesn't grow on trees, the week Yamil goes to do surveying I wash it less. But if Yamil's here I don't buy fruit for supper, he takes me out for an ice cream. If it only lasts me till after Estela's wedding, and then I'll use the taffetan for dances instead of the silk print which I can wear every other evening when I don't use the white, the white is when the Turk doesn't come with his hands. If it doesn't start falling apart after so much washing, or if it does I'll use it for the house, and the one I have now for the house I'll use for cooking since they take on the smell of grease and frying. That hole-in-the-wall stationery store was always full, always, and Dad in a bad mood because he couldn't get out to the café across the street, and now not a soul comes to the new store. A block and a half away from the other joint. A tile floor and the best of everything. But people don't want to pay the rise in prices. Laurita ordered her wedding announcements at the Spaniards' store, she could have come to us. I'll waste a whole bar of soap if I wash the cooking dress, sorry I didn't make an apron out of Dad's old shirt with the frayed collar, let the bums we gave it to get some good out of it. Doctor Fernández charged so little. How stupid Pirula is, being a maid and giving into someone like Héctor, who's not going to marry her. Every night. López was handsomer. What a lie he told me. Didn't that idiot realize Héctor wouldn't be seen with her on the promenade? Everybody knows the maids dance the last dances at the fairs. Those students. When the girlfriends have gone home, the students run around the fairs inviting the nobodies to dance. How could that jerk of a Pirula not realize the first time, gets hot easily the moron. She shouldn't even let them take her home, or touch her hand, or kiss, she must have felt like touching Héctor's face, real white not like the trash that could marry her, white but tanned from the swimming pool and on Sundays one of the best soccer players. Felt like touching the clothes Mita bought him the best in Buenos Aires, what she planned to spend on Toto she spent on Héctor because Toto didn't grow and still uses last year's. Héctor outgrew everything. But he's not handsomer than López. He has longer eyelashes. Now López's hairline's receding, Hector has a lot of hair and a sad look when he's looking into space, his eyes are always kind of moist, but not when he's talking and looks straight at you "I know that a guy gave you a line and then dropped you and now you're sewed up." Héctor seems to be reading my mind, looking straight through me with those piercing eyes, deep inside, where my thoughts are written. I once made López put on his bank glasses, and I took them off, an owl-face with the glasses, so serious he looked like the hardest worker of them all, not very long eyelashes but black, and green eyes and no spots on the white, some tiny threads of veins you could hardly see. You always have to keep at least one arm free, a maid like Pirula letting Héctor, a student, touch her, you got to be more than stupid. She gave in the very first time and now she's finished, she can't help herself, besides one time or fifty, it's the same difference. He must have looked straight at Pirula until he realized she felt like it and then she couldn't refuse because it was true. When López'd look at me there wouldn't be a thought written in my mind, I'd think about looking at him and looking at him and looking at him, a face without faults. At the table I feel like cutting off the bridge of Dad's nose, wouldn't it be great if his face was made of putty so I could squish it together and make it wider, that long, narrow face I got from him, eyes yellow from smoking and eyebrows stuck together, plink plink plink pluck those hairs out one by one even if the stubs come out, or burn them off with a match. Not a freckle on his face, a little turned-up nose, thin little mustache, white complexion, not even a little tanned from the sun, stuck in the bank all day, and that night at that moment it seemed I could stare at him and see behind his eyes what he was thinking; I wanted him to go back to the hotel so I could listen to the serial, I told him I had to iron but he refused, he didn't want to go back to the hotel, if he'd been living with his family OK, he'd go, and me all the time fighting off his hands with one arm, but he hadn't seen his family since the summer before when he went to Puán and he'd miss them if he returned to the hotel so early, he still wasn't sleepy and he'd be alone in the hotel, deep in his mind it was written he'd throw himself on the bed and cry his eyes out, only I could keep him from thinking about his family and crying, and deep in his mind it was written that he loved me because "Go to Puán for a few days, ask for leave," I said, "No, because in Puán I'd miss you" he answered, and I gave him a big kiss and threw both arms around his neck, like wings, two wings longer than my arms, to wrap him in; and at that moment it seemed we'd never never separate again, not even when it was time to go to the bank would he go, not even when it was time to go shopping or to eat or wash the dishes or sleep; and after his eyes got red, like full of veins from crying, but it's not that he cried, I cried, from the pain, and our eyes got that way, the two of us, because our hearts were choked with blood. That day I was able to read his mind, but afterwards I never stared into his eyes again. Poor Pirula, could Toto be lying? They mustn't send Toto away to school, Choli said, he won't be able to take it, Mita wants to send him away, Berto too. And the argument at snack time: "I'm not going to that awful instructor any more" Toto whining, "Shut up, you pest, can't you even learn to swim?" Mita serving him a cup of coffee with milk, when they got back from the pool, Héctor, Mita and Toto, the table piled with French toast, canned pears, toast and butter and jelly, in a second the piles of toast were gone, and the maid brought more, I had some French toast but no pears. "This little yokel doesn't want to dive," "I can faint if I bump against the bottom," and Mita telling me "I never thought this would happen, I asked the instructor how Toto was doing and he told me he's behind the rest of the class because he doesn't pay any attention, to the dive or the crawl, he always wants to have his head out of the water, frog style. Choli, the patience of a saint, taught him that last year." Mita was so angry she forgot to make me taste the pears to see how they'd come out, and I didn't go to the instructor anymore either, only one class, and on the very first day he wants you to dive with your head under water, the bully. Yamil says he scares people, the fat lady from the grocery store slipped and let go of the edge, right to the bottom, then she came up choking and went down again and not till the third time she came up did the instructor hold her up. I couldn't believe Yamil, but the fat lady didn't want to go any more either, Yamil says the instructor watched her sinking and laughed to himself. "Are you going to the movies this afternoon, Mita?" "Yes, I already saw *The Constant Nymph* in La Plata but it's wonderful, especially because she's so delicate" and Toto doesn't want to be left behind "They're always talking about the nymph but there isn't any, it would be nice if she came out like a ghost since the nymph is the soul of the girl, but she never comes out, I didn't like it, Delia, don't go" and Mita "No, it's a lovely movie, go see it, there's a lovely part when they, the three sisters, are discussing art and they go crazy over painting and music, the three who play the sisters are simply divine!" And five pear slices were left in the bowl and Toto grabbed all five, and Héctor had only eaten the one he'd grabbed with his fingers the moment he sat down at the table, "Mita, look at this shitty squirt, he took them all!" and Mita "Give three to Héctor" and Toto "I'll do it if I don't have to practice bicycle riding," he's had the bicycle since winter and he still hasn't learned how to get on it alone because it's very high and he doesn't grow and he's afraid of falling, and Mita getting angrier and angrier, "If you don't exercise you don't develop, you stay a runt!" if the new baby comes out disobedient like Héctor and Toto she's in a fix, Héctor and his boxing "From all he eats the runt'll be nothing but ass and belly if he doesn't get some exercise, but just try dragging him to the Baby Boxing at Playland." "*You*'ll be nothing but ass and belly, and you know what, Mom, yesterday I saw his weeny all cut from bad habits, the maid next door must have done something to him with her kitchen knife," out of the blue Toto started screaming, and I didn't know where to hide, Héctor threw the cup of milk in his face and Toto ran to grab Héctor's just-ironed suit and threw it into the well, and as usual he locked himself up in the bathroom. Mita, scared silly, went to tell Berto about Héctor's sore and Berto almost peed in his pants laughing. I got red in the face it was so embarrassing. What did Toto mean by the knife? After that, what happened the day before yesterday didn't surprise me. Later at six o'clock Yamil and I saw Mita and Toto arrive at the movies, they'd already seen *The Constant Nymph* in La Plata, "So lovely," I cried, the Turk as usual "Let's sit way in the back" and there was nobody way in the back, I had to hold him down all during the movie, he hardly even saw half of it between closing his eyes and looking at me, he laughed at my crying "Women always cry about such silly things," silly things my foot, there are times when you cry because you can't stand it any longer, and I began to realize López was avoiding me more and more, one day for one thing, the next for another and then that Friday night he didn't put his hand under my skirt, after not seeing each other for so many days, so I took his hand and put it between my legs and he pulled it away "We shouldn't do that any more, it's wrong" and me "Why?" and him "It just is, that's why," and he left. He left, just like that, the heel. . . . López! López! López! I didn't know then that the Sunday before had been the last time, the last time in my whole life, I still believed it was just one of many nights and in the dark vestibule I complained about his being sort of grouchy! And after five days of not seeing him, all of a sudden, on Friday, he didn't want anything to do with me, his hometown wedding day was coming up and all of a sudden he didn't want anything to do with me. I never thought that Sunday would be the last time, if he'd told me so I would've concentrated on every minute of it so I'd never forget it, I would have held him so tight my fingers would've hurt, and I would have told him all the things I'd do for him, not eat, not sleep . . . that I'd convince him to come back . . . But that was already too much to ask, I would have been content with simply knowing it was the last time, I could have worn my best dress for him, and silk stockings, and no holding back on the perfume, the vestibule floor shining like a mirror lined with flower pots—ferns—I'd borrow from Mita. . . . I would have played all I had. And I wouldn't have waited for him in the vestibule, I'd have waited for him on the street corner, that way I'd see him coming from a block away and he'd get bigger and bigger until he'd be so close

I'd start backing up, counting one, two, three, four . . . the time it would take him to reach me in the dark vestibule and take me in his arms . . . eleven, twelve, thirteen, fourteen . . . and as little as he was, faraway from the corner, he's so big now, in front of me, that he covers all the space in front of me, he covers all of me with his head and neck and shoulders, but I look into his eyes that reflect the waxed floor of the vestibule and reflected in the waxed floor is a man, where he begins and the floor ends nobody knows and my head starts swirling and I hold him tight so I won't fall. . . . And a big bruise I gave myself, for being just a foolish teenager. Mita's right that good character is the main thing. In my house there'll be a schedule for everything, and Dad won't come home after spending an hour at the bar because he didn't know the time and the Turk won't come late because there won't be any food to find, unless he looks in the garbage can, that's where he'll find it. And no maid, so never mind his calculation about not having enough for summer vacation, we'll have enough. That animal, he wants to spend it all on food, three courses like in the hotel, so much more expensive than one good big dish of one thing. I'll tame him, at lunchtime I'll say "we have three courses: lamb with sweet potatoes, meat potato pie and a homemade dessert," bread pudding, which is like a third course. And I'll make him eat lamb till it's coming out of his ears, and when I bring the pie he won't be hungry anymore, we'll just about eat half of the bread pudding so for supper I have the potato pie and half of the pudding, it's all set without spending a cent, and I'll keep fooling him till he forgets he had three courses in the hotel. Cold cuts, ravioli and beef stew at Mita's the day before yesterday, and cake roll with custard, a pity Toto ruined everything. She must have stuffed that swimming instructor good, starving on a boardinghouse diet, I told him I couldn't practice anymore because I had things to do at home, Mita kicked me under the table, of course, the guy still sees me at the pool, the bully. But he won't see me on Sundays, that's for sure, I'd rather be caught dead before I'd meet up with López and his wife. On the lawn sunbathing I looked to one side and there was a man with such a white body and I looked at his face, and it was him, the face I've kissed a million times but never without a shirt, the body was like that of any man, I thought it would be more delicate, and his wife came out from behind and from then on they didn't see hide nor hair of me at the pool on Sundays. And Berto made the instructor drink more wine than was good for him so he'd talk about the Páez girl, who he never wants to talk about, and Berto "Old man Páez sent his rifle to be fixed, he says a fox gets into the chicken house every night" and the wine didn't do the instructor any good "I'm around chickens all the time, you ought to see how this town is afraid of water" and he looks at me and dumb Toto gets red in the face and says "I'm not afraid of water, what I'm afraid of is the bottom of the pool," and Berto "But if you pay attention to what they tell you, you'll learn how to dive without bumping your head," and Toto "I already bumped myself once and that's plenty," and Berto "If we weren't at the table you know what I'd do to you" and the instructor "you don't learn to do the *crowl* either, and you don't have to worry about hitting bottom swimming," and Toto "It's pronounced crawl," and Hector "the genius has spoken," and Mita "he was learning fine at the beginning but then the diving came along and he got stuck," and the instructor "no Ma'm, what's wrong with Toto is that he's . . . jealous, jealous of the other boys who learn while he doesn't" and the instructor stood up and sat down again, nobody knew what he wanted, and then I realized the wine had gone to his head because he almost belched and I looked at Toto and he was white as a sheet. Then Berto "It's not nice to be jealous, the instructor is very fond of you, he always asks for you when you're not there, he likes all the boys the same" and the instructor "but I don't like jealous boys, or chickens, only women are afraid" and Toto's hand streaks to the cake knife and Mita screams and so do I, Toto stuck the knife right into the maid's arm just as she came near to take the dessert plates away. Nobody budged. The knife went into her arm near the wrist and then fell to the floor. A jump and Toto was already scrambling out when Héctor caught him by the arm but when he saw a furious Berto heading straight for him he let go. It's a good thing the girl covered her stomach with her arm, otherwise he would have killed her, this way he only cut her arm. If that boy's always so tied to Mita's apron strings, how did he become a murderer? And the maid who's so nice to him, why did he take it out on her? The tablecloth covered with blood and the poor little thing didn't even say "ouch," tears in her eyes, Mita bandaged her right away and when Doctor Fernández was about to come and give her a few stitches I got embarrassed and left. . . . And I wonder if doctors keep secrets, if the Turk found out, poor thing, how upset he'd be. Stupid things only a foolish teenager gets herself into. And all that's left are the hard feelings, that's what you end up with. Hard feelings eating you up day and night. For what it was . . . After he'd leave I'd sleep like a log till eight, no sooner was my head in the pillow than I'd be snoring away. Sleeping like a log every single night. In the morning I'd get up, have my *mate*, think about the night before, sweep, dust and mop, go to the butcher, the grocery store, go by the stationery store and you always have to buy thread or rubber bands or a dish towel at the five and dime and there I'd have a chance to ask Estela if she saw him going to the bank that morning, cook, wash dishes, take a nap . . . it's getting nearer, nearer to the hour, sew, take down my curls, take a walk around the promenade to get Mom, supper, put on my makeup, brush my hair, get dressed, leave the room, the hallway, the foyer, the vestibule, the street door, on our little corner I wait, and smooth down my dress, five, ten minutes go by and no one's on the street, still nobody, I count to twenty, thirty, forty and a man is coming, he's turning the corner and coming this way and it's not the policeman on the corner, it's not Mr. Nobody, or the newspaper boy, or the errand boy, or the Turk, or Héctor . . . it's him, green eyes, sweet little nose, the words written deep in his mind "If you make me go back to the hotel now I won't be able to keep from crying" and me "Go to Puán for a few days, ask for leave" and him "No, because in Puán I'd miss you" . . . that's me, not Laurita, not Mita, not Pirula, not the constant nymph, but me . . . And I throw both arms around his neck, I look at him, touch him, hear him breathe and I breathe and the two of us breathe, his sighs, or mine and it doesn't matter if I stop breathing since he can breathe enough for both, and he's inside me in the raw flesh and who knows where he begins and I end? that means he loves me, that he wants to see the inside of me, and reach to where it is written all over inside me that I love him so much, so much, so much; and I'm the best one for him and we'll never separate again and then he's really going to know what I think and I won't have to tell him that for his sake I'd throw myself off the Buenos Aires obelisk, and break into a thousand pieces just so he'll keep living and thinking of me and in the end that's all that matters to me, that deep in his mind it is written he loves me more than anyone . . . and without me he cannot live and will die from heartbreak . . . or whatever . . . whatever he feels . . .

oh my God, till when, what day, what hour, what minute is he going to make my life bitter, damn the moment I met him. And let him die if he wants, not that I'm going to die too, and if I do die it doesn't matter either, because everything's already gone to the dogs and life is a glorious pail of shit, fuck the bitches that burfed these bastard men a thousand times over. And even if I do sleep bad at night I still have to get up in the morning and if I don't have my *mate* I get drowzy and if there's no sugar I have to go to the grocery store and day after day of dust storms if you're not sweeping from morning to night you drown in the stuff, I wonder how Mita got the carpenter to fix the door so the dust wouldn't get through the cracks. As soon as me and the Turk set up house I'm going to get the doors fixed too. So Mom won't have so much work. I cook and Mom cleans and washes and Dad in the store, enough of that bar nonsense. So I'll be able to save on a maid and we'll have a lot for food and some extra for summer vacations, one year I'll see Mar del Plata, another Cordoba, another Mendoza, I'll do it while there's no kids; if they turn out to get the Turk's nose I'll die. Boy will I stuff that Turk, and I won't be far behind, the only thing he won't eat is pork, Mom and I when he's off surveying we'll make a good roast pork one night in the patio, no work at all, a little salad, plenty of wine, so full that I can't move, drowzy from the wine and roast . . . quick wash the dishes because I'm falling alseep already and as soon as I finish the dishes, jump right into bed, and with a full stomach I don't think about a thing because I'm already out, sleeping like a log till the next day.

VIII

Mita, Winter, 1943

And I'm not letting Héctor bring a single chum this summer, because if they start kicking that ball around in the backyard I'll kill them: fifty-nine degrees in La Plata this winter, and in Vallejos the plants in the new flower pots stood fifty degrees without freezing. You close the canvas shades at the end of the patio, open the glass doors and you don't see the bare backyard anymore. High ferns and indoor plants around the orange tree and a lot of blossoming branches of marigold on the ironwork over the well. And from further away, where the tangerine trees are, there'll always be cool air from the wet ground since the sun doesn't get in. It was the best place for the white arums, shady all day long. When the summer comes we'll eat in the patio every night, the air will be cool from the trees. And every day off to the pool, nothing worse than expecting in the summer. White all over with arums in the midst of winter under the bare tops of the tangerine trees, you can hardly see the lilies against the wall, this is the last time I'm planting them, white and dark violet; gloomy cemetery flowers, that's what lilies are. Toto and Héctor took white arums to the cemetery one day during winter vacation when it wasn't so cold, all those miles on bicycle. I'll never get up the nerve to go. Long naps in the winter and the whole newspaper, and two, three, four chapters of a novel every night, until I can close my eyes, and he spies on me, Berto pretends he's sleeping but I know he realizes when I cry, until I'll manage to forget, but how am I going to forget? I think maybe he's asleep now. You walk slowly twenty blocks going and twenty back a different way, you don't feel the cold walking under the nice two o'clock sun and the exercise is good for making you sleep at night, instead of a nap, and just two blocks from home the dirt streets begin and at four blocks the huts and a little more and you're already in the country with a little farm here and there. Not a leaf is moving today, yesterday the pampa wind started blowing a bit, so cold, and in another month the walks will be over, unfortunately, your mouth and nose get dry from the dust the wind raises, when spring begins in Vallejos. Have to wear dark glasses from the morning on to go outside, the glasses make the high storm clouds look black and the whirlwinds of dust reach over the houses, one day the dust is going to end up burying the houses, unless the strong winds stop blowing from west to east. They blow all over the pampas but they never get to La Plata, at the most a little breeze, and when the girls take a deep breath on the university street, they get dizzy with the perfume of the trees, one block before you're there the orange trees line the pavement from Fifth to Seventh Street and in front of the main hall the little square is full of orange blossoms in the spring and your head has to be as clear as a sheet of blank paper when exams are near, don't you breathe in that sweetened air from the trees, because it makes you feel like closing your eyes and opening them again somewhere else, riding through a forest in a coach, the Vienna woods, when the birds wake up in the morning and the sun rises behind the thickets that hardly let a few rays through, with so many trees the sun can't get in till a breeze moves them and they cover up one spot but leave another open and the rays of yellow almost white light gradually get in between the branches of dark green leaves, that are black at night and light green in the morning. What are the trees in the famous Vienna woods like? A little green grass thanks to the rains in Vallejos this year, and at the end of the street where the joint United Spain is you can see the broom farm, not the farm itself, just the two broom trees covered with yellow flowers and the farm disappeared, making pills this morning the sulphur was precipitated into a test tube of chromic acid and I felt like having broom flowers. Branches and branches of little yellow flowers that the Czech woman gives to me only, the little farm house shines inside, how can you compare a Czech or German woman with a dirty Spanish one? The good taste in cleanliness, gardening, housework, desserts made with fruit from the farm and Toto with his mouth full of mulberry pie looked at the tablecloth embroidered cross-stitch in many colors and he looked at the Czech woman and then at me as if to say she couldn't have designed the edge with peasants holding hands and jumping so the sparks from the bonfire in the center of the tablecloth won't reach them, the fire in green with little golden tongues, looks more like the sea than fire, waves with their tips burning. We kept looking and looking at the broom and the Czech woman telling me about all the illnesses she had since she set foot in Argentina and she didn't know what to give me first when I promised her the salve. More than twenty blocks away and coming back Toto carried a good bunch of broom and me another, and Toto told me the whole plot of *Hold Back the Dawn* on the way there and coming back he was going to tell me another one I hadn't seen, two months in bed, and almost every afternoon visitors talking nonsense. Nonsense about this one who gave birth, and the other one, and it didn't mean a thing to anybody anyway, yeah, that's the truth, it didn't mean a thing to anybody, and everybody forgot and now it's like nothing had happened. And on our walk today, about a heel who pretends to be in love with an innocent girl, a teacher, to escape from his poverty in Mexico and get to California to make it big, *Hold Back the Dawn* is the title. And coming back I told him about the Czech costumes and the fire on the tablecloth and the magic Jewish dolls and mad scientists. His eyes wide open, "more, more" he wanted to hear. Without a single defect, a perfect being was what the scientists wanted. Broom instead of sulphur in the test tube and the purest ruby red for the color of blood and drops of mercury to make the eyes shiny and a fresh apple for phosphorus in the brain, a dove's wing for good nature and something for strength . . . bull's hoof, into the test tube, to give whoever deserves it a good punch, and not run away . . . and to kick the ball over the goal harder than anyone, and have the skill not to fall off the bicycle even though the seat is high. But from the highest star, from higher than the stars we fell, the angora layette, and flying with our imagination is so easy, such illusions, the little face, how handsome he was going to be, the people who stop me on the street to look at him, the stuffed toys Toto wants to bring him so he doesn't get hurt, and Berto who looks him over and doesn't find not one fault because the baby is darling and strong and with a kick he can break all the windows in the hallway. I thought I was going to see *Hold Back the Dawn*, but it was the day I was admitted and the week that followed Toto didn't go to the movies either and afterwards it was better he had spent that time in the movies. A good thing I didn't send Toto away to boarding school. The landing of Maximilian and Charlotte, the bad omen in the palace garden, the firing squad and Charlotte opening the window so her husband's soul would come in, all came out very well: seven movies in picture cards to begin the new collection. "The *Juarez* pictures are the ones that came out the best" and he put them first in the whole pile. For tomorrow we have *Rage in Heaven* that he'll tell me about during naptime, let's see if it takes us all the way to the mill of the big farm. On the way back I don't know. Before, the first in the pile were *The Great Ziegfeld* cards, the title in letters like on a curtain, the sad telephone scene, and dancing scenes as fancy as can be, the lamé dresses, immense feather fans and long white tulle curtains that fall in cascades. Out of my mind with that pest of a Teté, down the sewer is where the other picture cards ended up, or was it because of the fights with Héctor? I threw them all down the sewer, the new *Juarez* cards aren't half as good. If Choli finds out I threw out Toto's picture cards she'll kill me, why is it that you lose the knack for drawing? Choli was here in the winter, then Teté and her parents, but I didn't get to tell Choli I was expecting. And Toto if you count the vegetables and fruit and meat he eats he'd be a fort, how was Héctor able to get so big? so badly fed in a boardinghouse, if fevers could make you grow Toto would have already grown. I was in my fifth month the beginning of summer, the sixth always nauseous, the seventh and that warm wind and dust and if classes didn't start in the fall who could have put up with them and their fights. At school some ragamuffin must have told Toto you can kill with thoughts, he asked me if it was true, and about the evil eye. And everybody has something to say, nobody wants to keep quiet, "It's better not to give the baby a name right away if he's born wrong, because afterwards he's harder to forget," everybody says, an angel face, not like a new-born baby, Berto and Toto thought, a very big baby, at the beginning Toto didn't like the baby's face, he says to me "the baby isn't so handsome" and I tell him it's because he's not too well, and there's some danger, and Toto says "If he dies it's like *The Great Man's Lady*, when Barbara Stanwyck's new-born baby dies on her" and I calmed him down saying he wasn't going to die and "If he dies it would be like in a movie, don't you see?" he says to me, and "If you could choose a movie to see again which would you choose?" Toto asked, and I read his mind and said "Hmmm . . . *The Great Ziegfeld*, did I guess right?", and he said "No," but then he said "Yes, *The*

Great Ziegfeld, me too." I think I'd die of sadness in the movies if I had to see *The Great Man's Lady* again. The nurse had so much to do and Toto would watch over the baby when he felt sick, all those days watching over him in case he had to call the nurse, and fanning him too, a baby they say was beautiful, and me on the other side of the room not allowed to see him, that room with the peeling beige paint, so ugly but worse with the vases of artificial gladiolas that I made her take out, I wasn't going to put up with homemade paper flowers for a whole week, I prefer the empty shelves against the wall, peeled as it is, and me on the other side of the room not allowed to see him, never, never, a mother who doesn't see her son because he was born with a breathing defect but he's beautiful, weighs almost eleven pounds and has a perfect little angel face "It's better for you not to see him, so you won't suffer and have bad memories" and I insisted yes, yes, I was going to see him the next day, or that very night if he got better. It seems Berto sensed something, Toto didn't want to go to school but Berto sent him, it's lucky he sent Toto to school that morning and he came in for a little while at noon, and said that now he liked the baby, I cried so much when I told him he'd almost died on us that night, and I sent him to English classes and that way he didn't see anything, God showed Berto the way, God in a manner of speaking because I don't believe God exists, being the way he is. Who knows where Choli is this winter. A good thing I didn't send Toto away to boarding school. Choli stands all those months without seeing her child, because of the sales trips, so she can pay the son's tuition. All the time talking Hollywood Cosmetics, but she can't see the boy not even on Sundays. Not to that closed-in boarding school downtown but one with more air, so he'll do exercises which Toto needs, Berto "and be faraway from your skirts," and I would have been alone all this year, and wouldn't I have had to take my naptime walks alone? Boys become men when they go to schools away from home, they say, so wouldn't I have lost my boy? at the end of classes would he have come back to me a man? and what right do they have to take a son away from his mother like that and return him in whatever shape they like? Fate can deprive me of whatever it wants, I know fate can take what it wants, when it decides to, but while I can avoid it they're not going to take my son from me to send back a big clod who's ashamed to go to the movies with his mother; Héctor went to

Buenos Aires with his father, and back for vacation he was ashamed to give me a kiss, and he left in the fall a little boy and came back in spring with hair on his legs, full of pimples and his nose swollen and again he went back, but the last time didn't even matter to me and when he came back a third time nobody recognized him, a man, I don't think there's another boy as handsome as him in Vallejos, a pity he's such a devil, "It's enough to look in his eyes, that sad look he has when nobody's noticing, to realize how good that boy is deep down" Berto says, and I don't know why he has that sad look if he's got everything he needs. Choli would go crazy over the new ferns in the patio, how I wish she could come and chat a while, with everything blossoming, flowers and more flowers in the middle of winter thanks to the arums it's all white in the corner where the sun hardly gets in, and with all those arums in the garden it was a pity not to take a bunch to the cemetery. It's not that Héctor doesn't have a heart, but he didn't want to bicycle to the cemetery during winter vacation, it had already been two months and home-grown flowers seemed more meaningful to me than bought ones, not for the money of course. And Berto "Tomorrow I'll take them in the car, since I have more time" but Toto had already cut the arums on his own, "Make them like a fan, like *The Great Man's Lady* when they put flowers next to the cross on the ground" his eyes almost in tears and Héctor "enough dramatics" and Toto "Because you didn't know him and also because you're an animal" and Héctor "And you, you little fag, when you cry you think you're in a movie." Cats and dogs, and the fighting is nothing, the worst part is that Berto forbids us to cry each time we remember. And where can you go during winter vacation? Everybody stuck in the house and the piece of chicken I serve one the other one wants and if there's no chicken and nobody is fighting "Fatso Mendez isn't coming to training today" says Héctor, and Berto "He played badly on Sunday" and Héctor "It's already the second time he's gone to get her at the ranch and when she gets to the midwife she feels better" and Toto "Her baby is going to die on her" and Héctor "Where did you get that?" and Toto "I heard the midwife say that at the drugstore" and me pretending it didn't matter "When? it's been months since the midwife's been to the drugstore" and Toto "You were in the back room preparing a cough syrup and you didn't hear her" and me "That's not true, the midwife isn't friends any more and she never comes to the drugstore now" and Toto "OK, I can't remember who said it, but he's going to die!" and Berto "Why don't they make Doggie play inside instead of Fatso?" and Héctor "Doggie's no good in forward" and I already knew that Berto was going to give me a side glance and how could I keep it in, all the plans we had and the hope that he might live, night after night, day after day, and Berto "The trouble is Fatso doesn't want to pass you the ball even if you're in the best position" and I ran out of the room, I just couldn't stand the midwife any more with that mug of hers coming to say he wasn't breathing any longer, the last thing I expected because it had been a bad night, but it was day and the weather much better, the first cold days of autumn but if the sun comes out it's very mild and how, I say how could this happen at three in the afternoon, a little baby who had been able to hold out all night could stop breathing at three in the afternoon; I was able to eat for the first time, at lunch, and it agreed with me, Toto came after school and I cried so much telling him that last night the little baby had almost died but now he was better and Toto went to English class and it did me so much good to cry a little, it calmed down my nerves and maybe I could doze a little thinking again that I was going to think about the name again for the christening which was better not to think about they said to me when he was born sick because then he's harder to forget, and what name could I give him, there are so many. The midwife caught me with my eyes dry, not a tear was left, of those tears of relief thinking he was going to live, and the midwife comes into the room, that room I hadn't liked from the beginning, and she tells me there's nothing left to do and I ask her why this nonsense, this crazy talk, and she answers that the baby isn't breathing anymore. And she stands there looking at me. And not one tear was left, there was no longer any reason to cry I thought, even my throat was dry, and there's nothing but the bars of the bed to hold on to and wring your hands on; the midwife didn't say a thing, it seems what she did do was rush forward and knife me with a scalpel and I hold on to the bars because I don't want to touch my chest and feel the sharp edge of the scalpel, but I can't stand it a minute longer "there's nothing left to do" she came to tell me, and she carved me up good like a butcher, "because he's not breathing anymore" she went on saying and she must have taken the scalpel out to disinfect it and put it away in the glass cabinet and just as well

Toto wasn't there, between the bed and the door, because when the midwife rushed at me he could have been between and received the blow and a child couldn't have stood it, he would have died, but I was alone when the midwife came in, when I was about to doze off, after the relief from the night before I didn't hear her come in at three in the afternoon when she came to knife me with the infected scalpel, it hurts so much it's unbearable, a wound made by a butcher, a wound that gets bigger; don't cry Berto says, and a wound hurts till it heals, when will it heal? a wound that doesn't heal is probably infected. It gets worse, it gets bigger and bigger and he doesn't let me cry, if Berto hears me and wakes up, it seems incredible but that afternoon I couldn't cry, if just a moment ago I hadn't cried so much thinking the baby would live, and not a tear, but Berto wakes up if I cry, and not even that? can't even cry? why not? when I can't stand it any longer . . . and what does it matter if he wakes up or if we're at the table, at least cry, now that I can cry each time the midwife comes to me with that nonsense, that crazy talk, cry till she stops looking at me and leaves the room. Running from the table to the other corner of the house, the furthest away so they won't hear me, you can't hear Toto's footsteps, you hear the weeping coming nearer because Toto can't stand staying at the table either when he remembers. And he sits next to me, crying until the midwife stops looking at us and leaves the room. The first day I made them take out the paper gladiolas, but in this total darkness with the blinds closed, wouldn't just a tiny bit of light help you sleep? only a little light would come in through the open blinds, if I turn on the night lamp Berto will wake up. With the blinds opened I could see the room, furniture, look at something and count sheep to fall asleep, every room is the same in total darkness, but the sun comes in through the open blinds in the morning and at six you can no longer sleep, I can hardly see the plaster ceiling with the black wet spot, the shape of mountain tops or Arabian tents you can't see in the dark, or boats sinking in waves with tips like triangles, the shipwreck of *Paul and Virginia*, "Who were they?" Toto asked, it's a bit vague in my memory, how did it go? one of the saddest books, in the university library, and if I would read it and cry? Berto would wake up, he wouldn't wake up for just the tears, falling tears don't make noise, movie tears, tears from reading *María* by Jorge Isaacs, it's the choking in the chest that rocks the bed and men reassure themselves thinking they can hold back the tears and that's what makes them real men, because they are real men, because they can hold them back, but they can hold them back because they can, since if they couldn't hold them back they couldn't reassure themselves thinking because they can hold them back they're real men. They hold them back because they feel less, or is it because they feel nothing at all? If I walk during naptime I sleep better at night, the two trucks paid off so Berto sleeps better at night now, for years and years he didn't, shouting, waking up from his nightmares, in a cold sweat, it's probably not good to smoke as soon as you wake up, the room full of smoke in his sleeplessness and the little lamp and another chapter, a good thing the trucks are paid for, years of no sleep counting sheep and pages of the calendar and piles of nickels, dimes, quarters, and deadlines, IOUs, bounced checks, from which sister? which brother-in-law? which friend who had a load and just gambled it away and Berto didn't have anything and why the hell help those good-for-nothings? and fly away calendar pages, deadlines, IOUs, and piles of coins on top so they won't fly. The night lamp on the little table half asleep the pages of the newspaper would crackle again, he had already finished the novel. Napoleon, Hindenburg and all Emil Ludwig's biographies, the crackling of the newspaper was too faint to wake me up completely, deep sleep that I had before, the pages of IOUs couldn't fly away because Berto wouldn't fall asleep and let them. Which is better, insomnia or nightmares? He's sleeping now, but he wakes up at the slightest noise and "It's your fault the boy doesn't learn that men don't cry, men keep it all inside, but they don't cry" each time we cried Berto "Pest, obey your father a little more, I don't want to see you cry anymore" and he's right because he and Héctor hold it back, I cry because women are weak and Toto because he's a boy. I can't remember if Héctor cried when his mother died, I broke the news to him, he was too young to cry, a year younger than Toto is now, but Toto cries because he has a grown-up's understanding. And I'm not going to let Héctor bring a single chum this summer, because if they start kicking that ball around the backyard I'll kill them, begging Mr. Héctor to go to the cemetery, don't go if you don't want to! imagine, his mother there! his mother, grandfather, Uncle Perico, and my little baby, I don't know how they're placed, all I know is my baby's in the basement, my little angel, there, among those people . . . all alone, in the hands of . . . because who knows what comes after death? who can be sure he's not suffering, and the dead aren't even worse than when they were alive? safe in his little box, but can't the spirits go where they want? and my little angel there alone, with Héctor's mother, who was so good, I agree absolutely but not when she died, sick ever since the birth of Héctor, a circulatory disease, and the blood didn't irrigate her brain, and she was one of God's souls, but when she died she was crazy, she didn't know what she was doing and she made holes with the scissors in her silk stockings, and locked up in the mausoleum with her is my little angel, and with the old drunk and Uncle Perico who died of anger and bitterness, and was capable of murder if he didn't like a joke and he burst out of fury, my poor little angel with those creatures? who can swear to me he's OK, that nobody's doing anything to him, that those dead people aren't . . . oh enough, please, I don't want to think a minute more about that prison of a mausoleum, with its crazy woman and disgusting old man and wild beast inside and my little angel by himself, a little angel face, and Berto put his christening outfit on, a gift from La Plata, Berto was going to be happy with this little baby, boxing, soccer right from the start, and no spoiling, Berto was going to be so happy with him, not like this weakling, this . . . chicken of a Toto, and Berto told me he put on the little christening outfit and told me he wasn't afraid of anything anymore, because if he didn't die from grief that day, he'd never die, but crying doesn't help any and if I cry I'll get weaker and weaker and I won't be able to do the treatment and exercises, since the specialist is sure that with treatment and exercises I'll be able to have another child, but meanwhile my little angel flew away from me, he left me and I could have killed that beast of a Delia when she says to me the saddest part is that unbaptised infants don't go to heaven but to limbo, and so I'll never see him again, but what kind of animals are these with their catechism and church and if they asked me who are the worst women in Vallejos, those who beat and starve their maids to death, stupify and deform them, I could tell them who they are right off the bat: just look at the ones who go to six o'clock mass every morning, the Caivano hag, her daughter, the two Leiva spinsters, and the rest of the mafia, and it's not only my word, they all know it, and everybody says so, and tomorrow morning I'm going to report them to the police, those inhuman hags, they confess first thing in the morning because they're afraid of dying with all the sins they've accumulated in one day, and those devils come to ask me why don't I ever go to church, and whether or not I go to heaven or hell I'll never see my baby again, because he's in limbo, let them say that to me and I'll tear their tongues out, those tongues poisoned with lies, how come God lets vipers like these be born? Choli on a visit to the Caivano hag's neighbor saw the poor maid, a hospital orphan, who started screaming that afternoon and saying she had knocked the milk over into the fire, and it wasn't true, and the hag took the stick to her and the maid told the neighbor the milk hadn't turned over and she laughed out of relief, she laughed as if she had done some mischief, the poor soul in her half language said she was afraid she was going to beat her that day because the hag was walking around in a bad mood and she lied to her about the milk to see if she was going to beat her or not, the stick because she had knocked over the milk, which wasn't true, but if the priest hears that in confession every day, doesn't he *have* to go to the police and report it? confidence of the confessional, and they call in the Caivano hag to teach catechism when there aren't enough nuns! how could God allow that, and also allow my baby to die, without seeing his little face, that little angel face, I wanted to see him, but after it was better not to, because he had suffered dying and didn't look the same, it was too late, better not to see him now, because he was deformed. And in this darkness with the closed blinds, how do I know I'm not in La Plata? How nice it is to be there, and I could be in any room, in the dark, how can I tell? and how do I know the walls aren't peeling? and that Toto isn't sleeping uncovered? if it wasn't for Berto I'd get up to see if Toto is sleeping uncovered. Make another picture card collection of famous couples? The collection of the capitals of Europe, and each one with a typical peasant girl in a typical dance, that's what Toto wanted, even more difficult, a Hungarian gypsy and the whirling hair dancing the *czardas* with the towers of Budapest as background, outlined against the sky and misty when reflected in the Danube, or the Eiffel tower and the two French *apaches*, she thrown to the ground, he looking down at her wickedly. And famous couples like Romeo and Juliet, the balcony scene I prefer, and Toto the vault of the chapel when Romeo had died and Norma Shearer sticks the dagger into her chest, for one measly second the tragedy happens, if Juliet had awoken a second before how happy they could have been, and Maximilian and Charlotte, when Charlotte has already gone mad and opens the window of the Viennese palace so Maximilian's soul will enter, executed in Mexico against the wall of a hut in the middle of nowhere, and Mark Anthony and Cleopatra, Toto wants Cleopatra alone, with the asp, and Mark Anthony in her thoughts, how she imagines him dead in battle, and will we have to hide to draw the new collection? "When he escaped from the birthday party because that big jerk wanted to hit him, I didn't say anything, but escaping from English class because Pocho wanted to hit him, no!" Berto back from tennis black with rage, "Pocho is the same age, his father comes to the tennis court and asks me if Toto invented it all to get out of English class. And I said 'yes'." Berto with his eyes irritated from playing against the wind and brick dust "so much trouble bringing him up and what's Pocho's mother? she worked in a store, and she brings the boy up better than you?", what do you mean better, what better! you don't have to be unfair, you shouldn't say what isn't true, you shouldn't lie! Toto's worth more than all the boys in Vallejos put together, but if someone's worth something everybody hates him, and I didn't answer Berto right away, Pocho is jealous because Toto's the best in the class, that's all, and he told him he'd push his face in, maybe Toto got scared because he thought he was going to push his face in with a hammer or some tool, I said to Berto, and he "I'm tired of being ashamed." There's nothing worse than being ashamed, poor Berto, "I'd cut my hand off to avoid an overdraw at the bank, you'll remember what I did to avoid embarrassment when my brother signed checks that bounced," he said to me yesterday talking about nothing in particular, and tomorrow I'll tell him that when he's older he'll change, so he won't worry, so he won't tire his brain out figuring how much boarding school costs and when he's older he'll change, I can't imagine him older, it seems to me he'll always be like this, ten years old already! but even though he's ten years old sometimes just looking at him for a moment you can suddenly see how he was before, at eight, seven, five, people were always stopping us on the street, so beautiful and charming he was, and it seems just looking at him a bit you can see through to the younger Toto, like a little onion, you take off one layer and there's an identical onion inside, but smaller and whiter, Toto at eight, when he started English and learned a whole bunch of poems right away, and at seven, when he started school, from the first month on in the honor group, and at five, removing the whiter and whiter layers of the onion, how his eyes opened wide when he saw the dances in *Roberta* and at three, at two, every mouth gaping in La Plata, they'd never seen such a beautiful boy, and now my little onion is tiny, tiny, there are no more layers to remove, because he's just born, only a bud is left, a sprout, the heart of the little onion, a white heart, pure, without the slightest stain, a perfect little baby, "a little angel face" Berto and Toto said, and the little heart grows, and takes shape, it's already a baby that walks, a stocky baby, and he talks, a little man's voice, and he grows strong and handsome, Berto takes him everywhere and back home he tells me he's the strongest boy in Vallejos, and he grows and grows and from one summer to the next nobody recognizes him because he got big, like Héctor, the same face as Héctor's, and his shoulders are like tree trunks, Héctor's shoulders, and I don't think there's another boy in Vallejos as handsome as he is, he has the whole town at his feet, and he has everything he needs and the sad look, but why does Héctor have that sad look when nobody's noticing, if he's got everything he needs? why will my little man have that sad look, if he'll get everything he needs? his white heart colored with the purest red blood like a ruby, my little white heart, what is there in the eyes of my little man? can it be that something of Toto got left in the tiny onion? Toto's heart? can it be that Toto is peering out from the eyes of my little man? is that why my baby's sad when nobody is looking? because Toto knows there are sad things, flying so much with our imagination, such illusions me and Toto, and from higher than the stars we fell because sometimes things turn out bad, because people are bad, and sometimes without bad people, sometimes things turn out bad and everyone had wanted them to turn out well, poor Romeo who kills himself because when he sees Juliet asleep he thinks she's dead, he didn't do it on purpose to make her suffer, he did it from loving her so much, but it was their misfortune, that he loved her so much, and there are so many things that turn out bad, why doesn't God change his mind and make everything turn out well? and make Juliet wake up in time when Romeo is about to kill himself, and then they can do everything they so much wanted, they're happy, and what do they do? have children? go live in a house? there must be something better than that, mount two horses, one white, the other red and gallop far, faraway on a hurricane cloud that takes them to the most beautiful place there is, a place that nobody's seen and so cannot know how beautiful it is, nobody knows the flowers they have there and the perfume they give off and nobody knows what can happen when you smell the perfume of one of those flowers, perhaps it's enough to breathe it in to become a flower yourself, and a bird of paradise opens its wings to land and sink his beak into the nectar and sink his wings into the air and high, high it flies with the best I can give, my nectar, in the delicate beak of the bird of paradise, whose arched feathers shine in the sun and shine even more in the moonlight, and it carries me high, high from where you can finally see how the country is, and the forests and rivers are letters that say what I want to know, what I most want to know, the rivers say what I most want to know, and those aren't red feathers that the bird of paradise has on its wing, it's a wound and we descend slowly to the earth and I take care of him, I tear my dress to shreds and make him a bandage . . . and there's a story in which the fairy rewards kind people and turns the bird into a prince, and a prince is what I want, a prince of men, a beautiful little prince wrapped in his soft angora layette, because now I know what the rivers are saying, the letters they form tell me the name I must give him for the christening and way up high I lift my eyes and I'm about to see what I love most, the most beautiful thing in the world, the handsomest little face, "a little angel face" Berto and Toto said, and what's a little angel face like? I want to think of a face so beautiful that it's an angel face but I can't see it, can't see it . . . "Toto's face is a painting" Choli says but I can't imagine a face so beautiful that you can see it and know right away it's an angel face, beautiful, beautiful but not a woman's face, an angel face! such an effort to see it . . . and it's complete darkness in this room . . . if Berto wouldn't wake up I'd get up and open the blinds, but complete darkness should help you sleep, and will we have to hide to draw the new picture cards? They're not going to come out like *The Great Ziegfeld*, I've never been able to draw like that since, I'm afraid Toto may ask me to re-do *The Great Ziegfeld* one day, it's not like before, but what if they show *The Great Ziegfeld* in Vallejos again? I would run to see it . . . If I refreshed my memory maybe they'd come out like before, the dancing scenes as fancy as can be, the lamé dresses, immense feather fans and long white tulle curtains that fall in cascades. But they won't come out, it's not that I have no patience, or even that I'm nervous from having to hide. I hope Toto doesn't ask me for *The Great Ziegfeld*, why is it that you lose the knack for drawing?

IX

Héctor, Summer, 1944

This drip fussing about my long hair, what comes out of her mouth is worth shit, what these broads have in their heads, hairpins, that's the only thing Mari has. I'll just drop her and the party's over, if she keeps pestering me, anyway I already fucked her and if they didn't fuck her before in Vallejos it's because they're only good for jerking off. And anyhow I just took her home twice, once after a walk around the square with her aunt tagging along and the other time after the club dance and how was I to know I was going to fuck her so soon, since her aunt went in because her heels hurt, and no sooner was she gone we pressed against each other again like the first time dancing the bolero "You and I" and me laying it on thick all I did was sing to her a little and presto! a little bullshit and she fell for it like a ton of bricks. Songs send her: "You and I, who are so much in love, we have to bid adieu . . ." that me and my aunt always sing while we wash the dishes, she says to me, they do everything for the old lady, all Mari does during vacation is cook, and schoolteaching all year around alone in the country and not one of them fucking her. Alone out there in the sticks and she told me she spent the whole year eating herself up thinking I was still with Pug-nose, what the fuck for, I dropped Pug-nose before school started, the smart aleck kept her mouth shut good and tight and dumbbell Mari all winter in the open pampas, never even gave her a thought but she was hot for me, she even remembers the first long pants suit I put on, two summers ago, and what the hell does it matter, only one more week and the next I'm already back in school, if it wasn't for Corky how was I to know Mari had the hots for me, Toto didn't know either and I certainly wasn't going to miss out on fucking the last two weeks of vacation. In the winter it gets dark by six o'clock when Corky finishes laboratory, she has to cross the square going home from convent school and with the whole winter and plenty of time to work her over in the dark from five-thirty on, nobody had fucked Corky, any old bullshit about going to a classmate's house to get the homework and between six and seven they could have fucked her all they wanted. In the summer it's not dark till nine and she-could-but-she-couldn't take a walk around the square, with her big sister, and something tells you that sooner or later a broad is going to give in, during winter vacation, the dog me and Toto met up with on the road to the cemetery was faraway and stared and stared, Toto didn't like him but I did, one hell of a greyhound, and how many times I wanted to swipe the brown dog on Fatso's ranch, but that dog wouldn't stare, full to the gills and happy where he was, and the terrier at the station, I'd put him in the car and be seeing ya, if I wanted to, but the greyhound was a better breed and hell, a hundred times better looking than the terrier. Dogs who haven't got a home or food follow you right away Toto said, but that's a lot of bull because The Kid's dog sleeps with him in the gutters and if he'd find a bone The Kid would snatch it from him before he could touch it, what happens is the dog stays with The Kid because The Kid lets him go everywhere with him and the dog couldn't care less if The Kid begs for bread from house to house. But the greyhound at the farm, he sure followed me, too bad Mita shooed him away, and then the store people got hold of him. Corky passed all her courses, me going to see her at home with her old lady busting my balls while the smart aleck explains me the theorems! is she crazy? Math, chemistry and physics, if I flunk two I'm up shit creek, flunking only one I can take it again next year Corky filling my bean with all this talk about them flunking me, come to my house to study and how could I tell Mita and Berto they flunked me not only in chemistry, but math and physics too. And play the smarty pants and honors and all that bull, almost the whole summer I squeezed Corky dry, fucking in the vestibule, you could hear if her big sister was coming and "if you don't change and start studying I won't love you any more" and I managed to drag it out, three weeks of vacation were left and was I going to end up fucking the maids. Dumbbell Mari why is she always ready to cry? A chick shouldn't be so sad all the time, and she answered she'd always been that way, bullshit, the deal is she's sorry for giving up her cherry so quick and keeps reminding me to write her, stuck in that school out in the sticks from fall to spring, she says last year was the first time away from her mother and all she thought about was me, that I'd be writing to Pug-nose every day in Vallejos, thinking how happy Pug-nose would wake up every morning waiting for the mailman, reading and re-reading my letters, reading and re-reading Dostoevski's telephone directories, *that* I believe. I made Pug-nose sorry she said I was a lamebrain and she gave me *Crime and Punishment* and I couldn't put up with more than ten pages of reading names and more names which always looked different and were the same, more names than a telephone directory and not one letter did I write Pug-nose, me being a lamebrain, "you didn't read the novels I lent you because you couldn't understand them," the novels the guy at the boardinghouse has, the hot ass, that I should go read in his room since he wanted to show me all the books he had, nuts for Dostoevski and also *The Book of San Michele* since I liked dogs, and if I didn't read *Man, the Unknown* by Alexis Carrel he wasn't going to say hello to me anymore, every position of chinky fucking in the *Kama Sutra* when he closed the window I figured the rotten old bugger would grab my crotch any minute, and in my room you can smell dampness but in his not only that but twenty pairs of shoes smelling from twenty years back, from spats to the sandals the shitty fag bought himself this summer, and bunches of dead flowers nailed on the wall, rolling his eyes "souvenirs of mine" and he acts mysterious, the big fag, according to him French movies with those ugly sagging broads are the only ones for intelligent people, and he asked me what actress I liked the best and he almost shit in his pants laughing since I liked Ann Sheridan, because she has a good pair of udders he says, getting bugged because I was moving away on the edge of the bed while he read the *Kama Sutra* and bull Ann Sheridan is good all over and isn't she a good actress? but he didn't dare grab me, he knew I got his number. "And to think we have to bid adieu makes me feel like dying," Mari said to me in the vestibule, "on the dance floor when you sang 'who are so much in love . . . we have to bid adieu . . .' I thought of running away to Buenos Aires and not going back to that country school, to die in the cold, and Mom insists I go back there since they'll transfer me to Vallejos in two or three years and then I'll get tenure, but how will I ever make it? and who can say that putting up with desperation for so long something won't happen to me?, what the country does have is dogs and I saw a big, hairy dog and it was you and I grab hold of the tail and run like crazy after you and then you weren't a dog but a wolf, or a tiger, but with hair brown like yours a little bleached from the sun and the chlorine of the pool, and you aren't a tiger no more because then I see you as you but with a woolly dog's tail," that Mari, who does she think she's kidding? she starts talking about coming with me and the woolly tail and she couldn't give a bigger hint if she tried. Then this cock-and-bull story about me taking advantage of her since she was in love with me and if I didn't really love her I shouldn't have broken her cherry, a week and a half before school starts again, her to the sticks and me to the boardinghouse, open the door and fuck the faggot's stinking clodhoppers. School, a noodle swimming in the soup, pumpkins stuffed with mashed pumpkins and a wad of sawdust, the fantasmagorically fantastic grub at the boardinghouse, to the poolroom and not even a buck for the rest of the afternoon, fifty cents from my old man's pocket he doesn't miss it if it's only small change and if I win the game I throw in the cue, rub the cue ball for good luck and five racks in a row I never won, but three or four I can make. Without dough you can't get a decent broad, to think that in Vallejos the swimming pool is full of broads, Pug-nose, Corky and Mari see ya later, baby, chicks in bathing suits, gams galore, in the summer a French kiss in the evening and at six o'clock in the winter you can French 'em all the way down to the pit of the stomach right smack in the middle of the square since nobody can see in the dark, and squeezing juicy jugs good and tight dancing in the club and loads of easy lays for a quick fuck at the country fairs, and in ten days back in that rotten boarding house waiting for winter vacation and summer is a gas three months in a row and I didn't pay any attention to Mita, what she needs is a few laughs instead of whining in corners with Toto and I didn't follow her lead and she started making cracks with García in a card game and we beat Berto, "see if you can beat this" and Mita "you'll get a beating on your ass, oh pardon me, should I say your backside which shows more class" and García turned red and Mita "a boy pissed in his bed and his ass's beaten red" and Berto almost died laughing and Toto so furious he doesn't want to learn how to play, but he stays in Vallejos while I'm stuck in the boardinghouse, fuck exams and not once did I go to the bar with the chemistry prof, he's going to screw me since I didn't play along with him and read Echeverria's fat books and *Das Capital*, me wasting my time blabbing in the bar from seven to eight? when the chicks are out on errands, half dark and not even God can see you in the winter, if not the maids who's going to notice you without a buck in your pocket. Five years in fucking Buenos Aires. Six since the boys' soccer team "Athletic Vallejos," every town cup the first year, playing center half I pass the ball to wing, the wing in wild play to the other wing who passes it to center half and goal! goal, folks! goal by center half . . . ! a brilliant play, game after game and it's ours the championship cup of 1939, and next year? who will be center half? I'm going to Buenos Aires and what the fuck am I going for, eh? that's what I say, I should talk Mita into it, talk your mother into it, Doggie, who was right wing before, pestering me with talk your mother into it, and she's not my mother, she's my aunt, and Doggie she's your aunt so that's why she wants to screw you into going to Buenos Aires to study, why? jackass, in Vallejos there isn't any high school and this year I finish sixth grade, and Mita is more than an aunt, she doesn't want to fuck me up and Doggie pestering that I should go with him to vocational school in Vallejos and that I should pester Mita into letting me go to vocational school, and three times a week to training and a sure bet we would win the second consecutive cup, and Doggie "talk her into it, talk her into it" . . . and Mita isn't like an aunt, she's more than an aunt and she doesn't want to fuck me up, does she love me more than an aunt? if I ask her she'll let me stay in Vallejos and ask and ask and ask but it doesn't depend on her she told me: she was going to write to my old man and talk to Berto and see what they thought but to be a mechanic was so low-class and I should think higher, "but don't you worry I'll write a letter to your dad," and Mita was more than an aunt, an aunt would fuck me up and send me to Buenos Aires, if she really loved me she wouldn't send me to Buenos Aires so we'd be together all the time, like she and Toto are always together, how great, win two championships in a row, center half is going to make all the goals, and two more championships from now we'll move from the boys' team up to . . . Third Division, and we'll play against the Third of River, Boca, and there and then they'll know who has the legs, and a talent scout sees you play when you lick them in the Second Team and center half Pedernera driving over to the field one day will crash into a pole and who takes his place?

asks the president of the club and the trainer gives him a knowing look, he already senses who will take his place, because that Sunday mighty River is going to win even if they play their sworn enemies: Western Railway! Mita and Toto came home from the store without a package and afterwards the errand-boy rang the bell and left a new, empty suitcase and Héctor dear, it's for your own good, think how I'm going to miss you, even more than you because you're going to wonderful Buenos Aires, think of me stuck here in Vallejos, and I said to her it was all my old man's fault he wanted me to go to Buenos Aires and what did he say to your letter? what letter? Mita asked me, what letter? the letter, the letter to the old man, the one you wrote to talk him into letting me stay in Vallejos! What letter? which letter? "I didn't write because you don't want to be a mechanic, it's so low-class, you've got to think higher" what letter? the letter, Doggie: she's more than an aunt and I'll stay in Vallejos forever, what letter? because I love you I'm sending you to Buenos Aires, I'll miss you more than you will me, you're going to wonderful Buenos Aires and I'm stuck here in Vallejos, because I love you I'm sending you to Buenos Aires, because I love you . . . I'm sticking you in a rotten boardinghouse, and every morning in the sonofabitch school. All year round in her letters if Mita would remember to tell me who won she'd forget to tell me who made the goals, Doggie? and how did they win? I didn't think they were going to win in Charlone, nor in Trenque Lauquen, and they won the last game, for the cup, they won the 1940 championship, two championships in a row, very few of the goals were made by the center half. He's not in Noziglia's gang, always with the gang, Noziglia, and ever since he saw the dirty look I gave him he doesn't even shit alone, the whole mill gang, about forty, but if there were only a few I'd call on Doggie, Beanhead and Blackie and we'd give it to 'em but good. Get hold of him for just once and bring up the subject, that he fucked the Mansilla and Echague kids, Toto saw it in recess, it's not allowed to go into the tall grass in the back of the schoolyard and the teachers check to see if somebody's sneaked in. But Noziglia's as strong as a grown-up and grabs one of the kids in his grade that he's been hungering for, seeing him so clean all the time with a starched uniform just like the teacher, and he's fourteen but he got left back and the kids in the class are ten years old and he looks at them during class and in recess he grabs the one he's had his eye on and takes him over to the wall and if the kid doesn't escape or scream he grabs him from behind right there, pulls his pants down a little and opens his own fly and hides it all with the little kid's uniform and his own and that's what Baldy López did in my time, in fifth grade he was already creaming in his jeans since he was thirteen and he'd plug the little guys who'd let him, the Asteri kid let him for a box kite and then Baldy the jerk didn't give it to him, I don't know how Baldy could get it in, with the tree trunk he had, and the mess of it was that if it hurt the kid would shout and a teacher could hear, but what shit, with all the shouting of recess and one day Baldy asked me why I didn't plug Indian, even if he didn't want to let me, didn't matter if he shouted or not, they would never know, Indian could give me his word and yell just the same, because of the pain, you got to be a son of a bitch like Baldy to find that fun, and Noziglia is the one who plugs everybody now, Toto saw how he fucked the Mansilla kid and that was the first time he saw fucking, he said he saw the Mansilla kid standing against the wall looking like he had an upset stomach and dripping tears, Noziglia behind him holding and pumping him and he saw Toto come near and said "giddyap horsy" Noziglia the bully making believe because he knew Toto was a dumbbell and didn't understand a thing, besides, it was all covered up with Mansilla's uniform, all plaited like a woman's. And another day he saw Echague, against the same wall, looking like he was having an operation, dumbbell Toto said, eyes like the boys in the hospital after they've had their tonsils taken out, half fainting and bibs like babies, covered with blood vomit, and he saw Echague's eyes and the mouth Noziglia covered with his hands because they had taken Echague by force, between Noziglia and two other smaller kids from the class, Noziglia's bootlickers, and with the other hand he clinched him by the stomach and was pumping away, one of the kids stood guard to see if a teacher was coming and the other standing on Echague's foot so he wouldn't kick Noziglia and Echague's other leg Noziglia had up high wrapped around his own. To torture him Toto said, but it was so he could put it into him and Toto went to call a teacher but when she got there Noziglia had already let go and the teacher didn't say a thing but that's when they must have put Toto on their list, I don't think they worked on him before. Going to the bar just once maybe I could have worked on the chemistry prof, about there being nothing better than the proletariat, the positive forces of the nation, and the stink of the maids bitches without a cent in Buenos Aires you have to take what comes, and the only thing that comes is you know what: maids, damn 'em! And about renouncing all personal ambition for the good of all, everybody will have the same salary and River is in serious danger, folks, Boca Juniors to the sound of thousands of *pesos* real currency is trying to rob the mighty team of its three stars—Moreno, inside Labruna, wing of wings Loustau—in an unheard-of maneuver in the history of Argentinian soccer, but the trio doesn't waver for a second, radio listeners of this sensational encounter in the Boca field, with the fans of the mighty team seriously alarmed by the sudden illness of its center half, substituted at the last minute by an unknown player, and discovered this morning in a vacant lot of the capital, no professional experience except a few appearances in a boy's tournament . . . and that's him, that's him now entering the field sure of victory, with the invincible hope of his barely seventeen Aprils, and the game is already starting, and the ball passes to the mighty River's side, the arch of the River Plate is in danger, folks, and yessiree folks, in barely two minutes after the start of the first half . . . goooal for Boca! goooal for Boca Juniors, the home grandstands roar! And the plays begin again, the ball's still on River's side, and yessiree folks in barely four minutes after the start of the second half goooal for Boca Juniors! five to zero reads the marker of this classic already a sure loss for the mighty team . . . but what's happening? in fierce play Moreno passes to Labruna, Labruna to Loustau and Loustau loses the ball for the umpteenth time, ignoring the presence of the new center half, who now for the first time in possession of the ball passes it to Moreno, Moreno returns it to center half who defies his Boca backstop with brilliant footwork and goooal, gooooal for River Plate! goal by the new center half in one of the most exciting *blitzkrieg* plays of the season and now Labruna takes the ball again, passes it to Loustau, who makes a skillful pass to center half and gooal, goooal for River Plate! now the two rival teams are tied and we are near the end of the second half: in these last two minutes anything can happen, folks . . . anything can happen in this field under the spell of the most brilliant quartet in the history of Argentinian soccer . . . but a player has fallen injured, Moreno has fallen injured, and now there are only ten men, ten men covered with dust and sweat that's the mighty team; will the marker again be in danger?

Nooo, nosirree folks, in brilliant play, footing along the entire Boca frontline he approaches the arch and goal! head-on goal brilliantly scored by the revelation of all time . . . the greatest center half yet in the annals of Argentinian soccer! and six to five the team wins, six goals, six, who gets six? not even five, I'd settle for four, passed and I'm off, three fours would save my life and just once that I'd gone to the bar and said any shit, that I read *Das Capital.* Like a kite that flies away, I would never be able to beat Pug-nose, who has brains like Pug-nose? no kidding, that summer, people really didn't recognize me because I wasn't a squirt anymore and I passed Pug-nose on the street and she stared, that's when it occurred to me and I asked Toto and he told me her father had gone away with another woman in the winter and afterwards her mother found out high blood pressure had screwed him in Buenos Aires, they went for him and now he's in bed but Pug-nose and he aren't talking, the old lady forgave him but not Pug-nose. Frogs are always panting for women Mita said, and Pug-nose looked at me and if the people passing by weren't looking I'd have patted her backside, I pat the terrier on the head and he stands still, real still, looking at me, and hee-hee tilts his head a little when he wants something, a little grub? for five lousy cents in the butcher I throw him a big bone and he follows me the rest of the day if I want. The terrier would come with me since his master never even looks at him and Pug-nose "Aren't you going to dance?", she asks me and in the club that Sunday I asked her to dance since I'd given her a good rubdown in the square and not a word about Dostoevski and "Let me look at you" she'd say to me "If you wanted you could have everything in life, you're not afraid of anybody it seems," and I didn't say a word about wanting to join the River Seconds, and she couldn't keep from blabbing about her old man and it was from so much reading he did what he did, I told her, and she looked at me, sonofabitch she-cat, she flashed me a sonofabitch look, cats are the crumbiest animals, she-cats even worse, they have it in for you, and there's not a chick who doesn't like rubbing, little by little, first the hand, then over her duds the tits, then under her duds, under the bra the nipples pop up like springs, and from the knee up, straight to strategic point number one and it said in the *Kama Sutra* it was enough to put one finger inside for the whole fortress to fall, one little finger, nothing else, let me, what does it do to you? . . . but tougher than Pug-nose it's hard to come by, eyes shut, her mouth too, between her legs for a month, all screwed up because she wouldn't let me put the fucking finger in, and one night, when was it? oh yeah, after Mita bawled me out at dinner for putting my foot in my mouth in front of the throat specialist, what a jerk I must have looked like, the Russians betrayed Hitler I got it in my head to say after dessert and it was the other way around, and Pug-nose felt sorry for me, didn't she? she squeezed my hand, I finished telling her what a jerk I'd made of myself and she stood still in the dark, a little light from her mother's window. Her father sleeps in the back and her mother's light went out almost right away, but the old lady wasn't sleeping because you could hear the radio from the open window, the news about Normandy and the Russians heading for Berlin and it reminded me how dumb I looked, shitty radio, and I squeeze Pug-nose a little and she's all limp, the first time she wasn't man-shy, and I put my hand under her duds and her two gams weren't closed tight, a little apart, and caressing her for the first time I reached my goal and not even daring to breathe since her mother might hear I made her, and I didn't tell anybody, not even Toto, and we didn't separate right away, holding each other tight, and like a jerk I cried but she wasn't wise to it I think. And two cherries more this year, Corky and Mari, to the collection of a humble servant, torpedo firer by profession. Only Toto knows, after what happened to him this year he sure does know, and about Pug-nose too and then Pug-nose comes out with the business about me being a lamebrain, that all I could talk about is soccer and that I don't even think about having a career, no ambition whatsoever and wow if she got wind of the River Seconds. And look at Toto he does have ambition she says, only eleven years old and a loose screw is what Toto has, "did you want your mom to die?" the squirt comes out with "your mom was always messy and didn't talk to you and didn't you want to kill her with your thoughts? I thought hard for her to die and so you'd stay in my house forever, like the other kids who have brothers," and that's when he was younger but now he's foxy and doesn't say anything but who knows what he's thinking? and who could possibly think that somebody wanted to kill his mother with his thoughts, I was fine with Mita but you'd have to be a fucking criminal and Mom was sick in another house, why would someone who's not a criminal want somebody to die? she was sick and I'd see her on Sunday mornings when Mita dressed me up and we always knew she was going to stay in that other house: when Mom died Mita told me my mom had gone to heaven and from there she was going to keep on loving me but on earth I had her and Berto who loved me like Toto, just as much, and the house was mine and we were never going to separate again, I was in fifth grade, and after I finished sixth, "you can't settle for being a mechanic, you've got to think higher," yes, and go to the club Pug-nose says, "in Buenos Aires go to the humanities club my brother-in-law's friends have" the club! the jerks' club with the Victrola listening to classical music, and Pug-nose with all this nonsense about going to the first meeting when they play the first classics of all and then continue on with Mozart and what's-his-face which you couldn't understand if you didn't listen to the ones that came first, and each one prepares a topic and talks to the others to enrich their culture and if the chemistry prof isn't one of them, I'd make him an honorary member, the drip humming Tchaikovsky's Concerto No. 1 he made me hate, it used to be the music I liked best and that Beethoven sonata God knows what it has that it makes me feel like throwing myself into a corner and never getting up again, because it's sadder than a sonofabitch, and I'll never get up again from the broken couch in the boardinghouse, you throw yourself down on it and they'll have to haul you up with a crane, old man, poor guy you'll sink right into the springs, but who knows if that's not what you want, to bury yourself there, so you don't have to look the others in the face, that bunch of sonsofbitches and "I'm going to manage some escapade to Buenos Aires to see you, dear, your dad tells me there's a couch for me in the boardinghouse, an old couch but what does that matter since it's more than a couch, it's like a bed, so when you least expect I'll come by for a few days" you don't have ambition, OK, but dragging Toto along the two of them couldn't sleep on the little couch and went to a hotel, because without ambition you can't do a thing, yeah, go to the humanities club, and it's more than a couch, it's a bed, she's more than an aunt, you see Doggie, she's a mother, she's more than an aunt, you got to believe it and throw yourself on the shitty couch to listen to the funeral march that's what Pug-nose wants, and don't get up any more, it's because I love you that I'm sending you to the boardinghouse, and not more than a month to go before the beginning of the second championship, in April, the boys' soccer tournament, and what the hell, I'll forget the old man's signature and sign up, let them all go fuck themselves, nobody's going to stop me from signing up for the River Seconds, even if there's a bunch of guys if you got the legs you got 'em, who can stop me? the jerks listening to classical music on a Saturday evening instead of fucking what's-her-face they listen to that funeral home crap, as if all the broads in the world had been wiped off the face of the earth and they had just closed registration for the River Seconds and there wasn't anything you could do to save your soul from rotting away . . . not even for that would I let them lock me up in that club, I'd shoot myself in the bean first since if my soul's rotting it's because it has to and there's no way out, but for me to go looking for it listening to funeral marches No! because if you keep moving you're bound to find something good and keep looking ahead because there's a few good things in life, the broads and two or three others and the rest is a screw job and the guy who doesn't shy away from the other things is screwed, and I'm going to tell Pug-nose what I think if I run into her before I go, I didn't read not even one of her dumb novels, "let's be friends, forget about what happened" the ballbuster and as a going-away present she shoves the books at me and "promise me you'll write from time to time" and if I run into her I'll tell her what they think of her in Vallejos, and if her old man went so cuckoo from reading Schopenhauer and all that shit about the Superman, she'll have it even worse because she's polishing off the whole Public Library and I'll tell her exactly what I think and I'd like to know what Toto thinks when he's listening to the grown-ups, before he always talked his head off, the first thing that came to his mind, and now not a peep, "Teté spoiled him that year" Mita keeps saying and "he copied everything from Teté" and if I catch Noziglia alone one day, without giving him a hint I'll bring up the subject and stare at him real hard, and a guy would have to be drunk to confess he took a little kid by force, but I'd realize right away if he got nervous and staring at him real hard I'd realize if he managed to do it or not, because before going out for recess Toto smelled something rotten, that they were giving each other looks, Noziglia and his two bootlickers, and Toto didn't want to go to the yard for recess and he told the teacher that some of the boys wanted to hit him and, which boys? he didn't say but he asked Corky's sister, the jerk he has for a teacher, to let him stay in the classroom and she said if something happened to look for her in the yard and Toto thought about all the shouting and if they managed to cover his mouth she wouldn't hear him and he went down the corridor to the yard to see if there was some teacher he could stand next to and there was nobody and he was almost in the yard passing the boys' john when all of a sudden the door opens and like three arrows out shoot Noziglia and the other two and scared Toto so much he jumped free and ran out screaming past the principal's office and split home and that was his story but Berto got hold of him and started asking what happened and that he should tell the whole story, that if they'd done something to him he'd kill Noziglia and Noziglia's father, and he grabbed Toto and shook him to make him swear they hadn't done anything to him that if so he'd kill the two of them, and from the minute he arrived Toto didn't stop crying and screaming no, no, that he'd escaped in time and Mita made the accusation at school but Berto wasn't satisfied with that, he wanted to beat Noziglia to a pulp, but when you come right down to it if nothing happened you can't do a thing. In short pants the big jerk, if he has a prick like Baldy López I don't know how he manages to fuck kids and you can't take Toto's word since I asked him if he'd seen Noziglia's and he told me "Noziglia always had it out, sitting in the last row, showing it to the kids and one day he put paste on the tip and it was big like a grown-up's and hairy, and he splashed paste on the floor" paste! and what does Corky's sister do that she doesn't see a thing? You got to be a little less of a dope to be a teacher, and Corky's going to be just like her, she'll never wise up, I never saw anybody so stuck on herself, the best in the class, the prettiest girl in town, everybody has the hots for her, and nobody's got the guts to make her, because in the end a stuck-up broad is the easiest of all since once you get her hot it's a cinch: she lets you because she's convinced that no sucker would dare drop her, I never saw anybody so stuck on herself, and she keeps knocking Pug-nose and how I wasted my time with that bookworm when *she's* the biggest bookworm in the school, you got to have nerve, the only job I had with Corky was making her hot, and afterwards it was a sure bet she'd let you, used to everybody throwing themselves at her feet, "after this I have more rights over you" getting on my nerves, that she passed all her courses and that she could explain the theorems better than anybody else and why don't I go to her house, and on top of that I have to put up with the old lady? let her go fuck herself, how could she possibly think somebody would jilt her? and now it's been two weeks since she set foot on the street her sister gave me the news, buried alive, let her learn what life is, laughing at Mari, who was a silly goose and crazy for me, thanks for the tip because she got on my nerves with "Are you going to write me or not?" and there's no way out of that since Mari is starting to pester me too, oh well, there's only ten days left and fuck the sonofabitch boardinghouse and school and eating shit and putting up with the old man who's always agreeing with the fag at the table. One day I won't put up with it any more, I swear, I'm going to tell that fag off and when he starts with "Your son should read good literature" and my old man "This one's a wild animal" and the fag "But he has intelligent eyes, I think he's more sensitive than he seems," go ahead, keep working over me, pester me more and more and one day I'll tell the old man about the *Kama Sutra* and all that jazz. And the chemistry teacher better not throw me any more hints about the ignorant people who don't have a political conscience is Argentina's ruin and long live the united jerks of my beloved country, gathered together in solemn masturbation Saturday night after club because on Sunday they can rest, and until next Saturday compulsory closing of flies and drips!!! if I feel like jerking off I will, Monday morning or whenever, but that's highly improbable while there still remains an eager fighting maid on the face of the earth, of course if they find out where you live you're done for, since the poor things lost and alone in Buenos Aires don't know a soul and stick to you and pester you and you have to keep telling lies, so boy don't you do your rounds in your neighborhood or trust anybody, only your mother, he who has one, and I'll tell the old man any fucking story and go to training every afternoon, since all the champions come from the second team, the great Seconds of the River Plate, not the dopey small-town champions: what do those guys know about soccer, how can they know what it is to enter a stadium with five million people looking at you, but never mind, let them look to their hearts' content so they'll know what a real center-half is.

X

Paquita, Winter, 1945

Within these green moss-covered walls and dirty stained-glass windows, where could God be to listen to all us girls, near the altar? today Saturday maybe near the confessional, at this very moment next to the grammar school girls, a sure bet that one or two confess the same mortal sin, and I'm adding one more sin, evil thoughts, I hope God doesn't listen to me until I'm ready for "the act of contrition is an act of total concentration, sins will not be pardoned unless the sinner is sincerely repentant" I swear I won't do it again and forgive me for swearing, all I do is sin but if I still feel like it even though I don't do it I already have evil thoughts and the devil is whispering in my ear because I still feel like it: I swear dear God I won't do it again. Still one, two, three, four left to confess, five, seven, nine, eleven from grammar school . . . I lied to Mom—deception—I stole raisins from the store, because even if I paid for the flour and sugar and coffee not paying for the raisins is the same as stealing—larceny—and I didn't lend the postcard to Toto—meanness—which aren't mortal sins. I'd kill him if he returned it with one little crease, Dad can close his eyes and still see his town, after leaving twenty-five years ago. Churanzás, province of Galicia, Spain is "so pretty, so pretty," always the same story, and damn the pampas, and was it true that Galicia was so pretty, then why did Dad come here? how silly, but they were poor and here we're so rich we can hardly afford the rags on our backs. But Dad will never know I have a mortal sin, because the priest can't go and tell what you confess to him. The postcard picture was painted in two colors, the mountains in one color and underneath a long slope where a river in another color was flowing and a village of uncolored stone huts and on top of the slope going to the top of the mountain the higher you went the less it cost to rent a hut, they didn't need the back wall because it was against the mountain and Toto "your poor father coming to the wind and dirt of Vallejos after this. Your godfather at least had money to go back for a visit, what's he going to bring you?" I didn't know Galicia was so pretty but Balán sent a postcard. "Dear friend: Everyone in Churanzás sends their love, they all remember us and the late Celia, may she rest in peace. See you soon, much love, Arsenio Balán" and when she was almost dying Teté says she was blue in the face from the choking fits you get from tuberculosis. Was she really a bad girl? if she didn't get married because of Dad, Mita "poor Celia was so good, but when I tended her in the hospital there was already nothing we could do, have you read *María*, Paqú? she also dies of tuberculosis, Celia the poor girl, everybody would talk about her, she never wanted to live in the country and put up with those relatives, but she had to stay there for more than a year until she finally died, do you realize how sad it is not to have a home?" Mita on duty at the drugstore didn't go to the funeral, otherwise she would have gone, not like the people in Vallejos. Dad didn't either. Balán and Teté's grandmother were at the cemetery. Did she leave a mortal sin unconfessed? "I don't know, but God doesn't need a man dressed in skirts to remind him that all the poor thing did her whole life was to suffer. And she had hands of gold for embroidering" Mita changed the subject, and would Celia embroider after a whole day of helping Dad make men's clothing? Mita is a member of the Social Club and Toto "come to my house, why don't you want to come? if I tell the instructor about Raúl García what would happen?" you swore by your mother and she'll die if you tell anybody! but he's too young to know that Raúl García and the instructor are like day and night, the instructor is good and Raúl is bad, did your mother tell you anything about Celia? "with what your father paid her she couldn't pay for her medicines, you're lucky there are no boys in convent school" didn't you hear your Mom and Dad talking about Celia? "Someone from my school escaped home during recess again" don't tell your Mom and Dad that I asked you about Celia "You shouldn't hide anything from your parents, I can't tell Mom about you and Raúl García because I swore I wouldn't but you didn't swear, why don't you tell Mom?" to his mother with all the gossip, what girl escaped from school? "I didn't say if it was a girl or a boy" from your class? "it's a secret" and I stayed a bit longer to play with his picture cards, the stupidest collection in the world and he thinks he knows all my secrets: in the hotel room the instructor opened the door "what are you doing here? you're under age, were you crying?" my father hit me, the crap-shooting tailor, whipping with his measuring tape, bread and butter on the customer's material! I did it by mistake, you can't imagine how it hurt, that's why I came to the hotel, are you angry? ooh, don't touch my back, it hurts, no, it's not cold in the room, I don't know why I got goose pimples, and he put his hand in my blouse to see if his cold hand would give me the chills . . . you know something? they're going to let me go to the Social Club next year, not this spring, next year when I'm sixteen, at home they don't let me go unless it's with Mrs. Mita, no! don't turn off the light, leave this pretty nightlamp on, it looks like a Chinese hat "if we turn off the light I'll open the closet and you'll see a bottle, it gives off light almost like a kerosene lamp" he turned off the light and in the dark took a bottle out of the closet "the country is full of them, look how they twinkle: fireflies are the cutest bugs there are" and he caught them at night in the country, the light goes on and off, I want to close my eyes because I'm ashamed to be in this room, do you leave these little bugs in the closet? a flock of them, he put the bottle back in the closet and you can't see the lights of the flock any more with my eyes shut I only see inside me, inside it's all dark but it doesn't matter, he touches me with one hand, Raúl García's gentlest caress can be so false, his big hand for chopping wood and his fingers stained from cigarettes, leaning against the truck in the backyard, you're not like him, you're much nicer, and another chill spreads all over inside me little bugs run through my veins, do you know there are thousands and thousands of veins in the human body? with my eyes shut it's not dark any more, a flock twinkles in me from the tip of my foot to the roots where my hair begins, thousands and thousands of fireflies, touch them Raúl, touch them Raúl García, Raúl, come, as much as you wanted me I want you now too, softly, touch me softly, their lights go on, their lights go off, on, off, on, Raúl! caress me please, caress me and all the little bugs I have inside, now, even though you hurt me, and a kiss that lasts until the flock feels like escaping and leaves me, then I'll fall asleep . . . "Paquita I don't want anything else to happen, let me hold you tight, like this" the instructor unbuttoned the collar of his shirt and nothing else happened! By mistake I left the novel *María* in the messy bedspread and Father Joseph "beware of she who confesses a sin without sincerely repenting for her error" but if I would have died after leaving the hotel I would have died free of mortal sin. Still five, six, seven, eight from grammar school have to confess before me, and if none of the students ask me to dance since Pug-nose "I swear, none of my friends will ask you to dance at the social" but all of them ask her what novel is the best and she knows about everything "are you sure you know the right things to read? you mustn't miss *The Brothers Karamazov*, but I'm not sure you'll understand it" Pug-nose, could it be true that Héctor did what he wanted? what does Pug-nose think about when she goes to bed at night? Corky thinks about next day's class, she covers herself because she's cold and the hot water bottle at her feet and Héctor's hands will begin to touch her and she already has a sin to confess: evil thoughts, which is not a mortal sin. Corky probably puts her hands under the blankets, between the sheets and her nightgown, because of the cold, and they are Héctor's hands when they lift up her nightgown and begin to rub her open wound, and she already has a mortal sin to confess, worse than evil thoughts. Mom, was Celia good? "a good tramp" then Mom knows what they say about Dad and Celia? and it's not true he comes home drunk, if he comes home furious at dawn it's because he lost the dice game, he sometimes loses what he made on a pair of pants, or pants and jacket, and he's such a stubborn player that he can lose everything he made on a pair of pants, jacket and vest at poker. "You shouldn't hide anything from your parents" Toto said. If they let me during vacation I'd climb almost up to the roof on a high ladder and scrape the moss off behind the altar and also on the sides and then a coat of paint, then if God would make it rain a little the dirt would come off the stained-glass windows after this long dry winter "its too cold to go outside" Mita with her belly from here to the other end of town and a cold, the doctor won't let her go out after the seventh month, afraid the baby might die on her again. By the fireplace "what book is that, Paquí? . . . *Marianela!* it's beautiful . . . how did it begin?" and she couldn't believe that I got *Les Miserables* out of the library and Dad caught me with the light on, coming back from the bar at three in the morning, "get up early and take advantage of the daylight, electric light costs money" but if I tell Mita all about the instructor and swear to her I won't do it anymore she'll forgive me and even if they come to tell her about it she'll take me to the dance just the same, Mita: I have to tell you something "Oh, Paquí, that poor girl Fantine who'd gone through so many hardships fetching water in wooden buckets for that hyena Madame Thenardier all day long from the frozen dawn of the French countryside to the ringing of the angelus." Mita remembers all of *Les Miserables* and she read it such a long time ago and why do I hesitate to tell her everything? and she couldn't believe that I read *By Order of the King* that one she forgot "I don't remember . . . Paquí . . . I'm going to forget everything and you know, already I can't remember how *Marianela* begins? how does *Marianela* begin? Paquí, I forgot so many novels in Vallejos . . . " Mita told me to read *María* "the best of them all, did you already read it? isn't it divine? but you'll see, if you stay in Vallejos you'll forget it" and I should think it's the same in Vallejos or China or Galicia, right? "No, Paquí, if you never talk to people about a novel you forget it" and Toto "she already told me all the ones she remembers." "I close my eyes and see my town," a landscape that looks painted, Dad came alone with Balán and the last person who saw his mother and brought him news about her was Celia when she arrived three years later but did he know her before or not? as soon as Celia's sister set foot in Argentina she immediately hooked Teté's uncle and only had to sew a few dresses while poor Celia worked as a tailor's assistant bending more and more over thicker needles and tougher mens' material, she caught tuberculosis instead of a husband, why didn't she keep her sister's customers? dressmaking is easier "when you have no taste for dressmaking it's better to work as a tailor's assistant" but after so many years of sewing if Mom doesn't have taste who does? at the sweet sixteen dance I'll hook a boyfriend, the richer the better, they live on a ranch, Teté's grandmother's, and another one finished confessing! only seven to go and Marianela throws herself into a well because she's ugly and her blind boyfriend is about to be cured and how afraid Mita was that the baby would die at birth, she doesn't want to go out in the cold, and she asked me only once "if you want to go to the Social Club, Paquí, we'll have lots of fun, but no going up to the terrace of the club with a boy because I don't want them to blame me for anything" if they find out in Vallejos that I went to the instructor's room, what will I do? "how does *Marianela* end, Paquí?" Marianela threw herself into a well, and I swear to Mita that I'll be a good girl at the club: just as soon as Toto leaves us alone I'll tell her everything "Marianela in a well where they didn't find her any more and the field rats ate her" before her boyfriend could come and see that she was a ghoul, but a well, how dirty! "better a well because if you hang yourself from a tree in the middle of the pampas swallows can fly by and look at you". "Paquita, dear" Dad doesn't look at me, he looks at the vest, the jacket or the pants he's sewing "if you stay at Mrs. Mita's house for supper say excuse me and call me on the telephone so I can wait for you on the corner, because now you shouldn't walk alone in the street at night" but Toto was with me when Corky came for the last fitting for her lace dress. Toto hadn't seen her for more than a year, since Corky didn't go out any more if it wasn't for school. And lying as usual "how tall and handsome you are, Toto" and Toto swallowed the bait right off, dumb runt, and him "I haven't seen you for such a long time, me and Héctor went by your house on our bicycles thousands of times last summer, and nothing doing" and her "really?" and the idiot "yes, you're first on the list" and the contest began "his list of the girls he liked the best, why didn't you go out anymore?" and the liar "I always go out" and Toto "do you love him that much?" and she "I'll never go out again" and the lace dress? did she make it for going to the bathroom? and Toto "Corky, you're the prettiest girl in Vallejos, and you're number one on the list," "no, it's not because of Héctor that I'm not going out, it's just that I don't like to" since lying is free, the whole year stuck in her house! and Toto "if you'd gone out this summer Héctor would have come back to you and not Pug-nose, anyway with Pug-nose . . . " and Corky sensed something and immediately "Paquita, can you leave me and Toto alone for a minute?" and I left, the fatal minute, in front of me nothing would have happened, with a glass against the wall you could hear everything perfectly from the kitchen. "Totie, you don't know how I loved Héctor, and how I still love him. That's why I don't go out anymore, when he's not in Vallejos there's nothing for me to go out for, and when he's here I'm afraid of meeting him again, and that instead of telling him to go to hell . . . I'll again be at his beck and call. But he's never going to look at me again . . . only I know why, Toto", and Toto, melting "why?" and a repentant Corky "because . . . it's hard to explain . . . boys get bored" and right there and then Corky probably covered her face with her hands what the hell for if she wasn't going to cry?, since Toto "don't cover your face, love is nothing to be ashamed of" and you could hear the kiss the phoney bitch gave him, and the melted candy "Corky . . . you don't have to be that way . . . he wanted to go back to you . . . and since he didn't see you, he went back to Pug-nose" and the queen of the hypocrites "yes, but maybe he found Pug-nose interesting" and him "why would she be more interesting?" and her "well . . . maybe Pug-nose was wiser, and hid things from him, secrets, and not knowing much about Pug-nose, not knowing her well . . . " and what I heard then makes me fit to be tied every time I remember: " . . . Oh Corky, how silly, he did everything he wanted to do to Pug-nose in the vestibule too, while her mother listened to the news!" ooh, ooh, I'll bet Toto's tongue stretches all the way from here to the North Pole and mad happy Corky now that she got what she wanted "no, you don't understand those things, you're too young" and Toto to look like a big shot "not so, the boys tell me everything, and that same year Pug-nose and you and the last days of vacation Mari, and this year Beanface Mascagno after her abortion, I found out about it in the drugstore and passed the word to Héctor" oh mother, good thing you caught me just then in the kitchen with the glass and I had to go back to the fitting room and Corky as calm as ever "I'm going to be a good advertisement with your dress, Mrs. Páez, at the Independence Day dance" and Mom delighted, ooh, if she only knew the advertisement Corky was and one day after school in the middle of the square there was a furious creature in my way, it begins with P and ends with e: Pug-nose! "so that's where we're at, gossip and slander!" me taking advantage of an innocent boy (!) to ruin her honor, she who always said nice things about me at the club, because she thought I was an intelligent girl, but now she could see that reading trashy novels had gone to my head and after the crime the punishment will follow "you cannot imagine what's waiting for you, the cold shoulder, none of my friends will even say 'hi' to you when they come back in the summer, you stinker" and reaching boiling point "you . . . you stinker" and a hard wallop on my head with her patent leather pocketbook, the atheist, and all the books she had in her other hand fell and I raced home while she gathered them up, because if she hit me with the hard cover volume of *The Brothers Karamazov* it would have been my last hour. And I'm the guilty one, since nobody can talk against the little stinker because of his cousin, and now nobody's going to ask me to dance at the social and I wish I had the luck Celia's sister had, and Celia wasn't bad! Mita had a cold up until the baby was born, Mita, how hot it is next to the fireplace! "don't come so close, you'll catch a cold like me" and to top it all off her layette was already complete from the other baby that died, she's got nothing to do after going to the drugstore in the morning for a little while, tell me, Mita: is Teté a relative of the late Celia? "no" what does tuberculosis come from? "*María* is one of the most beautiful novels ever, you must take it out of the library," Celia was still working with Dad after she got sick, Dad was lucky not to catch it "the old woman was only the brother-in-law's mother, but she took care of her till the end," did Celia have any boyfriend in Vallejos? "I've already almost forgotten the beginning of *María*" nobody wanted to marry Celia? "do you remember the ending? I can't forget it, with the fire red sun of spring that sets at seven in the Colombian mountains, almost night when the frozen winter air descends, galloping full speed to the grove that shelters white tombs and from the mountain peaks and from heaven you can see Efraín reach the tombs and look for the newest, and beneath the ground is María, dead at eighteen, Efraín who counted the days until he could return, leave his student's uniform and see her again, and he reaches the plantations and María's not in the house, not sewing, not embroidering, not going for water to the well among the cactus plants" did María let him touch her? did Efraín do to her what he wanted? "because to be near where she is now Efraín has to get on his horse again and with the last hours of sunlight ride and ride faraway into the mountains where the white tombs facing the setting sun are red and María, María, it's so easy to find the tomb of his María, poor Efraín, he has only to look for the newest" did she confess before dying? "and to know that she's so close, and not be able to speak to her, but Efraín must talk, talk until he has nothing left to say because María is going to listen to him, she's looking at him from the mountains, or the clouds, and one must have faith and think that she'll listen to all he says and if you only heard one word from María, meaning that she's been listening, what a consolation it would be, or to see her, see her just for a second appearing among the trees" and that would be one of the Virgin's miracles "since it's already night and the mountain frost has descended, Efraín's face wet with tears, tears big and round like pearls, and that would be the very mercy of the Holy

Virgin, if she existed: when Efraín suffers so much his tears run down his face and some fall on the tombstone and the grass, and in those pearl-like tears the Virgin causes the pale face to appear with the long hair that falls to her waist, and the rings of sickness under her eyes, the cheeks dry from fever, the white skin of consumption in the night of the quarter moon, in each tear María reflected, in each silver pearl, white like the dead but smiling at Efraín she tells him all he wants to know, every little bit?" yes, the Virgin does exist "since he only wants to know three things: if she's well, if she suffers no more, and if she still loves him, and one smile is enough to answer all three questions, María's smile, because she's well, not suffering, and loves him as much as ever, forever, because she's dead, forever smiling and forever dead, María's smile" the instructor's smile, so many smiles he's given me, but they don't mean anything, anything definite, a person who's still living can give you a little smile and then change his mind and I don't think the instructor's a married man. And it was almost at the beginning of school that I left *María* by Jorge Isaacs in his room. And he never came near me again. The librarian's going to kill me "why did it take you such a long time to return *María?* You're pretty damn slow," slow my foot, I finished *María* in two nights, and I'm going to read it again, five girls ahead of me on line: I'll take advantage and go to the library, and I'll read and touch every page, if the instructor tells me he read it I'll touch every page, gently touching each page with the tips of my five fingers, ten fingers, up and down and if he swears he read it all, that he ran his eyes over each word, his eyes looking out of his eyelashes, he ran those feather eyelashes—tiny feather dusters that swept the dirt off each word, and he returns the book to me clean as a slate: the instructor read every word of *María* and there's not one that I'm not going to reread. How much longer will it take the priest to confess all of us? my knees hurt from kneeling, but at night, alone in my bed, in the fitting room, only the mannikin saw me, what does Corky think about at night after turning the light off?, looking from my bed at any old thing on the sewing table, at the mannikin, the sewing machine, the tape measure, the scissors and Raúl García, Toto can't spy on me! shouldn't I take revenge on the stinker? "during recess a big kid ran after someone to do you know what and the little kid escaped and at home they complained to the school," don't tell me more because what you want is to bring up the subject of Raúl García "and this year the same thing happened and the kid escaped again" who escaped, the big kid or the girl? "what girl?" the one who they ran after, "right, the one who escaped was the girl" and the big kid? "no, the one who ran after her this year was a boy her size and her mother told her father and they told the girl he wasn't a big kid and why didn't she defend herself, but they didn't know the boy might have two friends who could help: one could hide behind the tree in the back and the other behind the bathroom door" and didn't the girl tell them? "yes, that was the third time they ran after her" but why do they always run after her? "because she has the highest marks, and her parents asked her the same thing, why do they always run after you? and they told her to learn to defend herself" why don't they send her to the convent school? "I can't tell you her name because I swore not to" but are you sure your Dad never said anything about Celia to your Mom? "that when she worked for your Dad they didn't deliver the suits late like now" I left home determined to see the instructor, Mom: don't tell anybody what I told you about Corky "those are the Social Club beauties, so many airs and they're common trash" but the better people go to the club "if I see you end up like them I'll kill you," I'm not going to have my milk with Mom in the fitting room, and in Dad's workshop with the cup of milk and bread and butter in my hand, I swear Dad it wasn't on purpose, the sticky bread and butter on the cashmere! and with the tape measure folded in two you can see the marks where he hit me "you have a mark down to where your back changes name, does it hurt when I caress you?" the instructor with his ringless hand, does he take it off to pass for a bachelor? in one of the rooms that face the hotel patio "they can take away my job for letting you come in, I should go see your father and tell him to take better care of you" and at the dance he doesn't ask me to dance because he's too old for me and the students don't either and Mita, please, make Héctor ask me to dance and make him tell the students, they're all friends of his, to ask me to dance, if they haven't already told Mita they saw me leave the hotel, I'm going to tell her without a minute to lose as soon as they finish the peaches and leave her alone, Toto, Héctor, and the little baby, what tiny little hands, he stretches them out to me so that I'll lift him out of his little chair, but Toto says that the baby who died was handsomer and Héctor doesn't want to go to the den to study because it's so hot and Mita "if you're waiting for it to get cold in the summer you're never going to pass the entrance exam" for the Naval Academy! Mita, I have to tell you something and Toto "good-bye River, your Dad cut you down to size, idiot that you are, not appreciating the better uniform" and "you, you little shit, don't start up with River because you're too young to talk about those things" Mita, listen to me, I'll hold the baby in my arms while I tell you something, but nobody saw that the peach skins were near the little baby and he put one in his mouth and swallowed it, and couldn't breathe, don't get frightened Toto, the baby won't die, why do you get so frightened? the little baby coughing since he's choking, and what could we do? instead of doing something Toto went out to the backyard to scream and cry as if his little brother had already died, the maid was the only one who knew what to do and she put her fingers in the little baby's mouth and pulled out a real long piece of peach skin and just the same Toto kept screaming, since screaming is free "you'll never know what the after-effects will be! the after-effects, if he stops breathing! all night long!" Mita, why don't we go to the kitchen so I can tell you something, "Toto, shut up", Mita shouted, you can hear Toto screaming all the way to the street "you have to watch over him all night, just in case the after-effects come!" and Héctor "enough already, enough hamming! I told you to stop screaming, you fucking fag, shut up, SHUT UP!!!" and Toto "fag your ass, and it's even worse to be an intruder, INTRUDER!!! Get out of this house, out!!!" with his finger like actors when they throw somebody out, since Toto was doing a little imitation of some movie on the side and right there and then I thought Héctor would leave him sitting on the floor with one whack but he was hurt, "I knew you would say that to me one day" and he locked himself in his room, a doormouse sleeps less than him always getting up at twelve in a bad mood, tak! he pulls a branch off the fern tree each time he goes by, tak! it'll be Toto's ear he'll pull off one of these days. Mita, listen to me, listen, I have to tell you something, it's not about Toto, no, I'm not going to stand up for anybody, it's another thing I want to tell you before somebody else does "don't come to me with your complaints because between the two big pests and the little one they're already driving me crazy" it isn't complaints! "I'm going to put this baby to sleep, he's sleepy that's what's wrong with him, God knows when this summer will come to an end" the truth is these pampas are as dry as rock, and when Dad came to Vallejos and saw this dusty town with not a tree in sight? I would have written Celia not to come even though Celia at least brought him fresh news from the village, how angry Toto got when I didn't lend him the postcard, I'm going to frame it, it costs 1.50 to put glass and a frame on it, if I knew how to paint with oils I'd paint it big, and from a window in one of the cheapest cottages way up you can see the river below and the orchards divided by rows of piled rocks, are the orchards big? "no, but the owners take very special care of every square inch of them and in the spring all the orchards turn white because they're all apple trees" and why in the world did he come to Argentina, he wears his thimble all day long in the pampas and closes the window so the wind and dirt won't come in: it's lucky he doesn't know the students are against me, what did I do Holy Virgin to receive this punishment? I saved myself from the instructor without Toto having to come and save me and next year he's lucky, going to boarding school in Buenos Aires while I'm stuck forever in the convent school in Vallejos "Paquí, Paquí, you can't imagine how marvelous boarding school is, at Teté's convent school they'd go to the bathroom at night to read novels, sitting on the john four at a time reading the same book together" and in the illustrated brochure the George Washington Private School dormitories are scattered all over a very big park and on Sundays Toto will take the train and in less than an hour he'll be in downtown Buenos Aires, no! I can't believe it! there are only two to go from grammar school! and then me! I stole, I lied, I didn't pray, and evil thoughts, and there's more, do you confess a mortal sin at the end or the beginning? for the father confessor wanting to sin is the same as, or worse than, sinning, there's no difference between thinking of Raúl García in my bed at night or going into his house early in the morning instead of going to school since Raúl's father sleeps until twelve like Raúl but in another room and Raúl is alone and I get in between his sheets warm from the night: the customers sit on my couch to try on basted dresses. God is everywhere and sees everything, maybe he was in the headless mannikin, God doesn't need eyes to see . . . that Raúl finally gets to do what he wanted! Toto, come tell me who's the girl who escaped from school "no one, I was lying" didn't they do anything to the big kid? "no, but God will punish him" what will God's punishment be? "I don't know, something awful" what will it be? "His face'll get full of scabs so everybody will realize it when they come near, like a dog with scabs" did the girls mother complain to the school again? "no, she complained to the teacher when she met her coming out of the movies" and didn't she complain to the principal? "no, my principal never goes out, she's never in the stores or the movies" and why didn't they go see the principal at school? "because the girl's mother was ashamed to go to the school again to complain" and now it's my turn to go to the confessional and tell everything, the second to the last in line is crossing herself, she must be about finished and it was Raúl García who did what he wanted to me with the help of my mind, and for the father confessor it doesn't matter if it's only with your mind, and it wasn't only once, every night I promise not to, not to think about him, but he slides in between my sheets with his big woodchopping hands, rubs me with his cigarette-stained fingers and goes right to my open wound, which is worse than evil thoughts: one morning I'm going to wake up with the fingers of my hands stained from cigarettes, and big woodchopping hands, a fifteen-year-old girl with big man hands hanging from each arm, that will be God's punishment! and the Virgin doesn't know how lucky she was, God's blessing made her have a son and stay a virgin forever, she stayed pure for all of eternity, looking everybody straight in the eye nobody can say she was common trash, "so many airs and they're common trash" Mom said, and Mita "God doesn't need a man dressed in skirts to remind him that all the poor thing did her whole life was to suffer" and in front of a customer Mom "Celia and her sister were a couple of tramps" how can Mom be so sure they were bad? now there's only one more left from grammar school to confess and I'll tell the nun I have a stomach ache and I'll sneak out of here as if I were going to vomit in the bathroom: Raúl is probably still sleeping and I'll get between he sheets that he washes himself, or does his father? the little window of the confessional with its little black grating doesn't let you see the priest sitting inside, but opening the windows in the houses highest up on the mountain you can see the town below with little white flowers, when it's autumn in Argentina it's spring in Galicia: they plant a lot of apple trees, now he doesn't let me go anywhere alone, if I stay for supper at Mita's house he doesn't even let me walk two blocks alone, on the corner waiting for me before going into the bar, but didn't I leave *María* in the hotel room? how come it's in Dad's workshop now? on top of Berto's new grayish jacket "Paquita, this book is from the library, right? go and return it, and from now on you must behave like a good girl, you understand? so nobody can come tell your father his daughter has done something bad: this better be the last time somebody comes to tell me to take better care of my daughter, luckily your mother doesn't know a thing" paralyzed, my heart stops beating, with the book in my hand to go to the library "no, go to the library tomorrow, it's too late now, and I can't take you because a customer's coming any minute now to be measured" yes Dad, *María* by Jorge Isaacs, and I never found out if the instructor read it or not, and did the instructor swear by his mother so that Dad would believe he didn't do anything to me? and Dad believed him, because if not, after a beating he would have taken me to the doctor to be examined, the instructor probably swore by his mother, or his wife? and Dad believed the whole truth of what really happened: nothing happened, and Dad forgave me for going into the hotel room of a man much older than me, and now I can't go anywhere alone, he's always watching me, God made him forgive me and not hit me, he didn't even shout at me or tell Mom, and luckily there's less to wait now: just as soon as the last girl from grammar school finishes I'll go first on the high school girls' line, if Dad had waited for me after the González girl's birthday I wouldn't have seen Raúl García "so nobody can tell your father his daughter did something wrong, you're still too young to know what's right and wrong" and he gave me the book to return to the library "tell your mother not to make dinner for me, I'm going to the bar to have a cup of coffee before the customer comes, I'm not hungry, go and tell her" and from my bed at dawn I could hear the street door open meaning he was already back, dear God, I beg of you for all that you hold dear, don't let him beat me, he might be angry because he lost at cards and get the tantrum he didn't have this afternoon and grab the tape and beat me: he went to the bathroom, came out of the bathroom, went to his room, he's lying down now, what could he be thinking about? that he didn't beat me? thanks dear God, thanks for telling him to forgive me, and Dad listened to you, maybe while he was cutting that expensive fabric for Berto, or while he was thinking he would have been better off in Churanzás? will he think about Churanzás till the day he dies? I'm not going to tell him anything and as a surprise I'll hang the picture of the postcard in his workshop, how come I didn't think about that before? and while the last girl from grammar school finishes confessing, dear God, I'm going to say a rosary to you, please tell me what's right and what's wrong, Teté said that the dead pray for us, she prays for her grandfather who died and her grandfather prays for her in heaven, Toto prays for his little brother who died, but his little brother can't pray for Toto because he died unbaptised and is in limbo, is that why Toto always has the devil right by him? maybe my dead grandma from Galicia prays for me and Dad, and does Celia remember me? no, I was very young, I'm going to say a whole rosary to the Virgin, no, to God our Almighty Father, for Celia's soul to rest in peace.

XI

Cobito, Spring, 1946

I'm going to murder these bastards, not a single one of them's going to get away when they step into the mousehole, that fucking garage crawling with criminals, they'll fall on the sidewalk, no time to sneak behind the newsstand, the lousy bastards, you'll learn what it is to fink out on Deadly Joe, one bullet in the leg (and they won't run), a second in the hand (and they'll drop their guns), they've had it, no time to raise the metal gate and crawl into the mousehole: they thought they were safe, in the secret passageways of the garage, rats inside the cheese, and what a cheese: a block long, full of holes inside but a bulletproof crust outside, and they screwed themselves since here only Joe is bulletproof, and when I catch up with these cowards I'm going to spit in their mugs, two slaps for every last one of them, once with the back of my hand, slam! and then with the palm which is even worse, damn bastards, didn't you know my callouses are hard from pulling the trigger? and *there* they'll be, lined up one by one, the doublecrossers of my gang, false as Judas, which doesn't mean Jewish, waiting to see what ol' Joe's going to do with their worthless lives. But waiting is so long, looking out the window is all I can do until nine-thirty? only thing on the street is a closed newsstand, who's going to walk by this rotten school anyway? Sunday even the shoeshine boys hit the road and leave everything a mess inside the newsstand, open cans of shoe wax rotting away faster than me and brushes left around, they're free, they don't have to put up with the supervisor, and if all the residents are away and I'm staying alone I don't give a damn, with my shoes dirty and the supervisor on Friday before class "So-o-o-, shoes unshined . . . and fresh answers" bastard, and right to Sunday black list, but at nine-thirty and a half-minute when the doublecrossers are back, a bullet in their legs and they're goners, a kick in the belly and their mouths bleeding they kiss the dirt on the Chicago alley, and another harder kick right in the stomach so they'll spill out the secret of the metal gate and all they had for lunch at home I'll bet on top of it some jackass hit the soda fountain in the afternoon, what do you think they ordered? a triple-decker banana split, in *one* plate, for *one* guy, shoving it in, the bastard, and with one single kick I'll make him spill it out, yeah man, Joe will dash into the garage the minute they spill out the-secret-of-the-tightly-shut-metal-gate that only opens if you step on the key tile of the sidewalk. And I charge in while the doublecrossers are still twitching in agony, what a bunch of fucks, huh? with family in Buenos Aires and gorging themselves on Sundays and to top it all off they finked out on Joe, who stepping into the hideout carefully checks out the passageways and . . . shit! if I'd only known in time that there was a way out of the art rooms Casals wouldn't have gotten away, and me wanting a fuck so bad, damn Casals. The perfect murder takes time to prepare, it must be like a watch that never slows down, hotpants Colombo wanted to grab him that very Sunday, the first Sunday off (*I* took off too, not like today) and me even hotter "Casals, you coming back for supper or at curfew?" and the bootlicker came at five to seven so he could be the first in line for supper, the first Sunday off and he wanted to be the first to get back, the first in everything, instead of coming in at nine-thirty and a half-minute, oh no, at seven sharp, the ballbuster, still sunny out and he was already the first in line, if I had gone out today I would have been the last to get back: I'd jump over the fence, make a one-hand landing on top of the list before that bastard supervisor could take it away, yeah man, the signature of Joe the last to arrive on Sunday at nine-thirty and a half-minute and a half-second post meridian: after the shooting I smashed the shit out of that whiskey shelf in the waterfront bar. And at five to seven, the first Sunday off, having relatives in town this ballbuster comes skipping into the dining room, with the heat and the sun still beating down, the lousy manager with what they charge in this fucking joint topping off a shitty Sunday for the boys without relatives with that cold shit, pure fat cold cuts, Colombo winks at me and when supper's over Shorty Casals looks blankly into space clammed up, what are you thinking about, Casals? "Nothing" with his squeaking violin voice, you're not crying are you, Casals? didn't you like the food? "Did *you?*" Why don't we play a little piano, Casals? "Where?" said Shorty, and Colombo's plan "In the music room, on the third floor of the old building" and Shorty "But that's where the art rooms and chem labs are" and Colombo "And at the very end a music room, didn't you ever see it?" and Casals flushed his tears and scooted up the stairs ahead of us to the third floor and between the third and second he quickly swung around because there wasn't any music room: Colombo covering the wall and me against the bannister we blocked the way. And then he read our minds, shitty Shorty, and with one leap he was back on the third floor but Colombo grabbed the tip of his fancy-tailed jacket. At last Joe had his victim cornered and told his lieutenant let him go! Hold your fire! No matter how fast this lousy skunk runs there's no escape: all the secret passageways in the hideout are blocked, and the cat is going to gobble up the mouse . . . and who the hell's the fucker that left the big art room open with the flower pots for drawing and the artificial fruit (meet my banana) and Shorty flies through there to the smaller room with casts of doric columns (grab my column) and Colombo after him like a rabbit caught him by the arm and held him so tight, this time he couldn't escape: there's nowhere to go after the smaller room, a wall full of shelves, another with a blackboard, another with windows and no exit: and Joe comes charging in with his fly open, gets his hands on the poor slob, and son of a bitch the jump he gave, he split through that one door to the flower pots room, but Joe's mistakes only happen once, next time he comes into a joint he's going to double lock the door behind him, and Colombo "Why don't you run after him?" forget it, let him go and fuck himself, because Shorty had escaped through the open door, and from there to the big room and from there to the second floor and from there to the first floor and then he didn't move an inch from the monitor until bedtime. And tomorrow's Monday! Botany, Math, Grammar, and Geography, they're going to sock me four Ds but what the hell do I care since I'm taking exams anyway at the end, and in the summer the Geography broad will be sure to give the exam bare-assed with her legs crossed. Want me to cool you off with a fan, Miss? now that I've looked all the way up to your tonsils from my seat in the first row. What's it to Casals to let me have a seat in the first row? only once he let me sit there in Geography, the seat next to the teacher's desk, it doesn't matter to Shorty Casals if they give a surprise quiz, he always knows everything, he doesn't have to cheat in front of her: the teacher's eyes can read even the lice in Shorty's head, not even Al Capone could cheat in that seat. And in the afternoon, Gym and Music, the year never ends, three more months of school and then soon everybody will start swimming in the Paraná River: on the shore the cricket is singing, I get the hell out of the house, lie down in the shade fishing and if I fall asleep with rod in hand, afterwards I can't open my eyes, they stick together if the shade moves away and I'm still there loafing but now in the sun, like the kid who once died of a sunstroke but it doesn't bother me except it's hard to open my eyes between the heat and the blearies, the sun shines strong until nine in Paraná, the time the old man closes the store, so he doesn't have to waste electricity, but now my brother is in charge "An extra month of tuition expenses since you won't pass without taking exams, during vacation at least you'll save me the money for an errand boy," Colombo goes up to the country, Casals to his home town, all they think about on vacation is getting up late, with school at seven all year round what the hell I already fucked up this term but they can still fuck me double in the fall, instead of only once in the summer, even if Colombo isn't coming I'm still going to the laundry during rest period, what's the fun in playing basketball when your bean's melting? in this heat the busty washerwomen strip down to their slips while they're washing, spying from the rear window, go on, scrub those undershirts, go on, harder, so they'll pop out, go on, you got to get that come stain out of the handkerchief, give it all you got, so your tit will pop out of its harness and I'll cream on you boy if it gets you in the eye it'll plug the whole thing up. "It weakens you," ballbuster Colombo, melting away running after the bare-assed ball, a good bare-assed broad is what I need after my bath, instead of going to study hall, tomorrow at this time in study hall and at this time the washerwomen will be on the loose, before dark the whores start blossoming like weeds under the dock lights. Bucktoothed, fat, shitty washerwomen, fucking fat Peronist, my sweet dumpling, come to me I'm all alone, not a soul in the school park today Sunday, I'll gab with the monitor and you sneak through the little side gate and wait for me legs opened behind the bushes, fucking fat maid, she has the cheek to come in those runover shoes with her apron still on, damn hot on the street I'll fuck myself before going with her, nobody, nobody stayed this Sunday, everybody cut out to grub with their relatives, Casals the first and he didn't come back until the very last minute on Sundays after that, but Colombo and the Paraguayan Wagger, shitty doublecrossers, who are they trying to kid with no relatives? at seven sharp they'll drop on the handouts of cold fried shit like flies, and for all her screaming the monitor won't hear the fat washerwoman half a mile away behind the bushes, a kick in her ass if she screams and I'll pinch her tit till she shuts up, that's where we should have taken Casals, behind the bushes. A quarter past six, the Paraguayan, who knows, but it's a sure bet Colombo has no dough, who's he trying to kid? watching the pool game in the station bar, Merlo, rotten one-horse town, no stores, no nothing. Bluffing I say to him "Colombo, why don't you come to Paraná with me during vacation?" my old lady'd kill me if I brought him and Colombo "no, I have a good time in La Pampa, a full three months in the country," "aw come to Paraná, we can fish all day long," bullshit, and the bastard keeps mum and me real smooth "you invite me one year and I'll invite you the next" to the country, this bastard saves his breath watching a fly in the pool room at the station, hard to believe but there are no stores, if my brother'd bring the store here to Merlo he'd have no competition, *The Magic Carpet* the only rotten store but the Turks don't have our know-how, the owners of the prosperous "White Bird" of the progressive city of Paraná, with a special section of Grade A homemade food products, pickled salmon and herring, meat pie filling, assorted pastry, since soup and stew, stew and soup I'm not eating any more in my whole fucking life when I get out of school, I pass my plate to Casals, let him put it where he likes, soup, veal cutlets acceptable on the outside and inside the surprise meat otherwise known as "fat," it's the only thing Casals leaves, "eat everything" his old lady told him, and he eats everything, because he's a ballbuster, stoops his noodle over the book and doesn't raise it again until the bell rings, and not once does he raise his noodle, if you don't raise your noodle, Casals, I'll split it for you with an axe!, and he's the type that wouldn't raise it, his old lady told him to study everything, why the fuck do you study so much, Casals? "time goes by faster that way," don't you like school? "no, and you're going to have to stay a month more for the exams, since you didn't pass," he's home before summer starts with nothing to do, his old man doesn't make him slave in the store, and me shine my shoes, and why do I have to pay attention to my sonofabitch brother? fuck him and his minding the store bit, my old man "go, Cobito, go to the river, and if you catch a good sole bring it back, don't bother with the minnows, they're no good for anything, go Cobito, but put something on your head, the sun is strong." If the old man were alive I'd write him, Casals writes the old lady a letter a day, I'd tell him there's only one store in this rotten neighborhood, Casals, what do you fill two pages with every day? and my old lady: "Dear Cobito: We're in good health and have plenty of work fortunately, you're going to have to help your brother in the store, it's been a very good winter, how happy your father would be if he were alive, but I'm very sad. If the summer is as good as the winter we'll soon be able to pay up the probate bills" and me behind the counter in the heat because I didn't study, Casals did and he's already stooping his noodle all set to write his letter, between the end-of-study bell and the dinner bell he finished off a page, and after dinner he sucks the dessert orange with one hand and with the other what does he do? jerk off? ha ha, smart aleck, he writes the second page and signs before the bell rings for the last study hall, ha ha, and why do you shit for two hours locked up in the bathroom Monday night after the quiet bell? writing another page! you fucking squirt, do you write your broad every Monday? "what's it your business?" ah, careful, careful, the girlie with her secrets . . . and rip! Wagger tore the page from him coming out of the shithouse, jerking off in the bathroom Wagger is in a fix because his bed's next to the monitor's and the creaking of the bed can be heard, even in the cold the shitty Paraguayan goes to the bathroom to jerk off and in the middle of creaming somebody flushes the toilet and out comes Casals armed with pen and paper and three whole written pages "Dear Mommy": ha ha!, "a new week begins which means one less to go before we're together again, how little to go, Mommy, one more week till the end of this month and then a couple of months more. If I were one of those boys who have to stay an extra month more to prepare for exams I'd die. The food is still second-rate but I eat everything so as not to get sick" Wagger read to the beat of his meat and I who had still not creamed came to see if he wasn't fucking and on the scond page ". . . yesterday Sunday Héctor waited for me at the station, as usual he arrived late and his father took us straight to lunch in the car. Uncle was angry with Héctor, they're not on speaking terms because Héctor is doing almost nothing to prepare for the Naval

Academy . . ." shitty tattletale! ". . . In the boardinghouse they served ravioli and then beef stew, delicious . . .", how the son of a bitch grubs ". . . and then Héctor wanted to take a nap because he went to bed late Saturday and we decided that he should sleep twenty minutes so we could take the bus at two-thirty to go to the matinee of *Spellbound*, a movie of suspense and romance. I tugged at him so much we finally got there but it had already begun and I missed the lettering of the credits, to see if they were like the posters outside the theater, with shaky lettering . . ." your mug will be shaky when I'm through with you! ". . . Some seventeen- and eighteen-year-old girls and classmates were in the theater, but no freshmen like me, they don't understand grown-up movies . . ." and out ran Shorty Casals from the kick the angry Paraguayan landed him and I grabbed for the third page but the bastard Paraguayan beat me to it and stuck the page in the slit of his ass and who was the third page for? ha ha, smart aleck, ". . . Today Monday the movie I have to tell you about is very difficult, instead of one extra page I ought to write you three or four, because the innocent man is confused and doesn't know if he's guilty or innocent in *Spellbound*, and I didn't really understand if he escapes because he thinks he's guilty or from fear that they'll catch him and sentence him, in any case he runs away immediately because if they catch him they'll definitely sentence him, if it wasn't for the girl who cleared everything up after hiding him, because it so happens everybody thinks he's the murderer and runs after him and he has something, a fog in his memory that keeps him from remembering the moment of the crime, but since he believes he's guilty every time somebody starts running after him he already started running ahead of time because he knows he's the murderer, or knows he seems to be the murderer . . ." fuck your murderer, and Wagger and Paraguayan finished jerking off in two strokes and tell me, Paraguayan, tell me about Carmela, the bratty bitch, bastard Paraguayan, last year his still hadn't grown on him and he screwed the little brat just off the boat from Italy, such whores in Chaco, the Chaco wops are whores to boot, and at the end of vacation the mailman fucked her, tell me about it, Paraguayan, what did the brat do? did it hurt her? how good was her ass? and when the Paraguayan goes home this vacation he's going to make her, faggy bastard, anyway, the mailman already fucked her before school, with the horse's prick he has. And mine's going into her too, and into Laurita, come to me baby, I'll make mincemeat out of you, you bitch, go with the seniors, whore, all the first-year broads want the seniors, bitches, they don't give a hoot for Colombo the brat either, Graciela has the best boobs, and what's Laurita fussing about if she's Jewish too, Whiskers sure gobbles her up with his eyes "Boys and girls, today we're going to talk about the Phoenicians . . ." and there's nothing Phoenician about Laurita's ass, what the shit is he looking at it for? put your missing teeth back in, Whiskers, you're starting to drool, and he comes to me with the sad story "Umansky, you're really giving me a lot of trouble, and listen, in front of young ladies you mustn't make those gestures, men don't do that, little boys do" bastard, and he sends me to Mr. Dean of Students who in turn takes my leave away for a month, the doublecrosser putting on the big act, our spiritual father: "Boys! in this moment a father is speaking to you" (father my balls), "The dean vanishes to make way for someone else who feels differently toward you, my sons, a father is speaking to you, boys" not for the life of me would I be your son, the biggest bum in Merlo his son is, the skinny brat burned out by smoking and jerking off, he must be doing it since he was nine years old, and when he's not doing it, it's because he has a cigarette in one hand and in the other dirty pictures he swiped from the Paraguayan, yeah, that's the one he can spout off to, his own son, with the tirade "I want to talk to you about sex, but not sex as this society corrupted by obscene posters understands it . . . Sex is love!" his wife's mustache, the beanpole, you kiss her and you get forked, the fire department has to come and unscrew you, "masturbation is a vice, which like all vices you can step by step get rid of, it's impossible to pull the evil out by its roots, we cannot with our humble strength pull a pinetree out by its roots, but cutting one bud off today, another tomorrow, letting one night go by, then two, clipping the smaller branches one by one, reduce that habit to twice a week, and then once, the larger branches start falling and then only the trunk is left: don't do it any more, don't even fornicate, if we're not in love with the girl who comes our way, because naked sex, without the marvelous apparel of love, is a purely animal act, and as such, degrades mankind." And if his beanpole of a wife takes off the marvelous apparel of her underpants and bra and the two hundred and thirty-three bones of the human body come into view, of course he'd immediately have to throw a sheet over her, or the marvelous apparel of a blanket if it's cold. He can cover her with the mattress too, and suffocate our spiritual mother to death, since I asked her if I could eat at Colombo's table on my birthday, and from up there the Beanpole shook her head and "you mustn't go against the rules" is it cold up there, fucking Beanpole? And when she turned around in the doctor's office I swiped the bottle of alcohol, now for the vaccinations she'll have to disinfect the kids' arms with spit, one gulp puts the balls in their place, two gulps of pure alcohol and the fat broad's tits get red, three gulps and it all looks the same with or without glasses, four gulps I jerk off and the taste lasts longer, fucking must be like that, the Garden of Eden, kill the broad if you overdo it, and you have to revive her, with artificial respiration, instead of oxygen I plunge it into her and she comes to life again, is Graciela a boozer? with one little sip, two sips, behind the bushes and she's not Jewish, that's what bugs me. From the first store to the last along the pier in Paraná where the stores begin all the chicks are Jewish, today Sunday the river is probably full, free and easy I'll take myself fishing, but not on her life would the old lady fry minnows if I brought her some, it could save money. And it would be better than the shit at school, me and Colombo can go to the river and live off minnows, fry them in any old can and for my birthday I'd swipe something from home, fresh minnows and assorted pastry. There's no way out of the store deal, visiting Colombo I'd save them the cost of my meals, fuck Colombo, he didn't invite me, after exams it's already summer my brother will screw me into the counter for making him spend a month more tuition, and at the end of summer it will already have been a year, poor old man, how thin you got a year ago, because of that sonofabitch tumor, until we opened the store again, only three days we closed for mourning, you had worked so much, old man, forgive me, as soon as I'm home I'll get behind the counter, you spent your whole life behind the counter after you came from Odessa with only what you had on and the "White Bird" is now an accredited establishment of the progressive city of Paraná, and I'm going to look at them when they come in: you'd focus on them with a clinical eye when they'd come in, you'd take an X-ray of their pocketbooks and the prices of the "White Bird" would go up like milk about to boil, but it would have to be done like you did it, taking the milk off the stove just before it boils over so the customer doesn't shy away, if you were alive you'd teach me. And all those days fishing and smoking after school, why didn't I go back to the store instead? I could have played the moron arranging rolls of oilcloth and boxes of curtain hooks while I'd take in the whole pitch: the act, what you'd show them before saying the price, then the price according to their interest, the shit you'd show them as second choice, and the jerks swallowed the bait, the little discount at the end, and ding!, cash . . . ! how much ding cash have you made in your life, old bugger? not the fixed-price ones, you know the ones I mean, besides the X-raying of pocketbooks: you'd see it in their faces! my brother hasn't got a chance, twenty-five years old, wearing that funeral face, what does he know about entertaining people? do you think he ever fucked a girl? an ice cream cone was all he treated me to when he came to Buenos Aires this year. Ten cents worth of rubber bands, twenty of string, forty of nails, this summer he's going to put me behind the counter and the first maid that comes in I'll take care of her, assorted pastries, pickled herring, whatever, and then I'll throw her on the floor, hit her over the head with a roll of oilcloth, lower the metal gate, pull off her Peronist button and I don't care if the first one's a maid, if I don't start fucking this summer my balls are going to rot, and what do I have to look forward to? the counter, and every two minutes my old lady or the jackass walking in, and the brats at the club are worse than Laurita, they want the older guys so's to get married and the whore on the island charges two bucks. I wouldn't give a whore two bucks not even at my last gasp, that's a business for you, but it's my sonofabitch lousy luck! while others are lucky, they already fucked, but the worst is working during vacation, wish to hell all the teachers would drop dead! and our spiritual father too, so nobody'd be left, only Big Chief! if I could only be in Big Chief's dorm I would have already made one of the laundry broads, the first time I saw Big Chief I didn't know he was a monitor, blond and his nose doesn't point down but he looked kind of Jewish, but with the heat in study hall he unbuttoned his shirt and you could see the gold chain with the cross, and he took the only two brats of his dorm who had never fucked, a broad waited for them in a construction lot past the station, a buck to the watchman and the kids got it out of their system, without paying her a cent, Big Chief fixed it with the broad and he doesn't want to let it out but he takes the long way around the block so nobody'll see him going into the laundry to see busty, if Beanpole or her venerable husband and spiritual father of us all catches him it'll cost Big Chief his job. Without his monitor job no dough to finish up law school, and I was a jackass to start a racket on him in study hall, he shouted so loud he made the whole building shake "All weekend leaves are cancelled if the students who belched do not come forward!", my belch wasn't so loud but for an echo the Paraguayan uncorked a bottle of cider, it must have been the most microphonic belch he produced in the whole year but near him it smelled like they'd taken the cover off the stew from last week. And Big Chief arrived Sunday and nobody was going to leave because of the rotten Paraguayan since we wouldn't confess and Casals messed up the works with our spiritual father, "I can't miss my leave after a whole week of studying because the monitor feels like it, it's his business to find the culprit," Shorty dared to call out Big Chief, he now knew what was waiting for him behind the bushes if he stayed the whole Sunday. The Paraguayan thought Casals was going to tell on him and he went up to Big Chief, and Casals didn't miss his uncle's ravioli, lucky dog. It would be great to get into law school, Big Chief looks real sharp when he goes to the university, I can make a great triangle knot like his, what fucks me up is my brother's ties, where I have to make the knot the fucking tie is full of grease, so the grease won't show on that fucking knot I have to make it with the wide end of the tie, the triangle knot comes out great but thick as a sonofabitch, and shit on my brother the fucking jackass, can't he give me a newer tie? Big Chief combs his hair to the side without pomade, looks real sharp but it doesn't work on my curly hair, too many waves. And nobody bosses him around, back in Paraná I'm screwed behind the counter. I'll bet you have to study like a sonofabitch in law school, with Big Chief's brains okay, he doesn't have to break his ass studying so much, but I'm not afraid smoking screwed up my brains, and the broad they say Big Chief has in the university is good cheese, he has a photograph of her in his room, according to Colombo she's not very busty, the stinking worm is all over the place, of course he wasn't going to have time to jerk off looking at the picture but he could have done it at night remembering. Smoking couldn't have done anything to my brains because in Paraná I'd smoke but here I can't swipe butts from the old man, here I have to buy them myself, straight to the river to smoke what I'd swipe from the cigarette box lying free and easy on the grass, and who can I swipe from here? and in Paraná? who can I swipe from when I go back in the summer? how much brainier than me is Big Chief? he said to the Paraguayan "read the lesson two times thinking about what you're reading and if you're not a moron you'll already have it down pat" and even though Wagger the Paraguayan isn't a moron from birth, his cerebellum is drying up from all his jerking off, does he do it twice as much as me? according to Colombo Big Chief keeps the picture right where he can see it from the bed at night to do his royal hand jobs, but what hand jobs is he talking about if he has busty from the laundry, what a jackass Colombo is, not to realize that a guy with brains like Big Chief couldn't have jerked off as much as the Paraguayan or Colombo and besides, what does a guy who already has his broad have to be jerking his jelly for? and fucking doesn't spoil your brain, I never heard it said, sonofabitch dog's luck, instead of Big Chief it could have been another monitor the day I belched in study hall, and now he's wise to me, if not . . . jerking off too much is the worst thing for your growth and mind but smoking fucks you up too, it must be bad for your growth more than anything and for studying too, I don't spend a cent on cigarettes, I'm not that dumb . . . and Big Chief must be wise to Casals too, when Shorty spoke up against him about not getting leave; but then again, if he stayed all Sunday . . . I'd get Colombo to help and if Big Chief sees us taking him behind the bushes maybe he wouldn't say a thing because he's wise to Casals. But he's also wise to me, fuck it. It would be better if Colombo'd take him alone so we wouldn't realize, pretty impossible, and I'd wait for him behind the bushes, and I'll shit bullets on the hostages, the prisoners of war condemned to death, it's war declared between the police and the president of the gunfighters, and the prisoner's on my list . . . I'll give it to him: Aim . . . Fire! might Casals be thinking about going to law school? well let him think, he's going to die any minute anyway, today Sunday I should make shit of him with a bullet in his belly, so all the ravioli he washed down today would come out of the bullet hole, and those two? they got permission to take him out of school one Saturday afternoon, two people waiting in the sitting room, a couple, could they be alumni? from four or five years back? the guy stood up when he saw the dean coming with his arm around Casals, and the guy who got up from the chair looked like Casals, he wasn't an alumni, he was his father, and the mother too, when she saw Shorty she began to smile as if she'd won the lottery prize, when she smiled she looked just like Shorty, and sonofabitch Shorty smiled too and why not, he was getting the hell out. Only once a year, even if they'd come only once what more do you want, they took him out to eat. I never ate frogs' legs, milk-fed ducks, tortilla jubilee, and then off to the theater. How sad it is when you're just about to finish the ice cream cone, one more lick and you're down to the cone, and where's your fucking ice cream? and no 1.50 for the movies, I came back to school for supper that shitty Sunday, what the hell! my brother was going to eat bologna sandwiches and my old lady cheese in the hotel in Buenos Aires anyway, much more expensive than Paraná, almost twice as much if you're not careful in Buenos Aires and a wad of dough they spent in less than a week with the lawyer and the probate business. "Mom, there's nothing to see in Merlo," and they came just the same, on Sunday in Buenos Aires all the rides in Japanese Playland are working and you can win something in the shooting gallery, it's not all spending, but "we're going to Merlo," we saw the square and the only store, the moth-eaten Turks, my brother didn't even get wise to the fact it was the only store in Merlo, but I always forget to write him to tell him that. I have time now, fuck Sunday supper, and if Colombo's not careful he'll be late for supper, and who can I ask for paper? putting up with Judas's and Beanpole's mug, I'll swipe all the bottles of alcohol, rotten Beanpole. And another little bottle of chloroform for the last day of school, before he wakes up I'll shove the handkerchief soaked in chloroform against Shorty's nose, so this time it'll work. A good thing he didn't go and blab about it, we didn't do anything anyway, he couldn't accuse us of anything, the chloroform afternoon: "don't be a jackass, Colombo, I'm telling you the best time is five-thirty, after the basketball game, he comes in for a shower and we have almost a half hour till six then the bell rings for study hall, and listen carefully: you hide behind the closet, and when he comes in from the shower with the towel wrapped around him wait a minute because I'll come in right after him" and "you, Paraguayan, come behind me and hold his legs, since Colombo will hold his arms while I cover his face with the handkerchief soaked in chloroform, all set?" . . . "wait, fucking Paraguayan, he might hear us, he'll be coming out of the shower right away, don't smell it, jackass, chloroform's stronger than shit, like ether, but don't attack Shorty ahead of time or you'll ruin everything, you have to wait till he comes into the room", ". . . !!! . . . son of a bitch, stay still, hold his legs down good, Paraguayan, great, Colombo, that's the way, hold him good so . . . smell this perfume, Shorty, take in a good whiff, it's good for the brains, we're making you smell it so you—our roommate—will win the prize for the best student, now that you're the best of the residents, you should win over the day students too, and you Paraguayan, don't loosen up, hold him, it's been five minutes but it takes a little time to make him sleep, go ahead, sniff some chloroform from your sister's cunt, don't loosen up, Colombo, this pipsqueak bookworm twists like crazy, he'll fall asleep soon even if he doesn't want to, and then I'll fuck him, then Paraguayan right after and you too, shitty brat you never fucked in your whole life, why doesn't he fall asleep, why does he keep twisting? son of a bitch, stay still, stop twisting!!!" "Paraguayan you're a double-crosser, don't let him go, if Shorty goes and tells I'll pass the buck to you, you're the one to blame, shit, if he had slept he wouldn't have remembered a thing when he woke up, we'd wrap him up in the towel like he had it coming out of the shower and no sweat, he wouldn't realize a thing, while now he could very well go to the monitor and tell him we tried to fuck him, and all hell will break loose. You're the one to blame, me and Colombo are going to say it was your idea, right, Colombo?, we'll say it was this lily-livered Paraguayan's idea, eh, Colombo?" and it's about time for bratty Colombo to show up for supper, what does he do a whole afternoon watching other guys play in the poolroom?, he'll show up soon, even if he has leave: without dough where can he go? he'd do better not to show off so much, he's in the same boat as me, anyway, there's nothing to see in Merlo, it's a small town I told the old lady and my brother, Sunday and I had leave from ten a.m. on, and they didn't show up in the visiting room that day until two, from ten to twelve watching our spiritual father teach his son to play chess, what's he gonna learn, that lousy brat? from twelve-twenty, when I finished lunch with the students who didn't have leave, till two nobody came to the visiting room, if the parents bring candy for some kid, they offer some to the other kids. Now her hair is all white, dressed in black, my brother wore the mourning arm band but she was in black head to toe, the grand tour of the students' dorms, the rugby field, the gym, the bushes and outside, Merlo square, the main street, and after the strawberry-vanilla ice cream cone how many hours is it from five to nine-thirty when it's time to go back to school? wouldn't there be time to go downtown and eat with them? "If your father knew that in the most expensive school you didn't pass and he had to pay an extra month for the fun of it, because his little boy didn't pass and had to take exams instead, and you think he doesn't see you but he sees you, even if he's dead, and if he could he'd give you a good beating, your poor father, not even for him dead and all can you behave" the old lady had a small glass of beer and my brother drank the rest of the bottle, it's bad for my old lady, "you don't love your father, when you were little how he spoiled you, I told him not to spoil you so much, to make you help in the store, all that sunbathing, the doctors are right that a little exercise is good for growing, but why spend the whole day at the river? in the sun and water wearing yourself out. Now he sees he wasn't right to spoil you so much, if you loved him a little you'd behave better, but you don't love your poor father who's dead" and what was I going to go to the hotel with them for? they bought bologna sandwiches to eat in the hotel and the old lady cheese because bologna's bad for her liver, and who came back to school for supper that night, at seven, the Sunday night special, double rotten cold food for the students without relatives in Buenos Aires? not me! let somebody else eat that shit! the oranges from the park are sour as hell but how many did Colombo wash down? three? and me two, and what makes you say I don't love the old man?, it's not true what the old lady said, and how the fuck did I know he was going to die like that, instead of smoking down by the riverbank I'd watch the old man closely to see how he'd raise the prices when a sucker fell in, and I'd learn, not like that jackass brother of mine, what does he know about selling? and who am I going to learn from now? who's behind the counter? nobody! because they can fleece my half-wit brother any time they want, and even if they don't fleece him, he thinks to sell he has to lower the price, that's not right, eh old man?, look old man, I'm going to raise it all I can first, and then little by little I'll give them a discount and what discount are you talking about? I'll just lower it to half the increase and thank you, and when summer comes, you'll see old man, I won't go to the river except for national holidays, Sundays and Saturday afternoons, the rest of the time, on duty at the counter, and my brother the half-wit drank all that was left in the bottle of beer "make sure you do well in the exams because if they give you 'incomplete' in the summer you'll have to take them over in the fall and that's two more weeks of tuition, on top of what we already have to pay for the extra month, and money doesn't grow on trees, plus all our probate expenses. You can sweep the floor every morning, run my errands and bring the rolls of fabric up from the cellar, at least help me save up on errand boy bills during the summer", me? run his errands? and Colombo, the three months of vacation with his family romping in the country with nothing to do and Casals stinking squirt the first to go home, he's counting the days, even the hours and . . . what I wouldn't give to be in Paraná now . . . getting off the boat . . . seeing the docks and the stores and eating at home, and there's help needed at the counter to sell half a pound of oilcloth, weigh a pound of herring, shit half a pound of shit, do whatever my brother says, and the Paraguayan?, he's the wisest of all, he's a real wiseguy, all his vacations with the broads in Chaco, hotter than bitches in heat, he already has Carmela lined up, the stinking bitch, and I could make her too, three months in Chaco, a hell of a lot better than Paraná . . . Paraná: fuck the goddamn sonofabitch hole! I don't want to see you again! not for a single day am I going back, they can have it. In Chaco me and the Paraguayan could fish all day long, and in the middle of the jungle there are two roads, "Hey Wagger, take this road to the lagoon where the clean water is, and fill the canteens" and the Paraguayan takes the road, sure, to the lagoon, what lagoon? shit, any road so he'll get lost, and take two days to come back, then I'll go back to town, waiting for night I'll go to that run-down neighborhood, my triangle knot loose, half untied, my hair neat with the part to the side and with my shirt unbuttoned you can see my chain with the cross, come on, what cross, I'll wait for her behind the weeds where it's thickest I'll hide and when she comes by I'll grab her by the arm: you can't even see your own thoughts at night in Chaco it's so dark and once Carmela's sure I'm the Paraguayan I'll start lifting up her skirt. . . . If Colombo doesn't come for supper I'll kick his ass in, who does he think he's fooling? If he doesn't come it's because he scrounged a sandwich from the bar at the station, or one of the guys playing pool invited him. He'll pay for this.

XII

Esther's Diary, 1947

Sunday the seventh—I should be happy and I am not. Sorrow, not deep but still sorrow, wishes to nest in my bosom. Could it be the fading light of this Sunday twilight? Sunday is already going, with its array of golden but unfulfilled promises . . . at night they shine no more, like my tin brooch. The "E" for Esther I carry pinned to my bosom. "E" for expectations? My newly bought initial shined like gold and now all I have is a tin letter pinned to my heart, its portal perhaps, "Esther!" they say to me gently, and do I like a fool open up for any voice? sincere and affectionate? or deceptive and false?

Night has already fallen on my suburb, as on the most aristocratic niche of cosmopolitan Buenos Aires, the sun has set for all, one of the many consolations of the poor. I hardly opened the geometry book, before supper I could have studied, Esther . . . Esther . . . I don't understand you, you have a good sister who prepared you supper before going to the movies, your little nephew is an angel who gives you no trouble, poor thing, if I could get my doctor's degree soon the first thing I'd buy him would be a bicycle, between finishing high school and seven years of university . . . poor kid. Sitting quietly on the sidewalk, while the boy next door goes around the block four times since he has a bicycle. For every four times he lends him one. What can he do . . . if he was born poor, and did his aunt by any chance have a bicycle?, it was not our lot to have one, but this spell of bad luck is going to stop, Dardito, your aunt had a great blessing, God chose her among all the children in her school, a crowded school of our weed-infested suburb. She would stop writing and take you there, by way of the vacant lots (you know something? with you I'm not afraid, you are a little man), treading on the narrow path, stepping around the nettles, after jumping over the fence gate all you have to do is slip through the barbed wire and cross the railroad tracks and facing the station is the school, forge of tomorrow's men. "A student of humble background in our section, shining example of dedication to her studies, good fellowship, personal hygiene and perfect attendance, in this year of so many storms she did not once miss classes: our young lady Esther Castagno is the winner of the new scholarship awarded by the George Washington Private School of the distinguished community of Merlo": the principal came into the sixth grade classroom and announced the winner of the scholarship. To an illustrious high school for rich people.

But my children are going to have bicycles, even though we didn't. And did I by any chance go downtown today Sunday? I came to your house, Dardito, to spend the day, for a change of air . . . five blocks from home. And we had a good day, even though they left us all alone, your mom went to spend the whole afternoon at the movies and our dad went to the committee meeting to attend to his duties. Naughty boy, if it hadn't been for you I would have gone with him, but how could I leave you alone?

Laurita and Graciela are rich, of course they must have gone downtown as they planned, to the three-thirty show, and no triple feature, or even double, oh no!, one only, first-run, nice and expensive, it ends at a quarter to five so they'll have time to spend more money, for coffee and those pancakes like in the American movies. And that's not all! at about five-thirty or six they go to listen to the Santa Anita jazz group at Adlon. Adlon! Those brats would do better learning to wipe their own backsides first. And where is the famous Adlon? I walked by all the elegant stores on the street where Casals told me it was and why couldn't I find it? He explained the following: "Opposite that big jewelry store, not on the side of the silver candelabra but across the street where the bracelets and rings and gold stuff are, and at the back of those fur display windows is the door to Adlon." But I simply couldn't find it. Besides, my sister was in so much of a hurry with her sheets and we would have gotten to the sale in time anyway. They were selling at bargain prices white sheets with a sky blue rim embroidered on the pillow cases and another sky blue rim on the top sheet, and nothing else, that was all, but what more do you need?

Monday the 8th—I knew it! For some reason the hand of fate was gripping me yesterday, almost choking me, hand that isn't a hand because it is a claw. Is our dean leaving? because he is sick? is it or isn't it true? what evil lurks behind all this? In the exam room silence I don't know how I drowned that cry that tore from the deepest pit of my insides, there where a sentinel is always alert: my gratitude.

I would have shouted "We want our dean! we don't want him to go!" and perhaps I would have been able to move those children—that's all they are, irresponsible children—who dared to rejoice since our dean might be dismissed, and all because he once might have suspended one of them.

But she who owes him everything would do everything for him. One day an old teacher with an impeccable record stamped his signature on a memo, announcing that the winner of the annual scholarship was a girl of humble background from a neighborhood school, daughter of a blue-collar worker, he placed his confidence in someone he knew little about, thus possibly jeopardizing a brilliant career in education, because I could have been a stain on his life record. A scholarship for her first year, which will be renewed for her second (and it was) if the student deserves it, and for third, and thus year after year, till the girl ceases to be such, since that day she'll enter college.

I was going to tell Mom but my heart sank to my shoes and I couldn't, why upset her, she'd stir the milk in the little saucepan especially for me (aren't I an unpardonable idler?) just as she stirred it a moment ago for the rest of her brood. Mom, leave out the curd, I don't want curd in my milk! she keeps the curd for me, she thinks I like it and that I need it more than anybody because I'm the student, but I don't like it! nobody likes it. In Laurita's house they throw it out. Curd is common and disgusting, do you think if we throw it out we're going to be even poorer? you think so? ah, maybe my sister would understand my torment, or maybe not, but my studies are in danger, I need someone to talk to, after sitting the whole afternoon within these four walls without even opening a book, and now it's late, too late to walk five blocks in the dark. Dardito does it in a jiffy, you might call us the tortoise and the hare.

I didn't study, and I didn't even talk to my sister, and if they don't renew my scholarship this year what'll I do? I don't understand, why C in Zoology, D in Mathematics and C in History? because the young lady doesn't study!, she opens her textbook, shuts herself up, makes her poor father turn off the radio . . . and in this silence smelling of stew—both stew and silence simmering hour after hour—her eyes pass over the printed lines of the day's lesson, while her mind takes its own voyage. It is the voyage—no goal, no reward—of another foolish teenager.

How foolish Graciela is! She thinks I'm going to believe everything she tells me, and if the recess bell didn't ring she would have continued. She promised to sit with me tomorrow in music and tell me the whole thing. Graciela and her stories, I didn't pay much attention and she draws an arrow from the line she's taking notes on to a little box and in the box she writes "I have something to tell you," and I already know that what she has to tell me wears pants, and I know the rest too, that "he's mad about me but I can take him or leave him." Yes, since her father has money in the bank she thinks everybody loves her. She believes all they say to her. Now she got over her crush for Adhemar, I can understand why they all like him, with those eyelashes and such black eyes and blond hair like a cornfield, he's sixteen and yet as mature as a senior, but . . . I am almost positive that Graciela is now thinking about someone whose name begins with H. Or better, Graciela and I are thinking about H. That sad look searching for a still surface upon which to rest a tear, his bosom is a forge tempered by the fire of suffering but from it buds and drops off a diamond, a purified and boiling tear, a man's tear. A long time ago he lost his mother, In contrast, I don't think Adhemar has ever cried, sweet and well mannered perhaps because his life is only a honeycomb, a castle of honey, and if one day those walls collapse I can see him crying like a helpless child; quite a different thing is a man's tear.

It seems strange for Graciela to like H, but all she needs is variety. Pitiful empty girl. But I saw her heart and there's nothing there either: "so they're sacking old baldy?" was her only reaction to the crisis of an old teacher. That poor old principal of mine.

My brother-in-law hardly said hello to me today, was he offended because I didn't go to the committee meeting as promised? In any case, the delegate from Matanzas was going to speak and at the last minute didn't appear. When was the last time I went? . . . during the summer, I believe.

Tuesday the ninth—Casals saved my life, he went to the blackboard in grammar and stayed there for almost the whole hour, he didn't once run out of string, if not, Butterball would have definitely called on me today. Esther . . . what's the matter with you? . . . what's the matter??!! snap out of it, hapless girl, knowing very well that today it was almost certain to be my turn, with my scholarship in danger, my dreams heaped up, a castle of cards at the mercy of the hurricane of misfortune. Dad thinks I'm doing my homework, and he doesn't dare turn on the radio, I'd die of cold if I sat in the bedroom to write, does this wood-burning kitchen unite us more than family love? and nobody turns on the radio so I can do my homework and who am I? the intelligent one, the student . . . who doesn't study! a raven has flown into the house and nobody realizes it, everybody quiet, and it's already after ten! ah my father, my poor father, missed the ten o'clock news for me!, with his mangled arm he holds the newspaper and with his left hand he turns the page. Now that we poor people have our newspaper, its many pages the expression of our leader, in a word the heart of a nation is contained . . . Perón! during the one year you've been our president there's no room for all the things you've done for us in the pages of every day of every month of this year of newspapers . . . and nevertheless in your heart there's room: toys for your children! all the needy children of the Argentine republic, and laws for the workers, not to be humiliated any longer, and welfare for those burdened with years and with want! my poor father, and his little universe, home to factory and factory to home and on Saturday night a game of cards and his one glass of *grappa:* my father is a real man and one *grappa* puts only a spark in his eyes, which one fateful day were beclouded with pain. . . .

Once upon a time there was a great factory and the best foreman that ever lived. His hands controlled the heaviest and most difficult tools, he'd bend them to his will and repair each and every machine of the establishment, the great forge that turns out millions of yards of fabric a day. One of those days in which the infinite production of yards (also infinite is Fate's treachery) was piling up as usual thanks to the efforts of my father and his keen eye which didn't let not one of those iron pieces slacken . . . in a moment . . . perhaps absorbed in something he saw which seemed to be working wrong, he let his right hand rest for the last time on the murderous roller that hacked it off, the oil cloth roller, the roller which in love with that strong hand took it away forever.

The handle that opens the elevator door is a simple one, and now with his left hand my father opens and closes the gate of the factory's elevator an infinite number of times a day . . . "An eight-year-old like Dardito could do it" . . . smiles my father, he who yesteryear ruled a whole infernal army of pistons, clamps, nuts, nails, racks organized into an army of industry, on the road to progress. And I saw it was ten o'clock and I forgot to tell him to turn on the radio, and he didn't say a word, so I could finish my homework, the homework I didn't do. Punish me, Dear God! because inside me a raven nests and night has fallen on my soul, tinged by the black of its feathers.

Casals says the best thing for overnight students is to study so that time goes by more easily. Watching Graciela go by he asked me "who do you like better, my cousin or Adhemar?", and that's why before Graciela told me I already guessed whose pants she was starting to talk about. If she finds out she'll kill me. At the intercollegiate championship game one Saturday, H was sitting next to me, between me and Casals. Of H I know that he likes to see soccer better than that volleyball game shamelessly lost by our representative team, I also know that he goes with Casals every Sunday to a movie matinee.

Casals' cousin, whose name is Héctor, the H is silent in Spanish, we know that the small letter is there, nothing more. There's something in me today, also, that is silent, but it's there. Perhaps it is just as well not to find a sound for it. Let's keep quiet. The car passing by this moment and shaking the water in the puddle is now moving away, I can no longer hear it, nothing but a void is left in my ears, it belongs to the past, a past it shares with a potpourri of young voices cheering a losing volleyball team, and he doesn't cheer for anybody, I know how much more he would have preferred a soccer game! and his silence, his voice that doesn't cheer, also left a void in my ears. Héctor, there's a strange shadow in your gaze, are you silent like the first letter of your name?, you barely said a word to me, of course, you thought I was a little girl, with my flat shoes and my white socks, how silly you must have found me!

A big fourteen-year-old girl dressed up like a little girl, yes, and I thought all I needed to be beautiful was to let down my pigtails, this loose mop, I look like an Indian, that's what I look like, and my sister what is she trying to prove, that imbecile, she thinks I should be grateful to her for the rest of my life because she gave me half a peso to buy eighteen inches of new ribbon, what is she trying to prove? that I was going to look the best of all? doesn't she know what these spoiled brats spend on clothes? that ignoramus can't even imagine that for the young lady of the house people spend what we spend to maintain the whole family for a month. Everyone of them has high heels, young ladies' hair-dos and tight skirts. While I have to go around saying thank you the rest of the year for a trashy piece of ribbon that can't even hold my big bush of thick hair.

When I turned the corner in the corridor to leave gym, Héctor was lighting a cigarette, silent, mature, he must get bored among us brats! He's nineteen, and he was looking thoughtfully at the display of championship cups. Héctor, I want to change your name . . . Jasper, or Joseph, or James, don't you see why? because that way your name will begin with J, like joy. . . .

Wednesday the tenth—Did God hear me? Yesterday our dean presented his resignation but they didn't accept it, why did he deem it necessary to make that step? Will I be saved? and what did I do for him in these fateful circumstances? but be quiet, Esther, quiet for once, who are you to help your dean? Be quiet and pray, since "the silence of prayer is God's favorite music" as someone who knew more than me once said. Does Héctor pray at night? would you have believed me, Esther, if yesterday I told you that . . . this Sunday you will be able to ask Héctor this and other questions? Casals, blessed are thou Casals!

I told him: "Casals, yesterday afternoon I had to go pick up the papers for my father at the Ministry of Social Security, as you know mutilated workers receive a pension, and on the way I walked down the Adlon street and I couldn't find it, I guess you must have given me the wrong directions," and I don't exactly remember how the conversation followed, but anyway . . . can it be true? is God a shooting star? what a thing to say! how dare I bring up that folly? Anyway, it was last summer: I was coming from my sister's house and he who has a great need of God always raises his eyes to heaven, a sea-blue heaven on a hot afternoon, and walking on the street decorated with a couple and some housewife coming out for a breath of fresh air looking up I saw a shooting star . . . a wish! right away! I must make a wish on the shooting star! but the mere thought of it makes me blush, and I don't know if I dare tell it in these pages. I could have asked for my mother to be healthier . . . for my scholarship to be renewed . . . even for more: that my studies continue until I receive my doctor's degree . . . I could have asked for, why not? a bicycle for Dardito . . . or a lottery prize, so that we all could forget about scrimping and saving and have a maid for Mother . . . and what did I ask for? I could only think of (in that moment which laid me bare) what Graciela would have asked for, and maybe Laurita too: four letters rose to my throat, intoxicated me like a sip of the strongest *grappa*, and one more foolish teenager . . . asked for Love.

Well, the thing is, yesterday, when the sun was at its zenith in a sky almost white with light, no sooner had we finished lunch when Casals came to the table. Laurita had already gotten up so he sat next to me and we walked around the park till the bell rang for class. The grass was still wet and there was a lot of mud but finally we could walk a little in the sun and take advantage of our enormous park after so many days of rain.

Casals then (without me asking him) began to talk about Graciela, that before Laurita would talk behind her back but now she defends her and that Graciela stinks. This is the way Casals expressed it: "Graciela you know, Esther, when my cousin and I were at the Canadian Cabin on Sunday eating pancakes after the movies, she came over to the table with that friend who went with her to the intercollegiate game, hook nose, and they started talking standing next to the table and my cousin told them to sit down and I could have killed him when they sat down and asked for pancakes too and my cousin had to pay with my money for Adlon" and Casals had to miss Adlon! and he told those two creeps he had seen the new Ginger Rogers movie. And according to Casals' words: "Ginger Rogers they said is an old bag, they looked at me with a face as if to say I was nuts and they asked my cousin if he liked the movie, and the idiot said no! and I thought he liked it and they ask him if I had chosen the movie and he says yes, that I always choose and they said poor thing, what patience, how do you like that!" and to top it off it rained and what were they going to do till it was time to go back to school if they didn't have money for Adlon and couldn't take a walk downtown because of the rain and were stuck there at that table. "And Laurita says that Adlon was great, Big Chief came with the two Kraler girls, the senior and the fifteen-year-old too." "I never talked to the Kraler girls, did you? their father is the owner of almost half the province of *Rio Negro*, he's German. The older one is prettier don't you think? and Laurita says the band played 'Shoeshine Boogie' and the Kraler girl knew the whole song in English and sang in a low voice at the table and Laurita says the other Kraler plays the drums with the spoons and glasses and cups and all the tables were looking at them because they were having more fun."

The poor boy told me: "Héctor left us at the station and you won't believe it but on the train hook nose bought a chocolate bar and I asked her for a little piece and she told me to go buy my own and I said I had bought her pancakes or had she already forgotten and then she gave me half and said I was too young to go out with them." And she's fourteen years old just like me and him! Casals made me feel ashamed when he added "I know that almost all of you like the seniors but don't you think they're too old for you, they're seventeen or even eighteen."

And it was then that I got up the courage, no wonder they say that without courage no war would be fought, and I told him I was dying to go to Adlon. And . . . "why don't you come with us one Sunday?," and flustered Esther "where?" to the matinee at the movies, and then if you give me money for the pancakes and two *pesos* more for an orange drink at Adlon, we can sit at the table with Laurita so my cousin can get a chance to talk to her." And I asked what boys and girls do on Sunday from the moment they meet till they part. And this is how he explained it: "They meet at the movies and hold hands during the whole movie, then they have a bite at the milk bar and afterwards to Adlon where they play special music for couples. At the table they say they love each other, talk about the movie they saw and plan what movie they're going to see next Sunday and the best part is if there's a holiday during the week they don't have to wait a whole week and the time comes for the boy to take the girl back to school and they kiss and hug on those dark streets." And I inquired: "Is that what Héctor tells you?" but I saw a kind of cloud pass over his face and he went on to say: "When Adhemar went out with the younger Kraler girl last year, he took her as far as the gate to the girls' dormitory since she's an overnight student and from there the girls' old monitor, who is very nice, spied on them, and the Kraler girl doesn't drink alcohol because she's protestant but Adhemar had a Manhattan, a mixture of whiskey and God knows what else and it seems that made him lose his shyness and he told the Kraler girl what all us overnight students already knew." And I asked what was it all the overnight students knew. To which he answered: "I asked Adhemar if he loved Kraler and he answered 'a kid like that should be loved for a lifetime.' Who knows why they broke up? . . ." And sly Esther says to Casals "the one you like is hook nose and you won't admit it, because she's prettier than Laurita, who I thought was the one you liked." And Casals answered with a voice coming out of the casket of his dreams: "Laurita is the best."

But she likes Big Chief who's twenty years old. And Casals asked me: "Isn't Adhemar the one she likes? Big Chief is a wild Indian," to which I added: "But if you like Laurita, why are you fixing her up with your cousin?" "My cousin has four hundred girl friends, what does Laurita matter to him, the most important thing is to get into the Kraler's and Laurita's clique. And this is a secret: my cousin won't be here next year because he's getting drafted, and I'll already be part of the clique."

Poor boy, he's fooling himself, and I told him so, why didn't he look for a younger girl, a thirteen-year-old, and he answered: "You can't talk about anything with them, they're too young." And without warning he took my breath away: "I'm going to phone my cousin to see if we can go to the movies this Sunday or if he's coming to get me after the River game, because now he lets me take the bus downtown alone, if you want to come then I'll tell him." Yes yes yes, you could hear a foolish school girl exclaim, and her heart, like a crawling baby, today ventured to take its first step.

I'll never forget it, Casals took me to the secretary's office to phone his cousin—I wanted to listen—and just then the office girl gives me the news that the dean is staying and she didn't let me hear a word of what Casals was saying on the phone. How nice he is.

Sunday . . . Sunday, Esther, is your first date with life: at three in the majestic lobby of the most splendid movie theater in Buenos Aires, a palace of the Arabian nights, where they are showing the movie Casals chose. In my soul I carry a dream—which fills my sails and pushes me forward like a strong wind—and as if it weren't enough another dream is on the screen, the dream of another girl or boy who like me . . . wants to love, is in love, or remembers having loved. Tears, smiles, for the heroine or for myself in her portrayed, and upon "the end" the lights go on again. Casals is by my side, did you like the movie, Casals? the whole week you waited for it while turning, one by one, the pages of your lessons, and now, let's get out of this multitude, a wave of people pours into the downtown streets of the metropolis, whose lights (blue and red are, above all, the lights of my city) gradually emerge against a darkening blue sky, upon an opaque blue velvet (the sky of Buenos Aires) jewels sparkle (its incandescent neon signs), which are the jewels pinned to the taffeta which, in turn, fitted to my flesh, does not let me forget it is a holiday.

And the hour for pancakes at the Canadian Cabin has come, "everything comes in its own good time" my mother always says, and a flawlessly attired waiter arrives with two American-style pancakes and two smoking cups of coffee. And the hour draws near, Casals figures that at a quarter after six he should already be here, who? Héctor! who else could it be? because just as soon as his favorite team finished its game he headed for the streets, hopped on the bus and he's already at the boardinghouse taking a shower and his short hair (just a tiny bit unruly) hasn't finished drying yet when he enters the warm enclosure of the Canadian Cabin. It's a little past six and pitch dark out, so where is the sun? we sure missed the warm rays of the brief afternoon in the shade of a movie theater . . . but if I extend my hand and caress Héctor's cheek I'll still have time to touch them, oh tepid rays, because the sun left his flaming color upon all the boys huddled in the grandstands.

And everything comes in its own good time, the moment also comes to ask him anything I want, his favorite team, what player he likes the best, if he plans to continue his education, and his political ideas to see if somewhere in his heart there's a place for the poor. My sister was right to say "don't marry young, don't marry young" because youth rules the world and the obligations and responsibilities will come soon enough, but now is the time to have fun, to live and give wings to the dreams that nest in our hearts, it's your moment, Esther, because after a lively chat we shall take a walk downtown (a milky way carved into perfect squares: the center of my city) and attracted by a magnet in almost no time we climb the stairs where you can already hear the electrified beat of a jazz band, and beneath the ultramodern indirect lighting of Adlon immersed in the gilded air, decked out in its best garbs is the triumphant youth of the George Washington Private School and thanks to Casals' maneuver when we sit down I am next to Héctor, and the band tackles a rhythmic fox-trot and maybe Héctor wants to change seats and sit next to another girl, how can a poor inexperienced girl know what a lady does in these circumstances? but oh God is it possible I am feeling what I'm feeling? . . . is this alone enough to sweep away my doubts—cobwebs of the soul—so easily? . . . yes, already everything is true and nothing false, ugly, sad or bad in the world, because . . . well, it's so simple . . . it's just that Héctor has taken my hand under the table, he's holding it tight and our hearts are beating to the rhythm of a fox-trot, and Esther, what more can you ask for? there is nothing else to ask for, because around every corner a rose bush and a couple blossom, and there is nothing else you can ask for, only one thing, oh yes, please, one thing . . . that the clock stop and time die forever, when it's Sunday.

Thursday—Felicity . . . thy name is woman, and should be then elusive, and also deceitful? do you promise and not fulfill? Let's begin with this: my mother doesn't want me to go, and on top of that my sister revealed for once and for all what she is: a poor slob, I hate her. Her mustard wrap, which she thinks is the finest thing around and makes you feel like giving her charity, a woman her age with an eight-year-old son and she wants to come and sit with us in Adlon. Imagine, she never heard of a fourteen-year-old girl going out alone with her friends, and she's the only one because the poor devil never got out of this God-forsaken neighborhood. And when she takes off the wrap she thinks she's going to look very pretty with that two-piece suit, the dye already running, the only thing that saves it from those red and yellow stripes, but you notice the dye because the material looks scorched.

As if I were a little five-year-old going with my sister so I won't get lost. I'd kill myself before going with her. And my brother-in-law green with envy, that's what he is, saying why don't I take "those good-for-nothing snots" to the committee meeting, so he can tell them off. . . . On a Sunday he wants young people to lock themselves up with a committee, and I told him so, and he answers me: "Bring those little broads to the committee, you'll see how the boys give them a good time." I'll remember his rudeness as long as I live.

And today Casals comes and asks me if I were going to let Héctor take me home, and he avoided my eyes. Not only that but: "Is your block very dark? but you're not going to be afraid because he'll hold you and defend you, right?", what do you mean? "nothing, my cousin will tell you the rest soon enough, you'll learn a lot from him." I couldn't stand it any longer and I gave him a good pinch in the arm, and Casals grabbed my braid and says to me pulling playfully but sort of hurting me: "Don't be silly, can't you take a joke? me and my cousin will take you, so don't worry, in front of me nothing can happen, unless you make me wait on the corner!" and he laughed. I said: "That's what you wanted to do with Laurita", and the snotty brat answered: "If I were Adhemar I'd have to choose between the Kraler girl and Laurita."

At home I should have said that it was a school party, any old fib but that it was downtown instead of at school. A party to celebrate the reappointment of our dean, how much my good dean deserved a celebration. But I'd choose death before entering Adlon with my sister, let a car run me over when I'm crossing the street downtown, even though the cars should really run her over, yes, let her step on a banana peel from those she's probably carrying in her pocketbook to eat in the subway, she would as long as she can fill her gut at all hours of the day. I can put up with hunger, if I don't have money for a snack bar, that's that, but I'm not going to carry a piece of cheese like she did the day we went for the sheets.

Well, I've come to the end of this cheap dimestore notebook (with its one or two grease stains) and it corresponds to the end of a day which has not far to go, I mean to say that my day also is stained.

Friday—They're right when they say you have to cry for your milk, you have to fight for everything in this world. A flash of intelligence lit up in the darkness of my mind and the argument that convinced my father came to me: if they let me take two buses and the train everyday to go to school at rush hour when it's full and I have to press against those pestilential bodies of dirt and lust, why couldn't they let me take the train downtown on Sunday when it's empty and I'll return home no later than nine?

On condition that I'm taken home, but Héctor will take me home, an angel called Casals dialed the number (I know it, I know it . . . Belgrano 6479), and after chatting a little on condition that I not listen (who knows what silly stories Casals is telling Héctor about me) another YES was added to the others, and on them I clamber higher and higher, those YESES which are the scaffolds of a dream. They say Friday is not a lucky day, day in which I begin this new diary, the dirty dimestore notebooks have ended, for a few cents I can have a notebook for a month. . . . And Casals, the brat, asks me if I'd ever been kissed by a boy, and he refused to believe I hadn't until I swore by my mother. "I have to tell you something, I have to tell you something"—what about? tell me already!—"You have to be careful with one thing"—what thing?—"Is your street very dark?"—pretty much so, why?—"and what's your house like? does it have a vestibule or is it one of those with a garden in front and a gate?"—my building has a long corridor with doors to each apartment, but there's no vestibule, there's sort of a garden in front, and a little gate, of course—"you have to be careful, Esther"—with Héctor? why do you say that? is he perhaps not a gentleman?—"it's not that and don't breathe a word to him!"—what is it then?—"you don't know what can happen to you with a boy in the dark"—not only do you treat him like a good-for-nothing but me like a . . . tart! are you crazy or something? We spoke no further.

Umansky's seat has already been taken, luckily it's a girl, she looks nice, she's from a Russian family, but she's not Jewish, her father was a Cossack of the Czar and they escaped with the mother when the revolution came. What could Cobito Umansky's mother have done to him? He's probably in Paraná by now, the creep, now I can relax if my skirt is hitched up or not, since that creature won't be there to look. I don't think there's any shame greater than being expelled from a school, but only Umansky could think of spitting on the monitor's clothes and putting feces in his shoes. Till tomorow, little notebook of resplendent, white, modest pages (beware of trespassers, I know you wouldn't like that, I know, I know, and that's why I'm hiding you between a fat Zoology textbook and my grammar looseleaf), till tomorrow . . . my notebook, till tomorrow . . . friend.

Saturday—It's all over. It wasn't meant to be. My neighborhood is still in the night, these modest calico curtains allow me to see the street through their flowers, as fanciful as they are faded. Dad says that in the factory you can't go near the machines where they're printing calico because of the smell of those cheap inks, not to mention that they use all waste products in the making of calico. Everything in life is a matter of fate, I can't figure out why, on such cheap material, they make such crazy designs of flowers that, if they exist, must belong to a very rare tropical species. But the colors come out blotted and the material is so thin you can see through to what's on the other side: the street and the houses across the way. From here I can see a door, two windows, the partition wall, then another house, a vestibule with a window to the side, two or three more, another house, with an iron gate, but all of them one-floor buildings, and if the roof could be opened like in the movie theater on the other side of the square, when the whole block would go to bed we'd all be looking at the same strip of sky, and my neighbors would confidently close their eyes every evening, without knowing it would be as impossible to touch those remote stars as to obtain what they most desire. . . . Looking at a star, looking at him, my desire was born on our first encounter, and that crazy desire wanted to fly high, a crazy kite, the string got out of my hand and the kite flew high, vain, pretentious, it wanted to touch the stars. I saw you today kite . . . and you're buried in the mud now . . . Is life just mud? is hope mud? my school park is all mud after it rains. It must have been for the rain storm that the grammar teacher was absent. Casals always takes advantage each time a teacher's absent to write home or do tomorrow's homework, but today, during the long unending period from ten to eleven he asked if he could sit next to me.

Immediately I sensed a cloud, but lifeless on that seat I could only manage to listen. He began to tell me the story of *Spellbound*, almost the whole film, for him it's last year's and this year's best movie, who cares? Ah, Casals, I thought you incapable of killing a fly and you killed me! you began talking about movies but suddenly you changed the subject: "We have to come back early on Sunday, so we'll have to skip Adlon" he said—"Why?" I answered—"It's just that there's not enough time, I have to take you home with Héctor and be back at school before nine-thirty" he said—"Then let's not go to the movies, let's go to Adlon earlier" I replied—"No, we're going to the movies no matter what, and besides, Adlon is empty before six o'clock" he added—"But it's not necessary for you to take me home too:

you go back to school and Héctor will take me" I added—"Are you kidding?"—"No, what's wrong with that . . . it's better for everybody, and you'll get to see your Laurita"—"No, if I don't take you home we're not going to the movies or anywhere" he roundly stated—"Because of your own silly whims, why do you have to come? I can take care of myself, I'll bet Héctor prefers going out with a girl without having to drag you along"—"What did you say?"—"That you're too young to be with the older kids all the time" and then he came nearer and said softly "You stinking scum, you shouldn't be in this school, riff-raff . . . go with the riff-raff in your neighborhood to Adlon!" and I said to him "I'm glad I'm breaking up with you, because I'm sick of your crazy talk . . . trying to court big girls and comparing yourself with Adhemar, and you have the nerve to criticize your cousin who's so good to you," and he tried to stop me but I went on "You think you're a big shot and you're just a little faggy sissy sticking to the girls all day long and what's all this talk about Adhemar? are you in love with him or something? well get it into your head that you'll never be like Adhemar, because all you are is a phony little fag." I got carried away, then I regretted it and was afraid he'd complain to the dean, who is his protector. But he clammed up, after a while he got up from the seat and went to the bathroom.

When he got back, giving me the shoulder, he didn't leave the new girl alone, of course she's the daughter of foreigners, white Russians, and her mother an opera singer, Casals was lucky to have her in the seat in front. He started off asking had she seen *For Whom the Bell Tolls*.

I feel sorry for the overnight students on Saturdays, they're left all alone, we day students go home and no classes in the afternoon, poor devils, they don't know what to do to make the day go by. Casals didn't once leave the new girl in peace: "Please stay, the dean will say yes if I ask his permission for you to stay and have lunch with the overnight students. This way afterwards we'll go to the park and I'll finish telling you about *For Whom the Bell Tolls*. He wanted to convince her at all costs and you can see he'll have a grudge on me forever because when Laurita, Graciela and I were leaving he says to them "see you tomorrow at Adlon's."

Is Adhemar handsomer than Héctor? beautiful black eyes and hair blond as a cornfield.

Oh well, let them keep their Adlon, let them go tomorrow Sunday, I'll go some other time . . . but when? when if not now? isn't this the moment to live and have fun? if not now, when?

My neighbors and I can't touch the stars, but others can, and that is my great sorrow. I'm going to spend the best years of my life behind this calico curtain.

Wednesday—Dear Diary: Many suns and moons have passed through heaven's arch without having had our usual meeting, the meeting of the soul with its mirror, and if in days past I have seen myself emaciatingly thin (egoism devours), or disheveledly ridiculous (dreams mess up my hair), today I would like to see myself not pretty (isn't that already progress?) but with an immaculate white apron (no plaits, nor vain adornments, just snowy white), neatly combed back, straight hair barely covering my neck and its tips a bit curled. The important thing now, dear diary, would not be the hair, nor the apron, but an intelligent and firm expression, firm like the hands that wield the scalpel, or the scissors, or the hated drill of the kindly lady dentist from the union.

I didn't think I'd be going to Buenos Aires today Wednesday, but yesterday my father saw the thoughtful dentist and fixed my appointment for today. How crazy! I thought, to go into town on a school day when tomorrow Thursday we have nothing less than Zoology, Mathematics and Grammar, but when the dentist told me that everything in life is a matter of organization, because there is time for everything, I realized how true it was.

On my way there by train I had already taken the opportunity to look over the theorems (fresh in my mind, thanks to the teacher's clear exposition and my own attention), and on my way back I read Zoology and after supper a half-hour for grammar and I made a clean copy of the drawing of the arachnids and now I'm free, at your side again. I have fulfilled my duties.

And wisely did the lady dentist say that there's a time for everything, even to take a little stroll downtown. Today had been a surprisingly hot day, with the first warm days you feel like throwing your woolen stuff into the garbage, fortunately last year's clothes are no longer small on me so I was able to put on the little sky-blue cotton with the short jacket. Undoubtedly it is my only decent dress.

How lucky I was to have already learned the theorem, in good spirits I arrived and strolled with no inferiority feelings along the elegant tree-lined avenue where Laurita said were the only imported fabrics from Paris there are in Buenos Aires. I saw them, reality and dream neatly separated by the glass of a display window. And I continued strolling, so many, so many beautiful things to buy and if they made me choose one, I wouldn't be able to decide, because to renounce the kerchief of purple gauze would be just as impossible as passing over the mink muff, and my head exploded, dear friend. How furious, how indignant certain things sometimes make me. That avenue is beautiful, wide, people walk without hurry—that nonchalant air of knowing where they're going—and the pavement rises as you walk towards the port, but the latter you cannot see, at the highest point there's an aristocratic square, drenched with sun, and a skyscraper closes the view, thus "decorously covering the view of the river and its tumultuous port," to use the words of Butterball, excuse me, the Grammar teacher.

In the shade of the square, however, I was aware of a sudden change of temperature, suddenly a wind started blowing from the river, not much more than a breeze, but penetrating. How I wanted to be back home, having a hot *mate*, imagine, me on the avenue without a coat, chills began to run up and down my spine, my dress felt like it covered me as much as a little cobweb. But I couldn't go into any of those houses, my city changes temperature without ever warning us, from one moment to another, it changes mood: laughter and tears like children laughing and crying at random.

So I had to run to the dentist's office and I ended up arriving twenty minutes early. What activity, what coming and going, how beautiful it is to be useful to humanity, that capable and besides beautiful woman who tended me doesn't rest a minute, on her feet at her patient's side, coming and going for cotton and medicinal fluids. She's the one who knows where she's going, not the useless indolent blockheads on the avenue, and I want to feel the feverish activity of the docks, Butterball, don't come to me with your tale about having to hide the worker and his sweat, and praising that skyscraper because it hides the savage (and until yesterday sad for going unrewarded) spectacle of labor from the eyes (and the consciences) of the wealthy.

How well the delegate for Matanzas expressed it in Sunday's meeting, "they can no longer deny the existence of a new force, the oligarchs will face the necessities of the worker even if the latter must hammer open their skulls and write it on their brains with his fingers and the ink will be their very oligarch blood!" Brutal but necessary words, which I rejected when I first heard them, before thinking them over. Brutal but truthful words. Because work is holy, and thus the worker is sanctified, his sweat bathes him in divine grace. You sweat with a shovel but you can also sweat in other ways, drilling or extracting teeth, and treating cavities, or better yet, operating on victims of peritonitis, or meningitis, or traffic accidents, in a few words: treating and caring for my people, my beloved people, all of whom I want to embrace in my arms, the arms of their little lady doctor.

XIII

ANNUAL LITERARY ESSAY COMPETITION
FREE SUBJECT:
"The Movie I Liked Best"
By José L. Casals, SOPHOMORE, SECTION B

That hot night in Vienna, the people didn't feel like going to sleep. Strains of a gavotte issued from the windows of a great ballroom but the heat was too much for even such a sedate dance as the gavotte, and the tenants of the neighboring houses, whether smoking a pipe, playing chess, or leafing through a newspaper, were gnashing their teeth they were so tired of listening to the same old music for twenty years straight.

The last couple is already about to leave the spacious premises, drowsiness has just about conquered its last victim when a violinist in the orchestra, young and impetuous, does not lower his bow on the last measure of the score but, winking to a chubby oboist, attacks a new rhythm, snappy, jolly and fast. The more haughty customers, shocked, raise their eyebrows, what is this? is it possible that a respectable place permits the playing of such a low-class dance? The neighborhood also hears and a hand puts down the chess piece, a newspaper lies idle on a table, and a pipe sends out snappy, jolly, and fast puffs of smoke: everybody has begun to dance. Absent-minded pedestrians stop in their tracks, carriages rein in their horses, everybody is asking what that unique music is, and from ear to ear travels a forbidden name, the waltz!

Then the furious owner of the ballroom sees no other solution than to call the police to throw the daring violinist out, but going towards the sidewalk a crowd prevents his passage. The coward wonders if they're coming to set his ballroom on fire but the invaders quickly split up into couples, rush onto the deserted floor and start spinning dizzily. The crinolines are stiff and the skirts quite heavy but to the rhythm of the waltz they become light poppies revolving in air and in a matter of seconds the ballroom is full, something has finally made them forget the heat! and the beer they consume will be a lot, to the benefit of the owner, more surprised than anybody else.

Johann swings his violin bow, now the baton, and after the last measure they burst out applauding: he feels like he's living in a dream.

Not far from there, an open carriage is riding past the imperial gardens, inside it an officer of His Majesty's Armed Forces and a lady with golden hair. Silence, only the trot of the horses is heard, the officer has attempted to distract the lady with miscellaneous conversation, she has answered yes or no, she feels hot, they are so far from the glassy and shaded canals of her Saint Petersburg.

A weak echo is suggested in the air, it sounds like Cossack violins drunk with blood and vodka, and because of that, minutes later the arrogant couple makes its entrance in the ballroom. She feels enraptured, they are not her Cossacks but it's the same joy and passion for life, what fire burns in the eyes of the young conductor! a lock of black hair falls over his forehead and eyes but does not prevent him from singling out among the crowd a radiant smile of approval in a frame of golden hair. He seems to recognize her, where has he seen her before? without knowing why, he imagines her on an enormous stage, but the lady doesn't dance, does she not like his music? . . . she comes toward him, gives him her pale hand to help her onto the platform and asks for the score.

"Dreams" is the title, and its first stanzas rest upon the orchestra notes like dew upon corolla, the voice of that dazzling woman is like crystal dew. Johann wasn't wrong, she is the great Carla Donner, prima donna of the Imperial Opera House. The poetic lyrics say that dreams sometimes come true and that a face so beautiful it can only be imagined may suddenly appear so close to you that you can caress it, her fair skin, her coral lips, "her green eyes—the emerald sea—where I submerged look for what? what is it lovers look for at the bottom of the sea?" And with the last note of the waltz Carla's last high note is also heard, the audience gives her an ovation but in spite of Johann's pleading look she disappears behind the severe figure of the officer.

The months pass, Johann triumphs with his orchestra and one day returns to his village to visit his fiancée and his mother. What joy reigns over the farmhouse, for days cookies have been baking, from the cupboard cold cuts are brought out as well as jars of preserves saved for special occasions. How long will Johann stay? Before it was all so different, Johann was jobless most of the time and would take shelter under their thatched roof and tell his mother about everything that was happening in Vienna, although she couldn't stop to listen as she was busy preparing bundles of food for Johann to take back to Vienna. But he no longer needs anything, he sits at the table and she anxiously waits for Johann's eyes to light up with that spark of joy which, you know, is so characteristic of the hungry man who is finally about to gorge himself.

No, this time Johann has not been saving up his hunger, and he eats much less than he used to. Panic spreads through the house, does this mean he doesn't love us any more? And that's nothing: the next minute Johann, used to telling mother everything, also tells her he met Carla Donner. And the spark lights up. It's as if it threatened to put fire to the vegetables in the orchard, and the fire might also spread to the fruit trees with all the green pears his mother was going to cut to make preserves for years to come. Of course she doesn't have to prepare bundles of food for Johann any more.

The family goes on eating but Johann looks at the kitchen and notices that it needs a coat of paint to cover all the soot and that the tiles should be scrubbed to uncover the colors hidden by a layer of grease, and he looks at his mother to tell her this and perhaps he should first tell her that the skin of her face is so dry she needs oils and that she should gather up that messy hair to show her high and noble forehead.

Time has passed, Johann has fulfilled his promise of marriage and lives with the gentle Poldi in a peaceful district of Vienna, his music has conquered the hearts of everyone but he hasn't written a new waltz for a long time. Besides, Vienna is in political turmoil, the people clamor for more bread and the old emperor lies in his bed most of the day, too weak to correct so many wrongs. The hope of the more liberal groups, among which Johann is included, points to the name of Duke Hagenbruhl, an important political figure in the court.

It is again summer, Johann makes his rounds of the taverns along the banks of the Danube, unhappy he searches at the bottom of each glass of bubbling wine for the new melody he has promised to his already impatient publisher. Drunk, he enters a fancy place, he's not sure of what he's seeing but at a half-hidden table among curtains of heavy damask there is Carla Donner with her usual companion: the officer. Johann wants to do an about-face and disappear into the night but it's too late, Carla has seen him and calls him to her table, after such a long time she still recognizes him.

Johann staggers near and after respectfully greeting her companion, invites her to dance. The officer is annoyed and calls him a disgusting drunkard, Johann tries to ignore him and repeats his invitation to the lady, to which the officer answers with a punch in the musician's face. Johann rolls on the ground and tries to find the courage to stand up and, in turn, knock down the sturdy officer; he tries to muster all the little strength he can and looks for a sign of support in the crowd, or perhaps a sharp knife on one of the tables to make up for the limited strength of his fists . . . when he hears the owner of the place shout "Throw out that coxcomb who's molesting the Duke of Hagenbruhl" what? Duke Hagenbruhl? is that violent monster his political idol? is he, Johann, thinking of plunging a knife into the man who is the hope of the Austrian Empire? if he hadn't been what he is, a musician, Johann would have wanted to be a brilliant politician like Hagenbruhl, but after much effort he gets on his feet without knowing whether or not to attack, and lost in his dilemma, takes one step forward and the duke, this time with even more force, plunges his fist into the cavity of the composer's eye.

Johann lies bleeding but some of the customers, upon hearing the name Hagenbruhl furiously rise up, they are opponents of the duke and like a rivulet of gun powder political furor flows. The fight moves from the tavern to the street and half of Vienna is shaken by a subversive movement, while Johann escapes in a carriage saving from among the shooting the beautiful Carla. Where could they flee? the coachman suggests the Vienna woods and under a downpour they leave the city behind. Carla cleans the wounds of Johann who, overcome by alcohol and exhaustion, falls asleep in the soprano's lap. She, in turn, lulled by the rhythmic trot of the horse, is overcome by sleep.

How dark the woods are, but not now, how dark they were,

the horse has been trotting for hours and the horizon is a pink brush stroke. Are birds the happiest beings of creation? It is possible, because when they wake up they sing, that they have the good fortune to forget each night in their sleep the evil that exists on earth. Besides, their nests in the leafy treetops receive the first caress of the sun's rays, so their trills descend drenched in light to wake up Carla and Johann, both victims of nightmares perhaps, mere human beings, unable to forget, neither asleep nor awake. They raise their heavy eyelids, and through the cobwebs of their nocturnal fears they faintly see the light of a different awakening, they have nothing to fear of each other, on the contrary, they'll finally be able to tell each other so many things. But they don't say anything, unable to find a word worthy of beginning such a special day.

Streaks of white light filter through the trees, trying to imitate the white of Carla's myriad gauzes, the tireless horse trots on rhythmically and the coachman turns round and says "good-day." "Good-day," they answer, and they've finally found the right words, "good-day," a good, beautiful, sweet day to come. Other dwellers of the woods announce their presence with sounds like the bleatings of sheep and the horn of their shepherd which grows louder in its echo. Goodday, day, day, day, day, and without a minute to lose the coachman pulls out a hunting horn answering with his not quite tuned notes "I love you" the coachman says to the woods, love you, love you, love you, love you, and Johann frantically wonders what it is Carla expects from him, him, him, him, and Carla says "only one of your waltzes could make me forget the morning voice of the woods" woods, woods and Johann already begins to feel inside a new melody, that is to say, the voice of a new waltz.

"Tell me, tell me, tell me, tell me what you feel for me, I daren't ask, I mean so little, I look at your eyes that look at the snow in Saint Petersburg and I look at all your features, lines sketched over your face with an especially light pencil, which doves then copy in the twists and turns of their ever restful flights, and oh! only once in its life did that streamer fly to repeat the grace of one gesture of your hands . . . but I, I'm nothing, my mother always said that in the whole wide world there wasn't a woman good enough for her son, in my cradle sleeps a baby protected by the web of a mosquito net, my mother guards me well from mosquito bites and thinks I am better than I really am, looking at me through the hazy web of a mosquito net, and she doesn't know I mean so little to you, my mother, because she's so kind, thinks it's not like that and if you were as kind, as kind as my mother, what would you feel for me?"

And so ends the new waltz, word for word Johann has been dictating it to Carla and she sings them, the notes rise to the leafy tops of the larch trees, beech trees, and linden trees and from there to the arch of heaven. Besides there are probably invisible creatures in the blue yonder who can hear this song of us mortals, will they pay attention to us? or will it be impossible for them to hear us? or will they despise us for being ephemeral and weak? Carla sings and pays so much attention to her high notes and trills that she doesn't realize what the words mean, since she goes on singing carefree and smiling, invulnerable like one of those creatures in the blue yonder.

Suddenly there's a clearing in the woods, where a typical hunter's inn stands, its enormous bower is tinted lilac by bunches of hyacinths. The coachman licks his mustache since he's already feeling very hungry, and he suggests to the couple that they stay there for lunch. In the shade of the hyacinths you can see a few couples occupying some tables, the young ladies drinking soft drinks, the young men beer, one couple seems to be students, their books heaped on a chair, perhaps they took advantage of the disorders in the city to miss school, he's drinking something alcoholic, maybe to lose his shyness so he can tell her what he's already surely told all his buddies, they are an enviable couple, she fair and serene, he elegant, with black eyes and hair blond as a cornfield, good-natured but he won't let anybody take advantage of that, with not only his wide shoulders but also strong and skillful arms for defense. The coachman says "I'm hungry" and only then do Carla and Johann think of the need for money and after making calculations afraid they won't have enough, they manage to put together the sum needed to pay for their lunches, the coachman's trip and it ends up they only have enough for one room, since they need a rest, and while the coachman withdraws to the stable the two of them go to the landlady and ask for the room, claiming they're married.

The malicious landlady takes them to a shady apartment, with a canopied bed in the center and sofas with pillows. Carla avoids her companion's eyes and retires to do her toilet. Johann sits on the sofa and can't believe that within a few short seconds he and

Carla will be alone together in a dark room. But how should he act? They still haven't even kissed, Hagenbruhl must have kissed her, and perhaps also made her his, they've certainly been lovers, that harsh man, with abrupt manners, rough features contracted even more by his monocle, has put his paws on Carla's delicate body . . . how could she ever permit it?, and if she did perhaps it's because that kind of animal appeals to her, and will Johann have to kiss her like Hagenbruhl did? taking her forcefully by her slight shoulders, leaving purple marks on her white flesh, which means that the squeezing has hurt her skin from inside, has provoked wounds under the epidermis and the purple color comes from the breaking of veins and arteries which amounts to small internal hemorrhages. And that's only the beginning, when Hagenbruhl has become as wild as an animal perhaps he has also used his teeth, and must have bitten her, and then better not to think of the final outrage, his fury certainly must not have calmed down till he saw blood run, and she, weaker and weaker, must have had little strength to defend herself, and was probably his victim several times, the victim of the raging executioner who wants to see blood flow. But how could Carla have given in to such a thing? There is something that escapes my understanding, some fatal secret, Hagenbruhl is perhaps in possession of a compromising secret of Carla's, some obscure spy ring debt of old Saint Petersburg, only for something terrible could Carla have let him trample upon her white skin.

Her white skin, and don't tell me that white means lack of color, because it is the most beautiful color, the color of purity, and of course white is not the lack of color: the physics professors have revealed to the whole world that in the immaculate white of a snowflake, the violet of the lilies, that is, sadness and melancholy, is nevertheless contained and hidden, and also the blue which signifies serenity when contemplating—reflected in the street puddle—the heaven that awaits us, because blue is next to green which is crystal-clear hope, and then comes the yellow of the daisies, which blossom without anybody planting them and appear without having to look for them, like good news when you least expect it, and the color of the oranges, which are already ripe by summer, is very appropriately called orange, the orange blossom yielded a fruit which ripens in the summer because of the heat, what joy to know that the seed germinated, the tree which is adolescence grew and is going to enter the youth of the fruit that yields the orange ecstasy, the juice and refreshing fruit of hot afternoons. But from there to the red of passion is only one step. Red is also hidden in white, it is also in her, Carla, who is so white. Is that why Hagenbruhl wants to see her blood and prove that she is as lowly as he is?

But things shouldn't be like that, if Carla is white like snow, the symbol of purity, she should be treated like you treat purity itself, *she must be treated like you treat purity itself!*

Thinking about all this Johann cannot stand the confinement of the apartment any longer, he's hot, the sun is burning down, you can hear the crickets singing, this means there must be a lake nearby, which, in fact, can be found behind a thicket in the woods and after making sure nobody can see him, the youth undresses to cool off. An almost imperceptible but warm breeze inflames his skin, but his image reflected on the surface of the waters irritates him: his sunken chest, skinny arms, slightly hunched-over back. He hates himself, but that breeze encircles him more and more in warm waves as he lies down on the grass.

Yes, yes, he silently confesses that he desires Carla, Johann has turned out to be an animal like the others, and he now wants to run to her, he stands up, determined, something tells him all will go well, that she will accept him as he is. Johann looks at the thicket and up at the sky reflected in the lake in which he himself is unavoidably reflected, and he again hates himself with even more intensity than before, he wishes he were that student he saw in the bower, strong and handsome, so there'd be no doubt that Carla would love him, and at that moment footsteps are approaching and Johann covers himself as fast as he can, spies through the leaves and sees that it is the student and his sweetheart who are passing by just a few steps away, heading for some lonely and quiet corner of the woods.

The student, emboldened by a little alcohol, must have already confessed all his love to his companion, and now, most probably, they are looking for a place where they can be alone. Johann thinks and thinks how will the student manage to make up for all the evil he may bring upon the innocent girl, how will he convince his sweetheart he won't leave her after a couple of meetings and then make fun of her with his friends? how will the student make her realize that he loves her physically because that is Nature's rule? he has to bow to Nature, when what he'd really want is to cuddle up next to her and take her hand to stop her from going into the woods, the student is afraid she'll get up to pick flowers unawares and go deep into the woods where there are so many dangers, and there might be hungry and ferocious beasts, so he holds her by the hand and asks her to talk about anything, and maybe they'll talk about Johann's waltzes which are now well known in all of Vienna and the student asks his sweetheart to tell him which waltz she likes best and because of that miracle, love, she chooses the same one the student likes best. They're never going to have an argument in this lifetime, and even less in the other, where love will change them into beings of the blue yonder on a visit to the Milky Way, or if they prefer, when summer comes they will soar to the four pale stars of the Southern Cross.

"Johann!" A voice is calling Johann and it is none other than Carla's, she has already changed clothes and is looking for him. Together they have soft drinks in the bower and since it is already evening the band plays Johann's waltzes one after the other without knowing that the composer is right there, and beneath the hyacinths Carla sings them with her voice that is truly unique and the air becomes filled with melodies, sound waves carry the refrains, one after the other, sending them who knows where, and wherever they arrive they will arrive laden with the perfume of hyacinths.

It's getting dark out and since the sun is setting the couple starts feeling a bit chilly, so before taking a walk in the moonlight they go to the room to put on something warm. But a surprise awaits them, the owner, a good businesswoman, has made a very nice fire in the pretty room and by doing this, she is encouraging them to stay and spend the night as well.

They don't have to turn on the light when they come in, the fire delicately but warmly lights up the room, they were already beginning to get the chills outside but here a gentle warmth perfumes the air, Carla reaches out to take her coat and Johann his, but suddenly their eyes meet, they step towards each other, and holding hands they draw near the fireplace. Then they put their palms to the flames to nearly touch those sort of vibrating butterflies that burst from the logs; Johann kneels before Carla and Carla kneels too.

She finally feels she's waking up from a nightmare, brutal beings and blood-thirsty ravagers are no longer around, and no longer does she have to practice so many hours to keep her voice in perfect shape, all that stayed behind, just like in a nightmare, and now her gaze moves from the fire to that being who loves her so, and who has told her as much with the excuse of writing words for waltzes. She gazes at him and how handsome he looks lit up by those golden flames, she had never seen him like that, those strong shoulders and two powerful arms that will always be ready to defend her, what a relief to know that she no longer has anything to fear, and the flames make his eyes and eyelashes look blacker than ever while it throws golden reflections on his hair and now the young man's hair looks as golden as a cornfield. Which means a kind of love miracle is happening.

And Carla embraces him without being able to completely envelop his powerful chest, and what words could express what his black eyes say?, she looks at him and has no reason to ask if his love is good or bad, because evil betrays itself in one's eyes, meanness causes the filaments of the iris to short-circuit, which never happens in his eyes; on the contrary, he has kind eyes.

Carla cuddles up in those strong arms and looks at the flames of the fire, but no, she is wasting time, she wants to look at him, wants to be in his arms and at the same time look into his eyes. Then Carla lies down on the thick rug and sees the flames reflected in his black pupils and something else, like a spark which, distinct from all the other sparks, does not die down, that spark in his black eyes shines constant, and Carla ventures to think it is his soul that has come forth to contemplate the flames in the fireplace. Carla has had the good fortune to be there, near the fire, and his soul is looking at her.

Yes, Carla falls asleep to undertake the dangerous journey he invites her on and it is as if she were falling asleep in his arms, within seconds she will begin to dream, and she is sure he is not going to abandon her afterwards, as sure as if he had sworn it before ten judges, and she cuddles up against him still more, full of impatience since she already wants to know what dream it will be her turn to dream that night, and she's already sound asleep. They both have the same dream: together they visit the stars of a constellation beyond planets such as Jupiter and Mars but which is in the reach of their bodies. Their bodies are one, a strong boy furrows the stratospheres, his cornfield hair to the winds and from time to time Carla is afraid of falling out of his arms and for that has asked him to look at her every once in a while so that she'll be able to relax by seeing that he's relaxed. His pupils are enormous since they no longer reflect the flames of the fireplace, but rather the whole cosmos in the dark night that he furrows in his flight.

But poor Carla is so used to not being happy that during the trip she dreams that she's dreaming something else: that he heads towards the furthest lights of all, the Galaxy, powdered stars colder than ice that make you shiver from just looking at them, and suddenly Carla feels afraid, and she asks him to change his course, she opposes his heading far out, and tries to turn him back towards the Three Maries, and because of that struggle she unwittingly breaks loose from his arms, she reaches out but can just about brush him with the tips of her fingers, and he tries to grab her but for some unknown reason bodies separate and move away from each other in the Galaxy zone, little by little they are already so faraway they cannot hear what each other is saying, Carla tries to make out the color of his eyes, but she can no longer see them clearly, she repeats to herself over and over again they were black, black, black, so as not to forget, and she thinks of his nose, the shape of his face, to keep him if only in her memory. She can no longer touch him, hear him, smell him, she can hardly see him, although something in her mouth lasts from the sweetness of so many kisses, and what was his smile like? how did he spread his lips when smiling? she can't remember! did his eyes look Chinese when he smiled? yes or no? did he get dimples in his cheeks? she can't remember! She had no more strength on the trip, she should have asked him to carry her on his shoulder as if she were dead, and then they could have continued the flight, she might have died, and he would have carried her on his shoulder, a dead weight, and drying up with time she would weigh less and less and would stick to his back, like a sheepskin, and he would master space for eternity with a sheepskin stuck to him as if it were his own skin. But not even that was possible, and lost in the Galaxy Carla looks toward him again, now just a dot in space.

Fortunately her sadness wakes her up and it was only a nightmare, and back from each one of these trips they ask each other what part they liked best, and they only have to quietly smile because they know it was the shooting star, and they think it over and laugh because they're not telling the truth, they had forgotten that, best of all, was when both dreamt of misfortunes but woke up and weren't separated but together, and they laughed at the nightmare, what a thing to do, lost among constellations, as if they were two kids giggling about nothing, and they don't even know the names of the constellations, and Carla doesn't have to look for the name of the constellations because what does it matter, if she's with him, to know so little about astrology?

Well, the months go by, instead of returning to Vienna the two lovers tour the capitals of Europe, giving concerts everywhere, from success to success, until there is so much demand for them to return to Vienna that they finally get up the courage to face the city where they first met. Their success is unanimous, Carla goes to her dressing room to change costumes for the final scene, Johann stays on the podium conducting the musicians, so that when Carla comes into her dressing room, she finds someone waiting for her: Poldi, Johann's wife!

She is a delicate and kind girl, who only wants the best for Johann and she tells the soprano that Johann is not for her, he's too sensitive a man, the day will come when Carla, carried off by her career that forces her to constantly travel, will abandon Johann and if she leaves him then, he will never get over it. Poldi tells her that on the contrary, if she leaves him now it will be more bearable for Johann because he is at the peak of his fame and he'll be able to forget her by again immersing himself in work, there, in his Vienna.

At first Carla is tough and haughty, but little by little she realizes the truth of Poldi's words. The prompter knocks on her door, like a symbol that her career is calling and she respectfully says good-bye to Poldi. The world premiere of Johann's new operetta in Vienna is a staggering success for both musician and singer.

Johann asks Carla what she would like to do to celebrate the triumph. They get into a carriage and Carla orders the coachman to go to the banks of the Danube, more precisely, to the docks. Yes, Carla is going away, for Johann there will never be a more triumphal moment than this and therefore he'll be able to forget her more easily.

He doesn't know that Poldi is the reason and bewildered, he watches her sail away into the night in that steamboat. What could have changed her like that, all of a sudden?, some political intrigue that escapes his understanding? it can't be anything that he did, but of course, as important as the reason was, if she had been madly in love with him she would have been deaf to any reason. The miracle of love has ended, Johann is Johann again.

That's the way it is, you are either madly in love or not at all, and on that dock dimly lit by torches of tallow he realizes that he never succeeded in making her fall madly in love with him, to be madly in love means to lose your head and do anything to stay close to your beloved. The torches are reflected in the river waters that run black with slime, carrying the boat that slowly moves away; Johann stays on the dock, he couldn't do anything. A dead man can't do anything either when he's struck down by a bullet, he receives a mortal wound and remains lying on the ground until someone carries him to his final resting place. But for Johann that final resting place will be difficult to find.

Searching for a way out of his despair he sets about to work harder than ever and creates his best waltzes, but this is of no help whatsoever. One day at home in Vienna, in his frantic but useless search he starts thinking about the house where he was born, the village, his early years, he can see his room, the thatched roof, his childhood toys, what a beautiful room, a sort of garret, his bright and colorful bedspread, and the quiet of the village.

Suddenly Johann trembles with the desire to return, he believes that he will recover his peace of mind there, in that house now abandoned after the death of his parents but which a neighbor keeps clean at Johann's request since he doesn't want dust to accumulate on all those objects after his mother spent her life trying to keep the house clean. And one day Johann gets up the courage and returns to his village, to sleep again in his childhood bed.

It is four in the autumn afternoon, so we are therefore talking about the last minutes of sunlight, nature seems still, if a baby bird moved in a treetop nest Johann would hear it; the silence is total. He enters the house, everything is in order, he goes up to his room, opens the door, the room is in darkness, he goes to the window, opens it and the dusky light comes in, but the room isn't as nice as he remembered it, the bedspread is the same, the toys are untouched, nothing has changed, memory has not deceived him, but unexpected shadows are hanging over those objects: you see, Johann left the door open when he came in.

Who has sneaked in uninvited? The despotic and contemptuous owner of that place that only played gavottes has come in, and his mother comes in, his angelic mother, but she is all disheveled, in the last years Johann had sent her fancy clothes and jewelry, but his mother has come into the room looking disheveled, her face wrinkled for lack of care, an apron as grey as her hair, Johann wants her to put on the new clothes but his mother doesn't answer, she puts herself in a corner and sets to dusting the furniture, while the ballroom owner looks at her. His publisher is there too, impatiently drumming his fingers on the night table, he has cheated Johann more than once, and is now going to lay his hands on new pages Johann has just written and brought from Vienna, Poldi is there too and grabs them first, to tidy up, Johann has told her a thousand times not to touch his papers and she is stubbornly piling them up so there won't be any disorder and through the door that was left open Hagenbruhl has just walked in, making his mother move aside so that he can examine everything in the room, he comes in determined to examine everything, and when Johann is about to tell him not to dare do so Carla comes in too, and doesn't look at him, she only has eyes for Hagenbruhl and lies down on the bed languishing from fatigue and Hagenbruhl comes near her and tells her to sleep, with an evil design in his eyes. And so, the room that Johann longed for in Vienna was exactly how he remembered it, but when he opened the door those beings came in with him, they are nothing more than shadows but they spoil everything, and the heartbreak is so painful that he throws himself into the corner with the toys and hugging them he breaks into silent and bitter sobs.

Many, many years have gone by, and the government has invited the glorious old composer of waltzes to a celebration in the palace. An elderly couple enters the throne room, it is Johann and Poldi who, accompanied by the aides-de-camp, approach the emperor and bow. What a surprise, the venerable old man who steps down from the throne is none other than Hagenbruhl, who embraces Poldi and Johann, he is a model emperor who has brought prosperity to his people.

He thanks Johann and Poldi for the honor of their company, to which Johann replies that the honor is theirs, to greet the monarch who has done so much good for Vienna. The emperor smiles and replies with sincere emotion in his voice that even if he has done a lot for Vienna, Vienna is another man's bride, and seeing that Johann doesn't understand he points to the closed balcony. One of the courtiers steps forward, opens the doors wide, and asks Johann to come out. Poor Johann, he's already an old man with very little strength, years and suffering have carried off his former drive, he can't get up the courage to go out on the balcony but upon the emperor's insistence he finally does.

The extensive palace gardens, the largest plaza in the city, lies before him, and a multitude, all of Vienna, waves its handkerchiefs in the wind. When Johann appears the salutes are fired, everybody was waiting for him, it is the homage the emperor prepared for him in secret, and the cheers little by little take on a rhythm, a waltz rhythm, the multitude sings those old love stanzas about dreams coming true and beautiful faces that can only exist in the imagination, and suddenly Johann seems to see way up high, above the multitude, a creature of the blue yonder, and the vision becomes clearer and clearer, it's a beautiful young woman, yes, it is Carla, singing his verses, and her lips aren't coral nor her eyes green like the emerald sea, her face is transparent over the sky of Vienna and Johann anxiously tries to think what color that heavenly vision is, he cannot make it out, and he begins to get upset, what are the seven colors of the prism? purple, blue, red, yellow, green . . . no, none of those, this is a color that doesn't exist on earth, it is a far more beautiful color, but so much effort and how can that old man possibly find a name for a color that doesn't exist? that doesn't exist on earth.

But the dazzling vision comes closer and closer, like reality once came close to being dream, and yes, "Dreams sometimes come true," Johann said to himself when he once had Carla in his arms, when for a few moments he had in his reach her coral lips, "her green eyes—the emerald sea—where I submerged look for what? what is it lovers look for at the bottom of the sea?" That is the question all of Vienna is happily singing on the esplanade, the city that knows how to love and what to answer to the waltz's question, and Johann, who never knew it, cannot join the chorus, to a certain extent since he's deaf due to old age, but mainly because it saddens him to die without knowing what he wanted so much to know, and his suffering becomes so great that he curses this world and the next.

But little by little the transparent vision of Carla in the color whose name is unknown comes so close, but so close, that Johann suddenly thinks if he asks her what the color is called, she will hear him, and answer.

XIV

Anonymous Note Sent to the Dean of Students of George Washington High School, 1947

It looks like you put your foot into it this time, big shot. Because it's not okay for you to recommend goody goody Casals, as the word goes, for best student of the year.

Let me open your eyes, maybe, you're going blind from so much reading, who knows. The thing is you don't know what a hellhole this place is becoming, the little sixth grade chick Leticia Souto is so she doesn't know where to hide, the same goes for the other one, Beatriz Tudalian, since Casals and Colombo made a date with them in the park last Saturday afternoon, after announcing to all the boys in the dorm that the chicks had given the long-awaited yes, get it, kid? the aforementioned had promised to let themselves get boffed, according to the two gentlemen cited. The thing is, the date took place and the chicks didn't let them touch their epidermis not by a long shot, but despite that, at night the two little sneaks said they gobbled them up.

Monday morning, in the class of one of the distinguished teachers you're acquainted with, somebody let the chicks in on it and right then and there Souto burst out crying. The problem's getting serious, kid. Because the word is getting around, and if the Tudalian girl's big brother finds out, there's going to be TROUBLE. And this happened quite a few days ago, the little time bomb can explode any minute.

So there's your best student for you, who we all feel sorry for because of his unrequited love for the Cossack girl we got this year, who denies she's Jewish but she must be more Jewish than the synagogue, because it's hard to be Russian and not Jewish, you know what I mean? Anyway, getting back to Casals the brat, that little louse also happens to be addicted to strange habits, if you don't believe me ask Adhemar, who's sick and tired of that kid telling him he wants to be just like him and what the big jerk wants more than anything is for people to tell him he's handsome. And good-boy Casals looks at him and asks him what he did to develop his chest and muscles and he asked Adhemar how many times a week he jerks off so that his prick will grow as big as his. And the kid must be jerking off so much no wonder he's losing his mind. I don't deny he was a smart brat when he started school but now he's like Colombo, who you know very well doesn't need an introduction. I heartily congratulate you, the one and only spiritual father of all the boys in residence, for how well your sons are turning out.

XV

Herminia's Commonplace Book, 1948

". . . Mary Todd Lincoln was one of the most admired and envied women of America, a logical fact since few women like her found such a favorable field for developing their personality. While she was single, Mary Todd distinguished herself in the intellectual circles of the then embryonic American culture, in which she was known for her intelligence as well as her impetuous character, in meditation she could be profound, in decisions startlingly impassioned. After a stormy engagement to Abraham Lincoln she became the First Lady of the United States, giving proof of her vitality and unique intuitive powers, for which they unjustly attributed to her powers of witchcraft. But she was loved as a woman and respected as the wife of the President, it could rightly be said that for her the lights of the world were always lit, as on festive occasions.

In fact, it was during a celebration, a theatrical production, that President Lincoln, sitting next to his wife in a box, was assassinated by a bullet. That night Mary Todd Lincoln saw all the lights go out, and some years later a committee of doctors declared her totally insane and therefore deprived her of the right to manage her own property."

This brief newspaper item saddens me and at the same time makes me ponder. Now I don't know whether or not it's better to see all the lights on even if only for a short time, and with the ever-present danger of momentarily lapsing into the dark, or as in my case—a common and dreary case of spinsterhood—to faintly see a weak light in one's early youth, that is already fading. I'm thirty-five and I've already been discarded. I think at forty I'll lose the little hope I have left and that will mean total darkness.

In an article in the Sunday edition of *La Prensa* the Danish thinker Gustav Hansen, whose work I must confess I'm not acquainted with, but who has already written for the same section of the newspaper, as I was saying, Gustav Hansen talks about the immensity of the material world compared with the insignificance of the spiritual one.

Such a statement originates in the impressions he gathered on a visit to the Alaories, a native tribe of Polynesia. There he had been taken to the archeological ruins of a tribal dwelling, where he found intact the piece of bread the chief had cut moments before fleeing his house when an earthquake hit the village and buried the aforementioned house, until another Alaori discovered it centuries after.

Hansen said certain things were conserved with startling freshness: the fold of a sort of tablecloth, human forms imprinted in cushions, stains on the same cushions, etc. Here Hansen points out he felt tempted, in a moment when the guard wasn't watching him, to leave a mark of his own course through that place, and he bit into a wooden shelf and stuck his right thumbnail into a table, etching a primitive circle. And he thought of the deep-felt impressions those ruins had produced on his spirit, but what else?, those emotions would pass, and even though he remembered them as long as he lived, after death his being would pass on to join a divine and unknown order, while those scrawlings and that bite imprinted on some material object would remain indelible for centuries to come.

Well, that digression bothered me a lot, not because it isn't true, it is, but now that it's been a few days since I read the article, I've thought of things which don't give me ground to refute Hansen but do make me see that his statement doesn't apply to all situations. Soon it will be seventeen years since I received the Gold Medal at the Conservatory, after performing the piano arrangement of the Prelude to "Tannhauser." If I had listened to everyone, and believed all their praises and predictions, my disillusionment would have been greater.

But there was a reason why I couldn't build up my hopes, it's not that I gave up without a struggle, because the doctor had already said that with my asthma I had to leave Buenos Aires. Nobody really dies from asthma, but it can attack your heart if you're not careful, and any concert pianist can die of heart trouble. As compensation, the dry air of the pampas around Vallejos allows piano teachers to live up to ninety years, even if they suffer from asthma.

But I didn't realize that the dry air had dried up my brains as well; Toto is surprised that I don't like modern composers. It's not nice of him to laugh at the romantics, a typical insolence of his young years, and Chopin, Brahms, Liszt, he discards them all, just like that. He's upset he stayed in Vallejos, to prepare for exams on his own instead of going back as a resident for another year.

Of course it's possible that the records he brought shock me since I haven't heard new music for such a long time. It's Vallejos' fault, you can't even listen to the radio here, except for the tango stations which can afford powerful antennas and so educate the public on how the ruffian knifed the maid next door. I don't own a radio anyhow.

Unintentionally, I have gone off on a tangent. I only wanted to touch upon one of the days before my final exam, struggling with the trills of "Tannhauser" that weren't coming out clean, and the octaves and ninths which are really for a man's hand, and despite the cough that had come to keep my usual chest disturbance company, I forged on, bent over the piano, and suddenly, while coughing, saliva mixed with blood spurted out onto the keys and my skirt. I couldn't put the handkerchief to my mouth in time and spat without meaning to. It was enough to frighten me, I already felt consumptive. It was just a false alarm, a flow owing to a throat irritation, my lungs had nothing to do with it, but in that moment, I decided to leave Buenos Aires.

Well, I wiped the bloodstains off the keys immediately, and we gave the skirt a good scrubbing in the washtub and those stains disappeared too. But, in my memory, they are still intact, I only have to recall that moment to once again see my saliva streaked with blood. Materially the stain had a short existence; in my soul it still lives. Of course as a true piano teacher I will die at ninety and that will be the end of my trills and my stain, but, Mr. Hansen, allow me to present you this small triumph of the spiritual.

Nothing of what I've read on dreams fully satisfies me. All the assumptions of spiritists and cheap astrologers are to be completely ignored and Sigmund Freud's interpretations, from the little that has come to my attention, sound a little too contrived for my taste; everything is so neatly catalogued to fit into his theories. My humble opinion is that it's much more complicated than he thinks, although dreams must have some meaning.

I haven't dreamt as intensely as last night for quite a while. I saw myself in my bed on a hot night and a locomotive was about to fall and crush me, but it was falling from the ceiling, and it fell slowly as if weightless, it was getting closer at an infinitely slow rate, like you sometimes see a leaf fall slowly from a tree, rocking in the air, but it goes without saying that it would crush me as soon as it reached me. And that vision kept coming back, over and over again, I would wake up and go back to sleep and dream the same thing again. Until I realized I was sleeping on my heart's side and I changed position, thus putting an end to the nightmare. Thank God I could go back to sleep since my chest wasn't too congested!

I would like to discuss it with a doctor. I figured out that when you sleep on the left side, oppressing your heart, the blood has difficulty flowing and after managing to get out of the heart, it can only make its way in spurts, and when it irrigates the cerebral cortex it does so with such force, I don't know if I'm making myself clear, that it reaches the most hidden zones, those sort of furrows or black convolutions. I think that's where all the bad recollections people manage to forget for the time being are, as if hidden in a dark basement.

Well, I would like to interpret my dream, but I've been thinking all day long, even during lessons, without result. After the last student left I was so tired I thought a bath would do me good, and I decided to warm two pots of water and then light the fire for a while to warm the air, since your chest closes up at night if you catch cold and I prefer any nightmare to not sleeping. It's awful not having a bathroom, bathing in a wooden tub is torture.

Finally I decided to wash my hair and do a general cleanup on myself but without going into the tub, I mean without waiting for more than an hour for the two pots to heat up. I looked at my hair in the mirror before washing it, and I couldn't believe how dirty it was. I've become a slob, my hair was smeared with my scalp's own grease and it really nauseated me. It took a mirror to make me realize how dirty I was.

I blame the lack of comfort. It's very hard to live in a room and to have only one toilet at the end of the yard and one cold water pipe, outside, especially now in winter. Mom doesn't feel it so much because she's so old and at that age you sweat less and accept things differently. This is the luck my love of music brought me. There was a phrase that Dad used only once maybe but which returned to my mind millions of times when I was studying at the Conservatory: "The life of Schubert has a sublime meaning." I don't think Dad would have cynically deceived me, he was convinced of what he was saying. On the contrary, for me Schubert was a sublime musician but died without enjoying the slightest recognition, after spending his few years of life in freezing garrets and washing the tubs which always leave a film of gray grease behind after each bath. Schubert did die of TB, and who knows if he didn't first get it by catching cold while taking a bath.

I think the train dream has a meaning, connected with sleeping on the left side. Yesterday was a bad day throughout, in part probably because of the news of Paquita's engagement. I'm not usually jealous, but to know that a sixteen-year-old girl, for me a mere child, is already building her life, with a boy who seems to be a wonderful person, depressed me. Toto told me that at first he thought the boy was already married, like most of the bank clerks who are transferred to Vallejos, but now that the future mother-in-law came to meet Paquita, everything is straightened out. I'm not saying that misfortunes, etc., are not waiting for her in life, but it's so different having a companion who also has a good job. Besides Paquita receives her teacher's diploma next year, and she'll be able to work too.

If I had studied to be a grammar school teacher instead of giving my whole self to the piano, I'd have a steady job at least. I don't blame Dad, the truth is he must have loved music more than I do, he really loved it, like a good Milanese. What upsets me is that Mom repeats what he said like a parrot: "For my daughter music comes first." How remarkable: when I won the Gold Medal Paquita was just born. I shouldn't say this, but how I envy Dad for dying. The last time I dreamt of him, I saw him reading a Milan newspaper, and he was saying to me that the war was about to end. It would have been even better had he died before the fall of Mussolini and all those Italian defeats. But at least he's in peace now.

The only meaning I find in the dream about the train is that I live under the weight of poverty. Since there's no money for clothes I go around badly dressed, although I could at least be more careful with my hair and nails, but even when much younger my eyes were always red, irritated by the always latent oppression in my chest, it affects me that way instead of putting color into my cheeks, grey like church candles. The locomotive was black like all locomotives and thinking it over carefully, the wood of my piano is the same black color, maybe the locomotive was the symbol of the piano. I shouldn't say this because thanks to the piano I earn my daily bread, but although it's not nice to say, I hate the piano.

It's remarkable that you can feel different things for the same person, or the same house, or the same piece of music. When I think about this forlorn room and its flimsy partitions, I hate it, for example, when some boy is doing his scales and gets distracted because we hear Mom behind the partition when she opens the little door of her night table to take out her slippers and then lets them fall on the floor, letting everybody know that she's going to get up and light the stove for the *mate*. It seems that the children know how nervous that makes me because until they hear the stove go on they don't continue their scales. I'm trying to explain that on those occasions I detest this room, but, on the contrary, if I think of this very room when I'm caught outside in the rain, afraid of getting wet and catching cold, I think of it as a cozy refuge. But this is not a very good example, Toto's case is much better for illustrating what I mean.

Toto is a boy who's capable of irritating me more than anybody else. It must be because he's so opinionated, about everything and everybody, being only fifteen and all. I really hate him when he criticizes people who only think about eating, sleeping and buying a car. It revolts him that nobody reads, when he reads almost a book a day, and also that nobody listens to music. He doesn't go out with anybody, he's not friends with anybody in Vallejos, he says, because there's nothing he can talk about with these people. I must be the exception because every evening he comes to chat with me. But he also criticizes me because I like romantic music. I don't know who could have infused this hate of Chopin in him. Maybe it's fashionable in Buenos Aires now.

But in part it's my fault, I've never dared to tell him that I would gladly change places with any of the housewives in Vallejos. It's remarkable, but each time I'm about to say that to him, there's something inside that stops me. I would change places with any housewife, and have my own house, radio, bathroom, and a husband who's not too common, who's merely tolerable, that's all. The car doesn't matter. Besides, if I could go to Buenos Aires once a year to see some good opera or a very good play, already I'd be more than happy.

But on the other hand I sometimes pity Toto, which shows me I feel affection for him. For example, when Paquita came to tell me I shouldn't have anything to do with Toto because he's a skunk. I don't doubt the truth of what she said: one night Toto came out of the movies and on the way home he started chatting with Paquita's fiancé, who sometimes chats with the students. And Toto told him Paquita had been involved with Raul García some years ago and that etc., etc. Paquita's fiancé told her he didn't care a fig about the past, but that she should never talk to Toto again, or even go to his house. I realize it was bad of Toto to talk, but he's jealous of Paquita getting married, she was such a good pal of his, and I understand him because if I weren't as old as I am, which restrains my impulses, perhaps, if I had met her fiancé's mother during her visit to Vallejos, maybe I would have stuck my neck out to tell her that there are better women than Paquita in Vallejos, more mature, and sensitive, some of my finished pupils for instance, who can cheer up his house with music. The fact that an intelligent boy like Toto couldn't help degrading himself with gossip proves to me that the poor thing feels very bad, I know so from personal experience. By the way, I have a tremendous curiosity to meet the little Russian girl, since Toto is so demanding, the girl he chose must be something. But he refuses to show me her letters, which makes me think that maybe it's all a fib.

To summarize, sometimes Toto irritates me and other times I feel sorry for him. And there are even other times in which it's neither one thing nor the other, I feel totally indifferent towards him, like a stranger, especially when he comes up with absurdities that I don't understand because only a madman could. It happened the other day. He came and first thing he said he'd been reading Chekhov's "The Madman" and I asked him what it was about, to see if he understood. I never read it but I know it's a short story about a sick man in a sanatorium for consumptives, and I never wanted to read it because those subjects make me sad. So, he starts telling me it's about a boy in Russia who's in love with a girl who lives in the capital and he feels very lonely in his village (here I began to suspect), and obsessed by loneliness one night he waits in the square for the next door neighbor's maid to come by since every night she takes the leftover food back home, which is a long walk after crossing the square. And when he meets her they start talking, and the boy knows the maid likes him, because she always looks at him, and in the dark he takes her right up to the gate of her employer's house. There, in complete darkness, he starts kissing the little maid, and despite his dream that the first woman he'd possess would be none other than his faraway sweetheart, he feels tempted to possess the maid. She refuses at first, so he begins to caress her, gently and roughly, on and off, trying to seduce her. But something strange happens: he's touching her and he isn't, because he puts the tips of his fingers against the maid's body and doesn't feel the touch, as if his fingers were made of air. And he stays there against the maid's body for an hour, and comes back the next night, but the same thing happens. Then he lights a match and puts it near his index finger to see if he feels anything, and he burns himself, and screams with pain. They hear him and the rumor starts going around that he's crazy, the people spread it maliciously, rejoicing that there's a madman in town.

Then the boy gets ready to go and see his faraway sweetheart and end his nightmares. So he writes to her announcing his visit and when he's about to leave with a knapsack on his shoulder, he receives a message from her telling him she's not waiting because she's soon to be the wife of another man. This is the final blow, and the hero goes completely mad, so that the townspeople, motivated by malice, had unwittingly guessed the truth. The End.

Why does he need to lie like that? I can't understand why a boy who has everything in life, or is going to have it, starts thinking that nonsense about fingers made of air and other absurdities, inventing a different and sad plot for a story that is already sad enough. That's what makes me feel indifferent to Toto, distant, as if we didn't speak the same language. Adolescence certainly is the age of unbalance.

Well, I see that I haven't said what made me think of all this. It was that yesterday Sunday Toto came to tell me we could listen to the radio because the soccer game had been suspended and his father wasn't going to listen to it. Then he suggested it was the perfect occasion to listen to the Sunday opera broadcast from the Teatro Colon, the only program broadcast from Colon on shortwave and that you can receive in Vallejos. Well, they were broadcasting the matinee of *Il Trovatore* with none other than Beniamino Gigli. We sat down and the reception was marvelous, as if you were in the theater itself, it had been years since I'd listened to live opera on radio. The first act was wonderful, and we were at the beginning of the second when Mr. Casals arrived and told us the soccer problem had been fixed and they were starting to broadcast the game. All smiles but we had to go, so he could have the radio, and we went from the living room to the patio because his mother wanted to cut some flowers for me and Toto's little brother was there playing with his electric train set that included tracks, stations, lights, etc. A very expensive and beautiful toy. The tracks make a circle and the train goes around, and different colored lights go on when the train goes by the different stations, over the bridges and past the railroad crossings.

That's the way it is, as the little train lights up red for danger, green for go and yellow for I don't know what, I also feel anger, affection or indifference for Toto when I think of him criticizing the middle classes, telling on Paquita or inventing nonsense about fingers made of air.

Today I felt like going to the movies but fortunately lessons ended late and I didn't go, which I'm happy about because if there aren't many people it gets cold sitting in the theater for two hours, and if you sit near the radiators it's bad for your chest when you go out.

I didn't know any of the actors in the movie, the title tempted me, that's all. And here goes the title: *Lust*. For me it's as if the movie had been called *Atlantis* or *El Dorado*, that is, something promising but totally unknown. Thinking it over, the word "Lust" always seemed somewhat dubious to me, as if it alluded to, with some exaggeration, something that exists but in lesser magnitude. What's all this about Lust? Some little maid's moment of weakness when she lets her employer make love to her.

But if I think it over I see that I cannot judge, I cannot talk about something I know nothing about. Besides, if I look around a bit I'll see that every morning I'm saying hello to a crowd of lecherous people. Let's begin with my neighbors: and with them it would be enough. Delia, for example. I'll bet Delia's husband is the only person in Vallejos who doesn't know she sleeps with half the town. And now with Héctor, a boy getting involved with a married woman!

But what am I writing today? A gossip column? Enough, I don't have anything enlightening to say so I better keep quiet. And I'm wrong to judge, yes, very wrong: in order to judge them I'd have to be like them, that is to say, I'd have to be healthy. There must be something about Lust which makes it irresistible to healthy people, I don't even know the meaning of the word "Lust," it must be something you feel when your blood is rich, when apart from not having asthma you eat well, especially a lot of meat and fruit, which are the most expensive items.

It's literally impossible to stick your nose out today, with the wind and dirt that's blowing you can't even walk the two blocks to the movies. My favorite proverb is "every cloud has a silver lining." Because of the wind I saved the twenty *centavos* for the ticket. Aforesaid proverb is my favorite because I can always apply it, according to my needs at the moment. Because I'm asthmatic I could never have embarked on the *Titanic*, since it's misty on the high seas and my bronchial tubes become humid. My bronchial tubes must be like paper, if paper gets wet it tears into pieces by merely touching it. Even if I hadn't been asthmatic, given my lack of financial resources I still wouldn't have been able to board the *Titanic*. Therefore I'm a doubly lucky woman.

Today being the only day of the week I don't have pupils in the afternoon I decided to pass the time reducing my overwhelming ignorance by reading the dictionary. At first I thought of beginning *The Magic Mountain* that Toto lent me, but the thought of beginning such a long novel tires me. I should save my patience for my pupils, I certainly can't waste it on novels.

Back to the dictionary, despite the exoticism of the letter "w" in the Spanish language, there was a word beginning with that letter which I always instinctively rejected. How can you possibly reject a word without knowing its meaning? It's something that's happened to me several times. All I knew was that the word "wyllis" was connected to "Giselle," the famous ballet, and I always refused to read its plot, something had put me on my guard against "Giselle," I only knew that Giselle was a wyllis.

Today I couldn't help finding out. Very simply, wyllises are the girls who die virgins and who after death inhabit the woods where they dance all through the night till dawn holding hands so as not to get lost, repeating the dance steps the wyllis queen shows them. To prevent the unlucky creatures from escaping with some stray shepherd in the forest, she invents steps which are more and more demanding and compels all the wyllises to dance and dance until they're all out of breath. When the sun rises their bodies vanish, only moonlight can again make them visible, at the fall of night.

What a fate, but how come, without knowing the meaning, I rejected the word? An inner voice was warning me it would do me no good to find out.

But "every cloud has a silver lining," so tonight when my chest starts torturing me and I begin twisting and turning in bed unable to fall asleep I won't think that above the faucet in the yard, under the mirror and on the shelf, behind the soap, is the little razor blade which, although slightly dull since I already shaved my legs with it several times, as I was saying, although dull, would be enough to open my veins and end the congested chest and the insomnia. But that could turn out to be a bad solution. So as long as I remember the wyllises, I won't think about the little razor blade, because there must be some truth in that legend. I don't want to go to the next life to keep on suffering.

Because I am asthmatic I'm not sure the queen of the wyllises would make me dance, she might be easier on me, besides, since I'm so breathtakingly beautiful, she'd probably think that no shepherd would try to kidnap me and that they would leave me sitting in a corner, without having to do so many pirouettes. I know perfectly well what she'd make me do: she'd make me play the piano so the others could dance.

At night you pay for what you've done during the day. It strikes me that tonight I'm going to sleep badly. All for having gone out this morning, with all the wind and dirt, just to wash my face in the faucet, and again after lunch to wash the dishes. The wind and dirt irritate the bronchial tracts and then you have to twist and turn in bed for hours until your chest loosens up. But it seems to me that the worst part for a person suffering from my illness, is when, after sleeping three or four hours, perhaps uncovered because your blanket fell off by accident, you wake up at dawn with a congested chest so that you can't go back to sleep.

That was what I went through last winter. Perhaps now that I put the brazier in front of the door the air warms up on its way in and the brazier doesn't go out the whole night because the gust of wind that creeps in through the cracks of the door keeps the coal burning. Before, Mom insisted on putting the brazier near the bed, and it would go out at two or three in the morning. I don't know why, but I decidedly prefer taking my time falling asleep—my chest closes up and scarcely a thread of air gets through, making a sort of whistling sound—instead of falling asleep for a few hours as soon as I get into bed, knowing that I'll be waking up at dawn—because it seems I have to help that thread of air get into the lungs—without the slightest hope of going back to sleep.

I haven't had an argument like the one I had the other day for quite a while. It's typical of conceited people to get angry for losing an argument but sometimes I can't avoid it.

Toto began talking about the uncultured man, who doesn't even have an idea of the absurdity of his own life, eating and sleeping in order to go through his long hours of work, and working in order to pay for what he eats and the house where he sleeps, thus closing the vicious circle. For the first time I dared to tell him I would have gladly married someone like that, since that very simplicity is the foundation of happiness, and there's nothing better than to live alongside of someone happy.

Since he didn't want to accept this I added that according to my modest opinion strength consists in living without thinking. He then asked me why didn't I myself begin by not thinking and I had to tell him that it was in spite of myself that I think, and that to be simple is a blessing from heaven that not all of us have.

His next argument was that to be simple is not to be strong. He had the nerve to say literally: "I am strong, stronger than a brute, because I think" because he who thinks is strong and knows how to defend himself.

I refuted this saying the more man thinks the weaker he becomes, because his questions don't find the answers, and he finally has to commit suicide, as has been the case of philosophers such as Schopenhauer and others.

This left him without a reply for a few moments, he struggled with himself like a wounded animal who wants to pretend that the bullet didn't hit its mark. As he didn't answer I kept telling him things, particularly how difficult it is for the intelligent man to act on earth, besieged by so many unknowns, while for a brute blessed by God everything is so easy: work, eat, sleep and reproduce. For his wife the task can also be easy, since she marries a brute and takes shelter in him.

Toto returned to the attack asking me what made me think God blessed the brutes, and how could I be so sure of God's existence in the first place.

To answer I used the Catholic argument, that is to say the existence of God is revealed to us in an act of faith, which is blind and alien to the rational.

He then asked me what I would do if I didn't believe in God, and I answered that in that case I'd kill myself. He then reasoned that I used the idea of God to reject the idea of suicide. My answer was that faith is the intuition that one has of God, and intuitions cannot be explained.

He then asked me if I had seen a certain French movie whose title he had forgotten. To try and make me remember it he told me the whole story. I never saw or heard of it. It goes like this: a very powerful feudal lord of Burgundy, highly respected by his serfs, brings up his many sons together with boys selected from among the strongest and most intelligent born on the fief. The feudal lord intends to mold them into true soldiers and strategists and during the day he has them trained by the best masters of France. But this lord has two faces, he's good and kind during the day but at night devotes himself to destroying what he creates during the day. While they sleep, he applies a different treatment to each one of his protégés (including his sons). He puts leeches on one boy's arms and neck, so they'll suck his blood and make him physically weak; he opens the mouth of another sleeper and makes him sip liquors, gradually creating the need in his organism for more and more alcohol, which will progressively damage his brain; in another's ear he whispers terrible stories against his comrades, he tells him he's the best student but that they all have conspired against him to deny it; to another boy, already an adolescent, he presents a half-naked slave girl who disappears through a secret passage the very moment the adolescent is about to pursue her; and so on to each one of them, taking advantage of their sleep because that's when their unconscious forces are on the loose and can follow the fatal paths the feudal lord appoints them.

Time passes. Despite everything, many of these young warriors have natural gifts which have developed as much as possible under the circumstances. Their first battle is soon to occur. The lord has promised endless riches to his men if they win; he has promised them a harmonious existence which includes the state most treasured in the Middle Ages: peace of mind.

To test the youths, the omnipotent lord has secretly hired an army of mercenaries in the service of destruction and at dawn after a black night he has the battle trumpet sound. The armies meet in a thick forest, the battle lasts for days. The women of Burgundy wait anxiously for their men.

And they return defeated. Some could not resist physically, others drank too much wine before the fight to steady their nerves, others poisoned by jealousy of their superior comrades attacked them when their backs were turned to test the edge of their swords before confronting the real enemy.

The feudal lord receives the conquered and reproaches them for not having the strength to avoid man's pitfalls: gluttony, lust, jealousy, fear, etc. The moment of retribution arrives, and for each of his warriors he has reserved a punishment appropriate to the offence. And the movie ends with the feudal lord leaving the torture chamber since it's already night and he has to tend to the new generation of boys, who are sleeping in another wing of the castle.

This was the plot. He asked me what I thought of the protagonist. I said he was a monster. And he answered that he wasn't so monstrous, if I compared him to God. I almost strangled him, but I contained myself and asked why.

He answered that the feudal lord took advantage of tender souls to inject them with the poisons of the earth and afterwards, when they reached the age of free will, submitted them to tests superior to their strengths. If there was a strong one who resisted, good for him, but the majority succumbed to temptation and ended their existence in atonement, that is to say, torment. And it all could have been avoided, if these warriors had been protected from the infections of evil. If the feudal lord had exiled evil from his castle, everything could have been avoided.

Well here, on a thoughtless impulse, I said something stupid: that even if the feudal lord did not put to effect his labor of destruction evil would still have creeped in through the cracks of the castle. Then Toto answered that's why God is worse than the feudal lord, because He does have the power to do what He wants, He's omnipotent, and He could therefore bring to an end evil on earth, but, on the contrary, He prefers to amuse himself watching the enemy crush His weak creatures with its superior strength.

I then answered with the Catholic argument, that is to say that man has free will, and that if he falls it's his own fault. Then Toto said that if man fell it was because of his own stupidity and vices, but no man wishes his downfall, and if everybody was born intelligent and immune to vice there would be no need of hell, because everyone would know perfectly well how to avoid it.

Toto's final thesis was that God made possible the existence of evil, and created imperfect beings, therefore He cannot be perfect, and what's more, perhaps God is a sadistic power that enjoys contemplating suffering. Therefore he prefers not to think that a God exists, because if He were imperfect He would be public enemy number one.

Well, this was his argument. I couldn't figure out a way of refuting his thesis so I cut him short by saying I would call him another day, when I was ready to continue the discussion. I'm sure I'll think of some valid argument.

Suddenly I got up from the piano stool and opened the street door. He asked if I was throwing him out, which hadn't occurred to me not even remotely, and before I could say anything he had already walked out, without saying another word to me.

He'll come back. It was a pity he didn't stay because I don't know if it was for the anger or what but I sat down to play Beethoven's "L'Aurore" and it came out better than ever.

It's already getting cool out, but in this healthful air of the Cordoban mountains all you need on is a little woolen jacket and there's no danger of catching cold. At this peerless hour of twilight, the mountains are turning blue before my eyes, and behind them one can imagine the sun that's going down beyond the line of the horizon, which is the only thing I like about Vallejos: its single unbroken horizon line. But back here in Cordoba, from blue the mountains will now be turning violet and when it's no longer light out we'll return to the hotel to eat some delicious food in the dining room, not too near the fireplace where logs are burning. During the day we went out in a chaise and the little brook had to be crossed on donkey's back. The sun gets stronger around three in the afternoon and I could stay out in a blouse only, nothing else, without risking a cold because the air is so healthy. The mountain stream is clear, fresh, and you can see the bottom despite the fact it's like rapids, coming down hard and fast from the spring. You have to be careful about covering your head to prevent sunstroke, that's the only precaution you have to take. Because of all the outdoor exercise during the day, at night we'd get to the dining room with a big appetite. And then we'd play checkers or dominoes until our digestion was well on its way so that we could then retire to bed, since we were truly tired. That's the life you have in the mountains of Cordoba. It's been eighteen years since I went with Mom and Dad for two weeks to see if I could get over the asthma, it will be exactly eighteen years in October. Back in Buenos Aires I felt as bad as before.

Paquita's mother will go to Cordoba this year, after her daughter's wedding. I would like to put myself in her shoes and go back to see the mountains. Almost an hour from our hotel you could go by chaise to the ruins of a mission and an old chapel built by the Jesuits. It seems that with the years each stone had come alive, and imbued with faith. The morning bells produce the most perfect sounds imaginable. Paquita's mother will go to mass with her husband, and both will thank God for a life full of sacrifice but set apart by God's blessing. It will be the first time Paquita's mother has taken a trip, and the first time her father has left Vallejos since he arrived from Spain. But they'll see that their sacrifice has been rewarding, they have fulfilled their mission: bringing up a child, giving her a good education, and sending her on her way in life with the right foot forward. Paquí's father is a man of few words, he makes very little small talk, but when you go by his shop he's always there tirelessly sewing.

I would have liked to have a quiet husband, it seems to me such a man must have a definite spiritual wealth. What an adventure for a woman to marry a man and gradually decipher his soul! When Paquí's mother goes to this chapel, which I'm going to recommend to her with great enthusiasm, she's going to kneel and she won't think "God is a sadistic power that enjoys the contemplation of suffering." She's going to pray and thank God for all the riches she's received, and it is even possible that out of pure joy, for which she feels in God's debt, she'll offer him some small gift or promise.

Even if Paquí's mother were like me, or let's just say, if Paquí's mother were me, with my bitterness inside her, and my doubts with respect to God's intentions, even in that case there would be a solution, because I would follow the example of my husband, a man full of silence, ready to accept his fate, which is why he's such a good worker. Just one such example in the family is enough, and resting my head upon his shoulder every night as I go to sleep some of his tranquillity and strength would pass on to me.

And so I repeat to myself that the beauty of the mountains, the clear water, the ringing of the bells, the music of Chopin and of poor Schubert exist on earth, just as there undoubtedly exist women who manage to rest all night, their heads upon the shoulder of a husband who will get up in the morning to go to work and give his family all he can. Perhaps I'm idealizing too much, all the married women complain about the life they have, but I, as usual, can't say a thing because I don't know how it would be to live next to a man my whole life. I will die not knowing anything of life.

I would like to talk to Toto about some of these nice things, but using some argument that could invalidate his thesis. Something inside tells me Toto's thesis isn't true, but I don't know how to attack it. It's really daring on my part to philosophize, and on his, too. He doesn't want to tell me the author he got his famous thesis from, now that he already made it clear it wasn't from a movie; when he came to show me the photograph his classmates sent him from his school (probably to upset me since he has people who write to him and I don't) I asked him and he didn't want to tell me.

In the picture is his famous Tatiana, two other girls from his grade, prettier than Tatiana, who looked a little colorless to me, and a boy who, according to Toto, is a monitor now getting his law degree, and one other boy, blond and very handsome. But all of them look too old to be Toto's friends, and Tatiana looks like a young lady already, definitely not for Toto. He was as puffed up as a peacock, proud of his picture; he came in without looking at me, his gaze was lost in space, like the harmony teacher at the Conservatory, Toto reminds me more and more of that unfriendly homosexual, he's very effeminate in his ways. May God forgive me for such thoughts but they look so much alike to me, and I don't in the least wish that misfortune on him, if all homosexuals were like the harmony teacher it would be terrible, such a nasty man so full of gossip and favoritism. He treated us women students like dogs, and right in front of our noses he'd look at the cleaning boy, who would come with his dustpan and broom, a caveman type, and he would watch him as if he were a chorus girl. He felt attracted to the caveman type because extremes attract. What a misfortune for a man!

That nasty idea came into my head when I saw Toto with the picture, it would never have struck me before, and I'm ashamed of my maliciousness. But I asked Toto who the blond was and he said he didn't know, and his face turned red as a tomato. Looking him straight in the eye I asked him why he blushed. He said the following: "I was too embarrassed to tell you but it so happens he's the most handsome boy at school and a girl told me I looked like him and that when I'm a senior I'm going to be just like him." Well, enough maliciousness! They're right when they say old maids have the worst possible imaginations. What I shouldn't do is let myself into certain kinds of arguments, if I have faith I have faith and that's that, who is he to come and examine it? His new idea about going to Tibet also annoyed me; according to him he won't achieve peace until he sees Tibet. Always asking the impossible.

I would be satisfied with just seeing Mar del Plata, since I never saw the sea. But I think that what would really give me the most spiritual satisfaction is something else. Of course if I ask for it I will also be asking the impossible. I would simply like to stay here in Vallejos and meet a good man. I speak of a simple man, someone like Paquita's father who works long hours in silence, without complaint, for my children. I know I am asking the impossible, if nobody wanted me when I was young they'll want me even less at thirty-five, with the word old maid written all over my face.

Who knows what recompense awaits old maids in the next world, or what tortures. I haven't done bad to anybody, nor good either, I don't know what God plans to do with my soul. It will be difficult for Him to judge me, because there's nothing to say about old maid Herminia's conduct, neither good nor bad, my life is a blank page.

I would be content if death were simply a rest, like sleeping. Sometimes it's nice to open your eyes in total darkness and rest your sight, but only for a while, because if not rest degenerates into insomnia, which is the worst torture. When I say rest I mean sleep. It would be a blessing if death were like sleeping forever without ever again being reminded that Herminia once existed.

XVI

Berto's Letter, 1933

Dear brother:
Although I still don't have any letter of yours to answer, I'm writing with the hope that all is well with you and that your wife is getting better in the healthy Spanish climate. We don't even know if the boat trip agreed with her, since as usual you haven't written for ages. I don't ask you to put a lot of details in a telegram, but at least the important matters.

Here we're having a hard time of it but we're all well. Mita is fine, my Toto is a darling, he's almost eight months now, a regular little butterball. As for your son, we are very happy with him, little Héctor is a very good boy and already feels at home with us. I wonder if it was your idea that you have to take your pants down and sit on the john to, as he says, "make a little fart." Mita saw him go to the bathroom a couple of times without flushing the toilet and when she realized what was going on we nearly laughed our heads off. What a refined son you have, not like his father.

The truth is I really cannot forgive you for not writing, it seems to me you're on vacation with nothing to do and I just don't see any excuse for not writing, you know that sometimes people like to get news, an encouraging word from time to time, because hungry dogs never lack fleas and with this year's drought in Vallejos I don't know where to start scratching. You'll remember what happened in '27, the same thing is happening now, the cattle are dying in the fields, the banks aren't dishing out the cash and the ones who are profiting from all this are those who have leftover bad cheese from last year, you should see the prices they're quoting. When I think of the cash we lost that year because you didn't want to listen to me, I could knock my head against the wall. I know the country and I know when a drought is coming, damn them, if you had listened to me that year and bought off the milk farmers' produce, having such a good friend in the bank manager, we would have been rolling in it by now.

This year I saw it coming again, but I couldn't count on any bank, and now the milk farmers remember '27 and are asking too damn much for their rotten cheese that nobody wanted last season. I mean it Jaime, every time I remember that mistake of yours, and not only that but with all the troubles I'm having now . . .

Well, let's change the subject, I can't wait till you see my little scamp, he's a handsome little bugger, every night I watch him sleep, and I watch his mother too, sleeping without a care in the world. She's fat from breastfeeding. Now because of the child she finally started eating like I want her to, and she's nice and round, before she kept herself from eating for the sake of her figure, but now that she has to think of feeding the infant with her breast, she's eating like a human being and her weight is where it should be, you know I never liked the bony type. Mita is very worried about money, and if she has her meals in peace it's because I don't let her see how serious the situation is, right from the start I trained her to trust me.

The one who's cashing in on this situation is the manager of the Regional Bank, you don't know him, he's been here for less than a year, he's a Basque son of a mother, he lent all the milk farmers cash so they could meet their expenses and make it through a few months without selling a single cheese until the price hit the ceiling. I saw the wop Luchetti's loan papers and the loan was at a three per cent annual increase, the lowest possible, so it wasn't wop excuses when he told me the earnings weren't so great because he had to divide them with a partner in Buenos Aires, what Buenos Aires is he talking about? A lot of bull! One thing's for sure; it's the crooked manager who's walking off with fifty per cent of the business.

I never told you before but at the end of the year I went to talk to the manager, as soon as I saw I'd have to close the dairy farm if it didn't start raining soon. I told him that seven field-hands would be out of work and he didn't care. I asked him for dough to go south where it was still raining somewhat so I could make a contract with some milk farmer there although freight would cost an arm and a leg, and he didn't want to give me a cent. What bloodsuckers some people are!

I didn't tell you this before because why should I give you bad news, and maybe you weren't interested either, what do you care if I go under? That's a joke, don't pay any attention.

God takes with one hand and gives with the other, you have to believe crime doesn't pay, of that I'm convinced, I don't care if that bloodsucker of a Basque is filling his pockets and there are seven fieldhands out of work, because for us it'll all come out in the wash while the Basque is going to keep suffering from diabetes till he dies. Every time you see him he's at the doctor's. I think God is going to help me, Jaime, I have faith, because I never did any harm to anybody. But I don't want the alarm to spread to Mita's family, everything was going so well, as soon as I sold the steer and bought the dairy farm Mita's mother wrote her from La Plata saying they were so happy they trusted me when I went to ask for Mita's hand. You know they wanted the best for Mita and they sacrificed a lot so that she could study, after that it's not so easy to give her away to the first bum that comes along.

Please excuse the length of this letter, but it's four p.m. and I have absolutely nothing to do, next week I'm taking one of the Englishmen who bought the Drabble ranch over to Juan Carranza's land, the Englishman's interested in buying pasture land now that prices are down, and I think the deal is already clinched, with the commission I'll have enough for half a year at least. Today Mita's on duty at the hospital till six, I'm going to pick her up. Luckily we found a maid who doesn't leave the baby for a minute.

I don't know if I told you in the other letter that we were expecting Adela, Mita's sister, the tall blond one, the one you liked. She was here for a month until a few days ago, but there's nothing like the three of us alone, me, my wife and my son. That's another story I'm not going to tell you, I don't want to upset you. Jaime, today I was thinking so much about Mom, as if it was just yesterday that she died, it seemed the years hadn't gone by and that I was still sitting in a corner at her wake and I was watching you receive the condolences of the people who came in. You were already a man, but I was a boy, and now that I'm a man and have a son I still can't accept the fact that Mom has gone forever and we're not going to see her ever again.

I'm sorry I'm talking about sad things, it's just that today I feel so much like reaching out and giving Mom a big hug. I wonder if she would be happy to see me as I am, she wanted me to study and get some degree but all considered I'm not so bad off, and Jaime I'd give anything to show her the wonderful grandson she has, with eyes like two grapes, Jaime, if you'd at least write more often, a letter from you would make me very happy, and I'll never forgive you if you come back from the trip without first seeing our relatives in Barcelona, when you're back I want you to tell me all about it, right to the last detail, like if they look like Mom and us. If they look like you they must be some bunch of heels. I imagine there won't be a sacred corner in Madrid when you're through with it, you must have already corrupted half the women there.

How different we are in that, Jaime. Since I met Mita I forgot that women exist, I swear I'm on the level, why would I lie to you of all people about this, big heel? But I think you're perfectly right to have a good time, in any case it's not my funeral.

I interrupted the letter a moment because little Amparo the maid came in with the baby just up from his nap. At six we're going to wait for Mita in the car in front of the hospital. You should see the tumbleweeds all over the road, there's not a green leaf in the whole place. When his mother comes out of the laboratory, the little bugger's face will light up, hope to God he has his mother for many years, so he doesn't have the bad luck I had, and she can bring him up properly and give him all the education she can, Mita studied more than enough for that. On that score I can't reproach her for anything. But just as soon as things straighten out I want her to leave the hospital, we can get along without her salary as soon as I have the situation under control. If I close the deal with the Englishman next week I may do something rash like forcing her to resign on the spot. I believe in God who can see which people deserve a little luck, if there wasn't any justice in the world and people like the manager, who calmly watches seven fieldhands lose their job, would always win out, well, this wouldn't be a fit world to live in. There must be some justice.

I haven't told anybody and I didn't want anybody to get to know this, but before Adela went back to La Plata something happened which hurt me very much. She left one Tuesday, and the Sunday before I had gone to play at the handball court in the afternoon, and when I returned Mita was talking to Adela, the two of them lying on the bed, and I stopped to listen to what they were saying. I quietly went over to the window facing the patio to see if they were sleeping, so as not to wake them up, but they were talking. Adela was saying to Mita that she was wrong to give me her earnings, you get it? She said she was making that money on her own and there was no reason to give me all of it, half at the most, for household expenses. What a bitch! Do you know that before things got bad I had Mita send all she wanted to her mother every month, but it's not my fault if the tide's against me, and lately she's been giving me her whole salary.

You'll probably say I shouldn't pay any attention to what that dumb blond says, but Mita should have stopped her short and told her to go to hell, and she didn't say anything, she almost seemed to agree. I didn't tell Mita I was listening, but she must have realized, she sure notices there's something wrong but I'm certainly not going to give her the pleasure of asking for an explanation. Adela also said I shouldn't have given a few *pesos* to the nun who came to the door that morning collecting for the poor. The bitch, she doesn't believe in God or anything for that matter. I don't think I made a mistake, Mita is the most sensible and well-balanced woman I've ever known, but she should have answered back to that hyena she has for a sister. Don't you think Mita's a fine woman if there ever was one?

How I wish you'd write me soon telling me about your travels, and tell me what I should do about this. You'll probably say why the hell am I dragging you into my problems. As for little Héctor, Mita's getting him ready for school next year, at seven they can go directly into first grade, so Mita is teaching him all of kindergarten. I think when mine starts school, even if I have to go out and hold people up in the street, I'm going to give him everything he needs so he can study, and get his degree, maybe he'll think his father's not good enough for him afterwards. There are sons who pay you off with ingratitude, but I don't care, that way he'll spare himself the dirty fight his father had to go through, without weapons, his guts only. The truth is, Jaime, I don't wish this fight on anybody.

Mita keeps harping on going to La Plata so I can get any job while I finish college at night and then go to law school, which I always wanted, but I can't stick her in her parents' house, living off charity, in a home that's not ours, living from hand to mouth, until I graduate almost seven years later. No, that's out of the question, I'm not going to make her spend the best years of her life in poverty, and I promised her parents I would give her everything she needed. It's too late to study now, I missed the boat. What a pity I left school at fifteen. I could never understand what made you decide that. If you needed help at the factory you could have gotten any honest boy, what need was there to take me out of school, simply because you needed somebody you could trust? No, Jaime, I could never figure that out, how could you take me out of school before I was fit to fight my way through life? And then you decided to sell the factory and go to Buenos Aires. The main thing is for the master to do his will, and you've always done what you wanted.

Well, why cry over spilt milk, it's too late now, there's nothing to be done. What makes me angry is that you haven't sent me news for ages, even if it's only for little Héctor, who's always asking for his father and if his mother's headache has gone away yet. Poor thing, he behaves better than his father, he doesn't give us any trouble.

Now I have to spend a fortune in stamps to send this letter, which is as long as my arm. And what for? so that you won't answer, like with the other letter? I don't know why I write you, you don't care about me, and I don't think you ever cared about me, Jaime, I'm full of bile today, and I don't think I want to send you this letter, I don't want to upset you, you must have your problems too, with your wife's health. But I'm telling you all this because it's the only news I have to offer, even though it's bad news, don't you expect a letter from me? It doesn't matter if you don't get any news from me, right? Why, if it didn't matter whether or not you took me out of school when I was a boy, which I can never forgive you for, and anyway, afterwards you suddenly had the inspiration to close the factory and there I was, out in the rain. I repeat to myself that you're the only one I have, my big brother, the only one I have left, and I say to myself too that you must have your own reasons for what you did, but no matter how hard I try I can't forgive you, Jaime, I cannot forgive you, damn your selfishness and damn all the whores you chase on the street. This letter is going into the wastepaper basket, I wouldn't spend a cent on stamps for you.

About the Author

Manuel Puig was born in 1932 in a small town in the Argentine pampas. He studied philosophy at the University of Buenos Aires, and in 1956 he won a scholarship from the Italian Institute in Buenos Aires and chose to pursue studies in film direction at the Cinecitta in Rome. There he worked as an assistant director until 1962, when he began to write his first novel. Puig's novels–*Betrayed by Rita Hayworth*, *Heartbreak Tango*, *The Buenos Aires Affair*, and *Kiss of the Spider Woman*–have been translated into fourteen languages. Now living in New York City, Puig has taught at City College, and, commencing in September 1980, will teach at Columbia University.